INTO THE

wrecked: book one

FIRE

MICHELE G. MILLER

Praise for the **From The Wreckage** series

Miller reminds me once again why I love YA books! 5 Heartbreaking and Earth Shattering Stars! - *I Read Indie* **Book Blog**

Everything about it tears at you and rips away your emotions until you are raw. You will feel every emotion with this book. From the Wreckage is definitely one hell of an emotional roller coaster. - *Consuming Worlds* **Book Blog**

It was so easy to get drawn into the feelings of loss, fear and confusion experienced, and observed, through the mind of Jules. She provided the story's point of view, and the feelings were filtered through her own perceptions and emotions. This seemed to evoke stronger feelings in me.
- *My Bookbag* **Book Blog**

A page Turner that will give you hope if you have had tragedies in the past. A must read!
- *Amazon Reviewer*

A page Turner that will give you hope if you have had tragedies in the past. A must read!
- *Amazon Reviewer*

Into The Fire

Copyright © 2015 Michele G Miller

Published by Enchanted Ink Press

Into The Fire is edited by Samantha Eaton-Roberts
Cover design and photography by Regina Wamba of
www.maeidesign.com
Cover Model: Savannah McBrayer

Other Titles by Author

From The Wreckage Series - Coming of Age Drama
From The Wreckage
Out of Ruins
All That Remains

The Prophecy of Tyalbrook Trilogy - YA Fantasy Romance
Never Let You Fall
Never Let You Go
Never Without You - Coming soon

Individual titles
Last Call - New Adult Romance

Visit my website for updates
https://michelegmillerbooks.squarespace.com/

"Life asked death,
why do people love me but hate you?
Death responded
because you are a beautiful lie and I'm a painful
truth."

~ Author Unknown

To the ones in pain. Hold On.
Life is beautiful and worth it and you are loved
dearly.

Today's reality… Doing something new
January 3, 2018

"Good morning, Danica. How are you today?" asks Dr. Green as he walks into his office, late as usual. His glasses sit askew atop his head, his salt and pepper hair sticking out in all directions. This is the man who has been counseling me to get on with my life. The man who scarcely arrives at our appointments on time. But I like him. He's easy to talk with: jovial, caring, and not nearly as pushy as other therapists I've seen through the years.

He seats himself in the chair across from me and I close my eyes, breathing in deeply. "I opened my email this weekend."

"Oh? Is that unusual for you?" he asks.

"My old email. The account from… before."

Dr. Green remains quiet, waiting for more. When it becomes clear I'm not offering up an explanation he does as he always does - he pokes at the hornets' nest. "What prompted you to do that?"

Tears jab the back of my eyelids, even as a small smile dances upon my lips. "I had a birthday Sunday," I remind him, knowing full well he's aware my birthday was New Year's Eve. "I turned twenty-one, and do you know what I did?"

He raises a brow in question, perching his glasses on the tip of his nose, and going to work jotting notes on the pad laying in his lap.

"Nothing. I did nothing. I sat in a dark room and watched the teenagers across the street set off fireworks." *I sound so lame*, I think to myself, shaking my head. "It's pathetic honestly. I know it and you know it and that's why I opened the email. I guess I wanted to know if anyone was thinking of me."

"You guess?" he asks, and I shrug indifferently. "And, what did you find?"

What did I find? I found years of accumulated junk mail and well wishes from people I've long left behind. I didn't stop to look at the messages, not all of them anyway. Instead, I clicked the senders into alphabetical order and searched for relevant names. More specifically, I searched for one name.

He'd sent three messages and as I'd read the words on the glowing screen before me, while fireworks popped outside my window, the truth of my life crashed down on me.

1

I'm weary of being this person, of living life alone, of being afraid to live.

I'm more afraid of letting someone in. Again. It's been five years.

Can I face the fear? Overcome the pain?

It's time to find out. Because if I don't… I'm not sure I'll survive.

Today's reality… I click and delete
January 8, 2018

"Weren't you supposed to start classes today?" Gram asks, pushing her way into my room with her hip, her hands laden with shopping bags. Gram sure does love her shopping.

"I wasn't up for it."

Dumping the bags on my bed, she rests on the edge. Clearly she's planning on staying a while. "Weren't up for it? What does that mean?"

"It means I wasn't up for it, Gram," I annunciate clearly, my eyes glued to the computer screen in front of me. Today's the start of winter semester at the local community college. Before the holidays I'd registered for two on-campus courses at everyone's urging. Stepping on campus will be a huge step for me; until now I've taken online courses. The idea of hanging out with cheerful co-eds all day has kept me from taking such a huge leap. However this morning, instead of getting ready for my first class, I'd pulled my email back up and began scrolling through the pages and pages of messages. I've been sitting here ever since. My fingers robotically clicking on each of the five-thousand-and-something messages in my inbox, deleting them one-by-one. I realize I could have done a mass delete. I'm not technology challenged. It would have been more efficient, and certainly less time consuming. But no, I click on each one. I'm not reading them, I don't bother to look at the senders' names. I just delete. There's something cathartic about it. About physically clicking on each message individually and pressing delete. Every checked box is a moment in time I ignored, pushed aside, or walked away from.

"Should I call Dr. Green?"

"No." *Click, delete. Click, delete.*

"How about lunch? Have you eaten yet? We could grab something," Gram suggests to the back of my head, her reflection in my computer screen. She's leaning forward behind my right shoulder, her hand rests at the base of her neck in worry. I should turn around and give her the attention she deserves, but I'm transfixed with my task. *Click, delete. Click, delete.*

"I'm good." Nothing matters except for emptying my email box of all the missed opportunities.

Click, delete. Click, delete.

The shopping bags rattle as Gram rises, and I follow her with my eyes. She wanders to my dresser and picks up a framed picture; it's the only one I keep of my parents. I wait for her to speak as she longingly stares at the picture. My hand stills. Her crumbling face reminds me that her pain is as acute as mine, and I feel guilty for being short with her. I love Gram, but she has a hard time letting me take care of myself. After the five years I've put her and Gramps through I suppose it's understandable for her to be skeptical. Understandable, but aggravating. I've been taking classes and keeping my weekly appointments with Dr. Green. I haven't slipped into my dark place since before my last stay at Crestdale.

I get stronger every day.

Not that it would take much for me to fall. I crave the release of the edge of a cool blade the way an addict craves his next hit. It's something that will never go away.

Today's reality… It's a leap in the dark
January 9, 2018

Leap - move quickly and suddenly
Dark - having very little or no light, hard to understand; obscure
Leap in the dark -- an action of which the consequences are unknown

Lifting my face to the sun, my eyes rove over the house I've lived in for the past five years. This house has been many things to me through the years: my refuge, my prison, my home. I allow myself one last glance before I slip into my car with a deep sigh. Today I take a leap in the dark. I need saving, and I have to save myself.

Between my conversation with Dr. Green and my birthday realization, I've come to understand one thing: it's time to move forward. Time to take action, to take charge of my life. I don't want to be sitting in a dark room alone next year on my birthday watching others celebrate.

My cell phone is plugged in, the GPS set. I don't spare a backward glance as I back down the driveway and pull into the street.

I'm ready.

Today's reality… My destination
January 13, 2018

The indention in the road, the one where the asphalt changes from new to old, that's it. That's the landmark signifying my entrance back into the town where my life began, and ended. I focus on the transition, as my tires make their way closer and closer to the bridge into Grove Pointe. At fifty feet away, I slow as the red hatchback in front of me crosses the threshold, its rear lifts and dips as its shocks absorb the change in the road. My pulse races as a blue and white wooden sign comes into view on the right-hand side of the two lane highway.

'Welcome to Grove Pointe.'

Peering in my rear-view mirror, I make sure there's no one behind me before I apply pressure to the brake pedal and roll to a stop a mere ten feet from the pavement change. There's no magical force field or mystical powers awaiting me once I cross the invisible line in front of me. It's merely a border on a map - a destination.

My destination.

I lift my foot, allowing my vehicle to roll forward, the incline of the road propelling me closer to my hometown. My palms, slick with sweat, grip the grey leather steering wheel for dear life as I take calming breaths.

Five… four… three… two…

bump… bump Front then back.

I cross the threshold, and my car pushes forward. In the distance, a pickup truck appears in the opposite lane heading my way and I force my foot to apply pressure to the gas pedal to maintain a normal speed. No need in causing a scene, or an accident, on the bridge. I've crossed this bridge thousands of times. Grove Pointe Creek - a small watershed which feeds into larger creeks before dumping into the lake south of town. As a child, I spent my days catching frogs upstream. The memory of hot summer nights, lightning bugs, and shared secrets of my childhood burn my eyes.

Bump… bump.

My car transitions from the bridge to asphalt and I hold my breath as the pickup reaches, then passes me. It rolls on toward its own destination, the driver never taking a second glance my way. Nobody notices me, the girl with the long dark hair pulled through a baseball cap. The girl who's returning home after five long years. Nope, everyone goes about their day, doing whatever normal people do with their lives, as I struggle to drive faster than fifteen miles per hour up a hill that will crest on the outskirts of Grove Pointe Corner.

"I can't do it!"

Panic assaults me and I veer to the right, the muddy shoulder of the road sucking at my wheels as I pull to a stop. Ramming the gear stick into park, I scarcely check for oncoming vehicles as I throw open my door in time to lose the small lunch and three energy drinks I've consumed all over the cracked edge of the asphalt.

I hang there, one hand gripping the door to balance my body as I lean out of the car, the other clutching my waist as I spit the rancid taste of bile from my mouth. Two cars breeze by, the second coming ridiculously close to taking out my door and I draw back, startled. Sinking deep into my seat, I close myself inside my vehicle. Inside it's quiet. The radio's not turned on, the car warning bell no longer chimes, and the singing of the wind - that moments ago touched my face - no longer fills my ears.

I hear nothing.

I hear peace.

I feel peace.

Peace? My gaze lowers to my arm. *Of course.*

My right hand grips my left, my nails cutting into the pale skin of my forearm, leaving it blotched red. The canvas, already covered in faded white scars, is now imprinted with half-moon shapes where I'm digging in, to give myself relief.

To give myself peace.

Positioning my head against the headrest, I close my eyes and mentally instruct my fingers to ease up on the pressure they're applying. Every muscle in my body aches as I will myself to relax. I'm drawn taut as a bow, anxiety spilling from every pore as my heart pounds violently, and I berate myself out loud.

"Get it together. You're fine. You can do this."

Several cleansing breaths later, I open my eyes and shake out my left arm, tugging down my sleeve. Another vehicle passes by, and the driver tilts her head my way, before she continues on.

It's time to go.

I shift into drive and move back onto the road. Trying to calm the frantic beat of my heart, I flip the radio on. An upbeat pop song fills the car as I come to the four-way stop atop a crest overlooking the business district of Grove Pointe Corner. I stop, sitting for longer than necessary.

My eyes touch on the row of brick buildings in the distance below me before I make an impulsive decision and turn right.

This unplanned route winds around town, around *the spot*, and through the residential areas instead of the business district. As I circle town, I notice all the new sub-divisions where farm land once ruled. Field after field of my childhood now in various states of development. The lot where we would park each year for the annual Fourth-of-July fireworks remains vacant though, and I grin at the knee high dead grass waving in the wind. My auto-pilot on, I drive and drive, taking the wide arc around the country town I grew up in before everything changed. Before I ended up in Texas, before Crestdale, before this black hole in my mind. In my heart.

It's early evening when I return to Charlotte's city limits and I make a drive-thru pit stop for dinner before heading to my hotel for the night. Today was a bust. Well, not completely. I made it across the town line. That's progress from last night.

Two days, two failed attempts. Tomorrow will be the day.

Tomorrow I'm going to make it to Grove Pointe Corner.

Tomorrow I will pass *the spot*. I shudder.

"You can do it," I tell myself as I crawl into bed in my temporary home. Switching on the television, I lose myself in a sitcom fictionalizing how life is supposed to be.

Today's reality… Right. Again
January 14, 2018

I turn right at the four-way stop. Again…

As I drive the same quiet road I drove yesterday my anxiety washes away leaving the devil, known as doubt, in its wake. Doubt laughs deep in my gut, churning the contents of my stomach as it mocks me. It scoffs at the courage I'd worked up before leaving my hotel this morning. The courage I *thought* I'd worked up. I want to scream, to kick this doubt out of my head because I'm sick of it toying with my mind. My arm prickles as doubt teases me, whispering in my ear. "Take the edge off. It's easy. Just one cut."

I adjust the volume of the car radio to drown out the commands.

'Turn left,' another voice, my voice, shouts in my mind.

I follow the unspoken order as I'm rolling up to an intersection. Tugging at the steering wheel, my tires squeal in protest as I cut the intersection with a sharp turn. The change in direction is so sudden it causes my bag to fly across the passenger seat and fall to the floorboard. My hand pats the wheel in a silent apology as I gain my bearings. *I'm on Chapman!* I realize as my brain catches up with the unexpected decision my hands and car have already made. *Chapman runs straight into Grove Pointe Corner. The back way. The way that doesn't take me past Burkeside Avenue, aka the spot.*

"I found a way," I say to the empty car, cracking a smile and calling doubt a few choice words. Excited now, I accelerate. I'm finally on my way to Grove Pointe Corner. I'm finally home.

In reality, Grove Pointe Corner is more than one corner. It's a small, quaint area anchoring a sprawling town filled with little more than horse farms, corn fields, and residential neighborhoods. Once known as 'the country', it's now home to more and more people who are relocating to North Carolina. Coming in from this direction allows me to see the town center from start to finish. The park to my right, the offices and small shops on the left. The family-owned Italian restaurant we used to eat at. It's all the same and a heavy sense of deja-vu assaults me as I drive through. The Fall Fest, held every October on these streets, the Fourth-of-July parades, the Founders' Day event. All memories of my old life. A life that will never be the same. I accelerate, leaving the memories behind and two minutes later I'm heading toward my old high school. I know I should have stopped. What am I doing back here if I'm not going to stop and see the places and people of my past? I don't have an answer to that question, and doubt laughs at me as it oozes its way into my gut once more.

That's the way it is with doubt and fear. One step forward, two steps back. It's like ants at a picnic, you think you've protected everything, covered it up, but turn around and there they are. Ready and waiting to attack whatever pieces you leave vulnerable.

Shut up! I tell the inner critic as I turn into my old school parking lot. There's no need to enter the building to recall the memories of my abbreviated time here. They assault me the moment I roll to a stop and look at the brick building. My senses recall the eclectic mix of sweat, perfume and soaps from hundreds of student bodies crushed together in small hallways. The cacophony of crowded halls, slamming lockers, students' laughter, and shouting fill my head. Each flashback is so real, so fresh, it's as though I never left. They're all memories of a simple childhood. My lost childhood.

I hit the gas, speeding out of the school lot, trying to outrun the memories bombarding me. The peculiar scent of photocopied worksheets, text books, erasers, and lead fill my nostrils. Memories of the gymnasium — all rubber screeching against wood floors and shouts of victory — as I sit with friends and cheer for my team. As I cheer for Jonah. It's too much to bare; the lost moments of my life. The moments I should have had; if it weren't for the one moment I did.

My phone vibrates in the center console as I turn back onto the main road and I debate the wisdom of answering it. There are a handful of people who have this number and none of them would be happy to know I'd left Texas without informing them. Decision easily made; I'll ignore it for now.

Today's been a better day. I made progress. There's no need to spoil that. Yet.

Something I can't ignore, not forever, is people. My fear of running into someone I knew before has kept me from doing much more than running through drive-thrus for the past three days. I need to stop hiding in my hotel. I'm running out of clean clothing and personal items, and I'm going to have to stop by a store soon if I plan on staying in Charlotte.

I tell myself again how large the city is and how unlikely it is that I would run into anyone. Kids I knew in school should be away at college. Plus, the city is filled with so many places to eat and shop, what's the likelihood someone will recognize me after five years? I repeat this mantra as I drive, debating on the best place to stop and take my first baby steps out. The internationally-known green and white circular sign makes the decision for me. Coffee. It's simple, requires speaking to someone, and is fast enough to keep me from lingering if I feel anxious. Done and done.

Finding the closest parking spot to the building, I park and hurry across the street, entering the small shop. It's a typical franchise with perfect looking baristas about my age wiping down fancy machines and calling out complicated drink orders as fast as they take them. The air has a hint of burnt coffee mixed with the smell of sweet mocha and I inhale, letting the wondrous scent comfort me. The majority of my coffee drinking years have been spent in group therapy rooms and rehab centers. I'm accustomed to bitter coffee, served by bitter people, so when it's my turn I take a cue from the tennis skirt woman in front of me and order a salted caramel mocha. Hot. Yes, whip cream - *duh?*

The shop is cramped, with two leather chairs flanked by three small tables up front and two more tables against a wall leading out the back door. Behind me shelves are stacked with mugs and coffee themed gifts, and I peruse them as I wait for my drink, feigning interest at their contents. A well-dressed man, carrying a leather portfolio, enters the shop. He looks at ease, normal, as he drops the portfolio in one of the empty chairs before ordering coffee: black. His dark eyes meet mine as the cashier swipes his card and he smiles with a nod. The moment feels awkward, but I return his smile before turning back to the wall of merchandise.

"Venti salted caramel mocha for... Danica," a male employee calls, jolting me from my window shopping.

"Thanks." I take the warm cup from his hand as he mutters a robotic 'have a nice day' and moves on to his next order. Now I find myself faced with a dilemma. Do I have a seat and pretend to be absorbed in my smart phone, similar to the lady sitting at the counter? Or, do I leave? Mr. Black Coffee, who's taken his seat, glances at his watch and shuffles some papers in the folder he's holding. The way he taps his foot to the beat of the soft rock music being piped through the store speakers makes me think he's nervous about something. He seems safe enough though, and I'm considering being brave enough to sit at the table near him when he stands abruptly, smiling as another professionally dressed gentleman enters the store. Realizing I'm standing in the center of the coffee shop staring at two perfect strangers, I decide to make my exit before someone notices my awkwardness. *So much for being normal today.*

Head down, I push my way out of the glass door and immediately smack into something. The impact causes hot coffee to splatter from the lid, scalding my hand as I stumble back on my heels. A grip of steel grasps my arm while a large hand covers my fingers, holding onto my cup, as a phone crashes to the ground between us.

"Holy… nobody told me there was a wall here," I gasp, biting my bottom lip from the sting of the hot droplets hitting the sensitive skin on my hand.

"Whoa, you okay?" The wall — who's actually a man, judging by his deep voice — asks at the same time, releasing my bicep now that I've regained my balance. I'm stunned by the large figure in front of me. He's built similar to a football player: huge arms, wide shoulders, and two heads taller than me. Very much the wall I thought him to be at first impact.

"Are you planning on snatching my drink?" I ask boldly, looking up at the behemoth. The sun casts his features into the shadows, but the tilt of his head shows his confusion at my comment. "I've heard of purse snatchers, but coffee snatchers? That's a new one," I joke, nodding toward his hand covering mine.

Catching on, he releases me and steps back. "Depends on the drink. I'll warn you though, the more words you used to order it, the less likely it is I'd want it."

My lips twitch at his witty come-back as I switch my coffee to my free hand and examine the red welts caused by the hot liquid. The black cell phone on the sidewalk catches my eye and I recall the clatter of it falling moments ago. "You dropped your phone."

"It's alright." He crouches down, picking up the chunky phone, and flashes it at me. "I sprang for the heavy duty case for moments such as this."

"This happens to you often, then?" The moment the words leave my mouth I wish I could swallow them back down. *I'm having a real conversation with a stranger.* My insides twist at the thought as he chuckles, and heat rushes to my face.

"It's best to always be prepared," he replies, but I barely hear him over the sudden pick-up of my heart. "Did you get burned?" he asks stepping closer. His long shadow overtakes me and, to my bewilderment, I find myself both excited and nauseous.

"No… no, I'm fine. It was a little splash." I hurry to spit the words out as perspiration pops up on my forehead. "Sorry for crashing into you."

"Well, how in the hell could you have known there'd be a wall in your way?" he teases.

If I were normal, I'd smile, twirl my hair and flirt, but I'm not normal. I give him a short dismissive wave instead of the smile I'm sure he's hoping for. "Sorry, I must be going."

"Uh, yeah… I wasn't watching my step, too busy reading email to uh… anyway, it's not your fault. Sorry." He stumbles over his last words, but I barely hear them. I'm already crossing the street and heading to my parked car.

My hands are shaking as I set the coffee on the roof of my car and fumble through my purse for my keys. Hitting the unlock button, I slide into the driver seat with a heavy sigh before I allow myself a glance back at the sidewalk. The stranger is gone, but my racing heart and sick feeling are not. The moment he invaded my personal space, his height towering over me, I panicked. I have no idea why.

Waiting for the traffic light to turn, I go over the interaction. The first few moments felt normal, the moments after first impact — when I wasn't thinking — I handled those moments well. It wasn't until I realized what I was doing that my body freaked out.

Baby steps, I remind myself. It'll get easier. I head back to the hotel, my mind working ninety miles a minute. *Tomorrow is Sunday. I need to call Gram and Gramps and tell them where I am and what I intend to do. Of course maybe I need to figure out what I intend to do first*, I admit. The rest of the afternoon and evening are spent sitting in my hotel room devising a plan. A life plan, as my various therapists would call it.

Step one — face the spot. Face the past.

Step two — …

Closing my eyes, I tap the hotel pen against my thigh trying to visualize my second step. Eventually I give up, scribbling 'figure it out once you make it past step one' on the notepad and throwing it onto the bedside table. Dejected, I do what I've done each night of my stay here. I switch on the television and flip the stations until I find another formula sitcom. I land on the same one I've watched the past two nights and lose myself, pretending my life is as easy as the twenty-something characters' lives I'm watching. From what I've seen in the past few episodes, they are a tight knit group of friends living out their lives and loves to a soundtrack of laughs all while maintaining perfect hair and drinking lots of coffee.

Damn unrealistic television shows.

Today's reality… Taking baby steps
January 15, 2018

Courage: Strength in the face of pain or grief.

*T*oday's the day. I chant the mantra as, once again, my tires roll across the indention in the road entering into Grove Pointe. *Today I will drive straight.*

My eyes focus on the towering steeple of the church coming into view as I arrive at my nemesis: the four-way stop. Behind it, the January sky is a crystal Carolina blue. Bright and clear. A direct contrast with the way my heart feels as I sit here.

"Today you're driving straight," I whisper into the empty vehicle, stopping my hand mid-motion as it moves to flip the turning signal. *Courage.*

Sucking in a breath, my foot applies pressure to the gas, and I glide through the intersection for the first time since I was fifteen years old. A burning sensation breaks out across my lower legs, and I shake the feeling off as I drive on, my eyes glued to what's in front of me.

Statistically speaking, the majority of car accidents happen within two to five miles from your home. A relic memory from my Driver's Ed class, the once useless fact pops into my mind as I pass the entrance to the Hall's neighborhood. Two-to-five miles. I grew up one point four miles from Jonah Hall.

My mind ticks off the directions automatically: leave his neighborhood and turn south on Grove Point Highway, making your way down and back up the hilly street for three-quarters of a mile. Burkside Avenue is the first right and my neighborhood was the first left. Turn in, take the first right, and we were the last house at the end of the cul-de-sac.

It was a simple trip; five minutes by car, tops. Once we hit middle school, Jonah would jog the route after school most afternoons so we could hang out. Who would have thought anything bad could happen on a trip we took for granted thousands of times before?

Today's reality… This is how life was
December 22, 2012

"If I'm forced to join in another sing-along I swear I'll jump off your back balcony."

"Aw, what's the matter? Not feeling the Christmas spirit?" asks Jonah, ladling punch into his antler covered glass. "Want some?"

"Punch?" I question. "Is the soda gone? Something less third grade party."

"No, Scrooge, there's a cooler full over there." He points toward the coolers sitting along the kitchen wall. "Help yourself."

I move to grab a can when Jonah's next words stop me. "However, if you want something more adult, I do suggest the punch."

My jaw drops as Jonah sends me a wicked wink. He lifts his glass, taking a sip, the absurd dancing reindeer picture catching my eye as he lowers it in a mock 'cheers' and my brows snap together.

"You spiked the punch?" I look over my shoulder into the living room where our parents and many of their friends are conjured together.

The musical high pitched laughter of several women rings out, mixing with the unmistakable bark of my father's, and soon other voices join in. Hands claps in merriment and I turn back to Jonah. He's holding a glass for me. The red liquid matches the boa the reindeer, Vixen, is wearing, and I accept the drink nervously

"Of course I didn't spike the punch. This is Virginia's special concoction, guaranteed to spread holiday cheer." He laughs, referring to his own mother by name, knowing she hates it when he does that.

"Danica?" My mother sings out from the other room, and I groan inwardly, knowing I'm about to be asked for another performance.

"No way, c'mon," Jonah says, his eyes twinkling with mischief. The look makes me question how many glasses of punch he's had.

He grabs my hand, pulling me from the kitchen in the opposite direction of my mother's voice, hurrying through the side hallway and up a back staircase. My heels click on the hardwood floor as we sneak away and I try to walk on my toes. At the top of the staircase, Jonah stops, leaning forward and looking down over the balcony railing into the living room below. His pause gives me time to slip off my shoes and catch my breath. Leaving my shoes by the stairs, I join him and peer down at the festive party below. I spot my father standing in a semicircle surrounded by his buddies, all in complementing poses; one hand

16

in a pocket with a beverage of some sort in the other. There are multiple identical groups scattered about the large room; sophisticated men talking about whatever sophisticated men talk about.

The women are perched on chairs and couches, their legs crossed daintily, wine glasses in hand. Their jewels and sequins catch and reflect the cheerful Christmas lights throughout the house. The hallway where we're standing is dark with the exception of the garland and twinkle lights draped over the balcony's wrought iron railing. I look down, catching the twinkling reflection of my red punch sparkling in the lights and I take a sip, nearly choking on the potent liquid.

"Good Lord! Is there any punch in here?" I sputter, taking a whiff of the cup.

Jonah's arm jerks me back into the dark shadows, his finger going to his lips as he nods downstairs. "Come on, Scrooge," he whispers. His warm hand takes mine again and tugs me down the hall.

I've known Jonah Hall my entire life. Our parents were friends before we were born, our mothers sorority sisters in college and our fathers golfing buddies. I've been in this house more times than I can count, but I haven't hung out upstairs in two years.

"Where's Kadence?" I ask as he pushes the door to the game room open and pulls me in.

The space is decorated for Christmas with a large tree full of handmade ornaments adorning the branches. The multi-colored lights on the tree provide the only illumination, filling the room with a rainbow of light. As children, we played Lego's and Monopoly in here. We watched movies and cartoons and shared countless hours playing video games, but as I walk in tonight, it feels different. Jonah is no longer Jonah, my best friend, the boy who built the best Lego ships or who taught me how to hit a baseball during recess in the second grade. He's *Jonah*, the guy who broke Carrie Hoyt's heart at the homecoming dance two months ago because, rumor has it, he's interested in someone else. He's *Jonah*, the sophomore class president and co-captain of the JV lacrosse team. The stud.

"She's at a sleepover."

The door snaps closed behind me and I spin on my toes, startled and unaccountably nervous. He takes another sip of the drink he's carrying and I follow suit, trying my best not to choke this time. I succeed, but not without allowing my face to pull back at the taste as a shiver runs through me.

"Dani, you're so freaking adorable," Jonah grins, crossing to my side.

"Adorable?" I cock my head, fighting the urge to step back as he closes in. "You say that as though it's a bad thing."

"Not at all, I like adorable things," he says suggestively. *Suggestively?* I shake the silly thought from my head.

My mouth chooses that moment to hum "My Favorite Things" from *The Sound of Music*. It's a horrible habit I have, I can't help it. It's as though I live in my own musical the way I break out into random songs. One time, my History teacher brought up Paul Revere's name in a lesson and next thing he knew I was whistling "Yankee Doodle Dandy". When you've grown up taking voice lessons most of your life everything reminds you of a melody.

"See. Adorable," he points out, wiggling his finger at me, one brow lifting to emphasize his point. "I forgot that about you."

I stop humming, feeling the burn of humiliation creep into my cheeks, and I'm relieved at the lack of lighting in the room as we stand there. His sudden scrutiny is making me twitchy and I change tactics, using sarcasm to get away from the spotlight of his gaze.

"You have a poor memory, Jonah Hall. I believe the last time I was in this room you did not think me adorable," I remind him, taking another sip of my drink. Now that the initial gag factor is gone the punch isn't half bad. It tingles as it goes down, landing in my stomach and spreading its warmth through my limbs.

Jonah's perplexed and I wonder if he's forgotten the last time we 'played' together. When he lifts his punch and drains the cup without speaking, I'm sure he has. Part of me is disappointed he can't remember, but then he clucks his tongue and looks me over.

He walks to the book shelves along the back wall without a word and I follow every move he makes, extremely curious. Squatting down, he opens a cabinet and I swallow back my laughter as he rummages around. After a moment, he stands, holding the somewhat battered blue box from our past.

"You do remember," I breathe out, falling to the couch as he walks around it and drops the box on the coffee table. Pulling up a chair across from me, he sits and pushes the Connect Four box my way.

"Rematch?" he asks.

"Hmm, that depends," I grin, pausing to take another drink. I lick my lips deliberately, my flair for dramatics duly noted by the boy across from me as his light eyes narrow in on my mouth. I find myself giddy at the way he's looking at me and I'm forced to draw a steadying breath before I can finish my thought. "Do you plan on cheating again?"

He erupts into contagious laughter, sitting back and stretching his long legs out. "You cheated, not me."

"Oh. No. I. Did. Not," I giggle.

I set my now empty glass down as I reach for the game, plucking the lid off and sucking in air as memories wash over me. Scattered inside the box, among the red and black chips and the plastic pieces of the board, are scrap pieces of paper with scribbles and tally marks. I'd nearly forgotten how competitive we used to be. I finger a small slip of notebook paper as Jonah pulls the game out and sets it up. He shoves the red chips my way with a wink, and my heart leaps. Red was always my color.

"Ladies first," he offers, and I'm struck by the intimate feelings creeping into me as I look at him. *Get a grip, this is Jonah,* I think as I shake off the feelings, again.

Leaning forward, I drop my first chip into the middle slot and he quickly drops one on the end. Back and forth we go, our initial moves swift, before we slow and strategy comes into play. A sharp squeal of laughter seeps into the room and I catch Jonah roll his eyes with a chuckle. I'm leaning forward, my elbows resting on my knees as I debate where to move next, but his slight movement lures my eyes to his face and I'm paralyzed by the look he's giving me. Girls are always swooning over the signature 'Jonah Hall gaze' but I've never had the privilege of seeing it in action. *Holy cow! I've been missing some good stuff, man.*

"Are you contemplating your next move or my last," I ask, sitting back.

He twirls a black chip between his fingers and I imagine those fingers interlocked with mine. I wonder what it would be like. To walk down the halls of Grove Pointe High on his arm. To share my lunch hour with him, to giggle at his jokes and swoon at his kisses, the way Carrie Hoyt used to.

I expect a cute reply when he drops his chip into an empty slot and crosses his arms. Instead he asks, "Why did we stop hanging out?"

"Why did we stop hanging out?" I repeat, as I spy the way he's set me up for a double win. All I have to do is place my piece in its slot and he can't win. "We still hang out."

"No, we don't. Not like we used to. How come?" he asks again.

I know what he's referring to. Although our families are always together, Jonah and I now have social lives. He used to spend the majority of his afternoons at my house shooting hoops. In middle school, we used to hang out on the weekends, playing games or swimming, while our parents grilled. Now when our parents get together, one, or both, of us tends to skip out, always seeming to have 'better' things to do. We nod at each other at school, chat during the classes we share, and hang out with mutual friends at parties, but we don't hang out like best friends the way we once did. Not anymore.

"I think we agreed it was this dreaded game," I tease, lifting a brow and claiming victory as I drop my chip in.

I want to boast, but the way he drops his own piece in, without looking, tells me he was already done playing and that he let me win. I take little pleasure in dropping the winning chip, but I do it anyway. I sigh, catching my tongue with my teeth to keep from harassing him. *Always so competitive.*

Sitting back, I finally allow myself to stare at him the way he's been watching me. He's dressed for his parents' annual party, he's never done that. As kids we used to hole up in this room with a babysitter, eating junk food and watching Christmas movies while the grown-ups partied downstairs. Then one year I begged to perform a special song for the party and they consented. I've been singing at the parties ever since. For five years now, I've come to the parties and sang and mingled with the guests afterward, but Jonah's never bothered to make an appearance. I recall seeing him the first year I arrived all dressed up to sing instead of to hang out with him. He frowned at me curiously, disappearing upstairs, but when it was time for me to sing I spotted him standing at the same balcony we stood earlier. He'd left before I finished singing that night and he's never watched since. When the parties were over he used to come down and share some cake with me while our parents cleaned up, but, as far as I know, the past two years he hasn't been home during the party. Tonight, however, he's here and dressed to perfection. His tall frame clad in dark slacks, his white dress shirt pressed meticulously, with the exception of the shirt sleeves he's rolled up to his forearms. His presence makes me curious, so I ask him about it.

Countering his question about us not hanging out anymore, I copy his tone and ask, "Why are you here tonight?"

"It's my house, you know." I let him see my frown and he pushes his chair back with a shrug. "I like the punch."

For some reason his flippant answer bothers me and I slide to the edge of the leather couch prepared to return downstairs. I'm sure my mother is more than curious about my whereabouts. I stand and Jonah pops up from his seat as well. I smooth the nonexistent wrinkles from my festive party dress as I mutter, "Always the jokester."

"Fine. I wanted to see you. I mean, we barely talk anymore and it kind of sucks."

It requires a fair measure of self-discipline to keep my jaw from falling open at his remark. "It does kind of suck," I agree.

I get the feeling he wants to say more, that he's about to say more, when the door to the room opens admitting both my mother and the party noise from below.

"Jonah! I didn't know you were here tonight." She smiles, her eyes tracking from Jonah's face to mine. "Danica, the Smiths arrived and would love to hear you sing. Would you please come down, sweetheart?"

It's hard not to show my irritation as I nod and pick up my empty glass. "Of course, I'll be right there."

She nods and flutters out of the doorway with a bright smile thrown Jonah's way.

"Contemplating that jump off the balcony now?" he teases dryly when she's gone.

"Among other things," I admit, and he smirks.

I pass him close enough to smell the cologne he's wearing tonight and I take a deep breath, sucking in the scent. He doesn't speak until I'm exiting the room.

"Hey, Dani?" I pause, looking over my shoulder. "Would you considering taking a different jump?" I give him a confused look and he clarifies. "Instead of going off the balcony."

I giggle, "What did you have in mind? I could drown myself or get sloshed on your mom's punch. They wouldn't want me singing drunk now wou-"

He interrupts my joke, his face one hundred percent serious as he says, "Go out with me."

I'm sure I've heard him wrong. I remain frozen there, flabbergasted, looking across the room at him. At Jonah Hall: my playpen playmate-turned best friend-turned chick magnet... and in that moment I realize we'll never be what we were when we were kids. This changes everything.

The sound of the piano downstairs warns me the crowd is waiting and I open my mouth to answer, but nothing comes out. So I flee instead, scooping up my heels as I rush down the stairs, both mortified for leaving him standing there and excited at this development.

The adults I've known most of my life greet me as I join my mother at the piano, her face full of pride. Smoothing my hair as the sweet melody of "Where Are You Christmas" begins, I allow the music to sink in as I prepare to sing. As much as I complained to Jonah earlier about having to sing for this crowd, it was a complete lie. I live for the adoration I see on their faces. Singing is what I do well. It's what I love.

The first lyrics leave my lips and I'm swept away, my eyes flitting around the room, touching on faces as I tell the story of a girl looking for her lost joy of the holiday. The chorus builds and I raise my head. Standing at the balcony watching me is Jonah, in the same spot he was five years ago, a beaming smile on his lips. Our gazes hold as I finish the last notes with my own smile. It always takes me a few moments before I come down to earth after a performance. The music transports me to my own world and I take deep breaths as the guests' claps and calls of 'bravo' break through my performance haze. Mom stands and we both curtsy, accepting their gracious praise. Afterward we circulate the room - something a performer should always do, so my teacher has said - and I answer the same questions I'm asked every year.

"Have you thought of Juilliard?" "Will you audition for any colleges?" "Have you ever considered going on that singing talent show?" I smile, thanking each person for their kind words and answering the same way for each one, "It's something I've considered."

Round and round we go, conversation after conversation, but my focus keeps returning to the balcony as I look for Jonah. He stood there for a while after I performed; I was taking peeks, trying to keep an eye on him, but now he's gone. I'm startled by how deflated his disappearance makes me feel.

"How about we do an encore?" My mother suggests at my side.

"Actually, Mrs. Evans, can I steal her away for a minute?" My spine stiffens as Jonah's voice sounds behind me. "I promise to bring her right back."

I don't dare look at his face, it would give everything away. Every feeling I thought I'd pushed down and locked away about Jonah a while ago. So I focus on my mothers' face instead and it tells an interesting story. She beaming, and I wonder if she suspects something is brewing between Jonah and me. The idea sounds crazy to my own mind. *How could anything happen between us?* The slow nod of her shiny updo is all the answer Jonah needs. His fingers take mine, not weaving between mine as I'd imagined earlier, but enveloping my smaller hand in his larger warm one. He leads me out of the living room and through the kitchen, pausing at the glass doors to the sun room. The room is occupied by a few couples and he tugs me forward again, mumbling under his breath.

"Where are you taking me?" We take five steps before he stops, looking around again. "Jonah?"

His eyes level on me, his brows raise and a smirk plays on his lips. I clearly remember the look from when we were eight and he'd convinced me to walk on the trunk of a fallen baby tree to cross an overflowing creek. It worked then and it works now. I trust him, and close my mouth. After a moment of looking around he hurries toward the small hallway on our left, throwing open the door to the laundry room and yanking me inside.

"Are you crazy?"

"Go out with me," he counters in the dark. My arm stretches around his body, searching for the light switch I know should be somewhere near his shoulder. The bright lights jolt us as I flip the switch.

"Jonah —"

"Go out with me," he repeats for the third time tonight.

"Why?"

He laughs. "Because you like me." He states it as fact and I don't bother to argue his point, not when it's the truth. "And, because I like you. I broke up with Carrie because of you."

"Um, you what?" His confession takes me by complete surprise.

"I don't know when it happened, D. One day I was sitting in Civics, minding my own business, and I looked back to ask you something and there you were flirting with Tate. I had this immediate urge to hit him. Really hard," he confesses, his face the picture of irritation.

Now I was the one laughing. "You did not."

"Oh yeah, I most certainly did. That same week I was on the verge of hitting at least three other guys I saw you with, and I knew. I knew I wanted to go out with you myself."

"You watched me sing," I blurt out, making no sense, but Jonah agrees with a nod. "You haven't watched me since the sixth grade."

His fingers skim my bare arm, giving me goosebumps, and he shakes his head. "Not true, I watched you last year, I just didn't let you see me. And before that I always listened from my doorway."

"Our parents will probably start buying us wedding china and planning our big day the moment they find out," I reason, but instead of terror his face lights up with a huge smile.

"Probably."

"Let's not tell them then, not yet," I suggest.

"That's a yes then? You're saying yes?" I nod and he shifts, settling back against the door and drawing me closer. "I hope you don't mind, but I'm going to kiss you now."

"You're kissing me?" I gasp as his shoulder hits the light switch, blanketing us in darkness again.

"Hell yeah, I'm kissing you," he chuckles as his lips meet mine and I lose all ability to think.

Tonight's reality… Did that seriously just happen?
December 22, 2012

After one long, and extremely pleasant, kiss in the laundry room Jonah and I carefully rejoin the party before our parents come looking for us. The next hour is spent throwing secretive glances across the room at each other as we socialize. I find myself walking to the food table every time Jonah's there. Each time we meet he makes some snide comment about something an adult has said. Half of the party is past their legal limit at this point and the jokes are becoming longer and bawdier by the minute. The way Jonah retells the stories has me returning to his side more than necessary, and by the time the party winds down, my dress is ready to bust at the seams from so much snacking. As always, my parents stay behind after every one has left to help clean up. Jonah and I take the opportunity to find a private moment.

"Did you seriously ask me to go out with you two hours ago?" I ask as he stalks around a corner, blocking me against the wall.

"Is there something wrong with that?"

"We've known each other all our lives. You can't tell me it doesn't seem a little strange," I point out. Jonah stills and his lips purse together. I've seen the look a million times through the years, I know he's thinking.

"Are you changing your mind?" he asks.

I dislike the trepidation in his question. Back in middle school there was a time when I'd come upon Jonah playing basketball with no shirt on after school. It was hot that day and he'd jogged to my house, his face splotched red, his hair plastered with sweat, and I'd run into the house to get him water. When I returned he was shirtless and dribbling a ball in my driveway. There was nothing new about my seeing Jonah Hall shirtless, we'd vacationed at the beach together every year of our lives. But, that day… that day there was something about him. Something that made my entire body light up like fireworks on the Fourth of July. I carried a secret crush, all queasy stomach and obnoxious giggles at his jokes, for weeks after that. When he punched me in the arm, as though I was one of the guys, I sighed and reveled in the attention he gave me. However, as quickly as the feelings came, they left. I chalked it up to hormones, PMS, to the new romance novel I was reading, or to my silly girlfriends and all of their boy craziness. Anything I could think of to explain why I'd crushed on Jonah, I used. Tonight, though, I'm admitting the truth; that crush never went away.

Giving him my best smile, I lean against the wall, dragging him back with me. He's stiff, his face full of doubt, but his hands land on my waist. "I'm not changing my mind. It's strange though, right? Like a fairy tale or some sitcom. You know, 'best friends fall for each other after years of friendship.' I never thought it happened in real life," I admit.

Amusement flickers in his eyes, along with something else. Hunger? He's eying me the way Tate, my-ex, used to before he'd lean in to steal a kiss. My tongue darts out, moistening my lips as Jonah moves in and I close my eyes. *This could be perfect*, I think with a sigh.

"Think your parents will let me pick you up for a real date tomorrow night?" he asks between quick pecks.

"Weeelll," I draw out playfully and he kisses me again, effectively shutting me up. When he pulls away I finish my answer. "You realize you're changing the roles here. When you're talking about dates you will cease to be good old Jonah. All bets are off once they start looking at you as my boyfriend."

"Is that what I am now? Your boyfriend?" His blond brows waggle in an exaggerated motion and I shove him.

"I dunno, I haven't gone out on a date with you yet, plus you're impossibly annoying. Do you think you could be boyfriend material? Come to think of it, I'm not sure I even *like* you," I complain with a shrug.

"I know all of your secrets, Danica Evans, you can't lie to me. You totally like me." He's so sure of himself.

Wrapping my arms around his neck, my fingers delve into the shaggy hair grazing his collar, and I smile. "I like kissing you. That counts for something, doesn't it?"

"That counts for a whole lot of something," he agrees as his lips claim mine once more.

"Danica, hun, let's get going," my mother calls from somewhere in the house, and we reluctantly pull apart. My mind might not know what to think about Jonah Hall right now, but my body sure as heck does. I'm breathless from his kisses, my limbs are nothing but jelly as his arms hold me.

Our parents' whispers carry through the foyer into the house as we wander hand in hand to the downstairs guest room where Jonah retrieves my coat. He's advancing on me, stalking me until my legs are pressed up against the bed, when the *tap, tap, tap* of heels alert us of someone's impending arrival. A moment later Mrs. Hall pops into the room.

"My goodness, you two sure do keep disappearing tonight. What are you doing, Jonah?"

"Helping Dani with her coat, what does it look like?" he asks innocently. I smother my embarrassed laughter, giving his mother a sweet shrug.

"It's late, honey. Your parents are waiting." She motions for me to follow, calling out "I found her" a few feet ahead of us.

Behind me, Jonah tugs my coat, leaning closer and whispering in my ear, "You're so my girlfriend."

And that's the scene our parents witness as we walk into the foyer. Jonah takes a hasty step back, putting space between us, and I'm grinning from ear to ear as though he's told the funniest joke I've ever heard.

Tonight's new reality… In a flash
December 23, 2012

"You and Jonah, eh?"

"What! Daddy, no-" My voice cracks in the midst of my unnaturally high-pitched denial.

My mother swats at his head. "Brad, don't you dare," she hisses. Something in her tone leads me to believe they'd already discussed Jonah and me when we weren't around.

The only light in the vehicle is the glow of the dashboard, but I don't have to see his face, to feel the burn of his stare. He must be chewing a hole in his lip, trying to keep from teasing me. Whatever he's doing only works until we get to the entrance of the Hall's neighborhood. Quiet isn't something my dad excels at. Nope, he can't keep his opinion to himself. "I suppose he's going to be calling for permission to ask you out now, isn't he?"

I knew they'd discussed us! It's probably what their conversation in the foyer was about. I snort at his suggestion. "Boys don't call and ask for permission to ask girls out anymore, Daddy."

"But he will be asking you out won't he?" he counters.

My mother groans in the back seat. "For goodness sake, would you let her concentrate on the road?" she warns. "Honestly… she shouldn't be driving at this hour or in this weather anyway. We should have stayed at the Hall's."

As we were leaving, my parents argued over letting me drive. The ground was wet from a short drizzle and the temperature was dropping steadily. Mom worried about black ice, but my dad pointed out how they'd both been drinking. I used my best Daddy's princess voice and puppy dog eyes to convince him to allow me behind the wheel.

"Yeah, I'm not thinking there will be any more sleepovers at the Hall's," Dad says meaningfully and I giggle in spite of myself. "Besides she was right, LeAnn, neither of us is fit to drive tonight and she'll be sixteen in, what, nine days now," he points out.

"Eight. I'll be sixteen in eight days," I correct him, taking my hand off of the steering wheel to point at the clock. It's after midnight, December twenty-third.

"Eight-" Dad mutters.

"Look out!"

We're cresting a small hill when my mother's warning shout comes and I jerk my attention from my father to the scene laid out before us. Sitting sideways in the dark road is a car, its emergency flashers blinking red on the wet asphalt in warning, but it's too late.

The rush of blood filling my ears and pumping through my body is all I hear as I clutch the steering wheel. Instructions from driver's education pop into my mind and I'm careful not to slam the brakes too hard. I tap the pedal, easing our speed and turning the wheels to the left, attempting to guide us to the other side of the disabled vehicle. It should have been okay, we should have swerved around the disabled vehicle and been on our way with nothing but racing hearts and muttered curses as a remembrance of this moment. But it's not to be. As I turn the wheel, perhaps a bit too hard, we lose control. The declining hill in combination with the slick, icy roads mix to create the perfect storm. We don't slow down, but instead the vehicle picks up speed and loses contact with the asphalt below us.

Everything happens in a flash, an arm — my father's — thrusts across my chest pinning me to my seat, my mother screams, my father curses, and I go into shock. Our headlights slash across the vehicle before us and I catch the unmistakable blur of a guy, his face full of fear, as we spin past him. Then my world turns up-side down.

I'm sprawled across a chaise lounge by the pool, the summer sun blazing down and warming my body as the smell of hot dogs and burgers on the grill fills the air. My eyes are closed as I try to sleep, but the heat is unbearable and I sit forward, deciding to cool off in the pool.

"Gotcha," Jonah shouts in my ear, his arms wrapping around me from behind and holding me hostage.

"Let go, Jonah. I'm going swimming." I flail and wiggle in his arms. He laughs, but doesn't release his grip.

"Mom, Dad," I yell for my parents' help to get Jonah off of me as the heat steals my breath. The air clouds with more and more smoke and I search for the grill, thinking to warn my dad of the burning food. I cough at the smoke. Jonah's face pops in front of me, even though I'm still trapped by his arms.

Confusion sets in as his face flickers in front of me, "Wake up, Dani, wake up!"

Wake up? Desperate for the cool water of the pool, I close my eyes once more and scream as I attempt to jerk free again.

"Wake up!"

I come to, Jonah and my backyard disappearing, as reality sets in. I'm surrounded by broken glass, a car roof that's too low, and a full blown fire that has engulfed our vehicle, the heat licking at my face. And I can't move.

"Mom! Daddy!" I cry out as the first stab of pain breaks through the shock my body is under. "Help!"

A voice shouts near my head and metal groans as something pounds into the door next to me, but all I can focus on is the acrid fumes burning around me. And the pain. The pain is the worst.

"Hey! Hey, it's going to be okay. I'm getting you out," the voice by my ear shouts, and I realize I'm in hysterics. Something thick and warm runs into my eye, marring my view, and I panic.

"Get me out. I don't want to die," I scream, my arms flailing as I search for whatever is pinning me to my seat. "Mom, Dad! I don't want to die, help me please, I don't want to…" I cry.

A thick cloud of smoke chokes me and I stop screaming, covering my face with my arm. A explosion pops, the snapping of the angry flames drowning out everything else.

"Hey! Turn your head," the voice outside the vehicle shouts, and I search through the thick cloud for his face as a window explodes. Shards of glass rain down, stinging my exposed skin. My eyes burn so I don't see, as much as feel, the body that falls across mine. He curses as he yanks at my waist, his arm slipping and jabbing into my chest. I reach out, grabbing at him as he pulls away.

"Don't leave me here, please," I beg.

"I'm right here. I'm not going anywhere. I'm pulling you out of this car right now, just hang on," he promises, his voice panicked and full of urgency.

"The damn door is stuck. Did you call 911?" His voice is muffled and I think he's talking to someone else, shouting orders I can barely process in my fuzzy mind. A crying voice mumbles a reply. Mine? I'm not sure.

A million pins and needles slash across my shins and I scream, "Nooo! The fire. Help me…"

"Court! The fire's in the car. Help me get her out. Court!" He shouts, his voice near my head again as arms yank at me.

I kick out, my feet crunching glass as I flail like a fish out of water. The floor below me becomes an inferno and instinct tells me to move away. I try curling into a ball, I try to slink away from the fire slowly eating away at my legs, but I can't move. The steering wheel has me pinned at the knees. The guy at my head is pressing my back into the seat. Curses and shouts, mine and the man beside me, fill the air, and I no longer know what's happening. All I know is pain and I want it to end.

The pressure against my chest is finally released as the guy helping me says, "C'mon. Come here." His arms tug and pull at mine until he's lifting and drawing me up out of my seat and through the broken window. His heavy grunts join with my cries of agony as my broken and burning body is hoisted from the vehicle and we fall to the ground. I writhe as I hit the ground and my rescuer slaps at my bare legs.

"My parents! Where are my parents?" I manage to ask.

"Get away from the car, it could blow," a girl screams, dropping to the ground by our sides and pulling on the guy helping me. They drag me away from the vehicle and every fiber of my soul wants to crawl back to the burning car to find my parents. Where are they? The sound of sirens fills the air as a chill, a numbness, seeps into my bones.

"Hey, stay with me. Okay?" my rescuer asks. "The ambulance is on the way. What's your name?" he asks, but I can't answer; I can't think. I can't move.

Blackness closes in as my hair is pushed from my face. My last memory is his voice saying, "Stay with me. Come on. Stay with me."

Today's reality… Nightmare versus reality
Date unknown

Nightmare - a bad dream that brings out strong feelings of fear, terror, distress, or anxiety.
Reality - the state of things as they actually exist.
My reality is a nightmare.

I'm in and out of consciousness. I have no idea what day it is, where I'm at, or who is speaking - even though I hear their voices. If I could make a tee shirt right now it would say:

Nightmare + Reality = my life.

The police report says it all:

At approximately 12:25 a.m., Friday, December 23, 2012 a car.. blah, blah, blah… driven by Danica Reese Evans, a minor… blah, blah, blah… Bradley S. Evans, 39, ejected from vehicle and dead on scene. LeAnn R. Evans, 38, dead on scene.

Cause of accident: weather related. No fault.

But I disagree. The fault is mine. I killed my parents.

Today's reality… Sweet oblivion
December 27, 2012

The scene in my hospital room is disturbing. Although I've been kept sedated, I'm occasionally lucid enough to catch sight of the spectacle. Flowers, plants, stuffed animals, and gift baskets of all sizes and shapes clutter every surface of the room I'm currently calling home. Presents for the girl who killed her parents. *Do they not know what I did?* My brain shouts the sentiment as I catch the polite smile of another nurse who's going over my condition with my grandparents.

As I know it, the state of my condition is this:

"Danica is a trooper, Mr. and Mrs. Evans. The burns on her shins and calves will be the most time consuming of her injuries. The process will hurt *(like hell)* blah, blah, blah, and as we continue blah, blah, blah, as the skin heals. She will be in some *(massive)* pain as we blah, blah, blah. But, with time and several surgeries and visits with a plastic surgeon she could minimize her scarring. She should be almost new *(as if)*."

Almost new... minimal scarring... the burns are the most time consuming. Apparently they teach creative optimism at whatever nursing school she went to. It all sounds like a bunch of crap to my foggy brain. Grams' usually perfect face and hair is haggard after several days in North Carolina with me. I want to tell her to go home, to get some rest, and forget about me for a while. To mourn the loss of her son and daughter-in-law and leave me be, but the drugs they have me on take that choice away.

I'm an empty shell right now, watching everything happening around me. Each time I wake Gram is dabbing at her red-rimmed eyes and Gramps isn't much better. His face is vacant as he takes in all of the information the doctors and nurses throw at him, and he looks as numb as I feel. The best part of my day is when 'little nurse sunshine's' speech comes to an end and she holds up a fresh IV.

"Let me load our girl up with more painkillers so she's able to get some sleep. Rest is the best medicine for her right now," she says with a smile, her eyes catching mine as she adjusts the machines by my head.

The sweet oblivion the drugs take me too are the one place I feel ready to handle right now and I bow to their power, slipping into darkness once more.

"Danica, sweetheart?"

Blinking, I open my eyes to find Gram sitting on the chair by my bed. She's wearing all black, again. She's been in full blown mourning since arriving at the hospital, but today is different. As I adjust to the light I realize she's dressed up, in a long black dress adorned with simple pearls at her neck. A wool coat is draped over the arm of the chair.

My throat is parched and sore, and I swallow several times before I'm able to speak. "Gram? Why are you dressed up?" I manage, my voice scratchy and fuzzy to my own ears.

"Honey, today is the funeral. Remember?" Her voice breaks and I hate myself for forgetting. My brain is loopy from the pain medication they keep pumping through my IV. Everything runs together.

What day is it? The accident was Friday and Sunday would have been Christmas. Has it been two days since Christmas, three? I can't seem to keep myself straight?

"Jonah asked if he could stay at the hospital with you. Would you like that? Do you think you're awake enough to see him now?" she asks.

My heart races at the thought. I'm conscious of the Hall's keeping vigil by my bedside. I recall waking one night to find Jonah asleep in the chair Gram is currently sitting in, but I let him sleep instead of waking him. I couldn't fathom seeing the pain I'm sure he's feeling, the pain Ms. Virginia or Mr. Ron are feeling at the loss of their best friends. I don't want to talk to anyone.

"Honey?"

"No. No, he should go to the funeral. His mom will need him. I'm tired and I just want to be alone," I tell her. "Thank him though, Gram. Make sure he knows how kind the offer was."

"We need to discuss your care moving forward too. Make some decisions."

"Take me to Texas," I suggest. Surprisingly, it doesn't hurt to think about leaving. There is nothing left to break in me. My heart is already dead, my soul is gone. "Let's go as soon as possible."

"Honey, you need to see your friends, say good-bye."

I shake my head, but I don't reply. I'm too tired to argue right now, we'll talk about it later; after today. It hits me again: today is my parents' funeral. A funeral I can't go to, and my head falls to the pillow. I close my eyes as Gram continues to talk. I don't hear most of what she says, I'm too consumed with my own words; the ones in my head telling me I don't deserve to be at the funeral anyway. I don't deserve to say goodbye. The words of guilt.

My eyes shift to the IV. The bag is full, no wonder I'm lucid, they must have changed it out recently and that's why Gram was able to wake me with such little effort. I should ask for them to lower the dose, tell them I don't need so much, but I won't. I love this little bag of liquid hanging from the machine. It trickles down through the tubing and into my hand. A magical concoction that keeps me as oblivious as possible to the pain, to the anxiety, and to the horror of my current existence.

Drop, drop, drop.

Gram is whispering something to me, but my head is heavy and I give up trying to focus on her. It's heavy as the numbness hits me, taking me away. It takes me to where I long to be. To where nothing else matters.

Today's reality… Candy conversations
February 13, 2013

I've shut everyone out.

Hours, days, weeks go by and I ignore emails, delete voice mails, and refuse phone calls. I can't comprehend everything going on in my own head, so how do I possibly explain it to others?

It's not easy. I'm not easy. Gram and Gramps are all too often on the wrong end of my angry tirades. I'm angry when the medical transport arrives to bring me to Texas. I'm angry when the doctors and nurses clean my wounds. I'm angry every time my heavy painkillers wear off and I'm reminded of my situation, again.

My injuries and burns heal as the days march by, but my heart, *my soul*, fractures. As each day rolls into the next, I'm painfully reminded of my truth: today is another day without my parents. Today is another day I'm alone.

I'm curled into a ball on my bed in my grandparents' house listening to the playlist my dad jokingly made for my driving lessons last summer when Gram peeks into the room. While I was in the hospital, they'd turned their guest room into a carbon copy of my old room. My furniture's here, my bedding, curtains, old stuffed animals, and picture frames. Everything from my room in North Carolina is now in Texas. I never asked how it all got here. When I walked into the room three days ago, after being released following my last skin grafting surgery, I stepped into the room and promptly threw up at the sight. It was jarring to see my life in this room, laid out for me as though I'd always been here. I crawled into my bed and I've barely moved since.

Gram looks about the room hesitantly, her mouth is moving, but I hear nothing over the heavy guitar from Dad's Van Halen song beating in my ears. I tug the ear buds out as she produces a box from behind her back.

"A package arrived for you," she says with a smile as she crosses the room.

She sets the brown box next to my feet at the end of the bed. I eyeball the package, wondering where it's from, but I'm not curious enough to sit up and see for myself. So I ask her. She does her best to hide her disappointment at my question, but I see it. I know I'm frustrating her.

She's standing there waiting for me to rip into the box, as though it's Christmas morning, and I raise a brow letting her know I have no intention of sitting up and looking at the gift myself.

Eventually she gives in with a frown. "The return address says it's from The Hall's. Why don't you open it?"

Hearing the name sends my heart into overtime. My palms turn clammy, my stomach flips, and I swallow hard as I drag myself into a slumped sitting position.

"Can I?" I nod from the box to the door in an unmistakable silent message for her to leave.

"Can you what?"

Apparently, grandparents don't know how to read silent messages. "Can I have some privacy?"

Understanding brightens her face and she agrees, patting my greasy head before stepping out of the dark room and shutting the door behind her. Popping my ear buds back in, I press play and lean against the head board, studying the box. There are no secret clues, no store names, or letters attached, only a printed label listing the sender and sendee information. I work up the courage to open it as a new song blasts into my ears. "Highway to Hell" plays as I use my thumb nail to slice into the masking tape sealing the package. How appropriate. This unexpected package feels a bit like hell. My mouth is dry as I slowly lift the lid and discover mounds of red and pink tissue paper. With a deep breath, I remove each wad of tissue, tossing them aside on the bed as I go. My movements are painstakingly slow, as though I expect something will jump out and bite my hand if I'm not careful.

When I reach a box, I stop. It's small, about the size of my hand, and covered in pink glitter. I'm curious now. I've always loved receiving presents and deep inside of me a spark of life kicks in as I anticipate this unexpected gift.

Flipping the box over in my palm, I find a curly-cued handwritten gift card:

To: Dani Love: Kady

Kadence, Jonah's younger sister. She changed the 'o' in 'to' and 'love' to little hearts and I smile as I pull open the box and a bottle of lotion falls out; pink cherry. My favorite smell from my favorite bath and body store. Digging back in, I find two more boxes of lotion, a shower gel and body spray too. Each one in matching sparkly boxes with a small notecard reading "We love and miss you, Virginia and Ron".

The sentiment brings tears to my eyes, but I have a feeling the best — or perhaps more accurately, the worst — is about to come in the shape of a small velvet box with a silver bow. It's taped to a larger red box and there's a pink envelope with the words 'open me first' sticking out in-between them. I'd know his handwriting anywhere and my pulse quickens.

The classic rock in my head is no longer appropriate so I shuffle the music, skimming through and finding my own favorite songs playlist as I remove a glittery card from the envelope. The front is covered with hearts and flowers, the words 'Happy Valentine's Day' emblazoned across it. It's gaudy and my smile grows because it's so not Jonah's style, yet I'm sure that's why he chose it. Bracing myself for the pain of reading whatever he's written, I hold my breath and open the card, startled to find two simple lines:

I miss you like crazy.
Please call me, Jonah

It's been over a month since I've seen or spoken to him. We haven't spent a month apart in our lives. As infants our mothers took us to 'Mommy and Me Yoga' together. We went to preschool together, we had weekly playdates and shopping trips. Our moms shared carpooling duties once we started school and we did homework together after school. I shake my head as I think about it. Even before the wreck, as busy as our individual social lives became, I saw him daily at school or we'd end up at the same parties.

One week. That's the longest I've gone without a Jonah Hall sighting in my sixteen years of life, until now. A one week vacation without his family, because even our vacations were usually spent together. An onslaught of guilt hits me for ignoring his calls since moving to Texas. Knowing how easy it is for me to get caught up in my feelings, I focus on the gifts he's sent instead. I choose the larger red box first, the velvet one makes me nervous. Like a child on Christmas morning, I shake the box, confused by the noise. It reminds me of a bunch of puzzle pieces and I shimmy the top loose.

"What in the world-" I jump as the bottom slips out, landing on the bed and scattering candy across my comforter. Except, it's not merely any candy. It's a box filled to the brim with conversation hearts. The candy my parents gave me every year for Valentine's, my favorite. I scoop a handful of hearts and lift them to my face, sniffing the chalky sugar scent. Memories come to life. My dad stealing all of the 'ur hawt' hearts years ago using the flimsy excuse of poor spelling. My parents using the hearts to leave me a poem. I recall having reading lessons in kindergarten at the table, my mom rewarding me with a piece of candy for each word I read correctly. Dozens of silly moments with tiny hearts taken for granted because I assumed I'd have more. My face is damp with tears by the time I set the candy aside and pop open the last remaining present. The velvet box. There's a gift card wedged in the top lid:

Hearts in memory of your parents...
A heart to keep us close...
You're in my heart. Always.

My breath catches in my chest and I lift my hand, pressing my palm to my heart in an effort to calm the erratic beats, as I focus on the necklace nestled on a bed of red silk. The intricate gold heart is stunning, made up of delicate filigree lines woven around a thick heart dangling from a delicate chain. I'm blown away.

There's a small button at the top of the heart and I press it, surprised when both sides pop open revealing a double locket. There are no words to describe my feelings at what I find within. The front side reveals two pictures of my parents' happy faces. I immediately recognize the shots from our beach vacation this past summer. My mom's wearing a straw hat pulled low over her face, but there's no hiding her huge smile as she laughs at the picture taker. Across from her is a picture of my dad. He's more docile in his shot. He looks as though he's contemplating life and someone caught him in his private moment. I stare at the shots in awe of the care Jonah, or whomever picked them out, took in choosing these particular memories. They are polar opposites of the way I would choose to remember my parents. My mom was the serious one, and dad the prankster, but these photographs remind me that wasn't always the case. These remind me of the parts I didn't always see, but always loved.

With the exception of my waking up to find the past months have all been a nightmare, I don't think there could be a better gift, ever. My grief has been unleashed and I'm beside myself, tears flowing freely now as I stare at my beautiful parents. Then I remember the back side of the locket popped open against my palm too. Clicking the front closed, I flip the heart over, and the last vestiges of strength I had is zapped. The sight before me knocks the wind from my chest and shatters my fragile psyche.

On the right is Jonah and I when we were roughly four years old. Our faces are pressed together, our eyes squinting, and our mouths wide with huge cheesy grins as we pose for the camera. It's a little raven princess and her fair prince, I choke recalling the nicknames our mothers' used to call us. They described us perfectly, me with my dark unruly hair and Jonah with his towhead. We were yin and yang, dark and light. I bite my lip, tasting my salty tears, as I gaze at the picture on the left side of the locket. It's one I've never seen before, although I recognize the scene from this summer as well. Our faces are all that's visible in the small trimmed down shot for the locket, but I recall the moment. I was sitting on a blanket, working on my tan, when Jonah returned from swimming and threw himself down next to me. In typical Jonah style, he shook his head, flicking water across me as though he were a dog.

"C'mon, get in the water," he'd urged, leaning over and trying to give me a wet hug.

It was in that moment his sister chose to run up and snap a few shots of us. I growled at Jonah to go away, pushing at his shoulders to get him to leave me alone, but he persisted.

"Stop fighting and smile," Kady whined as we continued to push and shove at each other. When she pouted and threatened to 'tell mom' we'd agreed to pose for one shot. I never saw it. Never even thought about it after that moment and yet, seeing it now, I'm tempted to say it might be the best picture I've ever seen of us. I'm scowling at the camera, my brows drawn and my mouth angry, and I remember I was still trying to hold Jonah at bay. His face though, is priceless. His mouth is arrested somewhere between a half-sneer, half-tongue-stuck-out, and I want to laugh. I envision him in that moment flipping his head back and shaking his dripping wet hair to the side as he posed. The cool ocean water smacking me in the face and making me angrier, hence my scowl. While his smile is ridiculous, it's his eyes that call to me. They're tilted to the camera and every golden fleck in their ocean blue depths are visible as the sun reflects in them.

This picture is of the couple who stole kisses in a laundry room forty-five days ago. I don't know this girl anymore. I no longer feel her emotions. She was alive and happy.

I'm dead.

Today's reality… A box is a box
June, 2013

"Danica?" Gram's voice calls out from the kitchen and I steady myself for another round with her. "Honey, have you not gone through that box of cards and gifts I set aside for you?"

There's a small sized moving box sitting in the dining room awaiting me. It's full of items Gram has decided is worth my time to look through. Things leftover from my hospital stay back in North Carolina. Several times, I've asked her to open the cards and mementos herself, because I don't care what they say.

I have no use for sympathy or well wishes from anyone.

I want to be left alone.

I don't deserve absolution.

"They're still sitting in the box aren't they?" I reply sarcastically.

The echo of her heavy sigh is the only reply I receive. I go back to staring out the front window again.

Today's reality… Where's the pain?
October, 2013

Physically my pain is gone.

My burns have been grafted and healed, and with the exception of minor dimpling and a few spots with heavier scarring, 'Nurse Sunshine' was right all those months ago; I'm almost like new.

Physically.

Yet, this is unacceptable to me. My parents, my strong, athletic father and my beautiful, regal mother, are dead and gone while I'm almost new again. It's unacceptable.

I long for the pain I once had.

I long for the punishment.

"She's withdrawn into her own mind most of the time. Her words are few and far between, and when she does speak it's angry." Gram explains.

I'm sitting in the office of Dr. Jan Panos, family counselor, with my grandparents' as Gram ventures to do her best at explaining what is 'wrong' with me to the good doctor. Keeping my gaze averted, I focus on scratching the purple nail polish I'd painted on last night from my nails. Beside me, Gramps' face is grim, his brown eyes flit about the room as he shifts in his chair every three minutes. Neither of us want to be here, but Gram insisted.

"She has no motivation to do her school work, she barely eats. She hasn't spoken to any of her friends from Grove Pointe or tried to have any sort of social life here since finishing treatment. Speaking of treatment, she was supposed to see a plastic surgeon to do some more cosmetic refining on the heavier scaring-" Gram pauses, looking my way with a frown, "but she's refused. We could have her scars removed and she's refusing!"

"Grace," Gramps warns as her voice raises.

His hand rests on hers and he flashes another glance my way. These days the looks he sends my way are sad ones. If I'm being honest, I long for the days when he'd look at me with amusement before launching into some absurd knock-knock joke the way he did when I was six. If I'm being honest… but I'm not. I haven't been honest with anyone since the day I woke up an orphan.

If I was being honest, truly honest, I would tell them all how I feel.

I don't deserve to be scar free, pain free, guilt free. I don't deserve to be social, to re-connect with friends, to open the stupid cards and presents sitting in the box — now in my room — collecting dust.

"Danica, would you feel more comfortable talking with me with your grandparents present," Dr. Panos asks, and I shrug. I have no intention of talking to her at all.

She asks my grandparents to wait outside and I stare at the floor, sinking further into the leather chair as Gram leaves the room. Gramps stands to leave, pausing beside me, and I inhale, waiting for whatever he's planning to say. However, after a moment he pats my head and exits without a word.

Dr. Panos clears her throat and I raise my eyes, keeping my face tilted towards the floor. She's looking at me. Studying me, as if she's attempting to reach into my brain and see what I'm thinking. So I study her in return. Her thick black hair is short and slicked back, curling under her ears, and I wonder what I'd look like if I chopped mine off that way. On her, the style is chic, grown-up, and sophisticated. I'm none of these things. Next, I study her gold earrings, her silk navy blouse, and the matching gold chain hanging in front of her chest skimming the desk when she leans forward. I move back to her face, her dark eyes are leveled on me, waiting patiently for my attention.

Once she has it, she asks, "Is there anything you would care to tell me? Anything about your grandparents, or your recovery, the accident… anything you want to talk about."

"Nope."

"No?"

I don't want to be here. I hate myself. Leave me alone. My internal voice shouts for me to answer her. In my head, where no one hears me, I'm honest.

I need help! That shout surprises me and I straighten, swallowing hard.

Dr Panos leans forward, her necklace once again falling on the desk in front of her, her eye twitches as though she heard my cry for help. "We can talk about anything, Danica. I'm here to help you and it's all confidential."

I give her a firm shake of my head.

Today's reality… Eleven months, but you still bleed.
November, 2013

"How about you tell me something that makes you angry. Doesn't matter what it is," Dr. Panos suggests.

Twice a week, Gram drags me to her office and forces me to spend an hour sitting in this black leather chair so I can be subjected to a barrage of questions I have no intention of answering. It's been going on for four weeks. Each session the same as the one before — a staring contest, a battle of wills. Dr. Panos stares at me, and I stare at the tiles on her ceiling — all one hundred and ninety-two of them.

"These sessions make me angry," I reply, immediately regretting it. I've answered a handful of her questions in four weeks; I'm sure she's delighted I've opened my mouth today.

"How about healing? Does your healing make you angry?"

Oh, she's a tricky woman. And scarily insightful.

Today's score: Panos: One - Me: Zip

I resolve not to answer her again.

Later that evening, I analyze the way I felt when Dr. Panos asked me to tell her what made me angry. I answered because she pushed a button. *Anger? That's a feeling I know.*

Her bringing up healing though, that was smart on her part. Does healing make me angry?

Yes! That's easy to answer. Explaining why it makes me angry is much tougher. Why should I be angry about my body healing? A few months ago I was in excruciating pain if I so much as moved wrong. For weeks I lay in bed, sedated, as doctors and nurses cleaned and prepped my burnt skin on a daily basis. It never mattered how much medication they gave me; unless they put me to sleep, I could feel the pain as they worked over the dead skin and soothed the fresh tender baby skin.

It's not something I'd wish on my worst enemy. But for me, the pain was comforting in a strange way because I deserved it.

The next week Dr. Panos asked me about the box full of stuff I still hadn't read or opened from North Carolina. "Is there a reason you're waiting to open those items?"

Evasion doesn't work, Gram keeps bringing me here, so I answer. Maybe she'll tell Gram to back off about it. "She opened them already, why should I?"

"Yes, she told me she opened them for you and set them aside because there are things in there you should see." Standing, Dr. Panos walks to her desk.

My eyes follow her and, for the first time since I arrived, I notice the box. It's sitting on the floor next to her desk and she lifts it effortlessly, carrying it over to me. She bends down, setting it before my feet and removes a yellow envelope from the top.

"Would you care to read it?" she asks, offering me the card. I refuse. "Very well… how about this one?" She pulls out a pink envelope, then a rose one, and then white. Each time she holds one up, I avert my gaze to the right and refuse with a shake of my head. She rifles through the box and I grip the arms of my chair, feeling unaccountably angry at her snooping in my things. I may not want to see them, but that doesn't mean she has the right to go through it all.

"Now, this is a sweet little guy," she says, her voice sounding mushy, and my curious eyes betray me. She's holding a brown fuzzy bear with a knit sweater and cute winter hat in her perfectly manicured hand. The bear is familiar and I recall seeing him sitting on the window shelf in my hospital room. "The envelope is sealed. Aren't you curious who it's from?" she asks, shaking the small bear in her hand. It reminds me of a would-be kidnapper holding out treats for his unsuspecting victim. My eyes fall on the small gift envelope tied to the bear's wrist, but I don't take the bait. Although I swore I wasn't going to explain myself or my reasoning for why I do the things I do, I find myself answering her with a question of my own.

"What does it matter now? It's almost been a year."

"These people cared about you, they wanted to be there for you. Don't you think it's time to open back up? To someone-" She motions to the box as she speaks and I stand, turning on her and interrupting her next sentence.

"No. Don't you get it yet? I don't want anyone to care about me and I don't want to open up. It's easier to be on my own." I storm out of the office, walking past my stunned grandpa and marching right out of the building.

Gramps is the one who takes me to my appointments now. His looks are no longer sad, they're angry. Not hateful angry, but the type of angry you get when you see something happening and you want to fix it and you can't. It's a frustrated angry. In contrast, Gram can't look at me without crying. My behavior is hurting them. I know this, but I don't try to change it. I'm not sure how to change it.

Box in hand, Gramps joins me at the car a few minutes later. I'm leaning against the door of his vehicle, waiting for him to unlock it when he steps toe to toe with me. He doesn't give me a choice, he simply pushes the cardboard into my chest as I stand there, arms crossed defiantly. He's always been the strong silent type and he doesn't change now standing there staring down at me, a menacing look on his face.

When I don't move to relieve him of the box, he drops it at my feet. The contents bounce about and something shatters, but he doesn't flinch. Behind me, the car door clicks unlocked and I step over the box, opening the door and sliding in. For a moment I'm tempted to slam my door and leave the confounded box sitting right there for whoever finds it, and then something happens. As I reach for the door handle, I allow myself to look down, it's a quick glance, but it's long enough to spy the handwriting on one envelope. My pulse speeds up as the familiarity hits me. I know that writing. My curiosity is more than I can stand and I sweep down, lifting the box and setting it on my lap as Gramps starts the engine without a word.

'Dani'

All the way home I stare at my name scribbled in familiar chicken scratch across the pale purple envelope. No one has called me Dani in almost a year. It was his nickname for me. Jonah. He started it when we were kids…

A memory from grade school flashes before me — *a crowded table at lunch and a gorgeous blond-haired boy frowning because he accidentally called me Dani in front of a bunch of boys in our class.*

"Dani? Oooooo," the crowd teases, and Jonah's cheeks turn crimson as he lowers his head. Giggles follow as one of the girls seated near me leans over, her lips forming a perfect 'O' before she asks, "Are you and Jonah boyfriend and girlfriend now?"

"Ewww, no! He's like my brother," I protest, and more giggles fill our table.

"Boys are so stupid," says Julia, a stuck up little pixie who always wants to be the center of attention. "Plus, Dani is a boy's name."

Now it's my turn to frown. "It's a nickname, and I like it," I argue back, perhaps a little too forcefully, and Jonah lifts his head, a lopsided grin on his face. We hold each other's gaze as though we're sharing a secret.

Perhaps we *were* sharing a secret back then. Our tight-knit bond was never understood by our friends, especially not at the age when they all thought members of the opposite sex were infected with cooties. The memory makes my heart hurt. After that day, my best friends took to calling me Dani. It stuck, but it was always Jonah's first.

My heart's racing as we pull into the drive of my grandparent's cozy home. Before my parent's death they'd been talking about moving into a smaller retirement community, now their plans are on hold. Everything changes when someone you love dies. Gripping the box, I kick the car door open and climb out, making my way to the front door without a word. Waiting for him to unlock the house, I look at Gramps as he walks my way. In him I see the man my father would have become. He's tall and handsome with distinguished gray hair, laugh lines around his dark eyes and still smooth cheeks. It's hard to look at him sometimes, and I turn away now as he shoulders next to me and wiggles his key into the old lock. He pushes on the door when the lock clicks, standing aside and letting me in.

I hurry to my room setting the box on my bed and pulling the purple envelope out. My fingers trace over Jonah's writing.

"Go out with me?" he'd asked that last night.

I'd been shocked at his request, asking why, even as my entire body warmed at the prospect, and he'd laughed at me.

"Because you like me." He stated it as fact and I didn't find the need to argue with him. "And, because I like you."

Oh, how simple that answer had been. Why couldn't all answers to questions be so easy? Flipping the envelope over, I find the seal is still set. Gram didn't opened this one? Obviously she knew Jonah left it. I work my finger under the seal, opening the card as I wonder if this is the reason they've been pushing me to go through these items. If they thought my reading something from Jonah would help. The moment my eyes touch on his words I'm transfixed. Standing there, in the middle of my bedroom floor, I read his thoughts:

"What do I say that would ever be right? You've been sedated every time I stop by. I just want to hold you. I want to tell you how sorry I am, how much I love you, how much I loved your parents.

How thankful I am that you lived. God, I'm so thankful we didn't lose you, too.

You've been my best friend since before we could speak. You'll always be my best friend and I will always be here for you. Your doctors said they'll wean you off of the drugs soon. I'll be here when they do. I'll hold your hand and wipe your tears and tell you everything is going to be all right. We all will. It's going to be all right, Dani."

My throat burns as I swallow back the pain. My mind pictures Jonah, his beach bum, blond, floppy hair, his light eyes with the mesmerizing golden flecks, and it's a painful memory. Every time I see Jonah I see two things: I see our happy smiling families enjoying years of vacations and parties, and I see the teasing look in my father's eyes the moment before our car went careening off the road and into a ditch. I hear the way he harassed me about starting something with Jonah and I see the joy on his face at the prospect. Jonah, as much as I love him, will forever go hand in hand with the night my parents died. That is today's reality.

With a shake of my head, I set the card aside and straighten, composing my thoughts and clearing my mind. I dig into the box, reaching in and pulling out a handful of cards, I begin the process of reading through them. One by one I'm reminded of the friends from my past. The friends I've ignored. Mallory, and her well-meaning gushing of sorrow. Veronica and her wordy store bought card with a quick handwritten sentiment. Notes from teachers, my parents' friends, an ex-boyfriend. Nothing touches me quite the way Jonah's card does, but that doesn't surprise me.

Reaching in again, I pull out a picture frame I recognize from home. The glass is cracked and broken, probably from Gramps dropping it today outside of my therapist's office. It's an old picture of my parents and I at the beach — the obligatory matching jeans and white shirts family photo. We're sitting in the sand among the sea grass, the sky red and orange as the sun sets behind us. Carefully, I place the broken frame on the bed and pick up the bear Dr. Panos held up at my appointment earlier. The brown fuzz is velvety and I run my hand over his arm.

"Ouch." I flinch as something pricks my finger.

A sliver of glass is stuck in my index finger, a drop of deep red blood pooling against my fair skin. *That's what I get for letting my emotions go,* I think as I drop the bear back into the box. Heading to the bathroom, I ease the splinter out and turn on the faucet. My hand stills midway to the water as my fascinated eyes study the blood, a river of red, as it gathers and inches along the lines of my imperfect skin. Around me everything stills and my insides go calm. It's a curious feeling.

I forget the box waiting for me. I forget the letters and gifts. My mind's held captive by the blood — the proof of life. I've felt dead — numb to anything and anyone — for a year, but here it is — life. I'm amazed at how this simple drop of blood makes me feel.

'You're crazy,' the internal voice whispers as I catch my reflection in the mirror. It's not pretty; my wide eyes are hollow, the shadows underneath dark and deep, against my unnaturally pale skin. My cheeks are gaunt, my hair's lifeless.

"You're a walking corpse," I accuse the unrecognizable girl staring at me.

Except you still bleed.

Today's reality... I'm marking the anniversary. Literally.
December 22, 2013

Thunder; earth shattering, window rattling thunder wakes me up. The sky is shedding tears on the one-year anniversary of my parents' deaths, how fitting. My pillow is damp and I push up, leaning against my head board as I swipe furiously at the tears running down my cheeks.

I was dreaming of happier days. Of the warm sun tanning my skin, the sound of waves crashing along the shore, the taste of salt on my tongue...

I prop myself up on my elbows, my toes digging into the hot sand and watch as Jonah, Kadence, and our fathers play in the ocean waves, body boards strapped to their ankles.

"Dani! C'mon," Kadence calls, waving furiously.

A wave sneaks up on them, and they paddle out, attempting to catch the swell. They scatter, like dandelion seeds on the wind, as they ride into shore, their laughter mingling with the other beach goers. Kadence, who has no control, ends up yards down the beach, while Mr. Hall has drifted the other way. My father missed the wave completely, and is now swimming into the deeper water. Then there's Jonah. As with everything he does, Jonah rides the wave all the way in. He steers himself right to the shallows, flips over as the wave breaks and stands. A moment later he's towering over me, his hair dripping cool ocean water down onto my burning skin.

"Do you mind?" I ask, squinting up at him. The sun is behind his head and I lean to the right, using him as a shield in order to see his face.

"Nah, I don't mind at all," he flirts shamelessly, his eyes perusing my bikini clad body. I sigh inwardly, I've become accustomed to this Jonah, the big flirt with a new girl every week. High school has changed us both. "Do you mind?" he asks, raising his brow.

It's impossible not to laugh out loud when he gives me that look. Of course I don't mind. This is Jonah Hall we're talking about. He should live in California with his ridiculously tan skin and too long, too blond -- yet I wouldn't want him to change it -- hair. This is the boy who played house with me when we were children. He stole my Halloween candy for crying out loud; I need to stop looking at him as anything but the annoying quasi-brother he's always been.

"You've grown up, D. You're filling out that bikini rather nicely," he says with a wink.

"Oh. My…" I bite my tongue with a grimace and stand. The need to cover myself after his creep comment is overwhelming, but I refrain. He waggles his brows at me again, this time with a smirk pasted on his lips, and I have to fight to maintain my angry face.

"Shut up, you idiot," I say, looking beyond him to the ocean.

He laughs at me and I push past him, punching his perfect stomach as I head toward the water. Two seconds later, my feet leave the sand as I'm picked up from behind, my body being flung around in a circle. Jonah growls in my ear as he drops me and I make a break for it, pushing and shoving each other all the way to the water. He chases after me as I run into the surf screaming for my dad to save me.

The thunder woke me before I could hear my father's reply and a terrifying thought enters my mind. I can't recall his voice, my dad's, and it shatters me to not hear it, to dream about it. How do you forget a voice you heard before you were born? I lay there, rain slapping against my windows, and my mind screams at me to remember. *Remember his voice, Dani!* I recall Jonah's voice. I hear Mr. and Mrs. Hall, Kadence, my best friend Mallory, even my mother's lyrical voice flutters to life within me, but my dad is nowhere.

Absently, my thumb rubs the scabbed scratch still lingering along my index finger from when I sliced it open two weeks ago. Behind closed lids, I picture the blood again. I picture the life dripping from my seemingly dead body, and my soul undergoes an awakening.

I want to know I'm alive. I *need* to know I'm alive.

The thoughts come from somewhere so dark and hidden within me, I'm not sure they're mine. It's as though I'm in a trance when I push my heavy blankets back and tip-toe across the dark bedroom to the box still sitting here. After the last time, I'd been unwilling to look at any more notes, so I dropped the broken frame back into the box and shoved it out of the way. There are a few unopened presents, a book of some sort, and a stuffed cat I haven't bothered to pull out, but I ignore those things as I sink to the floor. Watery moonlight sneaks into my room through a crack between my blinds and window frame. The image of the light being distorted by the heavy raindrops is fascinating, they're tears running across space.

I don't believe in alien encounters or abductions, but for a moment I wonder if I've been taken over. Invasion of the body snatchers? My brain skitters, pictures and sounds scrolling by, as though somebody has the remote and they're flipping through my life. I now know what is wrong - I've lost myself.

My mind is no longer my own as my fingers pull apart the distressed wooden frame holding my family. Small shards of glass sprinkle down to the floor, glittering in the moonlight, but I ignore them. I pluck a larger piece of glass out of the mess and drop the rest to the side. I'm trapped in this body, something within is arguing, pushing at me to *snap out of it*, but the rest of me moves forward, as though the voice is insignificant. For a while, I sit examining the glass in the moonlight. The edge that snapped and broke away is jagged, slanted and imperfect. Like me.

The moonlight and raindrops on my window create a sliver of light and shadows into my room and across the floor. I shift, positioning myself so the pattern is situated perfectly across my forearm, watching the way the rain forms and rolls down the glass. I find myself tracing the shadows on my skin, first with my eyes, then with the edge of the broken shard of glass. Little shadow drops of rain drip, drip, drip along my arm, and I follow them over and over, top to bottom, top to bottom. The staccato beat of the rain matching the racing beat of my heart. Adrenaline kicks in, daring my hand to apply pressure. Daring the glass to cut me.

'Leave a mark,' my mind mocks my hand as I trace the lines again and again. *'Do it.'*

I close my eyes and it's a relief when the first slice is made. I don't feel pain.

'Yes, there you are,' the voice inside sings, *'life.'* Yes, I feel life.

"Dani."

Gasping, my eyes pop open. "Daddy?" I whisper into my dark room. Nothing.

So I press harder… and my mind flies.

"You are my sunshine." My hand wobbles as I hear my father's beloved voice singing.

The room rattles with the sound of thunder and my sweaty fingers slip on the smooth glass as it slices down my wrist, falling to the floor. The moment my hand loses the glass shard, I shake my head, numbly clearing it, and look down through watery eyes. Blood falls onto my pale legs, mixing with the rainy shadows to create a beautiful juxtaposition - the rain created shadowy gray 'blood' of the dead mixing with the warm red blood of the living. My head falls against the wall, and I close my eyes, begging to hear Daddy's voice again.

"My only sunshine," I sing softly, waiting for him to join in. "Daddy," I call into the emptiness. "Daddy?"

Irrational anger washes up, and I shift my position, looking for the glass again.

"Where are you?" I ask, picking up the blood covered shard and slicing at my arm once more.

This time I cry out. There's nothing perfect about this cut. I wasn't following the shadow of the rain; I was angry.

"Where are you?" I scream again.

I'm sawing the glass across my arm as though I'm slicing vegetables for dinner. Every cut hurts, and yet each moment of pain is a moment of intense feeling I haven't suffered in months. I lived with acute pain for seven months after the wreck. It hurt, but it reminded me I was alive. I've been dead to everything for five.

This pain is euphoric. Each gasp I make as I slash at myself is one of pleasure.

I'm happy. I'm alive. I'm sick.

"You make me happy…"

I smile at his voice and join along with the singing in my head.

"Danica!" The light flicking to life in my room blinds me.

"When skies are gray. You'll never know, dear, how much I love you…"

"George! Call 911. Oh, honey… What did you do?" Gram cries frantically, falling to my side.

I blink her way before closing my eyes as she wraps my arm in a towel and applies pressure. The voice in my head fades, so I sing louder, hoping he will join me again.

"Please don't take my sunshine away…"

"Please don't… you are my sunshine… don't leave me… Dadddyyy," I cry on a whisper, rocking in my grandmothers arms.

Today's reality... I might be crazy?
December 22, 2013

"I don't know what to do, Virginia. They've got her on a forty-eight hour mandatory suicide watch."

I'm lying in a hospital bed, staring up at the white ceiling, when Gram's voice floats through the cracked door. Her voice is low and full of worry and I scan over the events of the night, trying to put it all together. Gram burst into my room to find me on the floor in a pool of blood. Her hysterical shouts for Gramps to call 911 echo in my head as I recall the way she wrapped my arm in towels and hugged me close while we waited. I must've been in shock or something because the rest is vague. We were transported to the emergency room. I was bandaged up and ordered to get rest in my small curtained-off space of the ER. A young female doctor, or maybe she was a nurse, told my grandparents I'd lost a good amount of blood, but not enough to need a transfusion and that was good. Since then everything else they've said has been whispered, in private, outside of my room. Away from my ears. It's been hours now, but I'm stilling laying here, waiting.

Hearing Gram on the phone, I'm getting my first listen to what the doctors have said to her. Suicide. They think I was trying to kill myself? I hold my breath, trying to eavesdrop on what else is being said.

"She's never been the same. No... she's withdrawn and moody. You wouldn't recognize her, she's so thin... No, no you don't need to do that. I... I know she's ignored them, I'm so sorry. You know if she were in her right mind... okay. Okay, you do that and call me back. Thank you so much, Virginia. Buh-bye."

Virginia? She's talking to Jonah's mom. Since when did she talk with her? I straighten as Gram says bye and wait, expecting her to enter the room. I hate the worry I hear in her voice and I resolve to be sure she knows I'm okay. That I wasn't trying to kill myself, not really. I was...

I take another deep breath, admitting the truth to myself - I have no idea what I was doing.

The clock reads eight a.m. and I'm fighting sleep when two young men wearing light blue scrubs enter the room with Dr. Panos and my grandparents in tow. One of the men, a redhead who looks no older than his early twenties, with his baby face, is pushing a wheelchair into the room. When I was released from the burn unit at General the staff insisted on my being rolled out of the door. 'Hospital regulations. All patients get a free ride,' the bubbly nurse, Robyn, told me with her one hundred watt smile. I sit up now, assuming I'm about to be discharged, before I realize I'm wearing a hospital gown. I'd have clothes if I were being released.

"Good morning, Danica." Dr. Panos' greeting is somber as she looks at my chart in her hands.

I force a smile. *Make sure they know you're fine*, I remind myself. "Good morning." Hopefully the fake cheerfulness isn't noticeable. "Why are you here? Can I go home now?" I'm not blind to the glances thrown around the room. "Gram? Gramps? I want to go home now, please." My voice shakes.

Their faces are set in stone, Gram's knuckles are white where she's gripping her purse. It gives her away. This isn't a friendly visit from Dr. Panos. The conversation I overheard between Gram and Ms. Virginia dances into my head and I know what's coming next.

"Danica, we're going to move you upstairs and then we'll talk. I want to understand what was going on in your head this morning. Do you think you could tell me what happened?" Dr. Panos asks.

"It was an accident. I didn't mean to cut myself like that." I look past Dr. Panos, focusing on Gram and Gramps, my eyes imploring them to hear me out. "I'm so sorry I scared you, it wasn't my intention."

They're statues. Nothing I say matters and nothing breaks their stony faces. So I beg. "I want to go home… it was a rough day and I lost my mind. No, I didn't lose my mind, but I just… I was sad."

Dr. Panos clears her throat, stepping to my side and giving me a sympathetic face. It reminds me of the doctors on television, all stoic and emotionless when they deliver horrifying news to patient's loved ones. She makes it clear there's nothing I say or do to change her orders and then, of all things, my grandparents walk out of the room as the strong male nurses approach my bed. I get the distinct feeling they will force me if they must and I give in. I'm too sleepy physically and too weary mentally to fight right now.

Twenty minutes later I'm settling into a new room. Dr. Panos gives me one last firm look as she stands at the door. "Get some rest and I'll be back to talk with you soon, okay?"

Nodding, I turn away from her. The door closes with an ominous click as a rogue tear rolls down the side of my nose.

What happened? Why would they admit me to the psych ward? I try to recall the events of the morning. *What happened when the ambulance showed up this morning? What did I say? What did I do?*

Everything is fuzzy, as though I were outside of myself, watching the girl in the shorts and tank top cutting herself. I'm not that girl. I hate needles. I hate knifes. I cut my finger slicing an apple once as a little girl and have shrunk away from them ever since. I didn't do this to myself. I couldn't.

But, you did.

I rip at the bandages covering my arm and gasp at the damage I inflicted. Raw wounds crisscross my skin, some small, others longer. There's nothing precise about what I did. I'd come unglued and wielded that piece of broken glass across my body as a painter uses a paint brush. I covered myself in wounds.

Dazed, I study the marks and think. Perhaps the most terrifying part of this entire ordeal is the lack of concrete memories of doing it. No memories coupled with the lack of pain and understanding is disturbing. Maybe I do belong in the psych ward. Maybe I am crazy.

I drift to sleep asking myself that exact question, *'Am I crazy?'*

Dr. Panos returns to question me some hours later, waking me from a fitful nap. I spend my time trying to convince her I'm not suicidal, nor am I crazy. *I don't think.*

"It was an accident," I insist as forcefully as a girl in my position is able. I'm small and helpless laying in my bed with her towering over me. I'm still in the hospital-provided gown from the ER, leaving me feeling exposed and gross. I long for a shower to remove the dried blood and overall feeling of fog off of me, but no one has been in to see me since I moved to this room.

"Danica, how were you feeling when you went to sleep last night?" Dr. Panos asks, ignoring my accidental defense completely.

Deciding it's best to get this conversation over with I shrug. "I don't know," I say honestly.

"What made you cut yourself? Were you trying to harm yourself?"

"I don't know," I say again. Her brows lift thoughtfully, and I blanch. "I mean no, no I'm not suicidal or anything like that. I don't know why I cut myself. I was sleeping, and the thunder woke me and I heard my dad's voice… or no, I mean I couldn't remember it and then I could.

The more I cut, the more I heard. I... I don't know what happened." The words tumble from my lips like cherry Kool-Aid on a white tablecloth. They stain my reputation in her eyes. I see it, her face doesn't fool me. She thinks I'm crazy. Something within me clicks. Self-preservation. I need to fix this.

"I think maybe I was sleepwalking. I remember I was dreaming. My parents were in it and we were at the beach... and happy. Then Gram was over me, screaming, and sirens were sounding." I'm not exactly telling the truth, but I'm not lying either. I work to flip everything around to sound as innocent as possible given the circumstances. However, the disbelief never disappears from Dr. Panos' face. She leaves the room an hour later after asking me the same question she did when she entered. "What made you cut yourself?"

My grandparents never come to see me and I sit there alone as afternoon creeps into evening. It's dinner before someone appears.

"There's a shower in the bathroom, am I allowed to take one?" I ask the middle-aged woman, with a pleasant smile, who presents me with my evening meal on a tray.

"Let me get a nurse for you, sweetheart," she offers, setting up my dinner tray and promising someone will return soon.

Fifteen minutes later, there are two soft raps on the door and a young brunette wearing scrubs enters. "Danica? You're wanting to take a shower?" she asks. Her eyes survey the room as though she's looking for anything out of the ordinary.

"Hi. Yes, please. I feel sticky and just plain gross for some reason," I explain, touching my messy hair.

"I'm sure you do. Here's the deal though, you can't get your arm wet for twenty four hours. We'll get your hair washed in the sink, if you want, and then you may have a modified shower. Do you think you can do that?"

I nod, the need to wash my hair greater than the embarrassment of having it washed for me. I'm grateful she didn't say I have to be given a sponge bath. She sends in another, younger nurse, an intern named Summer, who brings in a bag of my clothing and toiletries.

"Are my grandparents here?" I ask when she sets my things on the end of the bed. Why would they bring my stuff and not come to see me?

Summer shakes her head, giving me a sympathetic smile. "I'm sorry, I'm not sure. I haven't met them." At the disappointment on my face she adds, "I just came on shift though, maybe they're here and having something to eat in the cafeteria."

Doubtful. "Yeah, maybe."

Today's reality… I'm a lost girl
December 23, 2013

"I'm not talking to her anymore."

Those are the first words I speak when my absentee grandparents make their long overdue appearance the following day. They exchange scowls and I want to shout at them for avoiding direct contact with me. I'm skimming through some meaningless teen magazine when they walk in, simply biding my time as I wait for some answers from someone. Determined to keep them from seeing how much their desertion affects me, I straighten in my bed.

This morning, as I waited for them to show up, I vowed to make them understand my feelings, so I press on, "I'm not suicidal. I'm not. She doesn't believe me. I see it in the way she looks at me. I'm not talking to her anymore and I want to go home. Now!" Gram flinches at my anger.

They look tired. They always look tired. It's merely another thing I have to feel guilty about. They should be out enjoying golf and retirement — not raising their teenage granddaughter.

"I want to go home," I repeat, softening this time.

Gram meets my pleading gaze as she speaks for the first time. "You can't go home."

"Why not? I'm fine, I got a full nights rest, I feel better."

"Why not?" Gramps asks, his usually even voice cross. "You're under a forty-eight hour suicide watch, young lady. This isn't a game!"

"George," Gram gasps as Grandpa goes off, but he ignores her.

"You don't get to put us through what you did and then demand to go home, you have to face the consequences!"

"George, stop it."

I'm floored by Gramps' outburst, his face is bright red as he stands at the end of my bed. His hands shake, his back is ramrod straight. I'm not sure I've ever seen this side of him. "I can't sit by and let her behave this way, Grace. *We* can't let her do this anymore."

"Do what?" I scoot to the center of the bed and Gramps faces me. I raise my brows, wordlessly asking him to explain.

"You can't be dead to the world. You need to go to school, you need to think of your future."

The future. My head shakes of its own accord at the mere mention of future. Fear chokes me at the thought of going to school and I hate myself for it. For the doubt festering within me, for the fear of what others do so comfortably. "I can't."

"Of course you can." Gramps says as he enters further into the room. His demeanor softens now as he speaks. "We've all been a little lost this year, but it's time to move on. Your parents would never want us to stop living. They always wanted the absolute best for you and you deserve it."

"No, I don't. I don't want to move on and I can't." They wince and Gramps searches for the right words. He shakes his head, his jaw clenching, I see the struggle as it happens. He wants so desperately to say something that will make sense to me, but there's nothing to say. I don't know how to mend the brokenness inside, surely his simple words never will.

We stare at each other; three lost souls, none of which have the answers, when there's a knock at the door. Gram wipes at her face as she looks to the door and back and steps away from my bed.

"Maybe someone else can help you," she suggests, and Gramps moves to open the door. They look nervous, and my stomach drops as the tension thickens around me.

"I just want to go home." My eyes scour the room, as though an escape route might have popped up in the last few minutes, but it's a no go. Obviously, the psych ward wouldn't be secure if there were windows and secret passages. "I don't want to talk to another doctor," I complain, not caring if I'm overheard by whatever shrink has stopped by this time.

"Would you settle for talking to an old friend?"

A first kiss, a slow dance in the rain, a pillow fight with your best friends; none of these things compare to the way my body reacts to the sound of his voice.

"Jonah?" I blink rapidly as they verify what they are seeing. Jonah is standing in the doorway next to my grandfather.

Mrs. Hall slides around him, rushing me the way a Black Friday shopper rushes a sale. "Danica, sweetheart," she cries, her voice cracking, as she wraps me in a perfume-swathed hug.

My brain is scarcely able to tell my arms to hug her back as I look around her shoulder to see the entire Hall family walk into my room. Kadence who, a year ago seemed so young, looks sophisticated and grown up, her blue eyes shining with unshed tears. Behind her, his hand on her shoulder, is Mr. Hall, with his powerful presence and twinkle in his eye.

And then there's Jonah.

Jonah is… well, still Jonah. The all-American boy, sporting his too long — but just right — bleach blond hair and changeling blue-gray eyes. He's the poster boy of every teenage girl's dreams and the mascot of my childhood. Most of my memories have Jonah, and his family, in them and as Mrs. Hall eases back from our hug I'm painfully aware of what I've lost.

My head shakes wildly, as my soul plunges into despair. The feeling comes over me quickly, a tsunami hitting an unsuspecting seaside village, and I'm left clutching my stomach and covering my mouth as I stare at Jonah. My breath won't come, I'm drowning. Drowning in the memories, the pain, the realization of what I've done to myself. I'm the creator of my own private hell, my life.

Jonah moves from his stiff position at the door and within five steps is leaning over my bed and pulling me into his chest. His warm lips skim the edge of my forehead as he presses them to the top of my head and I wrap my arms around his waist taking solace in the lifeline he's extending to me. Voices ring in my ears, but I don't understand a word they say. All I hear are the words Jonah whispers, "It's going to be all right. I'm here for you, Bambi."

Bambi. His private nickname for me from our past…

Looking up, I note the way the leaves on the tree over the driveway have changed to bright, fiery colors. An early fall breeze knocks a few off the swaying branches and a bright red one dances back and forth as it glides to the group already landing near my knee. The bark of the tree bites into my back as I lean against it, taking a sip of my water as Jonah continues shooting hoops.

"Hey, Jonah?" I ask thoughtfully.

"Huh?"

"Do you think Nicole Remy is pretty?" The basketball leaves his hand, swooshing through the hoop, as I ask the question.

"Nicole," he repeats as he catches the rebound. "Sure, she's pretty," he says without missing a beat.

I bite the cap of my water bottle. Stupid Nicole Remy. She's the new girl at Grove Pointe Middle. The new girl with the pretty blue eyes, big blond curls, and bigger… assets than any of the other eighth grade girls. My eyes flick down to my own flat chest and I groan as my mother's voice echoes in my head, making my face heat up, 'I was a late bloomer, too. Just you wait.'

Dribbling the ball in a circle before shooting again, he asks, "Why?"

I can't admit my jealousy, he won't understand — stupid boys — so I shrug instead, kicking at the basketball when it drops to the ground by my feet.

"What's wrong with Nicole Remy?" he asks, falling to the ground beside me and swiping the water bottle from my hand, taking a long swig.

"Hey! That's my water, get your own."

"Geez… sorry, have it then." He shoves the bottle my way and I slap at his hand.

"You've contaminated it, it's yours now," I complain. I push up from the ground and dust off my back side angrily. Retrieving the basketball from the grass, I scoop it up and toss it from hand to hand as I try to calm my odd emotions. I feel off somehow.

Jonah laughs loudly and my flush returns. "Contaminated, huh? I thought I'd outgrown my cooties by now."

Rolling my eyes his way I sigh, "Oh, hush."

Turning my back, I dribble the ball around the court to cover my embarrassment, pretending to be as smooth as Jonah. Between my dad, Jonah, and his father, I've played enough one-on-one to get just good enough, and then middle school came. Once I had access to a cell phone, I stopped playing. These days, I prefer to sit on the sidelines and watch the boys, the ball feels foreign in my hands now. Physically aware of his gaze, I check over my shoulder and find him observing me.

"What?"

"Why'd you ask about Nicole?"

Of course he won't drop it. "No reason."

"Really? You're a terrible liar." Jonah jumps to his feet, slapping the ball away from my hand with a grin. His ball skills surpassed mine a while back and it's painfully obvious now.

"Fine. She's a freaking Barbie," I grumble, trying to block his next shot. "It's like all the guys in school have lost their minds over her, what little they have."

Jonah fakes a step right, then ducks and rolls left, eluding me and sinking his shot. He catches the ball as it bounces to the ground. "Not all of them," he says facing me.

"You said you think she's pretty," I remind him.

"Yeah, she is." He tosses the ball into my stomach, "You're prettier, though."

Choked laughter spews from my lips. "Ha, ha… you're not required to be nice to me, you know."

"I know that. I'm just telling the truth. I'm not the only one who thinks so either." My pulse speeds up and I can't stop the question from forming on my lips.

"Really, who?" I've told myself I'm not going to let boys go to my head. Too many of my friends have turned into boy crazy freaks, I'm not going to follow suit, but I find myself asking the question with too much enthusiasm.

"I dunno... guys."

"Which guys?" I prod, refusing to shoot until he gives me an answer.

"Dude, this is a strange conversation. I thought we agreed we weren't going to get wrapped up in the boy/girl crap." He lifts his arms, resting his hands on the top of his head, frustration clear on his face. "Can I have the ball now?"

"Fine," I toss the ball his way and move from the court back to the grass beside the drive way. "You're not pulling my leg?"

"Oh my gosh, D... stop being such a girl. What do you care anyway? I thought you were planning on remaining boyfriend free?"

"I hate to break it to you, but I am a girl."

"What! No way, you're not a girl... you're Dani, the annoying chick I've been stuck with since birth," he mocks with a wink and I force myself not to laugh.

Disappointed he won't give me more information, I lean against the nearby tree and contemplate the boys at school. Nobody's given any indication they might have a secret crush on me. Nearly every boy in our grade has been overheard talking about how hot Nicole is lately. Stupid Nicole, and stupid Jonah for keeping secrets. Stupid puberty for messing things up. Life was a heck of a lot easier without dating messing it up.

"Oh, stop pouting," Jonah says, and I look up to find him standing in front of me. "Scott Walsh was asking me about you last week, and Ben too."

"No way. They've known me for years, why would they be interested now?" I'm bewildered by this news.

Jonah's blue eyes roam over me boldly, from the top of my messy ponytail to the tips of my Chucks, and I cross my arms over my chest at his inspection.

"You've changed."

I know I've matured, so has he. We're different, growing up, and it makes me both happy and sad at the way things are starting to change.

"I'm still no Barbie," I point out unnecessarily.

"Not all guys want a Barbie. You know what makes you so awesome?" he asks, and I still as he moves closer until nothing except the ball is between us. Our eyes lock as he speaks, "You're not only smart and funny, but you can hang with the guys when playing sports. Plus, you look really good when you get all dressed up for your concerts. Don't let a bunch of stupid boys make you feel like crap, D. They don't know anything. I'd take you over Nicole Remy, any day of the week."

My eyes go wide as his unexpected compliments rock me to the core and he smiles, sending pleasant shock waves through my body. If my parents are paying him to compliment me like this, they can keep right on paying. I could get used to this.

I'm sure he's done when he says, "And those eyes of yours... no one has those."

"They're brown."

"They're huge," he corrects me with a grin, and I frown. "No, I mean that in a good way. Everything you think shows in your eyes, they're so... what's the word?"

"Huge and brown?" I deadpan, and now it's his turn to frown.

"No. Expressive, that's it, they're expressive. It's why you can't lie to me."

"Yes I can," I argue, although I know he's right. He always catches me when I try to trick him. He doesn't bother arguing, he merely gives me that look he has. The one that assures me we both know the truth, and I assent. "Fine, I can't lie to you. But still..."

"You remind me of Bambi, did I never tell you that? Remember how much I loved Bambi when we were little?"

"Yeah, you were obsessed, and I hated watching it because it always made me cry."

We laugh at the shared memory. "Exactly, your eyes remind me of Bambi. Plus, they're way prettier than plain blue."

My face must be ten shades of red by now. "Bambi, huh? My parents paid you to say all of this, didn't they?"

He snorts, finally stepping back from my personal space, allowing me to breathe again. "No, silly, you're pretty and you're just going to have to live with that curse." He gives me a shrug before he returns to shooting hoops without me, as though nothing of consequence was said between us. Leaning back against the tree again, I take everything Jonah said into account.

"Hey, Jonah?"

"Yeah, Bambi?" he asks, continuing to practice his shots. Bambi? I really love that.

"You're pretty cute, too. All the girls think so."

"Yeah, I know."

"Ugh, so full of yourself," I groan, pushing at his back when he steps close to me again.

"I'm totally full of myself, you're right." He grins and I slap the ball from his hands. "Ohhhh," he shouts.

"Focus on the game, punk," I laugh as I shoot and score on him.

"You're on," he promises, and soon we're back to shoving and pushing each other on the court.

Two weeks later Scott Walsh became my first boyfriend and not long after Jonah ended up sucking face with Nicole Remy under the bleachers after one of his basketball games.

The memory rushed in, the moment Jonah said Bambi, and I had no way of fortifying the walls around my heart before I let the past attack. The sweet innocent moments of yesterday batter me and the barrier fractures, causing tears to tumble freely from my eyes.

This time the tears are not for my parents or my injuries.

This time they're for me, and the girl I lost.

I cry until my throat is raw. Until my back aches from the convulsions of each body wracking sob. Until I'm totally and utterly spent. And Jonah stands at the edge of the bed, holding me through it all.

At some point the others left the room. I'm glad I'm not being watched, not being evaluated in this moment. The first moment of truth I've allowed myself in a year.

My truth: I need someone to hold me through this.

No words, no expectations; just love me through it.

I soak up every ounce of comfort Jonah's willing to give, all the while steeling my heart for the moment I'll have to push him away. And I will have to. Everything about him brings back everything about *them* and I can't have that.

Behind closed lids flashes of my parents whirl through my mind. They're more real than any dream or memory I've had in months and I don't want it to stop. I want the story of my life to keep replaying in my head forever — the story of a girl who has two adoring parents, tons of wonderful friends, and a charmed life. The fairy tale. That's me there, front and center, but I've been re-cast. *The role of Danica Evans will now be played by pitiful, lost, orphan girl Dani,'* a voice in my head mocks the imagery and my tears return. Jonah soothes me, his warm palm rubbing circles on my back as his 'it's all right' and 'we're going to get you through this' pierce the armor I've been wearing for so long.

I'm not sure how long we've been huddled in this cocoon of comfort before I manage to pull back and wipe my messy face with the bottom of my tee shirt. "Why are you here?" I ask through sniffles.

"Your Gram called Mom." His eyes flick to my bandaged arm before he refocuses on my face. He doesn't stop rubbing my back as he puts a little space between us and I notice the moisture around his eyes when he speaks. "Dani, we're worried about you."

"You flew here, two days before Christmas, because you're worried about me?" I ask incredulously. I wonder if my face is a mirror of the shock his displays. He steps back another space, his hands leaving my back. They float around, from smoothing his hair to tugging his shirt and finally sinking into his pockets, as though he can't figure out what to do with them. He's visibly shaken by my question.

"It's been a year. I haven't spoken to you…" I clarify and he interrupts me.

"By your choice, Dani, not mine." His reply is coarse, angry, and I sniffle once more. I shift to the side, making room for him to sit beside me, but he doesn't budge.

"No. I mean… yeah, I know that. That's why I'm confused. I've ignored y'all for a year. On purpose too. Yet, you came anyway. Why?"

His eyes soften, and he looks at me as though he can't believe I have to ask such a question. Moving to lean his hip against the edge of the bed, he takes hold of my hand. "We love you." I release my breath as he sits and, careful of my bandaged arm, pulls my hand to his lap, intertwining our fingers. "What's going on with you, D? Why did you do this?" he asks, nodding at my arm and giving my fingers a gentle squeeze.

"I wasn't trying to hurt myself." His brow lifts, challenging me, and I give in. "Not the way everyone thinks. I'm not suicidal… I just can't explain it."

"Not even to me?"

I shake my head, looking at the white wall before us and hoping he'll leave it alone. Jonah blows out a long deep breath, and I scoot forward, leaning into him and resting my head on his shoulder. His cheek touches the top of my head and I close my eyes, deciding to try and explain myself; for him, if not for me.

"I miss them," I confide. "Sometimes I can't remember them. I've forgotten their scent, their mannerisms, their voices. I just wanted to hear them… I keep thinking if it's this bad after a year, how will it be in five… or ten? Will I forget them completely? Will they soon become just faces in a photo album with fuzzy moments attached to them?"

Jonah doesn't answer, how can he? He's seventeen and doesn't know how to handle this situation any more than I do.

"Can you keep a secret?" I ask, my head remaining on his shoulder. His cologne drowns out the hospital smell and I want to bottle it up and keep it with me for after he leaves. It's clean, different than the scent I remember him bathing himself in when we were in middle school.

"Yours? Of course," he replies, matching my whispered tone.

Lifting my head from his shoulder, I turn away from him, too nervous to look him in the eyes as I make my confession. "When I cut myself, I heard my dad. He sang to me."

"D?"

"Don't say it, Jonah." I slide from the bed, untangling our hands as I stand. I see his disbelief as I turn to face him. "I know it sounds crazy, but the more I cut, the more he sang. It was a moment of weakness… I know that now, but I miss them so much and… "

"Don't do it again," he interrupts, running his fingers through his hair and standing. "I mean it. I don't care why you did it, just don't do it again."

I nod, "I won't."

"Promise," he demands as his hands take hold of my biceps. I nod again, it's all the promise I can give, and I hope it's enough as he pulls me into another long hug.

Today's Reality… You're not alone.
December 24, 2013

"May I come in?" Mrs. Hall asks, tapping on my cracked door and peering in.

"Sure."

I'm sitting on my bed, dressed and ready to go downstairs, but unable to make myself move. Yesterday, after I'd promised Jonah I wouldn't cut again, we were interrupted by Dr. Panos and our families. After a long lecture about how she was advising against it, Dr. Panos discharged me from the unit with the understanding that I'd return to her office in two days, the day after Christmas, for a follow-up session. Jonah's mom frowned, but remained quiet as I agreed with Dr. Panos' terms. I vowed to call her if I felt the need to harm myself again, but I swore I wouldn't.

I sat pancaked between a stoic Jonah, who held my hand, and a jubilant Kadence, who talked my ear off all the way home. It was because of the Halls I was able to leave the psych watch early. Jonah made sure I knew that before I excused myself to the privacy of my room the moment we stepped into the house. His parents stepped up for me, when my grandparents wouldn't, by refusing to let me stay at the hospital another night. Especially on the eve of Christmas Eve. I'm grateful for their assistance, but I'm not sure how much energy I have to thank them.

Closing the door behind her, Ms. Virginia leans against the frame and crosses her arms in front of her chest, as though she's hugging herself, as she looks around. "I helped your momma pick out this furniture," she says, her smile wobbling, as she crosses the room. Like Jonah, her hair is a gorgeous shade of white blond, the ends curling right below her collar bone. She looks as beautiful today as she did a year ago and I almost want to hate her. Almost.

"I remember," I reply as she picks up a picture of my parents from my dresser. It's the one from the box, the one with the broken frame. While I was in the hospital, my grandparents cleaned up the blood, removed the box of items from the room and put the picture in a new frame.

"We re-decorated your room while you were at camp. Your mom cried." She lets out a soft laugh.

"She cried?" Angling myself toward her, I pull my legs under me and wait for more, because I've never heard this story.

"There was a lot of wine, hun," she groans, as though that is all the explanation I need, and I smile at the thought. "A lot of wine. You were her baby girl and then suddenly you weren't. One day it was dolls and dress-up and the next it was boys and make-up. She struggled with that change."

"I remember how excited I was when I came home." My gaze floats around the room, and I take in my furniture with new eyes. These are the things my mother bought me as a coming of age present. The vanity table in the corner replaced a dollhouse. Books and picture frames replaced baskets of toys in a book shelf. A school girl left for summer camp and a teenager returned, and my mother needed wine to cope with it. I'd smile, if I didn't want to cry so badly.

"Jonah told me you're worried about forgetting them," I nod. "Oh, sweetie, I'm not going to let that happen." She touches my cheek. "Anything you want to know, any time you want to talk about them, you call me. I have stories upon stories to share with you." My eyes burn and she bends over, pulling me into a hug. "I miss them, too."

I'm not sure what to think. I've avoided sympathy for a year. I've avoided hugs and talking about my feelings. With the exception of my therapy sessions, I've avoided all things related to my parents. I sit there, motionless, while she hugs me much too tight, for much too long.

"Why don't you come down for breakfast? Kadence and Jonah are anxious to spend some time with you today," she hints, smoothing her perfect hair when she steps away.

I nod lamely and follow her downstairs, the steady chant 'act normal' on repeat in my mind. "Ms. Virginia?" Stopping on the bottom step, I fidget. My pulse is racing with the need to thank her. "Thank you for convincing them to let me come home. I know it was because of you and Mr. Ron."

She shakes her head, her face clearly telling me no thank you is necessary. "It's Christmas Eve, let's try to enjoy our time together, okay? We will talk things through later."

Her words hold an undertone, an intention I can't make out. I have this ominous premonition of a conversation yet to come, but I'm too tired to dwell on it and after a moment the feeling is gone.

We join the others in the kitchen, the normalcy of the scene spread out before me almost brings a smile to my lips. Kadence and Gram are rolling dough and mixing ingredients that, after a closer look, I recognize as Gram's famous Christmas morning sausage rolls, and the guys are sitting at the table talking basketball and eating large plates of bacon and eggs. I'd stand in the doorway and watch this scene all day if they'd let me, the perfect Hallmark picture of a happy family, but the moment we cross the threshold into the kitchen Ms. Virginia opens her mouth.

"Look who I found," she sings, breaking the happy spell that's been cast. The director of my new life just yelled 'cut', pitiful Dani is on-set, everyone stop and stare. I realize I sound cynical and horribly unhappy, also a bit paranoid. Then five pairs of eyes swing my way, pinning me to my spot, and I conclude I'm not paranoid. I'm the center of everyone's attention, no matter how hard they want to pretend life is normal. Jonah's the first to look away. He clears his throat and picks up the conversation he was having as if he were never interrupted and the men follow suit after saying good morning. *Action! Back to acting normal.*

I spend the next hour sitting at the table in silence. I feign interest in the breakfast Jonah's mom put before me. I feign interest in the baking Kadence and Gram are doing, and the conversation the guys are having. Eventually, I put my plate in the dishwasher and pick up a notebook and pencil. Returning to my seat at the table, I proceed to feign interest in socializing, when all I truly want is to gain the privacy — and peace — of my room. I pick up tidbits of conversations as I sit there. Talk of a quick shopping trip for Christmas dinner between Gram and Ms. Virginia. Kadence begging her mom to get the recipe she's working on, Jonah's next game when school is back in session. From what I gather, Jonah made varsity basketball this year, I'm not surprised. Then I recall Gram mentioned it to me a month or so ago, but I'd filed it away, as I did everything…

"Danica? Jonah asked you a question," says Gram, tapping my shoulder. I look up from my scribbles and thoughts.

"Sorry?" I ask, making eye contact with him for the first time since I stepped into the kitchen over an hour ago.

"I asked if you wanted to go for a walk?"

"Outside?" I look over his shoulder out the windows where the sun is shining brightly behind him.

"It's unseasonably warm out today. Go on, fresh air would do you good, get some vitamin D," Gram suggests, not so subtly. I agree, not sure if I'm doing it more to be with Jonah or to get away from everyone, and push back from the table as Jonah does the same.

"I want to go too," Kadence says excitedly. Jonah frowns, giving his mother a look I'm sure neither I, nor Kadence, were supposed to see.

Ms. Virginia coughs and wraps her daughter in a hug from behind. "No, sweetie, you stay here. I need you for secret Christmas stuff," she suggests in a conspiratorial whisper loud enough for us all to hear.

Kadence is still moaning about how unfair it is when Jonah and I close the front door behind us. Without a word, we make our way down the drive to the street before Jonah stops and stuffs his hands in his sweatshirt pocket. He looks at me and I try not to look at him, lifting my face to the warm sunlight instead.

"Where to?" he asks with a heavy sigh.

Instead of answering I turn left and he follows. We walk, turning down one street after another in my grandparents' neighborhood. The streets are crowded with vehicles, and we're greeted by several people with joyous shouts of 'Merry Christmas' as they unload families and cars, evidently visiting relatives and having parties. It's a good thirty minutes before we reach our destination, a small open park space with a pond and walking trail in the center of the subdivision. Tired of walking in silence, I make my way to the edge of the pond and sit on a boulder, pulling my knees up to my chest. I wrap my arms around my legs, propping my chin on my knees as Jonah stands beside me.

"You come here often?" he asks after a while.

I shrug. Truth is I come here several times a week, to think, to get away from my grandparents, to cry. I'm not sure why I brought him to this spot because now I'll think of him every time I'm here.

"You're not alone."

I keep my gaze on the water in front of us. "What?"

He moves to stand before me, his body blocking my view as he replies, "You're not fooling anyone, especially me. Why are you trying to pretend I'm not here?"

"I'm not," I lie, finally looking at him. He's wearing a Grove Pointe basketball hoodie, and black workout pants. Typical jock attire, and I smirk. Jonah Hall has become exactly who I knew he would become.

"Like hell you're not. You've barely spoken to me, you think if you don't look at me I'm not going to know how much you're hurting? I've known you forever." His soft, but angry, words are at odds with my thoughts and I have to take a moment to analyze what he's said.

"What do you want from me, Jonah? What did you expect, what did your parents expect, coming here?" I drop my legs to the ground, returning his angry stare as he shakes his head.

"A year. A full year, and you haven't called or written. Everything I know about what's happening has come from your grandmother and she's not particularly forthcoming. My mom's been going crazy."

"What are you talking about?" I ask, utterly confused.

"Just forget it," he groans, blowing his cheeks out in frustration and kicking a nearby stone into the pond. "Did you get my letter from the hospital? Did you get the package I sent for Valentine's Day? Do you know what you've done to me?"

"What I've done to you?" I ask. *He can't be serious?*

"It doesn't matter, I'm not mad, it just hurt."

"You're not mad?" I stand now, confused and angry in my own right. "What do you have to be mad at? I'm sorry, did your parents die in the car you were driving? Did you lose your home, your friends, your freaking entire life? Huh? Did you go through grueling hours of burn care and surgeries? Who do you think you are?" I shout, spinning on my heel.

"Damn it, Dani," he shouts after me, grabbing my arm before I get far. "I didn't mean that. I just…"

"You just what? What do you want?" I ask again.

"I don't know how do to this, D. I'm trying to support you, I want to be there for you, but I don't know how. I want you to know you're not alone! You're not the only one who lost something last year. My parents lost their best friends. Our moms were like sisters, you know that, and my dad… your dad was his go-to guy for everything. They lost, too." His hand moves up my arm and I jerk away at the tender touch, it sears my skin even through two layers of clothing. Jonah throws his hands in the air at my reaction. "You left, without saying goodbye. Kady was inconsolable, you've always been like a big sister to her…" He drops his arm, shaking his head with another shrug, as though he's finished with everything.

"I didn't have much of a say about when I left," I say and it's a lie. I was the one who chose to leave without saying goodbye. My grandparents originally scheduled my transport for later in the day so I could see some friends once I was weaned from the painkillers and a little more aware of my whereabouts. I'd begged them to leave as soon as possible instead. Running away felt easier than facing the truth. Facing leaving. Running feels easier now, and I'm tempted to take off. Jonah's eyes track me too well, he knows me too well, and I feel like a bug under a microscope right now.

"And what about you?" I finally ask, turning his own scrutiny back on him. "How did you feel?"

His jaw tightens, the muscle in his cheek flexing, as he exhales a long, deep breath and closes his eyes. "I missed you, Dani. I missed my best friend." His eyes open and everything about him has softened once again. His stance, his eyes, his jaw. My heart aches. "I miss us," he finishes.

He's said everything I feel. I miss him more than I can say. I miss what we could have become. I remember the kisses we shared our last night together and I curse life for the cruel hand I was dealt.

"I read your letter a few weeks ago for the first time," I admit, leaning back against the boulder again as I explain how I'd ignored all of the items from my friends back in North Carolina. "For a while I figured if I just pretended it wasn't there, I could forget it all. It didn't work though, I can't just forget everything."

His head cocks sympathetically to the side and I can sense his internal struggle. He's fighting with himself to stand there and listen instead of pulling me into his arms. He flinches and moves, before he stands his ground.

"I love the locket, Jonah. I love it so much and I wanted to call you and thank you... but I couldn't. I couldn't hear your voice, I couldn't think about you and your parents or Kady. You're right, you all lost something that night too and I'm so sorry. I'm so sorry I was driving that night -" I break, shaking now as I admit my sins to him. "I'm sorry I killed them. I killed my parents that night, it's my fault..." I crumble, folding into myself.

Jonah falls to his knees, pulling me to the ground and yanking me against him immediately, and once again I cry my pain out into his chest.

"Don't even go there. It was an accident," he says forcefully into my hair and I push away. Hearing another person say that stokes the anger in my belly.

"No." Scrambling to my feet, I back away, leaving Jonah stunned on the ground. He reaches out, his hand leaning against the boulder and using it to hold himself upright, as I continue to move away. "Don't you get it? I don't want sympathy. I don't want understanding and forgiveness. I don't deserve it."

The need to get away consumes me and I set off in a run as Jonah calls my name. A glance over my shoulder confirms he's rising to give chase, and I panic.

"Will you just leave me alone? I need to be alone, Jonah," I plead as I continue to run. When I reach the end of the street, I turn once more. He's standing there, watching after me. I turn left, never looking back again.

Gram's broken voice reaches my ears as I sneak in the back door after wandering aimlessly for a few hours, and I pause to listen.

"Virginia, I can't do it."

"Grace, we only want to help. I didn't fight it before, but I don't know if you two are up for this. She's not rebelling or depressed. She's endangering her life," Ms. Virginia says.

Fight it? Fight what?

"We're trying the best we can," Gram says defensively.

"Of course you are, but you said it yourself, it's not working. She's getting worse. You heard Jonah, she blames herself for their deaths. And those cuts, I don't think it's the first or last -"

The bright kitchen light snaps on and Kadence gasps as she spots me standing there, my back pressed against the door. Before I stop her she's hurrying to my side and hugging me shouting out, "She's back."

"Are you okay?" she asks, grabbing my hand and pulling me away from the door.

"I'm fine," I assure her as the Halls round the corner into the kitchen. Their faces are filled with worry and relief and mirror my grandparents' who enter not far behind them. "I'm fine," I repeat louder so they all hear.

Gram and Ms. Virginia speak at the same time and I hold up my hands, shaking my head, "I don't want to talk. Is it almost dinnertime? I'll go up and change, then I'll help set the table." I smile as warmly as I can manage, scooting past them. Their eyes burn holes into my back as I walk away, the silence I leave behind, deafening.

Emerging from my room a short time later, I fully expect to find a group of shell-shocked people standing right where I left them. Instead, I find dinner preparations are in full swing and I dive in without a word. I'm able to keep myself busy doing the little things needed without having to speak. I pull out silverware and set the table. I fold the stack of festive red linen napkins sitting on the counter and place them around the table, too. Christmas music plays in the background as Ms. Virginia mashes potatoes and Gram works at the sink. Their eyes track my every move and I send bright smiles their way each time I look up. It's Kadence who pays the most attention to me, giving me suspicious sideways glances whenever she thinks I'm not looking.

"Where's Jonah?" I ask as she sets a bowl of olives on the table.

She returns my smile with a black look. "He wanted to be *alone*," she replies, adding extra emphasis to the 'alone' letting me know he filled her in on our earlier fight. I swallow, biting the inside of my cheek. I hate how my actions today have hurt him further.

Our Christmas Eve dinner is tense, to put it mildly. Jonah doesn't materialize until the men carry the steaks in from the grill. He sits across from me, doing his best to ignore my presence, and I tell myself it's for the best. I'm able to smile and hide my pain from everyone but Jonah. He knows better, and I find myself relieved he's chosen distance instead of inquisition. The adults at the table are no better, and other than a few murmured compliments on the meal, we eat in silence. More than that, it's cold. I'm not sure what's put so much tension between the Halls and my grandparents. They were a united front at the hospital yesterday, but after the tidbits I overheard earlier I feel as though I'm missing something important.

Today's reality… So this is Christmas.
December 25, 2013

Merry Christmas, I tell myself, waking up before dawn on Christmas morning. My memory of last Christmas is non-existent. I was in a medically induced daze. I'm in that daze now, I admit to myself as I pull a sweatshirt over my head. I'm indifferent to everything. Creeping through the dark house, I make my way downstairs, grabbing a blanket and throwing it around my shoulders as I sit on the floor beside the Christmas tree. There are presents scattered around the bottom that weren't there last night, but I ignore them. I ignore the stuffed stockings, the twinkling rainbow of lights, the glittering stars and snowflakes adorning the tree. I ignore everything, everything except for the void in my chest. My parents loved Christmas and all of the hoopla that goes with it. Presents, decorations, food, parties, and more food. We did it all, and then some. I haven't let myself think about the celebrating we'd have done if they were here. As with everything else I've built up a wall, telling myself it's merely another month, another day. But it's not simply another day and I miss them so.

"Merry Christmas, Momma and Daddy," I whisper to the tree. To no one. I sit there for hours, until the ceiling above my head groans, alerting me to the others being awake and then I sneak back to my room.

Christmas morning is anti-climactic. My grandparents and I originally agreed to a quiet day, with a few presents. The things I open make me feel awkward. Some new books, a purse, gift cards; all little things with little meaning. The Halls left all of their gifts in North Carolina, planning on doing Christmas when they return home. They did present me with a small package and my eyes mist over at the representation of the gold double heart earrings.

With nothing to do, we agree to watching classic Christmas movies and relaxing. I sit on the floor, my back against the couch, snuggled under a throw blanket, and lose myself in the mindless classic, but I feel like the main attraction at a zoo. Eyes are constantly looking my way. They watch and evaluate me, so I smile and laugh at all the right moments hoping I look normal. Midway through the second movie of the day, Kadence plops down next to me on the floor with her laptop.

"You're never online," she says as she logs in.

"Yeah, not really," I shrug, not sure what I'm expected to say and she smiles.

"I can't live without social media. Between my phone and laptop… no way."

"She's like a fish out of water without her phone in her hand," Jonah says drily across the room, speaking to me for the first time since saying 'Merry Christmas' when I first walked downstairs this morning. Kadence sticks her tongue out at him.

"I've noticed you playing on your phone, what's so interesting on there?" I ask conversationally. I'm tired of the tension in the room and as the time for them to leave draws closer I'm starting to panic. I haven't spent enough time with them. Suddenly, I want to make up for the lost time. Kadence's eyes go wide when I ask her to show me her online social life and soon she's talking my ear off with site after site I've never heard of.

"This one," she gasps, pulling up a website where people make what she describes as 'virtual bulletin boards' and 'pin' things. "If you only use one site I've shown you, use this one. Look… I have my whole wedding planned. You can find clothes and art and all kinds of funny quotes and things."

"Maybe you'll find your virtual husband, since you're too annoying to ever find a real one," Jonah teases, but Kadence ignores him. A pillow slaps him in the face a moment later as Mr. Ron whacks him upside the head and I turn away from the devilish smile I see cross Jonah's face as he watches us.

Returning my attention to Kadence, I nod as she goes on and on showing me everything she likes to pin and smiling at the life she's building herself virtually. Her dream wedding, dream house, dream wardrobe and vacation spots. My heart flips and I close my eyes saying a silent prayer that she'll make these dreams come true one day. I hope they become a reality for her. I know firsthand how life doesn't always go as we want. Her fairy tale life looks eerily similar to the one I built up at her age. *I want my fairy tale. I want my Prince Charming, my happily ever after…* the thoughts sweep into my head unbidden and I snap my eyes catching Jonah studying me perceptively

"Excuse me," I mumble, hurrying from the room and rushing upstairs, planning to stay hidden until dinner. *Silly Dani, your fairy tale dreams are gone,* the evil voice in my head mocks, pressing down on my heart and soul until I'm drowning in it and begging for release. The one release I know how to find…

After an early dinner, an hour later, I offer to do the dishes to get out of sitting around and talking again. To my surprise, Jonah jumps up to help. Checking her watch, Mrs. Hall shakes her head, reminding him of their plans. "You need to pack up. We need to leave in less than an hour."

"Already done," he tells her. "I'll help Dani, you go pack."

We work in silence as we clear the table, scraping food into the sink and loading the dishwasher. Jonah carries leftovers in as I dig through the cabinets for containers to store them in. He's an efficient helper, lining each dish up on the counter and wiping off the table once he's done without my having to say a word. Once we've put the food away he offers to help hand wash the few dishes and wine glasses we couldn't fit into the washer.

He's testing the water temperature and soaping up a sponge when he speaks directly to me about something, other than our chore, for the first time. "Do you remember Missy Lamb? We dated for what, two-point-o seconds freshman year."

"Sure, she was kinda emo for you," I recall with a grin, picturing Missy. Pretty girl, but exceedingly dark and unlike anyone Jonah'd ever shown interest in.

He chuckles. "Yeah, well you know I had to test out the waters at some point. There were so many new faces. I seem to remember you doing the same."

Leave it to Jonah to remind me of the disasterous trail of guys I crushed on in ninth grade. Grove Pointe was a small town with one high school serving the majority of the area. Three middle schools converged into this one school creating a new and large dating pool when we entered high school. Everyone tried something new freshman year, it was awfully 'CW teen drama' of us all.

"Anyway, Missy," he gets back on topic, nudging my shoulder as he hands me a glass to dry. "She was… um, troubled."

"Yeah?"

"Her moods would swing from high to low, sometimes in the span of an hour." I wonder why he's telling me this as he sets down another wet dish for me to dry. "I chalked it up to PMS, at first, and then I saw them."

Them? A warning bell goes off in the back of my head at a long forgotten memory and I bite my lip, preparing myself for his next words.

"I'm not stupid, D. I followed you yesterday after you ran away from me. It took me a while to find you, but when I did, I watched you. You looked ready to jump off a bridge, hell I honestly thought you might try. I hated standing idly by, but I knew if I intervened you'd either run or yell at me. I didn't want that, so I let you be."

He sets the sponge down, leaving the water running, as his hands grip the edge of the sink. Looking out the window over the sink, he speaks, "I thought it was crazy, how happy you seemed last night. The way you offered to help with dinner and the way you chatted with Kady. I wanted to think maybe the fresh air and alone time had helped you clear your mind, but I knew better."

Shaking my head, I drop my dish towel preparing to leave. "I don't know what you…"

"Don't," he enunciates clearly as he grabs my arm, making me wince. "Don't lie to me."

He turns on me, pushing my sleeve up revealing three small fresh red cuts along my forearm. His eyes narrow on the marks before looking at me with sadness. Sadness and hurt… and something else. Pity, maybe?

"Stop." I slap at his hand, yanking away. "How dare you judge me. You don't understand."

"Understand what? You don't need this. Let us help you. Come home and let my parents take care of you and let your friends be there for you."

"Wow," I snap, keeping my voice low. "You know nothing. I don't need your parents or my old friends. This," I slap at my arm holding it out to him, "has nothing to do with you or going back home and everything to do with me. Me, Jonah, and my need to feel alive."

I hurry from the kitchen, afraid I've said too much, a fist stuffed in my mouth to keep from screaming. Rushing to my room, I kick at the door as panic rises in my chest, I expect the door to slam shut, but it doesn't because Jonah's hand stops it.

"I thought you'd be coming back with us."

"Why?" I ask, confused.

"My parents wanted you to come back, to live with us. That's why we came, they're worried your grandparents can't handle you."

"Can't handle me? I don't need handling," I deny. "Plus, they're the only family I have left, what makes you think I would leave them?"

'Shooting him would have been easier,' my inner voice scolds as Jonah's body jerks back, his face crumbling. He shakes his head, his messy blond hair falling into his eyes, and he brushes it away.

"It's never going to be the same again, is it?"

"Jonah -"

"I should have known. I'm sorry for pushing you." He crosses his arms as his eyes roam over me. They touch every inch of my body from the top of my head to the tips of my toes, and I get the feeling he's taking a mental picture. That he's saying goodbye. Permanently. He opens his mouth, drawing a shallow breath, when his father appears behind him, startling us both.

"Son, we need to go," he reminds Jonah, as he gazes my way. "Ms. Virginia and Kadence are downstairs waiting to say goodbye, honey." I nod and his eyes flick between Jonah and I before he steps away.

"I don't want to say goodbye down there, in front of everyone," Jonah says, stepping further into the room and I match him step for step until we're standing face to face. His hands slide under the hair at my nape, his thumbs forcing my jawline up as he brings our bodies into contact.

"Just one more time... I have to," he says, leaning down and pressing his lips to mine.

I let him kiss me. I don't merely let him, I give into him. My hands grip his sides, my mouth yields to the sweet caress of his as my heart races to the beat of the thousands of basketballs we played with in our lifetime. We don't take the kiss any further. It's one long lingering touch of his mouth and mine. Yet, I know I'll never have a kiss as sweet as this one in my entire life, because this kiss is his goodbye. It's my goodbye. Goodbye to Dani and Jonah and the kids we were. Goodbye to the unfulfilled dreams we might have had a year ago to be together.

I know it, and the moment he pulls away, I know he does too.

"Do yourself a favor, if you're not going to talk to me talk to someone, please," he whispers, placing a kiss on my cheek. "I love you, Bambi."

I love you too, I reply in my head as he walks away.

His parents and Kadence hug me fiercely as we stand next to their rental car. Jonah's already in the back seat and it takes everything I have to keep myself from looking at him. I can't give in to the weakness pulling at me, telling me to yank his door open. The weakness telling me to let him help me. To let the Halls help me. *They can't.* They can't give me back what I lost, they only remind me of it. I push Kadence toward her door after she hugs me for the third time and turn to her mother once again.

"Thank you for being concerned for me and coming here. It means a so much," I tell her honestly and she shakes her head, waving it away.

"We'll always be here for you if you need us, you know that right? If you need anything…" Her eyes are swimming in tears and she gives me one final hug before sliding into her seat. I nod, plastering on a smile for her benefit.

When the engine cranks, Jonah's head snaps up, his eyes meeting my gaze as I'm helping shut his mom's door behind her. My hand slides along the car, from her door frame to his window, and I manage a wobbly smile. My fingertips brush against the cold glass as we stare at one another. The car shifts back an inch and I step away. I step away, but not before Jonah's fingers press against the bottom of the window too, for a brief moment. Then he turns away and he's gone.

Today's reality... I have a secret.
January 16, 2014

After the fiasco that was my hospital stay and the Hall's visit, I promise Gram I'll try to do better. I promise to be more social with them, to be a part of the family. Each evening I eat dinner with them, sticking around afterward to watch television game shows and all sorts of DIY shows. I stop complaining about my therapy sessions, too. I refuse to open up to Dr. Panos, but I go, and I listen. I sit at the kitchen table most days, while I do my schoolwork. Being in Gram's view while I do something so simple makes me look normal or so I hope. I'd started homeschooling two months after the accident, while still in the hospital, to keep up with my schoolwork. My grandparents had hoped I'd be ready to start my junior year at the local high school here in Texas, but I'd refused, begging to continue doing online curriculum instead. They balked and attempted to argue, but this is one area where Dr. Panos had become my ally. She convinced my grandparents school would be an unnecessary stress for me for the time being and so they stopped pushing. On the outside I'm trying my best to look like a girl who's finally healing from the trauma of the last year. But on the inside, I know it's a lie. It's my New Year's resolution - Fake it till you make it.

Night is always the hardest time of the day for me. When the only thing I hear is the beating of my heart and my mind can't stop the replay of memories, that's when my fingers itch to hold a blade.

In the three weeks since the Halls left, I've graduated from my original tiny shard of glass to a perfect little X-Acto knife. The small, pencil-sized tool was the first item I'd bought from a store in more than a year. Using the excuse of needing some school supplies, I convinced Gram to drop me off at the office supply store one afternoon a few days after Jonah left. My pulse raced when I found the aisle of drafting supplies and the neat rows of knives. It was equivalent to seeing your crush at the mall when you're thirteen or being asked to dance at homecoming — my heart sang. I purchased the knife and covertly stashed it in my back pocket, under my long sweater, when Gram picked me up. The hard metal pressed into my back side all the way home and I couldn't wait to test it out, some day.

That's my secret.

It's not every day that I feel the need to press the cold tip of the blade into my skin and watch my blood bubble up. It's only the darkest days. The days when I sit for hours staring at the sky, the ceiling, the dent in the sheetrock of my wall. The days when nothing anyone says or does will pull me from the dark abyss of my own mind. Those are the days when I wait until the house is quiet, before finding absolution at the tip of the blade and the slice of my skin.

Tonight is one of those nights.

I'm sitting on the floor, classical music playing in my earbuds as I lean my head back against the wall and close my eyes. This is cut number seven and I've yet to hear my father's voice again. The cuts Jonah saw were ones made out of desperation. The pressure I'd felt having his family here had been overwhelming. After we fought at the park, I walked around for hours trying to figure out how to handle my feelings. I'd come to one conclusion: I needed to take control. Jonah made me feel things I couldn't figure out, Kadence made me miss being a normal girl, Mr. Ron and Ms. Virginia made me feel as though I needed to be the old Danica. Their expectations washed over me, drowning my senses and making it hard to breathe, and then I had a thought. Wandering back to the house, I recalled the clarity I'd felt when I'd made my first cut and I knew what I needed. The moment I walked back into the house I put my plan in action. I went upstairs seeking my clarity at the end of a sharp edge, to deal with my emotions. The funny part was, it worked better than I'd remembered. The cut calmed and soothed me, filling me with a subtle joy at the way life seemed to awaken within me as my blood spilled. Since that night the feeling has intensified with each subsequent cut.

Tonight I bask in the pain as I gently trace a new line across my thigh, directly beneath the scabbing wound from last week. Back and forth, back and forth until the music builds to a crescendo, and I apply the pressure necessary to gain my release. Teasing my skin, the build-up leading to the cut, it's a drug. And the making of the cut is me pulling the proverbial trigger. I revel in tricking my senses, baiting myself by dragging the knife around as though I might back out.

But, I never do. When I want to cut, I cut.

As I sit there, Jonah's last words tumble around my mind. 'If you're not going to talk to me talk to someone' he'd said before telling me he loved me and walking out the door, and seemingly out of my life. In the beginning, I tucked his comments away in the dark recesses of my mind, but they won't stay hidden for long. The words remain, popping up when I least expect them, and I'm forced to think about them. I've let them marinate until I can't stand it anymore.

We haven't spoken since he left. I've had two somewhat brief and relatively tense conversations with his mother and one pleasant chat with Kadence. But nothing with Jonah. There are a few times when I've overheard Gram giving 'Danica updates', but she never mentions the calls to me. I get the feeling whatever argument they'd had on Christmas Eve, when I was missing, has carried over.

Cursing, I shake the thoughts away, angry my last cut didn't clear the mess from my head. Usually I rely on my cutting to push the bad things away. It's frustrating. I have something I want to do tonight and I need the clarity to do it. Picking up the cell phone lying by my hip, I type, delete, and re-type a message before I'm happy with it:

"Hi Luke, this is Danica Evans… from the car wreck last year. I know it's been a long time but I was hoping you would be willing to talk some time."

Expelling a heavy sigh, my shaking hand lingers over the phone before pressing the send button. When a little blue box with my message pops onto my screen I want to throw up. It sits there, mocking me, and the text causes me to second guess everything. I re-read the words, wondering if I should have said more. Maybe this was too brusque, or maybe he has no interest in speaking with me, it's been more than a year.

I've been toying with contacting him for a few days now, ever since I found the card he wrote. I'd been listening to music, lying on my bedroom floor, when I turned my head, spying a little brown bear. It was on the carpet, nestled between my bed and the wall and I recognized it as the bear from my hospital box. He must have been pushed aside and fallen when my grandparents cleaned the room after the cutting episode. Curious, I rescued him and opened the small card attached to its wrist. I expected to find another note from a friend or teacher back in Grove Pointe, instead I'm punched in the gut at what I've found.

Danica,
I wanted to stop by and tell you how sorry I am. I'm the guy who pulled you from your car. I'm Luke. I'm so so

sorry for everything. I feel so responsible for the accident, even though there was nothing I could have done differently.

The hospital staff won't tell me much, but they do tell me you'll be okay. I hope when you feel better that maybe you'll send me a message and let me know. I'd like to know how you're doing.

If I could go back to the other night and change things I would. It was a crazy slick road and we spun and... well, it was an accident and I'm so sorry we caused your wreck.

Please forgive me,

Luke Claborn

The same stranger who saved my life that night had been the one whose car had caused it? How did I not know this? Holding the card in my hand, I thought back to the police's description of the accident scene. The driver of the other vehicle, a young college student whom they didn't name at the time, had lost control. The rear end of his car sunk into a ditch enough to prevent him from moving the vehicle on his own. He'd called for towing minutes before we came upon him. The driver was not being charged because everyone agreed it was an accident. Evidently this 'mysterious college student' was Luke Claborn.

'Please forgive me' his note said. That was a year ago. I felt ill thinking of this poor guy who probably thought I blamed him for the wreck since he'd never heard from me. Sitting up, I resolved right then to contact him and let him know I held no ill will toward him.

So, here I am, reaching out. It took a few days for me to work up the courage and still my anxiety is rising. I feel as though there's a monster tearing beneath my skin and trying to crawl out as the seconds tick by and I wait for a reply. I ache to make another cut. Beneath my long sleeve the last bit of healing skin from previous cuts itch. I scratch at the opposite arm, trying to trick my skin into feeling relief, much like one would if they had a mosquito bite. It doesn't work, the more I scratch, the itchier and jumpier I become. *You've lost it, Dani*, I laugh internally as I get to my feet and pace the length of my room.

The bear Luke left sits on my dresser where I placed him. He's wearing a Christmas sweater with a matching red and green hat. His little ears stick out of holes in the hat with a soft, white pom-pom sticking up between them. He makes me smile; his blue eyes and pink nose, the crooked smile sewn onto his happy face. My anxiety lessens in my chest as I stare at him. Spotting an odd glittering speck on the top of his leg, I reach for him and flick at his fur, dislodging a stray shard of glass.

The broken picture frame.

Upon further inspection there are several sparkles of glass covering the bear's legs and sweater and I shake him out over the dresser. I inspect him carefully after the last bits of glass come loose from his sweater. Satisfied he's clean I toss him to my bed, grabbing a wet sheet of toilet paper from the bathroom to pick up the small shards of glass and discarding them into the trash. Save but one. I keep the largest sliver, examining it as though I've never seen something so amazing. Roughly half an inch long, the shard is a triangular shape with one pointed end and one flat edge.

Walking back to the bed, I check my phone, there's no blinking light, nothing to tell me Luke has replied, so I slide to the floor and wait. I use the glass as a pencil, tracing the lines in my palm, the sharp tip tickling my sensitive skin. Following each line from left to right, top to bottom, and I wonder which lines mean what. Is the short one my life line? Does the line with the branches represent the children I might someday have? My eyes drift to the freckles on my bare leg and I shift the glass from my palm to my thigh. There I draw the outline of my own constellation, connecting the dots of my freckles again and again until my pale skin is bright red from the scratching. Then I apply pressure; the bite of the glass is a relief to my senses as I add yet another line to the collection along my thigh. A rush of air releases as I breathe out the adrenaline and lay my head back against the bed. Contentment washes over me in waves and I let myself sink. I allow my mind to wander in a euphoric daze. I picture a guy standing in the dark one fateful night. I see the stunned look upon his face as my headlights cut across him. For the first time, I visualize the way the ground shimmered, wet, black, and icy after the late night drizzle and drop in temperature. I see the ice before I hit it. Flashing forward, I shiver recalling Luke's appearance in the driver's side door. His face isn't visible, but I hear his panicked voice and see the shadow of his body as he rushes to unbuckle and pull me from the burning car. More than a year later and the acrid scent from that night fills my nostrils, but I'm not scared anymore. Behind my eyelids I see the orange flames lick up under the steering wheel, I feel the anger of the flames as they touch my bare shins. But whereas panic overtook me back then, tonight I find peace.

The muffled vibration of my phone behind me breaks me free from the memories. Twisting, I reach for it, my heart pounding once again. The screen illuminates with an unknown North Carolina number and I'm at a loss. *He didn't simply text me, he's calling me!* My mind screams as I glance down at my leg. While my brain was wandering, I cut my own freckle constellation into the pale skin on my thigh. Small drops of blood well up along the markings and I smile as I survey the work. My entire body tingles in an indescribable way; it hurts, yet I'm high on the pain. So I answer the phone.

"Hello?"

"Danica? Hi, it's Luke," he says in a thick country twang. I try to reconcile the voice on the line with the one that saved me. "I realize it's late, but your text worried me. I thought I better call."

"Oh," I ask, checking the time on my cell. One in the morning. "Wow, I'm sorry. I didn't pay attention to the time. I didn't mean to worry you. I just…" I'm not sure what to say. His admission of worry has surprised me.

"How are you?" he asks after a moment of silence.

"Um, hi. I'm good, I… I just found your card actually. The one with the teddy bear," I fumble. The cuts on my leg burn and I wipe at the blood.

"Yeah, I know what card you're talking about." There's a touch of humor in his voice before he clears his throat and asks, "Why'd it take you a year to open it?"

My fingertips smear the blood across my skin, drawing circles as I think of how best to answer. Evasion, works best. "I moved after the accident… to Texas."

"I heard."

"So my grandparents boxed up my things and… wait, you heard? That I moved? Were you checking up on me?" I ask, both curious and confused.

"We were," he replied.

"We?"

"My girlfriend and I. She was with me that night, too."

I vaguely recall him yelling at someone for help. "Oh." I nod as if he can see me through the line. "Well yeah, so I'm fine. Um, I live in Texas with my grandparents now and I just wanted to thank you for stopping by the hospital back then. I'm sorry I wasn't able to see you and thank you for saving my life."

'Thank you for saving my life?' How ridiculous is that? Thanking someone for saving your life.

He clears his throat again as though I've made him uncomfortable. "You don't have to thank me."

"I do," I start and he speaks over me.

"I've spent the last year wondering if there was this girl out there somewhere who hated me," he sighs into the line.

His forlorn tone tugs at me, makes me feel... something. Pulling my knees to my chest, I apologize. "If I'd known, I would've called earlier. It's kinda been a bad year, you know."

He huffs, "Sorry, I didn't say that to make you feel bad. You don't owe me anything."

The way his words roll off his tongue, with his heavy accent, brings a smile to my lips. "You're wrong," I disagree wholeheartedly. "I owe you my life."

"Thank you," he replies, his voice soft and I feel the tug again. It feels like hope. Like something within me wants to think there are brighter days ahead.

"No, thank you," I counter, pressing the end button as a wall of emotion crumbles around me. I'm not sure I can bare to have hope. Hope is the light at the end of a tunnel, and I've been in darkness far too long to believe there is any light left.

Today's reality… I'm in too deep
January 18, 2014

Two nights later, I'm slipping into bed when a text lights up my phone. "Texas, huh?" It reads and I recognize the unknown number immediately, it's Luke. I take a moment to think and add his name into the contacts as the phone goes off again.

Luke: you're not a Cowboys fan now are you???

What the heck? I re-read the text three times and check the number against the card, I left sitting on my nightstand, thinking perhaps I'd remembered it wrong before I reply.

Me: Luke? Are you drunk or something? Wrong number??
Luke: Ha, yeah it's Luke and I'm 19, I can't LEGALLY drink. I thought that was an obvious question to ask someone who's moved to Texas, no? I suppose I could ask if it's true what they say about everything being bigger in Texas, but I figure that might be inappropriate
Me: is this a prank?
Luke: not at all. You hung up on me the other night. I wanted to say hi and let you to know I'm around if you ever want to talk

Biting my lip, I'm considering his offer when the phone buzzes again.

Luke: don't say no. Think about it

I reply back that I will and clutch the phone to my chest, rolling over, a smile playing on my lips at the odd interaction. My brain mimics Luke's thick accent as I repeat his text in my mind. *Are you a Cowboys fan? Are things really bigger in Texas…* a giggle shakes my shoulders as I try, and fail, to picture his face. My memories of the accident have always been sketchy, the pain and shock I went through overrode everything else, causing me to only see flashes of the scene. I have two vivid memories of Luke Claborn: the overall terror on his featureless face as my headlights swept over him before we crashed, and his voice telling me to stay with him. I hear the words in my dreams weekly, but now they're in his real voice. Before the other day they'd been in a generic tone, passionate and filled with fear and worry, but it was a generic male I didn't know. Now, as I lay in bed, I place Luke's southern drawl with the words he spoke. Texas people have their own unique accent, different than the southern accent I've known all my life. Texas guys are cowboys, their tone sharper and quicker paced, whereas the southern boys I've always known have something softer and sweeter about them. Like a lazy day under the sun. The thought warms my face and I find myself typing a message back to Luke with a smile on my lips.

Me: I'm insulted you think I'd go to the dark side so easily... hint: I'm NOT a Cowboys fan. I'm still a Carolina girl at heart!

Luke: I knew we would get along.

Me: did you?

Luke: sure did. Now how about an answer to my other question?

Me: ??

Luke: are things bigger in Texas?

Me: oh that. Well, I don't know. I don't get out much. I do see a lot of cowboy boots and hats…

Luke: LOL, yeah I bet you do

Me: and Im convinced my grandparents own stock in the cattle industry the way we eat meat around here!

Luke: sounds like I need to visit Texas

Me: you don't get enough red meat in North Carolina?

Luke: in college? No.

Me: ahhh, yes you live off Ramen noodles and pizza, right?

Luke: with a liberal helping of cereal

Me: Lucky Charms?

Luke: Special K, I'm trying to keep an eye on my boyish figure! Wanna see?

Me: lol. Wanna see? A picture of your boyish figure?

Luke: yeah, I realize you probably don't have a clue what I look like. I want to make sure you don't get the wrong idea.

Me: what idea would be wrong?

Luke: I get mistaken for movie stars a lot with my devilishly handsome face and windswept hair. It's a curse really, some girls can't handle it. It's best you know now what you're dealing with.

Me: Oh, okay I suppose I can understand that. I'm not sure if I can text with someone who is prettier than me.
Luke: Handsome! I said handsome, not pretty!
Me: Okay, gorgeous then send me a picture.
Luke: fully clothed?
Me: OMG! Yes creeper, fully clothed! Please.
Luke: okay, okay stop begging.

I flip to my stomach, rolling in my laughter as I wait for a picture to come through. When my phone vibrates, my heart picks up and I take a deep breath as I click on the attachment. I expected a picture from Facebook or something saved on his phone, instead he's sent me a selfie. He's leaning up against a wall and making this face only a guy makes. Some sort of 'what's up/head nod' face I've seen on hundreds of boys through the years. And he is devilishly handsome, he wasn't lying. His dark hair is short on the sides and kinda messy chaos on top. His jaw line is covered with dark masculine stubble, something I'm not used to, but oh my word I could get used to his. Luke is gorgeous, in this dark way, and I smile because in all honesty we could probably pass for family.

Luke: Did you pass out from shock?
Me: You lied about the windswept hair, I'm disappointed.
Luke: Ha! Well as long as that's the only feature disappointing you. So your turn.
Me: Ummm, my turn?
Luke: Yep. Picture now and clothing is optional for you too, you know.
Me: …
Luke: I kid!

I'm laying in bed, in my dark room. Oh why not, I think holding out my phone and taking a shot. I press send with a smile because I know he can't see much of anything in it. It takes him a minute before he responds.

Luke: Is that your hair I see? It's pretty dark.
Me: well, I'm in bed, in the dark. Maybe I'll send you one of me sticking out my butt and boobs next time, okay?

91

Luke: promise?
Me: lol. Here, I have this one from Christmas.

I attach a bathroom mirror selfie of Kadence and I on Christmas day,
it's one of the few pictures I've taken since my parents death. She'd
forced me into it and then sent it to me after they'd left Texas.

Luke: You're prettier when you're not covered in glass and blood.
Me: I'm the brunette, btw.
Luke: I know. I remember that hair of yours, and those big eyes. Your
eyes will forever be etched in my memory…
Me: as will your face.

We fall into silence. The humor of our first texts broken by the
seriousness of the last. I don't want to think about the crash scene or the
accident. I want to be light and happy. So I text him changing the subject
and asking him about where he goes to college and after a moment he
responds and proceeds to tell me about his crazy roommates. Our
conversation goes back and forth for two hours. We text about his
school, then mine. We chat weather, sports, music. Mostly Luke makes
humorous comments on things and I laugh and agree. I've been so out
of touch over the past year that I'm not familiar with some of the pop
culture references he makes, so he explains them. Everything we say is
superficial. He makes me laugh multiple times and I find myself typing
replies to his comments that remind me of the old me.

In a few hours time I feel as though there's a part of the girl I was left
within this scarred and lonely shell I call my body. A few hours and
hundreds of text messages between Luke and I and I'm more alive than
I've been in a year. And like that, Luke Claborn secures himself a spot
in my life.

Luke: college sucks

The text pops up on my phone as I'm climbing into the car next to
Gram after a therapy session. It's the first less than chipper text Luke

has sent me in the three weeks we've been texting each other. My fingers itch to reply as Gram asks her typical post therapy questions.

"How was your session?"

"Same as usual," I say, turning to look out the window. She knows better than to ask. Therapy is confidential and I never tell her what we discuss, but it doesn't stop her from asking. If I weren't so afraid to get behind the wheel again I'd drive myself to my appointments and save her the heartache of her fruitless questions I refuse to answer.

"You know we have a group session next week," she reminds me needlessly.

"I know. Hey, Gram, will you drop me off at the pond? I'd like to get some fresh air, I'll walk home."

"It's too cold out."

I lean over to read the temperature on her dashboard. "It's fifty-two. That's not bad and it's sunny, plus I have my heavy jacket," I remind her, reaching into the back seat and grabbing the thick black jacket as proof. "I'll be fine, promise."

Twenty minutes later, she drops me off at the pond in the neighborhood, the same one where Jonah and I sat two months ago. "Don't be long, an hour?"

"Tops," I agree, shutting the car door and stepping away and waving as she pulls off.

Concerned, I pull my phone from my pocket and reply to Luke asking him what's wrong. The park is empty and I wander to the swings while I await an answer. Kicking the ground with my toe I glide through the air, pumping my legs to gain momentum.

Luke: call me?
Me: really?

I'm not prepared for the way my heart races at the thought of calling him. We've never once discussed the idea of speaking on the phone since the first time he called me. 'Too much?' he texts back and I lower my feet, dragging the ground and coming to a stop on my swing. Is it too much? There's something about the way we text late at night when I'm lying in my bed that conveys an intimacy between us. Nothing romantic has been said, but I feel closer to Luke now than I did to boyfriends whom I saw and spoke with on a daily basis. I'm worried it will change something between us, but I dial his number anyway.

"Sooo, not too much then?" he asks, the sound of his voice putting an instant smile upon my face. He says the words in the same playful tone I always hear when reading his texts and suddenly the worry is ridiculous. This is Luke.

"Not at all. I was surprised, that's all," I say.

"Well, hi then."

Oh, I forgot how heavy his twang is. Sigh. "Hi. Everything okay?"

There's a pause on the other end of the line and I pull my phone from my ear to be sure the call didn't drop.

"School's a ton of pressure. I'm tired of these classes and I keep thinking if I hate this now how will I feel when it's my job? You know?"

I think about the few times he's told me how much he hates his classes. "You're only in your sophomore year, change your major if you want," I suggest.

"What if I dropped out?"

"Whoa, that's a huge decision."

"Yeah, I just don't want to be stuck doing something I hate. I don't want to sit in an office all day. I want to be outside, moving, enjoying life." He speaks with such passion it makes me curious.

"What do you want to do? I don't know of a whole lot of jobs for college dropouts that involve those things and decent pay," I tease.

He chuckles and I hear a muffled shout. "I have an idea actually. You know what, I'm sorry, but I need to go, thanks for listening."

"Oh, okay…" my cell beeps in my ear signaling he's already hung up before I finish speaking. This is why talking was probably a bad idea, I tell myself. Like a helium balloon hanging around after a party, my heart deflates bit by bit all the way home. I try not to let the abbreviated phone call bother me, but it does. My conversations with Luke are daily hits of happiness for me. They lift me out of my darkness, each joke or update sustaining me enough to hold my head up out of the deep end until his next text. He's become a life preserver of sorts. I didn't mean for him to, it simply happened. I kick at a rock on the sidewalk as my mind races with this new development. Is it one-sided? I have no idea. Maybe I'm projecting too much onto our texts? I resolve to ask him, feeling it's best to know where we stand before getting in any deeper. As I walk into the house the voice in my head laughs at me, '*You're already in over your head, Dani. This could be a disaster for you.*' I sigh, because I know it's right.

Today's reality... Weeks move forward, I do not.
February 24, 2014

"You've been in a dark place the past two weeks. Did something happen?"

"No." I bite at my thumb nail, my eyes following the slow moving minute hand of the clock on the wall in Dr. Panos' office as I answer shortly. *Unless you count the complete and total silence from Luke.*

"What do you want with your life?" she asks out of the blue.

"I'm sorry?"

"Have you thought about it? What you want to do after high school? Your grandmother told me you've worked through your classes so quickly you're able to graduate early. So what is it you want to do?" She cocks her head to the side, her inky black hair slipping over her face and she pushes it back. It's grown longer in the four months I've been seeing her, the front angles forward whenever she leans down to take notes. "Danica?"

I blink swiftly. "Sorry," I reply as I focus on her question. "My future? Uh, I have no idea, I'm trying to get through this week first." *In reality, I just want to hear from Luke. I want answers.*

Dr. Panos' face scrunches up, a semi-frown on her face as if she doesn't know how to feel. "I want you to come to a group meeting."

"Group meeting?" My eyes check the time again and I straighten in my chair. *Five minutes.*

"Yes, I run sessions once a week with survivors of events like the wreck you were in. Survivors or family members who lost someone in a horrific way. I think perhaps you could learn a great deal from listening to others who have figured out a way to move on."

A huff releases from my chest. "I'm moving on, I have no choice," I say sarcastically. *Or I could slice a little deeper tonight. I could end it all.* I gasp audibly at the internal thought and she levels her always probing eyes on my face, as though she heard my threat. Saying nothing, she stares until I give in and look away. Then she speaks again. "Not just moving on, but moving on and living. You can go about the rest of your life moving forward, Danica. Look around, we're all moving, growing one day older, going forward; but we're not all living. I want you to live. Do you want to live?"

Two more minutes. "I'll think about it."

"About living or the group meeting," she asks, not letting me off the hook.

"Both," I tell her with a shrug.

I'm lying.

Three weeks. Four weeks.

It's almost April and I haven't spoken to Luke in one month. At first I sent him texts, all carefully worded, and neutral, trying to ask if he was okay. I told him I hoped school was okay, I hoped he was figuring things out and I was here to chat if he needed to. He never replied and I stopped asking, stopped sending, stopped caring.

No more letting people in. The demon in my head curses at me each night as I lay there waiting and hoping he'll finally call. He hasn't. So when my phone vibrates during lunch as I sit at the kitchen table eating a sandwich and doing history classwork, I'm momentarily frozen. Thankfully, I'm alone this afternoon, Gram would jump all over me wanting to know who I was talking with. I flip the phone over, seeing his name on the caller ID and every single part of me with an ounce of reason says 'ignore him.' My fingers know no reason though. They don't think twice, sliding over the answer button before I can stop myself.

"One month," I say crisply, my angry tone making up for the quickness of my eager hands.

"I know, I'm…"

"Don't you dare say you're sorry. One freaking month, Luke. If you didn't want to talk anymore you could have replied to any number of my messages and told me so. If this was nothing but a joke or a time waster then you could have just said something." I sound like a shrew harping at him, but I'm mad. More than that, I'm hurt. He hurt me and for that I'm angry at myself, because I let him.

"Danica…"

"I know you thought we were just texting, just chatting, but I counted on you. I looked forward to your messages each day and then you tell me to call you. Then nothing, you just…"

"Danica!" he shouts again and I stop. Tears spring to my eyes as I realize what I've been admitting to him. "If you'd shut up I'll explain it all to you."

"Shut up?"

"Yes, shut up and let me talk. I'm sorry, I never intended to hurt you. I was hoping you didn't feel that way about me."

I was hoping you didn't feel that way about me? I blow out a breath as I choke on a reply to that painful sentence.

"*That* way? What way?" I ask curiously, as if I don't already know. The line is quiet and my thumb toys with the idea of hanging up on him. Then he speaks. "The way I feel about you."

"Well, I'm sooo sorry I care… wait, what? The way you feel about me, I'm sorry did I miss something?" I gasp as his words sink in.

"May I explain now?" he asks sweetly and I agree numbly with a grunt.

"I had some massive decisions to make after I talked to you last month and I needed to take time. I was stupid not to contact you, to not let you know, but I was dealing with a ton here. I quit school. My parents were pretty ticked, of course, and then I had to move home and deal with Courtney."

"Courtney?"

"Of all the things I just said, you pick up on my ex-girlfriend," he laughs.

He's right, I'm focused on the girl. "Ex?" I ask for clarification.

"Yeah, we broke up. We were dragging it out, it was time."

In all the times we'd texted each other, he'd never confirmed they were together. I assumed they were, but I'd never asked. I'd let myself fall for a guy and I didn't bother to find out if he had a girlfriend. *Idiot.*

"I wasn't trying to keep her from you, you know. We've been on and off for the past few months and once you and I met…"

"I don't know what to say."

"Don't say anything. Or say everything, whatever you want. I'm the jerk who disappeared for a month."

"Why? Why did you do that?" I ask, trusting he would answer me honestly.

"I needed to get my head on straight. You wouldn't know it based on our conversations, but I was barely passing school. I was partying too much, wasting time with Court, being miserable in my classes. I needed to make a choice and to do that I needed time. I didn't think it would affect you, but I gather by the way you went off on me, it did."

Lie! Lie to him, tell him you were fine, it was no big deal. You're friends, nothing more. "I missed you. I didn't realize how much I relied on your calls until that last day. I've been working so hard to keep people out, Luke, but you worked your way in. I don't know how or why."

"You don't have to explain it, because I feel the same way."

I slap my hand over my mouth to smother a laugh. "You said that already, didn't you? Seriously, you said you felt something for me."

Luke laughs and I join in, giddy with the news. "You're a little slow in the uptake, huh?" he teases.

"And you quit school? Oh. My. Gosh. You quit school! What are you going to do now?" Everything he said is registering as my head clears and I'm floored.

"I'm doing what I've wanted to do for a while. I've decided to become a firefighter."

"A fire…" The word dies on my lips. I can't be near a candle since the wreck and Luke is telling me he wants to run into flaming buildings? "No. No way, why do you, why…"

"Hey, hey, calm down."

"Calm down? I hate fire, I was burned by fire, or don't you remember. What are you thinking?" I ask. My body's shaking, trembling at the visual of Luke fighting fires. Not because it's Luke, I'd feel this way about anyone I know, anyone at all. Fire equals bad in my eyes.

"I'm thinking of you." He shushes me. "The one moment I'm most proud of in my life, Danica, is rescuing you, saving you. Ever since then I've thought about how amazing it would be to be a hero to others."

"You don't have to be a hero to others," I tell him selfishly. "Just be my hero."

"Aw, babe…" The endearment must catch him by surprise because he clears his throat before continuing on. "I can still be your hero, but I want to do this. I've already signed up. I start training in a week."

"So it's a done deal?" He tells me 'yep' and I swallow hard. "It's what you really want to do and your parent's are okay with it?"

"We fought, but yeah, yeah they're okay. They know me well enough to know I wasn't going to be happy working some sales job and wearing a suit. This is more my style. My mom even reminded me of my fireman phase from when I was a kid. It's not as far-fetched as it sounds."

I can't form a sentence that doesn't sound horrible so I sit there.

"Hey, I'm sure the idea stresses you out, I understand your fear of fire. Honest, I get it. I won't talk about any of it if that will make you feel better."

"I'm happy for you, Luke. If you're doing what you want, then I'm happy for you. Terrified, but happy." I know saying I'm happy three times is overkill and I'm surprised when he doesn't catch on. But, who am I to tell him no?

"Great. I'm glad I could finally get all of that off my chest. The past few weeks have sucked. How about you, I mean besides some jerk cutting you out. How's school?"

And like that, Luke Claborn worked his way into my life again. This time though, it was deeper. Weeks turned into months, winter into spring, and we chatted every day. Sometimes it was for a few minutes at night after a long hard day of training for Luke, when he could barely keep his eyes open, but he would call and say 'hi' and tell me he was thinking of me. Other days, his off days, we'd talk for an hour or more, mostly random things — movies, music, my school. I don't tell him how much I still hurt, because little by little I'm starting to think, that maybe the pieces are being glued back together and soon I'll be whole again. I also don't tell my grandparents or Dr. Panos about him. He finishes fire academy and starts a job, he's thrilled and happier than ever. I'm terrified. I still have my secret, I still cut, but the need has lessened as time goes by. I have more strong days than weak.

Life keeps moving forward and I move forward with it. Some might say I'm living. Even if it's in secret — I'm living.

Until summer comes.

Today's reality… The six month plan
June 2014

There's one room in my grandparents' house I've ignored for the past year and a half. I can count on one hand the times I've been in there. Today, though, I'm feeling strong, brave. My feet sink into the plush carpet as I step into the formal living room, for the first time in months. The room's decorated in pale colors: pinks, beiges, a touch of whimsy with gold sequined pillows I helped Gram pick out during my 'sparkly phase' in middle school. The one contrasting piece of furniture is the reason I've avoided the room for so long. Sitting along the wall, a gallery of framed family pictures above it, is a beautiful dark walnut upright. The ivory keys call to me, making my fingertips tingle as I move closer. I haven't touched a musical instrument since the night of the accident. Music — something that once upon a time made me me — died along with my parents. No singing, no playing, no writing… nothing.

Today though, I'm taking another step forward. It started with a conversation between Luke and me about my dreams for the future. Like Dr. Panos, he's been asking what I plan to do after I turn eighteen and graduate. I could graduate by summers end, if I wanted. I've spent all of my spare time taking classes and getting all of the credits I would need. All that's lacking are two core classes and the extra fluff classes colleges look for. College, something I don't have plans on doing, not right now. Luke doesn't argue with my choice, he doesn't ask me why, he just asks what I want to do. Every time I close my eyes and allow myself to contemplate my future, a future I'm finally beginning to believe I deserve, all I see is music.

I graze the keys, hitting a few notes and humming with them. My pulse pounds in my ears, building like the crescendo of the very music I love. Closing my eyes, I don't think, I simply play. It's nothing specific, notes strung together into a melody, making me smile.

I play until my fingers cramp and palms ache. They're weak from disuse so I stop and sit there, replaying the song in my head. I glance up at the picture hanging directly in front of me on the wall, seeing my reflection in the glass. Beyond my face are my parents' from years ago. I look to the left at a picture of Gram and Gramps, then one of me as a baby, and two candid shots of me with my dad. Looking to the right, I'm startled when I see Gram's reflection in the glass. I turn on the stool.

She's standing a few feet behind me, her hands clutched in front of her chest, her face wreathed in a smile, her eyes are red with tears.

"You still play beautifully," she says.

I shake my head, "It was nothing."

"No, it was beautiful, sweetie. I've missed hearing you sing and play."

I want to be indifferent, to shake it off, but I don't. Today I allow myself to be vulnerable to my Gram for once. "I've missed it, too. I've been thinking maybe I want to play again. I sort of forgot how music makes my soul feel," I confess with a shrug.

"We could look at colleges with music programs," she offers. "If you want, that is."

"I might."

We stare at each other before Gram rubs her hands together, taking a step back. "I'll leave you alone then."

As she turns to leave I call after her, "Gram?"

"Yes?"

"I know I haven't been the easiest person to deal with. I'm getting better though, I'm feeling better." She opens her mouth, but nods instead of speaking. Giving me another smile, she takes her leave.

Rummaging in the piano bench, I remove an old notebook and pencil. Carefully, I draw a blank music staff across the page. Five straight lines with equal spacing to chart the arrangement. I'm a bit lazy, not worrying with bars and measures or dynamics. Today I just want to remember a tune. Setting the pencil and sheet in front of me I begin. I tap a few keys, then copy the notes to the staff. The notes come to me effortlessly, one after the other, as my mind hums the haunting tune of my life. Words I didn't say, things I didn't do, the loss, the pain... everything pours out of me in the universal language of music.

When I'm done, I tear the sheets of paper from the notebook and fold them. I don't play the completed piece, I don't need to; it's perfect. My soul felt every note as if I'd played them already. My lead smudged fingers are sore and I stretch them out as I get up, pushing the bench back under the piano. I leave the room the same way I entered — full of apprehension and longing — only it's reversed. Now, I long for the music. To sit and play all day, to touch the keys, feel the vibrations. I'm apprehensive of the strong emotions playing again has evoked, though. In eighteen months three things have brought me to life — Jonah, cutting, and Luke. Am I finally waking from my nightmare after so long?

Excited at the prospect, I hide my song away in the top drawer of my dresser and call Luke. I want to share this new accomplishment with him. I've kept my truths from him, the extent of my damage, the cutting, the dark thoughts I have in the middle of the night when I awake from another nightmare. I hide all of these things from him daily, worried he might think of me differently or that it might hurt him too much. His guilt in that night is eclipsed only by my own. We've recently made it to the point where we're able to talk about the accident. Over the past few weeks we've discussed it thoroughly, what he was doing that night, where he was going, how fast. In the end it was ice, a product of Mother Nature, and bad timing that put us both off of Burkeside Avenue that night.

The phone rings four times and I'm about to hang up when an unknown female's voice answers. "Danica?"

"Uh, yeah." Pulling my cell from my ear, I double-check the number to be sure I didn't dial someone else, the way she answered saying my name perplexing me. "Who's this?" I ask, my hand tightening around my phone.

"Courtney."

Courtney? Why is she answering Luke's phone? The soaring freedom I felt moments before sinks into the pit of my stomach. "May I please speak to Luke?" I ask. My voice is tense to my own ears and I picture some girl sitting in North Carolina with a satisfied smile on her face.

"He's in the shower." There's no obvious malice in her voice, but her reply is damning on its own.

I tell my heart to stop freaking out until I clarify things. "The shower? Okay, I'll call him back then."

"Don't." That one word breaks the civility I was trying to maintain.

"Excuse me?" I ask angrily.

"Don't call him back. What is it you two are doing? What do you think is going to happen with him? You're seventeen, he's twenty. You're across country and you've never even met," she says evenly. Her points are valid, but I ignore them by asking the one question I want an answer to right now. "Are you two back together?"

There's a moment of silence. A moment where everything stops and I wait for the bomb to drop. Finally with a heavy sigh she answers me, her voice soft as a whisper on the wind, "No."

No. "No? So why do you think…"

She cuts me off. "I love him. I've known Luke for years and I just want what's best for him."

"And that's not me?"

"I'm sorry, but no it's not."

I want to be angry, who does she think she is to say these things to me, but I can't be mad. She said something I've said to myself many times. Luke's a good guy and he deserves happiness — I'm a mess. My chest tightens, clearing my throat I ask on a shaky voice, "Has he said something to you?"

"Look, I'm not trying to hurt you, but since you two started talking he's changed. He quit school, he broke up with me, he…"

That's right! He dumped her. The reminder lessens the blow of her previous comments and I strike back. "So is this the jealous ex speaking or someone who wants the best for him? I had nothing to do with his decisions. He made them when we weren't talking. Also, when you two were together Luke and I, we were friends."

"Friends?" Sarcasm finally pokes its way into her remarks. "You were exchanging daily texts with *my* boyfriend. He didn't dump me because you two were talking about the weather."

"Actually, he did."

"Whatever. I'm not jealous. I'm not saying this to get him back. I'm saying this to help. He's with you because he feels guilty and he's using you to make himself feel better."

There are moments in life when something is said or done and your jaw simply drops. Where you sit speechless and stunned, helpless to process what you now know. This is one of those moments.

"Please just leave him alone. Finish school, find a new life away from the pain of that wreck. It will never work with you two. You're both hurt and in the end you're only going to get more hurt. It won't last… let him go, please."

Wordlessly, my thumb slides over the 'end' button and I drop the phone from my hands.

'You're not good for him.' 'He feels guilty.' 'What do you think is even going to happen with you two?' Each argument she made hits me in the chest. A kill shot. My original thought of her being a jealous ex flits away as I allow her words to penetrate the happy fence. She's right. What are we doing? I still cry myself to sleep, I still have nightmares, I still cut. *I'm not better,* I think with a bitter laugh. Behind the fence my darkness lingers. Today, the piano and music was one moment, one small victory amongst a

mountain of failures. He deserves better. Rolling to my side, I hug my knees to my chest and close my eyes, willing the night to come so I can create my own brand of relief.

6 6

A steady drum beats around me as I open my eyes to a dark room. Confused, I blink the hazy cloud of slumber from my brain and the drumming above my head melts into vibrations. The moon glows beyond my open blinds and I realize I'd fallen asleep for hours. Rolling to my stomach, I slap at the bed until my hand lands on my now silent phone. I hit the button, and the screen lights up, revealing twelve missed calls, all from Luke. I attempt to ignore them, dropping the phone to my chest, only to pick it up a moment later. Pulling up the call log, I study the times. He called three times back to back around six-thirty, that was close to when I spoke with Courtney. I wonder if she told him about our conversation or if he's merely returning my call? Then he called an hour later, and thirty minutes after that. *He's nothing if not persistent,* I think as I see his calls every thirty minutes up until two minutes ago. It's five minutes after midnight. I trace over the screen on my phone, my mind debating the wisdom of calling him back. As if on cue, the phone comes alive, Luke's hazel eyes staring at me as his picture pops up, alerting me he's calling again. *So much for the every thirty minutes, he must be desperate.*

My finger slides over the green arrow, instead of the red I wanted to press, and I put the phone to my ear.

"Danica?" Luke's strong voice says into my ear. "Danica, please talk to me. Are you okay?"

The tension in his voice tears at me, directly at odds with the dry tone of Courtney's as she told me to leave him alone. I can't bring myself to speak.

"Babe, please. Courtney told me what she said, it's all crap. Please talk to me," he pleads.

Squeezing my eyes shut, I ask, "What's crap?"

He sighs, "All of it. She had no right to say those things to you." I maintain radio silence. "I swear nothing happened. I'm sure you were confused by her picking up my phone. We were going to have dinner, she came into town yesterday and called asking if we could grab a bite. She was supposed to wait for me to call her, but when I returned home she was here. I just got off shift and needed a shower, I swear she waited in the living room."

"It's not that, Luke," I finally say. "You don't owe me explanations... we're not..."

"Not what? Not a couple? Not real? Don't tell me you listened to her."

"Listened to her? Of course I listened to her, although she didn't say anything I don't already know. I've ignored the truth for too long."

"The truth? What does that mean?" he asks, tension returning to his words.

I groan in frustration, "What are we doing Luke? What is this... a way to pass time? A way to make ourselves feel better for something? A way to alleviate guilt? I use you, you use me..."

"No. No... I could kill her for making you think that."

"Don't blame her, she cares about you. She's worried. I understand where she's coming from."

"Stop," he growls.

"Stop what?"

"Stop running away and fight for what you want."

"Luke..."

"Am I wrong? Do you not want me? Is this nothing? If this is nothing tell me and I'll hang up right now, but don't lie to yourself and don't lie to me."

"I don't know what I want," I admit. "Gah! I'm not who you think, Luke. I'm so messed up. I've been lying to you all this time, I'm not okay, I'm not even close to okay..."

There's a low huff on his end cutting me off. "You think I don't know that? I'm not deaf, babe. I know you're hurting. I'm not pushing you and I'm not going anywhere."

My breath catches. "Why?"

"Because we need each other," he says earnestly. Biting my lip, a strangled cry throttles me, the emotion of his words overwhelming. "Courtney thinks we're doomed. Did she tell you that?" he chuckles.

"She might have inferred that," I say sarcastically.

"Look, I don't know where we're going to end up. Nothing about our relationship is normal, I know that, but I figure we have six months before we need freak out about anything."

Confused by his time table, I frown into the dark. "Six months?"

"Six months till you're eighteen and I'm hopping the first plane I can get to Houston."

A few hours ago my heart was heavy, now it's dancing. *Six months and we'll meet, is that a reality?* "Really?"

"Yes, really," he sighs, as if I've exasperated him. "I meant what I said. I would never want to insinuate that what happened that night was for the best or, you know… part of God's plan or something. But, it happened and maybe since it did, and we can't change it, we can at least find something positive in it. Maybe we were supposed to find each other."

Like fate? I'm not sure if I believe in fate, not the good kind anyway. I'm reminded of so many sessions with Dr. Panos and her telling me how I can't change the events of that night, but I can make the best of them. I was offended at first. Make the best of my parents' deaths? What the heck is that? After a year of discussing the same questions at every appointment, I'm finally understanding what she meant. I need to make the best out of my life, with what I have left. Be the best I can be, find the silver lining - I'm alive - and run with it.

"Okay," I whisper.

Luke repeats my soft words. "Okay?"

"Six months."

I swear I hear the smile he must have on his face when he replies, "Six months, it's a deal."

My stomach growls, reminding me I slept through dinner earlier. Scooting out of bed, I tiptoe out of my room and make my way downstairs to grab something. Luke yawns in my ear and I recall he said he'd gotten off a shift earlier.

"You're probably exhausted, huh?" I ask, careful to keep my voice low so my grandparents won't hear.

"A little. I didn't get much rest at work, it was busy," he says.

My chest tightens thinking of him going on calls, running into fires, seeing mangled cars and bodies after wrecks. Those things would be flashback hell for me, but he loves it and I'm happy he's found his 'best of the situation'.

"Danica? I want to make sure you know I'm not interested in you out of guilt. I'm not going to lie and say I wasn't trying to make myself better the day I left that bear for you, but since then… since the moment I heard your voice and got to talk to you… since then, I've been in it for you. I can't wait for January."

I sink down to the kitchen floor, a granola bar and water in my hand as I listen to him. Could I blame him if he said he was sticking around out of guilt? Something in my gut, in my soul, tells me I'm using him for that exact reason, but I push it away. He makes me smile and laugh. He makes me look forward to each day. Guilt or not, I won't give him up.

"So, what happens in January?" I ask playfully.

He laughs, a low masculine growl. It's husky and full of want, making my body twitch at the lust he emits. "I take you in my arms and I kiss your beautiful mouth."

It's going to be a long six months!

Today's reality… The cookie thief gets caught
June 16, 2014

"Can you tell me about Jonah?"

Whoa! Say what now? My inner voice goes crazy. "Excuse me?" Surely I've heard her wrong.

"Jonah. Your grandmother tells me you've been back in touch with him for a few months now. Why haven't you told me about him?" Dr. Panos arches her brow, her accusation-filled eyes pinning me to my seat.

"No… um, no. I'm not talking to… Jonah." Hearing his name hurts, saying it? That's downright agonizing. I have to force it from my lips as I shake my head in denial.

She looks at me skeptically and I shake my head again. "I'm not."

"No? Then who *are* you talking to from North Carolina?"

The cell phone bill. Evidently Gram's finally paid attention to the call log for my phone and she leapt to the conclusion I was talking to *him*. I don't allow myself to think his name again. *Why does it hurt so much? His name, my mental picture of his face…* I push the thoughts aside, reminding myself of January and Luke.

"I … this is confidential, right?" I confirm, always distrusting of what she might share from our sessions.

"Danica, everything you've told me has always been confidential. The only thing your grandparents get to hear is what you tell them and how I feel about your progress based on what you've told me." Her voice is soothing again. The coaxing voice of a doctor telling her patient to trust her.

"Luke Claborn."

"Luke Claborn? That name is vaguely familiar. Who is he?" she asks.

My arm itches, the idea of sharing Luke with her has my pulse doing overtime, and I wipe my sweaty palms on my thighs — wincing when I put too much pressure on a fresh cut — before I answer. "He's the driver of the other car. The one I almost hit. He's the one who pulled me from my vehicle."

One, two, three, four… I count the seconds it takes for Dr. Panos to reply. Her lips tighten before forming an 'o' as she opens her mouth. There's an audible intake of breath as she prepares to speak, and then she closes her mouth. *Five, six, seven…*

She hesitates so I inhale a deep breath and explain it all. The teddy bear, the note, the first text, and his return call. I provide her with the

108

five minute recap of our relationship and I'm startled by my word vomit. I'm spilling everything about him.

"I have no idea why I spilled my guts to you," I confess after I tell her about our six month deal.

Dr. Panos releases a slow breath, finishing whatever notes she'd begun jotting down while I talked. "Wow," she smiles. "That sounds both romantic and scary at the same time."

She studies me before her pink, glossed lips crack a wide smile. It reaches her eyes and I find myself joining her. We both laugh and the tension breaks as relief replaces the worry I'd built up as I unburdened myself.

"Why scary?" I ask after a few good chuckles.

"It's a big step, Danica. Putting yourself out there again, after so long, would be scary no matter who it was and for you to have picked Luke... that's..."

"Crazy?" I insert for her when she pauses.

"Possibly," she nods. "But, I was going to say brave."

"Nah, it wasn't brave of me. I didn't want him to feel guilty. When I saw his note... you could feel his pain looking at his handwriting. It was tangible. I needed to make sure he knew I didn't blame him."

"Why the secrecy? Why haven't you told your grandparents about him?"

The question makes me laugh for the second time in one session — a record — and I lift my arms, pushing my hair up out of my face. "Could you imagine me telling them I was speaking to the guy who, in their minds, played a part in the death of their son?"

The unexpected narrowing of Dr. Panos' eyes cause my arms to drop. Her mouth goes tight, little white lines pop up around her lips and I shrink back at the change.

"I mean, they've never said they blame him outright. I just thought it was best..." I trail off. She's looking at me with unexplained anger. Her eyes scan from the top of my head to the tips of my toes peeking out from the long hem of my maxi skirt.

"Danica, I'm going to ask you a question and I want an honest answer," she says dryly.

"Ooo-kaay."

"Why are you wearing long sleeves?"

"Why. Am. I..." *Crap.* I pull my arms into my chest, my fingers tugging at the sleeves. They're long, but the fabric is loose around my arms and I freeze, knowing exactly what's happened. I laughed, felt at ease — carefree for a moment — and let my guard down. When I lifted my arms to comb through my hair, the sleeves slid down and she got a front row seat of my private show.

"It's the middle of June," she points out unnecessarily.

"I'm always cold in here, you know that. I always wear a sweatshirt or cardigan." I'm relatively sure anything I say will only make a case against myself and when she sighs I know I'm right.

She stands, silently walking to her desk and picking up a thick file, flipping through it. Page after page she turns, saying nothing as I sit there. Seeking a release, my fingers twitch, wanting to press down on the newly made cuts lining my forearm, wanting to inflict pain. Mentally, I command them to be calm as my eyes check the clock: fifteen minutes before this session is over.

"Always covered up. Sweater and jeans, long dress and sleeves, day after day," Dr. Panos says as she closes the file and leans her backside against the edge of her desk. "A few weeks ago your grandmother mentioned she wanted to book a fun vacation for you all, she was contemplating a beach trip or cruise, but then she mentioned how you prefer wearing long clothing and how she feared you wouldn't be comfortable." I avert my gaze as she continues. "We thought maybe you were having a hard time dealing with your burn scars. It's why I brought up the idea of you going back for some more cosmetic surgeries two sessions ago, remember?"

She shakes her head ruefully and I don't answer because I know she isn't looking for my reply. "All this time," she breathes out, pushing from the desk and walking back to her chair across from me. "You've been hiding more than Luke from us haven't you?"

Unbidden, my head shakes in slow motion and she closes her eyes, reopening them as she drawls, "Push back your sleeves."

I know it's ridiculous to lie. Like a child who's caught stealing a cookie, my instincts shout deny, deny, deny. "I thought we were talking about Luke?" I counter, my eyes flicking to the clock once more. *Eleven minutes.*

"Danica." It's the forceful tone of an angry mother. The guilt trip eyes leveled on the cookie thief.

Deny. "This is silly. I wear long sleeves because I'm cold. Can we get back to Luke and my grandparents? Do you think they would take it…"

"Are you going to make me go to them?"

I break off my rambling. Unlike a child, I know when I've been caught red-handed and I know I can't win. "Go to them?"

"Your grandparents," she confirms what I already knew she meant.

I verify the time — *nine minutes*. Turning my head, I close my eyes and push my sleeves up and over my elbows.

Her horrified gasp fills the room.

My shame-filled tears streak my face.

Today's Reality... I'm a prisoner.
June 19, 2014

I step into the small room I've been assigned while my grandparents stop outside the doorway. Everything is white. White walls, white bedding, laminate white bedside table, desk, and dresser.

"You can add your own touches," says the nurse I'd seen earlier at the main desk when we walked into the center.

My arms hug my midsection as I shrug. "My Gram brought a few things."

"Well, good. I'm Jackie, I'm at the desk Monday through Friday so we'll get to know each other well while you're here." She gives me a toothy smile, her dark eyes wide and friendly. Jackie's ebony skin and hair contrast with my new living space. She's full of warmth and my room is ice cold. Like my heart. And soul. I shake my head, rolling my eyes at the direction my thoughts have taken. Jackie doesn't notice, or if she does she pretends not to. I imagine she sees her share of strange things here, I'm merely another crazy to add to her list. She's talking to me, pointing at things around the room, and I try to focus on her words. She moves to the door on the right, showing me a small private bathroom. There's a single shower, toilet, and small sink. All white.

"I thought yellow was the color of happiness," I mutter and she laughs. The sound is unnatural in this quiet, sterile building.

"Color stimulates happiness. We don't want artificial happiness, hun. We want you to *be* happy."

"Good luck with that," I mutter.

Jackie goes on with the tour of my box of a room as though I said nothing. "The button on the wall by your bed is a call button to the main desk. We prefer you get out of your room and walk down if you have a question, but you can always call if you need something. Any questions?"

My grandparents step in at that moment and I lock eyes with Gram as I ask Jackie one important question. "Am I a prisoner here?"

"Danica," Gram pleads.

Jackie shakes her head. "It's all right, Mrs. Evans, we get that one a lot here," she tells Gram with a small pat on the arm. I feel betrayed by the touch of sympathy Jackie's voice contains for Gram. *Another person against you,* the demon in my head reminds me.

"You're not a prisoner here," Jackie says, turning back to me. "There's a courtyard and a game room, you're free to wander, make friends — spend time in their rooms. This room is not a cell. We'd prefer you spend as little time as possible in here." Expelling a long deep breath, I nod. "Get settled and when your grandparents leave I can show you around some more."

Gramps steps forward. "Thank you…"

"Jackie," she offers and they smile at each other before she leaves the room, pulling the door shut on her way out.

"You two can leave now," I mutter, turning my back to my grandparents as soon as Jackie's out of the room.

"I'll get your bags," Gramps says, followed by the creak of the door opening and closing.

Gram's heels click on the linoleum floor as she steps to my side. "Danica, we're doing this for your own good honey. I wish you could see that." Her hand touches my shoulder and I flinch

Scooting around her, I jerk the door open. "Gramps will need help. He can't carry everything himself," I tell her before chasing after him.

I walk down the hallway to the sliding glass doors, tapping on them when they don't automatically open for me. Looking around at the nurses' station across the entrance I point to the doors as a small blond nurse meets me gaze.

"Sorry, Danica, patients aren't allowed out the front."

"What? Oh c'mon… my grandpa's right out there unloading the car. I wanted to help him." The nurse smiles sympathetically before picking up her black desk phone. A moment later she's asking someone named Lee to come to the front to help unload. She murmurs something else I can't hear and then looks my way again. "Lee's on his way up to give your grandpa a hand."

Jackie rounds the corner a moment later and I glare at her as she sends me a smile. "Not a prisoner, huh?" I complain, sliding down the wall and sitting on the cool tile floor as I wait for my stuff. My eye catches Gram leaning in my doorway down the hall, so I face the other way. Today I'm determined to be the worst granddaughter in the history of granddaughters. What do they expect after committing me to a nine week program for depression and self-harm? Crestdale Victory Center, the silvery white letters on the glass doors in front of me proudly exclaim. This is my new home. Pulling my knees to my chest, I rest my head on my arms and wait for my belongings.

The mechanical whine of the outer glass doors opening startles me and I sit up, seeing a luggage cart heading for me as the second set of doors open. Scurrying to my feet, I greet Gramps and an unknown male, who's pushing all of my belongings for the next nine weeks into the building. Without a glance my way, they pass by, heading toward my room leaving me to trail behind them. When they reach my room, Lee empties the cart at the door. He shakes hands with Gramps before looking my way. He's young, early twenties I'd guess, with dark hair and eyes. He's wearing dark blue scrubs and I assume he's a nurse too until he introduces himself.

"Danica, I'm Lee. I'm what you might call a jack of all trades here at CVC. Maintenance, bouncer, champion chess player. If something calls for muscle, they call me."

I fixate on the dark bronzed forearms and biceps flexing under his tight work shirt. "Bouncer?"

"You'd be amazed at how rowdy Friday night in the game room gets." He winks, causing a frown to cross Gram's face.

"So you're security then," I smirk.

"Yep, there's two of us. You'll meet Clint tonight. He's not as fun as I am, though I do recommend challenging him to a board game. He's horrible at them — not enough patience."

"Noted."

"Okay." He smiles, his eyes touching on each of us. "Danica, it's nice to meet you and I'll see you around. Mr. Evans, don't give up on the Rangers yet, it's barely mid-season." He nods again as he backs out of the room, the wheels on the cart squeaking as they roll away.

My grandparents' eyes are locked on me as I turn away from the open door and I drop the grin from my face as I survey my pile of belongings on the floor.

"Let me help you unpack your things," Gram offers, reaching for my suitcase of clothes.

"No, I'd rather you go ahead and go." I try to soften my tone this time, but it's hard to cover my anger with them.

That day in Dr. Panos' office, after she saw the extensive cuts lining my arms, things changed. Leaving me sitting in tears, she picked up her phone and asked her receptionist to escort my grandpa into the office as soon as he arrived to pick me up. Then she sat across from me again and bombarded me with questions. The why's and how's apparently mattered a great deal to her, but I remained silent. I remained silent through her explanation to Grandpa, as he stood and pushed back one of my sleeves to see the marks himself, and as he drove home and then repeated Dr. Panos' story to Gram.

Silence.

It's been my answer over the last few days. Until yesterday morning when the three of them — Gram, Gramps, and Dr. Panos — sat me down, intervention style, in her office and informed me I was being sent to Crestdale Victory Center.

Blinking rapidly to hold my tears back, I sat slack jawed and overwhelmed with their decision.

"It's a lovely facility, Danica. Many of my patients have been treated there and come out healthy and ready to commit to a successful future. I have no doubt you can do the same, but you have to buy into it. You have to want to get better," Dr. Panos points out, leaning forward and running her hand over her leg as she stares at me.

I'm silent.

"Danica, I told you after last Christmas we weren't going to stand-by and let you hurt yourself," Gramps reminds me, his voice gruff.

Silent still.

"You don't have a say in this young lady. You will get better, you need to stop." Gram is the angriest with me. Her voice shakes every time she speaks since seeing the cuts, her eyes sad every time she looks at me.

"Grace," cautions Dr. Panos, tipping her head meaningfully. "Do you have any questions for us? Now is the time to talk with us about this because once you check in you won't see us for three weeks, at-least."

This makes me chuckle lightly and my eyes drift from the spot on the floor I've been staring at to her face. "You promise?"

"You're angry, I understand…"

Wow, a mind-reader! "You think?" I can't control the fury I've kept locked up any longer. "Do you hear yourselves? You want me to stop cutting, you want me to be happy, to live a normal life. You want to know why and you push me and push me until all I want to do is run away." My head falls into my hands and I tug at my hair, combing my fingers through the thick mass as I try to calm myself.

"We want to understand."

"You want to understand?" I echo with laughter. "YOU. Want. To. Understand. What do you think I want? I can't give you answers I don't have. I don't know why I do it. It's a drug, an addiction I'm helpless to control. On my best days I want to cut, to prove I'm alive. Listen to yourselves… you want answers? Well, get in the damn line because I want answers too. Okay. Why did Mom and Dad have to die? Why did I have to live? Why can't I move on? I want answers too, so you know what, take me to this, this… place. I will be glad to let them pick and nag at me for the answers you all want so badly."

"Please leave now," I tell them once again. Gramps nods, clutching at Gram's elbow to drag her away from my room. She looks over her shoulder as she exits and my heart cries out, not wanting this angry good-bye. If I learned nothing else from my parents' deaths, it was how fragile life is and how utterly alone I'd be without these two, no matter how angry I am with them at this moment. My sandals slip on the floor as I rush to the door and call after them. "Gram. Gramps."

They turn a few doors down the hall and my hand clutches the door frame to anchor me in place. My legs want to run to them, to hug them and beg for forgiveness, while my heart breaks from the betrayal of their leaving me here. I'm torn, so I use words instead of actions. "I'm angry with you both." They stand there and I add, "But I do love you. I just wanted you to know that."

Gram's body moves as if she's going to come back to me — slowly leaning away from Gramps — before she pauses. Her hand taps at her chest, over her heart, and she nods. "We love you to, sweetheart, so much."

"Gramps?" He's looking away, but I need his confirmation so I'm able rest easier at night.

After a moment, his brown eyes, the same as my father's and my own, lift to mine, holding me there. "There was never any doubt, kiddo," he assures me. I want to crumble to the tile floor. His words reassure me, he knows how much I care — regardless of how horrible I've been. This bitterness in me, the anger and pain, it rules over me often and, as my grandparents walk away, I resolve to rid myself of it. I resolve to find the answers *I* seek.

I hug myself. Now that I'm alone it feels as though the temperature's dropped twenty degrees. I've unpacked my belongs — my comforter, throw pillows, some books, a journal and writing material, and my clothing — and now I sit and wait. For what, I'm not sure. Do I wander the halls, find Jackie and get the tour she promised? My limbs ache from shivering and I pull out a sweatshirt, slipping it over my head. It's almost July and I'm dressed for winter — always so cold.

Deciding to get acquainted with my new space, I open my door and peek into the hall. It's quiet. Across from me the rooms are all closed. I step into the hallway and make my way to the front desk. The blond prison warden who wouldn't let me out of the glass doors earlier has not moved from the desk. She taps at a keyboard, engrossed in whatever work she's doing, her back to me, and I slip down the hall to my right to avoid her. I spend the next hour walking corridors and reading the signs next to doors, acclimating myself to the layout of the facility. I come across the game room, a cafeteria, several large empty rooms with letters for names, and a large living room type area. The living room contains two couches and several groupings of chairs. The back wall is lined with bookcases and there's a television that's currently set to some talk show. I count three heads around the room and continue on, not wanting to make small talk with strangers today.

I find a door leading out to the courtyard Jackie mentioned and push my way outside, half expecting an alarm to sound and Lee, the 'bouncer', to come running around the corner. The oppressive Texas heat swallows me the moment I'm free of the meat locker facility and I peel off my sweatshirt as I survey the area. Benches and gardens are laid out before me in glorious summer splendor. There's a vegetable garden to the left and I hear the unmistakable smack of a basketball on concrete in the distance. My legs carry me to the noise, bringing me to the back of the courtyard and around the corner of the building. Tucked in between a large fence and a brick exterior wall is a full-sized court. I'm reminded of a prison yard for a moment and I scan the area for barbed wire and weight benches. There are five guys shuffling around and I step back, hiding in the shadow of the building and watch. They all look to be around my age or early twenties and I wonder why they're here. I'm not sure what type of people come to Crestdale. Will I be surrounded by recovering addicts? Depressed suicidal people? I have no idea and the unknown makes me nervous as I back away from the basketball area.

"There you are," Jackie's voice startles me. "I see you've taken your own tour of the facilities."

"Um, yeah… I think I've seen it all. I hope that's okay."

"Perfectly okay. I told you you're free to wander about. I do need you inside though so we can go over your schedule."

"My schedule?" I ask, following after her back to the building entrance.

"There's group time, meditation, meals, your therapy sessions — I've got all of that information for you."

We stop by the front desk where she grabs a file before returning to my room where we go over my daily schedule. Each day is full of group

117

and individual therapy session ranging from grief counseling to coping skills and life management. There's morning meditation, organized recreational times, and at least two educational speakers each week.

"So apparently being in rehab is a full time job," I muse out loud, scanning over the schedule after Jackie reads it to me.

"Yes, it is, and then it's not always enough," she says somberly. "It takes a lot of work to get better, Danica. You have to want it."

I nod. *Now or never, Dani.* "I do."

"Then let's get you started."

Today's Reality… Week by week, I'm getting by
June 2014 - August 2014

"Hey, I keep missing you," I frown as I leave yet another voice mail for Luke. "I miss you. I'll keep trying to call when I'm able. Stay safe, Luke," I whisper, hanging up the phone sitting in the corner of the common living area. In the three weeks I've been at Crestdale I've been able to speak to him three times. It sucks, but there's nothing I can do. I have to wait for the phone to be open and I have to wait until after dinner to make the calls — same as everyone else — which is why it's so hard to get time on the phone. Celia, another self-harming patient is watching me, her fingers tapping on the arm of her chair.

"Do you need the phone?" I ask, getting up, and she nods hurrying over before someone else grabs it.

"Thanks," she smiles, immediately dialing a number and turning her body toward the wall away from everyone. I overhear her, her happiness clear, as she murmurs to whomever she called, and jealousy flairs to life in my chest because she's able to talk to her loved one.

"That's not a happy face," Lee says, his hands lifting to stop me before I run into him. "Where you running off to?"

"I hadn't realized I was running," I admit as he drops his hands from my arms. "I was heading back to my room."

"You and your seclusion," he shakes his head. "Why don't you go to the game room and play a game or something? Make some friends."

"I don't want friends."

"That's not the way to getting out of here, you know."

I shrug, indifferent. "Six more weeks, friends or not, and I go home."

"Six weeks and you plan on spending them all alone?"

"Why not?" I ask.

His brows raise. "I've seen you sitting out by the basketball court when there's a game going on. You a fan?"

"You've seen me?" Every day I sit in the shade of the building where I can hear the game, but not be seen by the players. I didn't think anyone paid attention to me there. He nods. "Yeah, I'm a fan… or I used to be. It's a memory."

"Why don't you play then?" he suggests, his dark eyes full of question.

"I haven't played in years. I… it hurts too much." Lee squints, looking about the room before he motions me to follow him.

119

"Where are we going?"

"Follow me and you'll see," he smiles over his shoulder. He leads me outside into the lit courtyard. It's almost eight and most of the residents are in their rooms at this time of night, so with the exception of two girls sitting on a bench talking, we're alone.

"Why are we out here?" I ask, causing him to laugh.

"You ask too many questions. Why do you think we're out here?" We walk around the building to the basketball court. "You ever played horse?"

I look back over my shoulder before stepping onto the court. The lights are out over here, but the full moon and clear sky provides ample lighting. Lee grabs a ball resting on the grass and dribbles it three times before tossing it to me. The ball feels foreign in my hands after so long and I fight the urge to bring it to my nose and sniff the familiar rubber scent I grew up with.

Shaking off the sadness the thought brings, I smile. "Have I ever played horse?" I mock as I step to the line and bounce the ball before rocking to my toes and taking a shot. The ball swoops through the air in a perfect arc, hitting off the rim before swooshing through the net. "Of course I have." I shrug and send him a wink.

I'm not flirting with him, not really. This is Lee, it's the way he is, playful with everyone he speaks to at Crestdale. During the first week I wasn't sure if he was coming on to me or if he was simply a charmer, but after watching him for several days I realized that was simply his personality. I imagine it's part of the job, staying upbeat for all of the depressed souls wandering around here. He's come to my rescue a few times when he's spotted me feeling down, pulling me into a checkers game or bringing me a late night brownie. I'm grateful for him, he makes me smile. He fills the void created by a missing Luke.

"Alright, game on, girl," he claps grabbing the rebound after my shot. "So how are your sessions going now?" he asks, shooting a perfect basket.

Swoosh. Another basket for me. "It's going," I reply.

"That good, huh? You finding the answers you're seeking?"

I frown at him as he sinks another ball. My second day here, he came upon me by accident when I was huddled in a dark corner of my room crying. I was supposed to be at dinner, but instead I'd crumbled onto the floor and cried out the misery I felt after my first full day of sessions. I was exhausted after trying to discuss the wreck, my past, my cutting,

120

and I simply wanted to drown in my sorrow. Lee knocked, which I didn't hear, and entered my room to change an overhead light. Instead, he found me in the corner and immediately came to my side where I threw myself into his chest and cried out my misery. He's been rescuing me from myself ever since.

"I don't know. Some, I guess."

"You'll find them, I have faith in you," he promises. I'm not sure what he sees in me that I don't see.

We shoot back and forth for a while before his hand-held radio buzzes. "Lee? Mary needs a hand please... two-three-five."

"On my way," he replies, glancing at his watch. "Time to get inside anyway."

"Thanks again, for coming to my rescue," I tell him as we enter the building. The air conditioning causes chill bumps to raise along my arms.

"Anytime, D. See ya later," he offers with a wave when we reach the main hall. He turns left, rushing to his call. He called me D, one of Jonah's nicknames for me. A deep sadness crawls under my skin. *No, no, no,* I tell myself as the blackness slinks in. It's similar to curtains being closed over an open window. One moment there's light in the room and the next the shades are pulled, enveloping me in darkness. My heart is dark and I fight it. I fight the feelings of Jonah invading my thoughts. I fight the pull of the scars screaming for release. *Dang it!* I rush to the living area, my eyes falling on the open chair next to the phone and there's one thing on my mind. Luke.

Luke will make it better. I'll call, hear his voice, and tell him I miss him. Luke will make me laugh, he'll banish Jonah to the deep dark corners of my heart and mind. He always does. I don't pause to think about how messed up that sounds, my using him as a means to keep another from my heart. I'm messed up, this I know. I'm in rehab for a reason after all.

"Tell me about your guy," Lee mentions out of the blue as he slides a black game piece forward. We're playing checkers in the game room after dinner during week five of my nine week sentence.

"My guy?" I falter, pushing my red circle into an empty spot.

"Yeah, the one you rush to call each night."

I laugh, "You notice everything, don't you?"

"Security, remember. It's my job," he winks, jumping and capturing two of my chips.

Dang it. "You're trying to distract me, aren't you?" I survey my options as Lee drums his fingers against the table. After a moment he playfully hums the Jeopardy theme song and I bite my tongue, finally making my move. "His name is Luke."

"Luke? Is he the reason basketball's just a memory?"

"Nope, that's… another guy."

His eyes go wide. "Two guys, huh? King me," he gloats. Surprised, I look at the board. He's jumped two more of my pieces and, sure enough, he needs to be kinged.

"You didn't lie when you said you were a checkers champion," I mumble, topping his piece with another.

"I get a great deal of practice time."

"Speaking of… you don't get in trouble for spending so much time with us?" I've wondered how he gets away with hanging out with me, and others, so often.

"Nah, as long as I run when I'm summoned on the black box," he teases holding up his radio, "I'm cool. I do most of the maintenance jobs when you guys are in sessions, or at meals."

"Is it part of your job? Hanging with patients?"

Lee sits back, sliding down in his chair and forgetting his turn for a moment. "It's a perk. I don't get paid to hang out with you, if that's what you're asking."

"So why do you? You could be hanging out with the nurses on your downtime, or watching TV in the break room, but instead you hang out with us. Why?"

"As I said before, it's a perk." He leans forward and moves again. "Your turn."

I'm no longer interested in the game though. I study him, he turned nervous at my last question. Wonder why? I stand, "You know what… I'm going to check the phone and see if I'm able call Luke before he goes on shift tonight."

"Sure. You up for game of horse later?" he asks, standing.

"I'd like that," I tell him, waving as I leave the room. At the door I look back and see two of the other girls already standing over him, flirting wildly. Do I look like that? I hope not. I enjoy his company and he's certainly easy on the eyes, but another guy is the least of my needs right now. Laughter rings out at his table and I leave.

Thankfully, the phone is open and I dial Luke, my brain chanting *answer, answer, answer* with each ring.

"Hello, gorgeous," Luke's deep voice answers. Angels sing and the sun shines down on me when I hear him, my heart and stomach leaping.

"It's Danica," I tease dryly and he curses.

"Awe man, sorry. I thought it was my girl, my bad."

"Hardy, har, har. I'm surprised you knew it was me." Pulling my legs under me, I clutch the phone to my ear as if it's a lifeline. There's *nothing* like hearing his voice.

"Are you kidding? I know this number by heart now, babe. How are you today?"

"Good. It's been a good week. I suck at checkers though."

"Checkers... okay, I'll start practicing. How's therapy?"

Luke's support was the one thing that kept me going when I first learned I'd be going to Crestdale. The day of my little 'intervention' was the day I called Luke and filled him in on my reality. I told him I'd been cutting on and off and how my grandparents finally decided I needed help. It was a bit of a fib since I didn't tell him the extent of the damage, but it was a step in the right direction. He was upset I'd kept my pain from him, but he was understanding and supportive. He swore he was sticking by my side and we're continuing to count down the months until we get to see each other.

"It was therapy."

"You're trying aren't you? I don't want your grandparents to force you to stay longer." His voice is worried and I sigh. He doesn't find my flippant attitude funny.

"I'm trying, Luke. I promise. They keep telling me how much I deserve and I almost believe them."

"Almost?"

"Habits die hard."

"I get that." Something in his voice is off, as though he's holding back on me.

"How's work? Save any lives lately?" I ask.

"Wow, you're asking me about work?"

His sarcasm is palatable and I cringe. "I'm sorry. I never ask, do I? You know it's not because I don't care." *I'm terrified of what you do*, I think to myself instead of speaking out loud. "I'm trying."

"I know and I love you for it… "

Holy wow! "You love me? Did you… um, did I hear?"

"Ohhhh." Luke sputters and coughs. "Wow, I did, didn't I?"

"Um, yeah you did. Did you not mean it?" I question, nervous as all get out now.

"I think I do."

"You think."

"Danica, this is freaking crazy right? We said six months."

I can't help but laugh at him because I feel it too. The crazy feelings his voice awakens within me. So many feels. How will I feel when I see him face to face?

"It's an eternity," I groan.

"Damn straight," he agrees. "I'm not going to tell you I love you. But, I will tell you I'm falling for you. With every phone call and every letter you mail me, I'm falling harder and harder for the girl I haven't technically met yet."

"Not true, we met. Once," I counter.

"I'm more grateful for that meeting than any other in my life, but I'd prefer a simple coffee date next time if that's okay with you."

"I think that's a good idea."

"Kay, I need a shower before I'm on shift. Talk to you in about twenty-five hours?" He works twenty-four hour shifts at the fire house and I try not to call him while he's on duty unless it's an emergency.

"Be safe," I tell him, as I do every time we end a call, and he replies the same as always. "Promise."

Today's Reality… Goodbyes are never easy
August 24, 2014

Crestdale's perception of Danica Evans: She's closed off, but making progress and ready for out-patient treatment. Receives the proverbial gold star.

My perception of Danica Evans: Nine weeks, hundreds of hours of therapy and group sessions, yet my hand continues to itch for something sharp.

"Tomorrow's the big day," Lee says, his breathing heavy as he pushes against me blocking my shot.

We're playing one-on-one for the last time. It's hot and muggy this mid-August night and sweat stings my eyes as I swing around him using my backside to push him off. "Yep." I duck and shoot, missing wide. "Water break?"

"I thought you'd never ask," he sighs, falling to the ground with relief. "I'm too old for this."

"As if," I laugh, grabbing our water bottles and joining him on the court. The sun set an hour ago, but the asphalt remains warm to the touch. The Texas heat has been relentless the past few weeks, the trees, grass, and flowers all wear the effects of the searing sun. "Wait, how old are you anyway?" I question him as he sits up and takes the water I offer him.

Gulping half the bottle in one long swig, he wipes his mouth with the back of his arm. "Old, twenty-six."

"Oh, yes… you're decrepit. Now I know why you're so good at checkers. Geez, I'm surprised you can keep up with me on the court. Are you going to be able to get up?" Water hits my face as Lee flicks his wrist and bottle my way. "Hey!"

"That'll teach you to be so mouthy," he laughs and I lay back laughing with him.

Above us the clear sky is splattered with white dots. Stars as far as the eye can see, twinkling as they hang there for the world to wish upon.

"Make a wish," Jonah whispers, startling me as he comes up behind me on the dark beach outside the beach house our families are sharing for spring break our freshman year. I'd sought the privacy of the peaceful beach an hour ago after spending the entire day surrounded by flocks of girls watching him. I should be used to it, but it's exhausting, answering all their questions and listening to them prattle on and on

about his abs and hair and 'OMG his God-like eyes'. Gag me, my IQ lowered twenty points today.

"What the flip, dude?" I look up at his dark silhouette standing over me, clutching my chest and making sure my heart is firmly in place after the scare it just took. "You scared the mess out of me."

He sinks into the sand next to me, his knee and shoulder bumping mine as he practically sits on top of me. "Sorry. Wow, there must be a billion stars up there, huh?"

"More like a trillion, science wiz."

He knocks into me again, "I just meant we never get to see them all at home. Look out there over the water… stars as far as we can see. It's crazy how huge the universe is, I forget sometimes."

Out of the corner of my eye I study his profile. "Feeling philosophical tonight?"

"And you're feeling a bit snarky, huh?" he mocks as he rests his forearms on his raised knees, clasping his hands between them.

"Touché." I stretch my legs out in the sand, my toes reaching right to the edge of where the waves wash up. "Do you wanna make a wish?" I ask after a few minutes of comfortable silence.

"Yeah, we should." His hand covers mine and I'm thrown back to our childhood when I swore the only way a wish would come true was if we held hands while making them. It worked for maybe two years before wishing on stars, dandelions, and lightning bugs became child's play.

My throat goes dry as he teases the back of my palm before turning it over and lacing our fingers. "Let's pick the same star. Big dipper, top of the handle. Got it?" he asks and I murmur 'yeah' although my eyes are staring at our hands, barely visible in the dark.

"You're not looking," he chides, his head leaning closer to mine. His breath wafting over my cheek as I lift my chin and find our faces inches apart.

"I…" Whatever words I was about to say are cut off by our proximity.

"Make a wish," he urges, turning his head and squeezing my hand.

Closing my eyes, my mind races ninety miles a minute. This stolen moment is so random, so out of the blue, I can't focus on a thought to wish for. I simply keep my eyes closed and take little gasps of air.

"Did you make one?" he asks, letting go of my hand when I nod. "What's your wish?"

Another fib I managed to convince him when we were kids. 'Wishes only come true if you tell your very best friend.' I'd lied one day when I'd blurted my big wish to him and he wanted to keep his secret. I've never liked secrets.

"It was your idea, you tell me first," I manage. I sound breathless — and I am — *I'm trying to recover from the touch of Jonah's hand, the husky way he's speaking to me.*

He doesn't hesitate, "I wished for things to always be this way with us. That we'll be sitting here when we're in our twenties, wishing on stars and holding hands."

I drop my head to his shoulder, my arm lacing through his as I lean into him. "Me too," I tell him. "That's my exact wish."

A hot tear rolls down my cheek and I swipe it away as the rogue memory fades and I return to Texas, Crestdale, and the basketball court with Lee sitting there watching me.

"You okay?" he asks when I turn my head his way.

I bite my lip, contemplating that question. "I'm gonna miss this place. It's grown on me. Crazy right?"

"Nah, it's pretty common actually. Most patients walk in hating us and leave crying."

"There's safety here. Acceptance for the things I can't explain. I don't know what to tell my grandparents," I admit, sitting up and taking a sip of my water.

"About what?"

"About why I cut or why I kept cutting. The first time was somewhat of an out-of-body experience and then I did it because I felt all this pressure to be healed, to be okay, so I cut to relieve the pressure. Now, I don't know why I do it. I should've been happy, I found Luke, I was doing well in school, my therapy sessions were going fine and yet, I cut anyway." *I continue to want to cut,* I add mentally.

Lee fidgets as though I've made him uncomfortable opening up to him this way. "You may never find an answer."

"That's comforting," I groan. The therapists I've seen over the past few weeks have all said the same thing. "It's probably about curfew, huh? I should head in." I stand and offer my hand. "C'mon, old man, let me help you up."

We walk to the doors quietly and before I pull them open, Lee places his palm on the glass stopping me. "Hey, Danica, don't worry so much about why you do it and simply focus on stopping, okay?" His voice is full of pleading, his eyes worried as they roam over my face.

"I'm trying."

His hand touches my shoulder and slides down my arm. It's not romantic, it's comforting — a soft touch of encouragement between friends. "If you're unable to handle it, come back. Okay? There's no shame in needing help."

He opens the door and before I enter I press a kiss to his cheek. "Thank you for being a friend, job or not, I will truly miss you."

"Hey, I told you, it's not a job, it's a perk."

It's after noon by the time my belongings are loaded up and we're pulling away from Crestdale. I didn't exchange goodbyes with Lee today. I wanted to leave with a smile instead of tears, and seeing him would only bring tears. Goodbyes are never easy, but that one felt impossible the more I thought about it. We did one last exit interview as a family, signed some forms, and then I was free to walk out of those front double glass doors. The same blond nurse, Carrie — although she remained prison warden to me — sat at the desk today and I was tempted to re-enter the building, merely so I could walk out again.

I feel strong today. Strong and capable. The cell phone clutched in my hand is a huge part of that. I powered it up and unlocked the screen the moment I closed the car door and buckled up. There's a long list of texts from Luke and I smile, anticipating reading each and every one, but I'm satisfied with the last one he sent, for now.

"I'll be waiting by the phone for you all night. I can't wait to hear your beautiful voice. Welcome home."

Glancing up from my phone, I catch Gram staring at me in the rearview mirror. "You look good, sweetheart. You got some color."

There's nothing to say so I give her a half smile and she continues on with small talk. She complains about the heat and the drought, then mentions us taking a vacation before she moves on to my schooling.

"I went ahead and set up your classes for school. I put you down for your final math and English courses. You are set to graduate by the end of the year if you don't want to add any other electives. Of course we should check requirements if you've changed your mind on college."

"I haven't."

"Danica, we should talk with Dr. Panos about that. Discuss your options before we finalize anything."

"I don't need to talk to Dr. Panos about it. I'll do college, but I'm not planning on enrolling at a large state school, Gram. Please don't pressure me right now." I throw the word pressure out on purpose and Gram's face loses two shades as her lips tighten and she diverts her gaze out the passenger side window.

During my exit interview my therapist, Dr. Thomas, specifically cautioned them on not putting too much pressure on me. He explained that the reason Crestdale feels so comfortable to most patients is the freedom we feel there. I was able to be myself, to roll my sleeves up and lay in the sun without worry of my scars, to breakdown, or be upset without having someone assume I was a danger to myself. No pressure — the new golden rule of the Evan's house. I can't help but wonder how long it'll last if Gram can barely make it across town before she starts in.

It's odd to be walking back into my grandparents' house after nine weeks, almost as though it's not home anymore. Everything's the same though and as Gramps carries my bags to my room I walk aimlessly through the downstairs.

"I need you to call the Halls today," Gram says out of the blue when I find my way to the kitchen. She's leaning against the counter, a glass in her hand, her face grim.

"The Halls?" My eyes narrow. "Whatever for?" I haven't personally spoken to Ms. Virginia in seven months. I wasn't aware Gram kept in contact with her. Evidently she has.

"Because you need to."

"Gram, I really don't…" I start to protest, but she straightens, her face turning red as she looks at me.

"Danica, I don't want to start out your homecoming with a fight. You have to call the Halls, end of story. Call Virginia and tell her how you are and that'll be the end of it."

The way she said 'have to' as though it's a requirement, didn't escape me and I don't argue again. After giving Gram one last questioning look, I leave the kitchen, retrieving my cell from the messenger bag I dropped on the couch in the family room. Returning to the kitchen, I pull up Ms. Virginia's contact number and press send. Gram rubs a hand over her face as I stand in front of her and the motion sets off a myriad of warning bells. *Why is she so upset?*

"Danica?" Ms. Virginia's excited voice picks up on the third ring.

"Yeah, it's me." Gram's head lifts, her face is void of emotion, but her eyes are panicked, reminding me of a caged animal, and my heart lurches for her. I hate seeing her in pain and I have no idea what's bothering her.

"How are you, honey? How was Crestdale?" Jonah's mom asks through the line. There's a faint commotion behind her, I swear I hear Kadence shouting Jonah's name and I picture them all crammed around the phone trying to hear me. Her question angers me. How is this her business? Why did Gram force me to call her?

"I'm fine, Mrs. Hall. Gram said I needed to call you, is something wrong?" I evade, purposely using her last name to distance myself.

"Wrong? No, honey, I… we were worried about you. I wanted to see how you're feeling. Are you getting everything you need, can I do anything?"

"Can you do anything?" I repeat. Looking at Gram again, her panicked face and tense posture, I make my decision. "As a matter of fact there is something I need."

"Of course, sweetie. Anything," she replies.

"Back. Off," I pronounce each word clearly and purposely. "My life, what happens to me, isn't your problem. My grandparents and I will deal with it. Got it?"

Gram's hand slaps over her mouth, her eyes wide as I speak. On the other end of the line, there's silence.

"I'm sorry, I know you loved my parents. I know how much Mom meant to you, but you can let go now. I need you to let go now. I need to move on."

Gram makes her way around the counter as I wait for a response from Mrs. Hall. All I get is a shaky breath and sniffle — *she's obviously crying* — and I swallow down the guilt I feel. "Maybe someday I'll feel differently, but for now this is what I need. Do you understand where I'm coming from?" I ask, attempting to take some of the bite out of my voice.

"Okay," she whispers and then with more force, "okay, if that's what you want. Take care of yourself."

"I will, thank you."

"We love you. Don't forget that, please. We miss you so much and we love you." She rushes the words out, trying to get them in before I hang up, and I don't reply. I hit the end button, letting out a long, deep sigh. Standing next to me, Gram has tears in her eyes and I do something I haven't done willingly in months. I pull her into a hug. I may be angry at them for the way they handled things with me and Crestdale, but this is my family, my blood.

"What was that about?" Gramps asks from the doorway.

Gram doesn't release me from our hug so I turn my face and speak to him from her embrace. "I don't know what's going on with you two and the Halls, but something is going on and it's not necessary. We have enough to deal with without them. No more pressure, right?" I remind them.

"We're going to do better. We're going to get through this together this time," Gramps promises gruffly, joining our embrace and making me the meat in the center of a hug sandwich. My eyes close and I imagine a small speck of light at the end of my dark tunnel. *Hope? Maybe.*

My optimistic hope withers away not thirty minutes later with the ring of my cell. Dropping the clean stack of shirts I'm unpacking, I throw myself across the bed, expecting it to be Luke.

Jonah shouts the moment I answer my phone, "What did you say to my mom?"

The sound of his voice, although angry, halts my breathing and causes my world to tilt. I give as good as I get though, giving him the same attitude as I reply. "I asked her to back off and leave us alone. It's obvious your parents fought with my grandparents when they were here at Christmas and whatever happened is affecting Gram to this day. She was terrified watching me call your mom, but she forced me to do it. Said I *had* to."

"Seriously, D?" he growls, cursing under his breath. "We did back off. We gave you six months. We gave you space and waited for you to come around… when your doctor called Mom and told her about you being admitted to that rehab place it all made sense… or so I thought."

"Dr. Panos called your mom? Why? Why would she do that?"

"You don't know?" he asks incredulously. He huffs. "Of course you don't, they're not gonna bother telling you."

"Oh my word, you're talking in riddles, Jonah. Tell me what? What's going on?" I fume.

He scoffs, "Screw it, it doesn't matter anymore. You've spoken. You want us out? We're out."

No, no, no! "Jonah?"

"I'm not doing this with you anymore, D."

"Am I supposed to apologize? Do you think this is the way I wanted my life to go?"

"Damn it. You know… I let myself hope… again, that you'd come around. It's our senior year. You're supposed to be here. Homecoming, prom, graduation… everything we were supposed to do. The stupid spring break trip we swore we'd take… I'm done. I'm done hoping for my best friend to wake up and return to me. It's not happening, is it?"

"I can't, J… I just can't," I confess in a broken whisper.

"The girl I knew, *my* Dani, never would have made my mom cry. She never would have kicked us out of her life the way you have."

"The girl you knew died in that car along with her parents. Why is that so hard for you to understand? Why do you keep refusing to see that?" My tears break free.

"Because I thought I could make you better! Damn it, I wanted to save you…" he says, his own voice breaking.

"You can't save me. I don't want you to." I shake my head, gasping between my heavy sobs now.

"Okay," he replies on a sharp intake of air. The defeat in his voice ripping at my heart. "Enough said."

I want to take the words back the moment they come out of my mouth, but I can't get enough air between sobs before my phone beeps and he's gone.

"Jonah? Jonah?" Throwing my phone across the room, I fight the urge to scream.

My brain goes crazy, I pull at my hair, squeezing my eyes shut as a little voice tickles the back of my mind. The little voice that tells me to find something, anything, sharp and puncture the balloon of pressure filling my body. *Get some relief,* it mocks. Mopping up my tears, I hurry from my room, flying down the stairs… *head to the kitchen, one small cut…* and rounding the corner of the foyer, my socks slip on the wood floors in my haste. I stumble into the family room, catching my grandparents sitting on the couch, their faces startled by my sudden presence, and they exchange worried glances as I freeze before them. My body plays tug-o-war, one part begging me to move to the kitchen. The other — the part that spent nine weeks at Crestdale, the part that wants Luke, Lee, and Jonah and his family, to be proud of me — that part orders me to fight the urge.

Like a toddler, I rush to the couch, breaking down as I throw myself into my grandparents' laps. "Jonah called me," I explain brokenly. "We fought… and, and… I told him, I… he's gone. I think he's gone for good."

I'm enveloped in a warm hug, as Gramps pulls my soaking face to his shoulder. Gram lays a blanket over my legs, rubbing my back the way she did when I was little. Somewhere in the corner of my mind the little voice keeps goading me to make a cut and I shout back telling it to 'shut up'. I accept the comfort my grandparents give me. It's the first time I've given them everything. All my hurt, my tears and pain. I hold back nothing, pouring everything within me into their laps. "I miss Mom and Dad, I miss home. I miss… me," I confess. All of it pours out of my black soul and when I'm through, I'm spent. I'm exhausted mentally and physically and my grandparents are sitting right there with me. Their eyes red and their faces full of hurt for me.

In the coming weeks, my grandparents become my rocks, my support. Them and Luke. I don't know how I didn't see it, their love for me, their wishes for me. I think they were too lost in their own grief when I first came to Texas, so I tried to handle it on my own. But, not anymore. As the months pass by — August, September, October, November — I find music again, I apply myself to my final high school classes, I attend therapy, and I fall farther and farther into a relationship with Luke. The six month deal has six weeks left now and I'm giddy with anticipation. When I'm feeling down I stare at my scars, I contemplate a cut, but I've been good. I start considering auditions for a conservatory education, I run errands with Gram and Gramps the way a 'normal' person would. I sit and converse with a few of their friends who stop by the house. I'm living. Except for one small, dark hole in my life. Jonah. Each new month is another month I fall further from him. The pain of our last conversation has never let up. It wasn't a fight. It was final.

Today's Reality… Finally!
December 2014

The second anniversary of my parents' deaths is marked vastly different than the first. There's no blood, no ambulance and ER. There's only reflection. I crawl into bed beside Gram that night — secretly I worry I won't be able to stay strong on my own — and we watch old black and white movies. That morning we eat Dad's favorite omelets from his childhood and my grandparents take turns telling stories about Dad, and some about Mom too. We pull out family photos for the first time since their deaths and Gram and I start working on a album using all of the old photos from their younger years. Luke calls during dinner, he's on shift, but he didn't want to let the day pass without sending me some love. I see the way my grandparents frown when I excuse myself to talk with him. I told them about him after Crestdale, deciding it would lesson my anxiety if I didn't have to keep it all secret. They must have talked with Dr Panos on how to handle it because, thus far, they've reserved their opinion on the subject.

Christmas and New Year's, my birthday, pass with little fanfare. We have a small tree, exchange some presents, but we spend the time alone this year, just the three of us. Both of my parents were only children too, so extended family is limited, but I don't mind. I enjoy the peace, I enjoy not feeling pressured to smile for anyone on what is the hardest time of the year for me. The one thing that keeps me from falling is knowing I'll be meeting Luke in days.

I'm standing at the end of the arrivals terminal waiting for Luke to come through the double door that keeps security checked travelers separated from the non-flying guests and family members in the airport. My pulse hasn't stopped its marathon race since the taxi dropped me off thirty minutes earlier. The arrivals board shows Luke's flight as having landed five minutes ago, and now it's a waiting game. The best part is — he has no idea I'm here.

For the first time since the accident, I'm overly conscious of my scars. I haven't wanted to impress anyone in so long, but now I'm tugging at my clothing, wishing I were in a sexy, little dress instead of the tight jeans and chunky sweater I have on. It's a silly thought, another little nugget of doubt wiggling its way into my brain. *Gah! I wish the doubt would be gone for good. I'm so tired of it.*

The passenger terminal doors open, a steady stream of people pour out and I forget my clothing. I feel as though I'm strung on a wire, pulled taut as I watch and wait for sight of him. Distinguished business men with suits and ties, their briefcases slung over their shoulders come out, joined by women in pencil skirts with oversized purses and tennis shoes on their feet. There's a mother pushing an umbrella stroller with a chatty toddler, a few casually dressed passengers all too heavy, or too blond to warrant a second glance, as my eyes search eagerly for his face. And then there he is. I know him immediately, his six foot frame towers over the people around him, and if that didn't give him away his 'UNC' hoodie does. Everything about him is familiar to me, his dark hair, tanned skin, the thick brows over light eyes, a year of phone calls and texts has made him second nature to me. He's looking to the left, and appears to be reading directional signs as his steps slow. I can't take it. I yelp, bouncing into action and rushing him. My hand covers my mouth as another half laugh/half cry escapes. My emotions are going haywire and that's before he sees me. When his head turns my way it's instant. *BAM!* As though lightning has stuck. My vision blurs, but I see the huge smile cross his face when he recognizes me. He scarcely has time to brace himself before I throw myself at him. His large duffle bag drops to the ground as his arms reach out and haul me into his chest. My arms wrap around his neck and his arms clasp around my waist as he lifts and twirls me around, my legs dangling.

"Hiiii," I cry, burying my face into his neck and drinking in his scent, his warmth, his everything.

"I can't... this is unreal..." His reply is a muted, emotional grumble of whispers as his lips skim my ear.

"Nooo," I choke, lifting my face an inch from his skin so he can hear me. "This is real."

His arms tighten briefly before he touches my feet back to the ground. "Come with me," he orders, unwrapping my arms from his neck. He bends down, grabbing the handles to his bag and hauling me into his side with his free arm. He starts to the left, before stopping abruptly and moving to the right.

"Where?"

"Just, come with me," he repeats and I hug my arms around his waist, letting him steer me wherever he wants. We're walking away from the

135

rest of the crowd, heading toward luggage claim and the parking decks and away from our exit. I start to correct him when we round a corner and he pushes me back. His bag thuds against the floor, at the same time as my body hits the wall behind me.

"First things first," he says, descending upon me and running his hand over my cheek as his face lowers to mine. "I want to kiss the breath out of you. May I? Now, please?" he asks as his left hand digs into my waist.

My breath is already gone and I nod, my hands already winding up around his neck and pulling him to my mouth. When his lips are an inch from mine, I feel his neck fight against the pressure of my hands. He pulls back from my face, looking at me.

"Hi, by the way," he smiles and I laugh out loud.

"Hi… " the word is swallowed by his lips covering mine. They swallow my words, my breath, my every thought. *For the love of all that is good and noble in this world, this boy can kiss!* His large frame covers every inch of mine as he presses me into the wall, his lips and tongue taste and memorize every inch of my mouth and I chant random words in my mind, least I forget where we are. When his hand lowers to my hip and then slides lower, toward the curve of my rear, I finally awaken.

"Mmm," I mumble into Luke's mouth, "airport… public," I remind him as I rise onto my toes and sink my fingers into his short hair.

He shakes his head, groaning and smiling into my mouth as he pulls away. "Good Lord, that was one hell of an introduction."

"Well, we do tend to do everything bigger and better, don't we?" I tease, dropping my hands so he can straighten.

He stands there with one hand on my hip, staring at me, and I shuffle from foot to foot as I return his piercing gaze. When his scrutiny becomes to be too much I take the bait. "What?"

"Nothing," he smiles. "It's just… you. I'm here, we made it. Six months and here we are."

"So crazy," I smile.

"So perfect," he counters, and I agree.

Stepping back and taking hold of his bag again, Luke throws his arm around my shoulders as we head for the exit. "So, what are you doing here anyway? I thought you'd be waiting at your grandparents."

"I lied."

"You lied?" he scoffs playfully, his voice rising.

"You realize if I'd waited at home for you, our first meeting would have been with George and Grace front and center."

"Ah ha, you're an extremely smart woman, indeed."

"They are waiting on us, though. I promised to bring you straight home. I'm pretty sure they were afraid I'd accompany you to your hotel first and that idea gave Gram heart palpitations."

"No hotel, got it. So we need a cab then?" he asks as we exit the airport and I nod.

I don't drive yet. It was a conversation Luke and I had when we were discussing his trip here and what we would do. I'd hoped he would stay at our house and be able to use Gram's car when we needed it, but that proved to be too much for my grandparents. They were reluctantly accepting Luke into my life, and they swore they didn't blame him for the wreck, but they haven't gotten past who he is. It's funny how, for me, he's never represented anything other than another person who knows how horrific that night was. Two years later and I can't think of Jonah, or his family, without dying inside because I see Mom and Dad and all the memories of my life, but with Luke I don't feel pain. I see the guy who saved me. Maybe he was right all those months ago, maybe we were brought together for a greater reason. Maybe life is all about fate.

Luke wavers by a cab before waving him off. "Change of plans. I'm gonna rent a car, come on."

"Rent a car? Isn't that expensive?"

He shrugs, dragging me to the shuttle that will take us to the rental facility. "And a cab isn't? I don't want to be stuck all week relying on taxis, or your grandparents, for rides. How will I take you out without a car?" he asks.

"Out? On a date?"

"Yes, a real date. And I'm going to want a whole lot more of that kissing we did back there."

My face heats up at the prospect. "Well, alrighty then, a car it is," I agree.

♦

The evening with Gram and Gramps turns out relatively pleasant after the initial awkward greetings. As if we'd all agreed not to speak of it, the accident doesn't come up. Most of our conversation revolves around talk of Houston and news or sports. Luke's good at guy talk, probably because he spends much of his time around a bunch of firemen, so he and Gramps keep the conversation flowing most of the night. I study Luke, the way he smiles, the ease of his movements, the tilt of his head when he's thinking — all things I couldn't learn about him by phone and text. We tried video calls a few times over the months, but neither of us cared for it much, so we agreed to stick with calls.

"Danica tells us you're a firefighter," Gramps comments, and I flinch, struggling at the mention of his job.

"Yes, sir. Thanks to her."

Oh no, thanks to her? Worry where this conversation may lead bubbles up within me.

"Oh?"

"After the accident I had trouble for a little while," he stops, his brows gathering as though he realizes he may have stepped into deep waters. "I'm sorry, maybe… " He stops speaking and shifts a worried gaze my way.

I'm trying to think of a subject change when Gram speaks. "Please continue, I'd like to hear your side of the story." I'm not sure if she's actually interested in what he has to say or if she's being polite. Her face is unreadable, but Gramps nods his agreement so Luke goes on.

"Well, let's just say things were hard and school wasn't particularly my thing. I thought of your granddaughter often, wondering how she was doing and if she was all right. Then she called me." He looked at me then, a soft smile of his face. "It took her a year, but it was perfect timing. I needed direction and hearing from her and getting to know her, well it opened up the idea of being a firefighter."

"I think he has a hero complex," I tease, and Gramps laughs.

Luke nods, "It's scary how well she knows me."

"I should head to the hotel to check-in," Luke says a few hours later as we're all sitting quietly watching some outdoor reality show. "Mr. and Mrs. Evans thank you for the meal."

"Should we expect you for lunch tomorrow?" Gram asks.

Luke looks at me for direction. "No. We're gonna do some sightseeing and hang out, I promised him some real barbecue. Can you believe he keeps arguing with me on which is better Carolina or Texas style?"

"By all means, you need to set him straight on that," Gramps orders, rising and shaking Luke's hand.

"I'm going to walk him out," I tell them, grabbing my jacket and slipping on shoes. The moment we're out of sight of the front door my hand is in his.

"That wasn't so bad," he admits as we walk to the driver's side door. He leans against the car and pulls me into a hug. "But, tomorrow I want some alone time. Thank you for telling them we're going out."

Resting my cheek against his chest, I sigh, "We've got four days. I'm not spending them with my grandparents."

"Okay, then how early is too early for me to pick you up," he asks.

"Twelve-o-one a.m.," I play. His chest vibrates as he laughs silently. "I'm sorry you can't stay here. It sucks."

"Hey, it's okay. I wouldn't want some strange guy under the same roof as you either." His chilly fingers tilt my chin up. "I'll pick you up at nine? We'll do breakfast and then you can show me all around Houston. Deal?" he asks, giving me a quick kiss.

"Deal. Good-night."

Today's Reality… Passion
January 6, 2015

"I swear I'm going to have to put in overtime at the gym when I get home to work off all this food you keep stuffing into me," Luke groans, lifting my hand and clutching it to his lips before pressing a kiss to my knuckles.

The reminder he's going home tomorrow afternoon wipes the smile from my face. We've spent the last three days touring Houston. The Space Center, aquarium, malls, museums, we've done it all. I've seen more of Houston in the past three days than I have in the two years I've lived here.

"Getting in?" he asks, holding the door open for me. Blinking the thoughts away, I slide into the car. Luke moves around the vehicle, looking my way as he climbs in. "Where'd you go out there?"

"You're leaving tomorrow."

"I am," he agrees, his hand reaching out and taking mine again. "But, I'm here now. What should we do next?"

Looking at the time as he starts the car, I count the hours. Thirteen. Thirteen hours before he walks through those glass doors at the airport and who knows when I'll see him again.

"Let's go back to the hotel," I tell him. The parking lot is dark so I'm able to make my request without him seeing the flames creeping into my face at the idea.

"You don't sound so sure of yourself. We don't have… "

"I know," I interrupt, turning in my seat. "I want to. I want to spend every moment I can with you, alone… together."

- ❦

Luke slides the key card into the door of his room, flipping the switch and holding the door open for me. We've been quiet since leaving the restaurant parking lot, letting the radio fill the air between us all the way here. My fingers slip through his as I walk by him, entering the large room he's occupied this week.

"This is a nice hotel. I don't know why I kept picturing you in a seedy motel."

He laughs behind me. "I'm not sure how to take that."

"Ha, I don't mean you look like a seedy guy or anything. I guess I didn't expect you to pay... oh that sounds worse." I stop speaking, afraid I'm digging myself a large hole to climb out of.

"I know what you meant. How many twenty-one year old guys spring for the expensive rooms unless they're trying to impress someone?" he winks.

The gesture serves to both calm my nerves and crank up my pulse. "So you planned to bring me back to your room this whole time?"

"I hoped to, but I didn't have plans," he says, kicking off his shoes and emptying his pockets. "Make yourself comfortable."

Nodding, my heart races as I look around. I eye the king bed before pulling off my jacket and choosing to sit in the one chair in the room. *Baby steps.* Luke grins at my seating choice as he dumps his keys, phone, and wallet on the dresser. He removes his jacket, dropping it on his suitcase that sits on a metal luggage holder against the wall. I note the way every move he makes is painstakingly slow. It's as though he's giving me time to adjust to being here, in his room. Alone.

"So," he finally says as he crosses the room and stands over me. "Should we go ahead and have the chat now?"

"The chat?" I feel as awkward as a middle schooler when he holds his hand out to me.

"Come sit with me," he says and I place my hand in his. We move to the bed, sitting on the edge, and Luke turns my way, his face serious. "What do we do now? What's the plan?" Uncertain, I shake my head and he continues. "We made a six month plan, now we need a long term plan, babe. Do we do this thing long distance?"

I giggle, my sigh of relief putting a frown on Luke's face as he watches me. "Oh my gosh... I'm just..." I swipe at my forehead mouthing 'phew' dramatically. "I thought you wanted to have a sex talk. I was kinda freaking out about how to do that." Luke's eyes go wide and he swallows down a horrified laugh. Slapping my forehead, I realize what came out of my mouth.

"Ugh... how to have the talk. Not how to have sex. I know how to do that... I mean, not that I've done or... Gah! I'm shutting up now," I moan, trying to hide my face.

Luke surprises me by leaning forward and kissing me. It's a quick peck, barely a kiss, but it silences me. "Nervous are we?" he asks. "I frowned because I thought you were laughing at me." He admits, his vulnerability making me forget my embarrassment.

"Awe, no. I'm sorry." I stare at him, sitting here in Texas with me. He flew across the country, took vacation time, and spent hundreds of dollars to meet me. Me. This beautiful hero of mine is sitting here asking me how we move forward and I decide it doesn't matter. Reaching up, I take hold of the back of his neck and pull him down as I stretch forward and kiss him. He complies immediately, his mouth opening to mine, his palm cupping my check.

Eventually we fall to the side and Luke rolls to his back, pulling me half on top of him. His hands roam over my body, sliding from the center of my back down past my jeans-clad rear to dig into my thighs before they head back up. Up and down, up and down. His hands match the speed of our kisses — slow and languorous — mostly innocent and then, sexy and shocking. He mumbles into my mouth. "I don't know if I can go back."

Pressing my palm to his chest, I put some space between us. "Luke?" He scoots back on the mattress, sitting up, and I follow suit. He sighs, pinching the bridge of his nose between his thumb and index finger. "What's wrong?" I ask him.

"I… this, us."

My heart plummets. "Us? We're wrong. Did I do something wrong?" I ask, pressing my palm to my stomach. *I'm gonna be sick,* I think as I look at him. He looks as though he's seen a ghost. He's spooked and my eyes burn as they fill with tears.

"No, damn, babe. No," he promises, shifting closer to me. "You've done everything right. Everything," he reiterates. "I don't know if we can do this," he motions from us to the bed. He's referring to us getting intimate. "How do we go back to phone calls and texts after this week? After tonight?"

He's right, I can't sleep with him. I'm not sure if I was going to — although with the way he's making me feel I imagine I'm not far from caving in.

"Can I be honest with you?" he asks. I nod, terrified of honesty. "I didn't expect this."

"Am I supposed to be relieved or offended by that?"

"And there it is, that sassy bit of spunk you have. You don't let that girl out often enough, you know that?"

He's paid good attention to me, I think, amazed at how well he's gotten to know me over a few months. "So are we talking about you or me? My spunk or your lack of expectations, which is it?"

He grins, raising his brows in a clear 'I told you so' to my reply. "Okay, tough girl, let's talk expectations. What I meant was there's no way in hell I could've ever expected this. Did you?" My lips form a reply and he stops me. "Be honest. Did you think when you sent me that text a year ago that we'd be here tonight?"

"No."

"No," he repeats with a smile, and I try to understand his point. "I kept thinking this is going to fizzle out, that one day you won't call or you would and suddenly your voice wouldn't make my stomach flip and my pulse race anymore. I thought we'd get past this. When I got on that plane I honestly thought I'd come here and we'd realize what we thought we had isn't real.

"I'm not trying to hurt you by saying this. I'm trying to be real with you. I've been in love once, and the way I felt about her is the exact way I'm starting to feel about you and that scares the hell out of me."

His roundabout admission of love finally placates me and I push at him, swinging a leg over his lap to straddle him and bring us closer. His eyes flare with heat at my move. *I'm bold, didn't know that about myself.* "I'm scared, too. Believe me, I'm scared every day, but I keep going back to what you said months ago."

His hands grip my hips as he shifts beneath me asking, "What did I say that was so meaningful?"

"You said that maybe our meeting was fate. So every time I miss you, every time I hang up the phone with you, and every time we say goodbye as you go to work — I just tell myself this might be fate and I have to trust it. Trust us."

Luke closes his eyes, inhaling deeply and exhaling slowly. "Stay the night. No expectations, I want to hold you while we sleep."

"Hold me and nothing else?" I repeat skeptically.

"Weelll," he grins. His warms fingers move, skimming the bare skin at the hem of my sweater. "Hold you, touch you... taste you," he whispers easing to his back and pulling me down with him, our lips tumbling into each other.

Passion is new to me. I know pain. I know darkness. Hate, love and loss. Those are feelings I know, feelings I've dealt with intimately. Passion? Passion is different and it's scary as hell. As Luke's lips bite and tease their way along my jaw and down the curve of my neck, every inch of my skin erupts in goosebumps. He ignites a million fires within me, and I shiver as his hand pushes my sweater higher and higher. His hips grind into mine, his throat releases a low growl and I'm well aware of where this is leading. If I don't stop now, there will be no stopping. *Do I want to stop it? Yes! No… oh mylanta! Don't stop kissing me there!* My mind screams jumbled thoughts as Luke tastes the skin along my collar bone.

"I need to call Gram," I blurt, bolting up when his thumb skims the edge of my bra. "I need to tell her what I'm doing." Luke's eyes go wide. "Oh! No, I mean to tell her I'm staying the night. Not to tell her about what I'm… we're doing," I clarify.

Luke nods, laying back on the bed and scrubbing his hands over his face. "Wow, I kind of forgot about them. It's been a while since I've thought about answering to parents. What are they going to think?"

They're probably going to want to find you and drag me home. "I'm eighteen, it doesn't matter what they think, they can't do much about it. Don't worry I'll handle it."

Luke rolls off the edge of the bed, grabbing the purse I'd left on the dresser when we walked in. Handing it to me, he smiles and presses a kiss to my temple. "I'm gonna change then."

I dig for my phone, dialing the number as Luke closes the bathroom door. Gram answers on the fifth ring, her voice low and sleepy. "Gram, did I wake you?" I realize I have no idea what time it is.

"No, no, I was resting my eyes," she lies. She's said the same thing each night this week when I've found her asleep on the couch upon my return from my dates with Luke. "Is everything all right, sweetheart? Are you not home yet?"

"No. I'm with Luke. Um, listen, Gram… I'm going to stay here for the night. He leaves tomorrow and I want as much time as I can get. I'll have him bring me home before he heads to the airport in the morning."

"You want to spend the night? At a hotel with a boy we barely know?" Her voice is calm considering how bad the idea sounds coming from her lips.

"Gram, I'm eighteen. We want to talk and have as much time as possible together." Luke chooses that moment to come out of the bathroom and my jaw drops. He's wearing a grey pair of loose fitting sweat shorts that ride low on his hips, and nothing else. I swallow hard, my throat dry as he winks at me. Clearly he knows exactly how freaking hot he is.

"I'm supposed to believe that? I know I'm old, hun, but I was young once too. I'm not a fool."

"I know you're not a fool. I didn't have to call you, you know. I didn't want you to worry and I don't want to argue over this. I want to stay and I'm going to. Okay?" I catch the frown on Luke's face and I try to smile his way, mouthing 'it's fine.'

It's takes Gram to the count of ten before she answers, "It's not okay, but if I can't stop you without dragging you home then it'll have to be. You're right, you're eighteen and you're out of school." Relieved she didn't put up a fuss, I thank her profusely. "Danica, please make wise choices. If you choose to... do something... "

"Gram. I'll be careful. I promise. Love you," I tell her before hanging up the phone. "Wanna have a sleepover?" I offer playfully, dropping the phone into my purse and leaning back on my elbows.

The corner of Luke's lips lift, as though he's thinking before he crosses his arms and smiles, "Well okay, but I call big spoon."

The thought of being hugged into his naked chest all night is certainly a pleasant one. "Deal."

For a moment we're both motionless - Luke standing in the open doorway of the bathroom reminding me of an Adonis with his perfect golden abs and muscular upper body, and me sprawled on the bed, leaning back on my elbows with my legs hanging over the side. It's a contest of wills, I feel it. One of us will make the next move and everything within me tells me whatever it is will chart the course of our night.

"I pulled out a tee shirt and shorts for you and set them in the bathroom," Luke finally says.

What does that mean? We're done fooling around? Are the clothes for now or later? I bite my lip thinking, *Why is this so confusing?*

"Don't hurt yourself trying to overthink everything, babe. I thought you'd want something more comfortable than jeans and a sweater to sleep in," he says, obviously seeing the hesitation on my face. "Change, don't change, sleep naked... it's totally up to you. I won't tell you my opinion."

"You're a flirt," I accuse.

He bends down, setting his hands on my knees and squeezing them causing me to jerk up.

"Gah! That tickles," I laugh, slapping his hands away.

"I'll make a note for later," he winks, stoking the fires he lit within me earlier back to life. "I'm trying hard not to kiss you right now."

"What's stopping you?" I ask, my fingers itching to touch his skin.

"You are. One moment those brown eyes of yours are warm, melted chocolate as you stare at me and the next you look frightened, unsure of yourself and I'm afraid you're as skittish as Bambi and... "

I gasp. If he says anything else I don't hear it. *Bambi. Jonah's nickname for me.* "I'll go change," I say shortly, standing and scooting around him. I enter the bathroom, locking the door behind me and collapsing against it. Lifting a shaking hand to my mouth, I take deep breaths. "I can't get away from him," I whisper to myself, smoothing my hair back.

Taking my time, I splash my face with water before changing into his clothing. The shorts he set out are drawstring and while extra baggy, they fit fine, and hit me about two inches below my knees. My burn scars will show and I have to think twice about that. I'd pulled up my jeans his first day here and showed him one shin, but he hasn't seen everything yet and I can't help feel self-conscious about them. He wasn't revolted by the scars before, in fact he admired them, telling me how brave I was that night, and afterward, to go through that. Being a firefighter he knows all too well the trauma of burns. I make the decision to wear the shorts. They will be way more comfortable than jeans and the lighting in the room will be low, or off, anyway. My next mini-crisis comes in the form of Luke's tee shirt. Short sleeves. Pulling my sweater over my head, I survey the neat rows of scars lining my pale forearms. Most of my cuts have always been superficial, deep enough to draw blood, but not enough to cause much more than a pale line. There are a few, such as the ones I made on the first anniversary of the wreck, that are larger, deeper, uglier. I hate them. I hate the very sight of them and so I keep them covered, usually. Two years of wearing long sleeves, or light cardigans, anything to keep people from seeing them. In rehab the standing joke in group therapy was how we all needed to move north, to Alaska or somewhere frigid, where it's acceptable to wear fall and winter clothing year round.

Luke knocks on the door lightly. "Babe? You planning on sleeping in the tub or are you coming out here."

Grabbing his tee, I pull it over my head. "Ummm, yeah, I'll be out in a minute." His scent clings to the cotton tee and it envelopes me, calming my nerves.

It takes a few more minutes to gather my courage and then I open the door. Flipping the bathroom light off first, I step out of the bathroom,

146

my arms crossed tightly against my chest. I'm careful to keep my scars facing in so he won't see them, but the worry is unnecessary. Luke's turned off the lights, leaving the glow coming from the muted television as the only light in the room. He's standing with the remote control in his hand, flipping the channels and barely glances at me as I walk toward the bed.

"I can't find anything worth watching." He shrugs, setting the remote down and leaving the blue and white scrolling channel guide on the screen. It's the poor man's version of candlelight. *This is one of the good guys.* The sudden thought crosses my mind in my mother's voice and I savor it, agreeing mentally.

"You look good in my clothes," he compliments me, his eyes never leaving mine.

"Thank you."

"You're more than welcome."

"No, I mean thank you for turning out the lights. For complimenting the way I look in your huge baggy shorts and boxy tee shirt, for not making a big deal out of seeing my... "

"Don't," he says and I stop speaking. "You would be beautiful in anything. All of you," Luke reaches out to me, running his index finger over my arm. "All of you, no matter what. I don't care about them. Okay?"

There are no words to adequately convey my appreciation to him for the consideration he's shown me. So I don't use words. I follow my gut, my heart, and do what I've been wanting to do since the moment he stepped out of the bathroom half-naked. As though I'm reaching out to touch something priceless and fragile, I take care to stretch my hand out, allowing Luke's body to have a moment of anticipation before my fingers make contact. When the tips skim along his ribcage, he sucks in air. I reach my left hand out, copying the right before running them both down his abs, along his waist and up his back. I have to step in closer to touch his back, his heat radiates through the tee shirt I'm wearing, making the skin underneath jealous of my hands' freedom to feel this man. *Holy cow, I want to feel this man. I want to touch him. I want to feel him. I need him.* The animalistic thought rips through my body unexpectedly. I'm simultaneously afraid of the passion and in awe of it. *I need him.* Wetting my dry lips, I lift my face to his.

My eyes search his face silently, telling him to take charge. "I have no idea what I'm doing," I admit. *Oh hell, I didn't mean to say that out loud.*

His lips touch my forehead as his hands finally wrap around me. "Don't worry, you're a natural. Just the way you look at me makes me want you. I'm trying not to scare you, though. I'm trying to go slow and let you make the moves and choices."

"Then kiss me," I whisper, my hands rounding his bare shoulders and tugging him down so we are pressed tightly together.

If there were a scale to rate passion it would be off the charts the moment I give him permission to kiss me. His mouth swoops down, crashing into mine, while he lifts me up and swings me onto his bed. We move so fast I'm hardly aware of what's going on. One moment I'm standing, the next he's laying over me kissing me senseless.

"We need to stop," I murmur some time later. My skin is on fire, every part of my body is tingling from his touch. "Luke," I jump, pushing against his shoulders when his hand skims my thigh, brushing over the scabs and scars and I jump.

"Stop... really?" he mumbles, slowing his kisses to my neck and sliding back over me. "You said stop, right? Okay... are you sure? Sorry, you are... I'm stopping." He groans and I feel horrible.

"We can't. We're not ready for this," I touch his cheek. His eyes, glowing in the light of the television, say differently and I correct myself. "I'm not ready, not yet. Maybe this can be part of our next deal?"

Luke falls to the side, his hands covering his face as he growls into them.

"I'm sorry," I tell him again, sitting up and tugging his tee shirt down around my hips.

"No, don't apologize. I'm the one who's sorry. You're simply too desirable for your own good, and I'm a guy," he says leaning up on his elbow. Sitting up, I yank the covers over us and settle into the crook of his arm, snuggling into his side and breathing him in. "Thank you."

Today's Reality… Everybody falls
January 7, 2015

I'm pulled from sleep with a start, my heart racing as though I've been running a marathon. The room is quiet and dark, the bed warm and soft, and beside me Luke's breathing is slow and deep. *What woke me?* I close my eyes, moving to snuggle back into Luke's side, when it hits me: fire. It was a nightmare: a building, a fire, me and Luke. It seemed real and I sniff the air searching for smoke as I pull away from him. He shifts, rolling to his other side as I move into a sitting position. Focusing on the dream, I rub my arms from the chills running up and down my body.

Luke and I were standing in a long hallway. Him on one end, me on the other, and I'm begging him not to go.

"I don't want you to leave," I beg the Luke in my dreams.

"Babe, I'll be back soon. We'll make plans and you can come home to North Carolina and visit me, too." He smiles, turning his back. He walks away, into a hazy cloud of smoke, and I scream. "No. Luke, please don't leave."

There's no reply before I feel an intense heat at my back. I turn, finding the hallway in flames and panic. Twisting back to where Luke disappeared through the smoke I see flames licking the floor and ceiling. And I run. I run toward him yelling his name and cringing as fire lashes out at my arms and legs.

Then I woke. No wonder my pulse is doing triple time, I realize as I grind my fists into my burning eyes. Tears fall as an unwelcome darkness invades me. Its heaviness settles into the pit of my stomach, making me sick and with another peek at Luke I stand, quietly walking around the bed. Grabbing my purse, I go into the bathroom and carefully shut the door behind me.

My actions are driven by a sharp pain in my soul and I slide off Luke's shorts before sinking onto the cool tiles of the bathroom, digging my make-up bag from my purse and pulling out the hidden razor I keep there. The moment I lay my eyes on the silver blade my heart rate picks up. I'm a junkie craving her fix. I look at my bare legs and don't think twice as I cut.

I cut and I cry as I sink into euphoria. ✒

149

The pressures too great, the imminent loss of watching Luke walk away too painful to consider, and I need a release. A cry escapes my lips and I look down, biting my lip. Blood seeps through the cuts I've made, running down my thighs and pooling on the floor. I've gone deep, the last one painful enough to pull me from the hazy high of adrenaline coursing through my body. I'm twisting to grab a towel from the rack above my head when the bathroom door flies open.

"Danica? You okay?" Luke asks, barging in and sliding to a sudden stop. "Babe? What the... what did you do? Oh my... " Luke springs into action mode, grabbing a handful of towels and dropping to his knees straddling over my outstretched legs. "Drop the razor, hun."

I raise my arms, splaying them wide as though he's a cop telling me 'hands up' and I stare at him in shock as he speaks with more force. "Babe, drop the razor."

My eyes move to my hand. It's covered in blood, thick streaks running down my palm and over my wrist. My hand shakes as my fingers loosen their grip, dropping the razor to the tile floor.

"I... um, I..." I struggle to pull my knees to my chest before I realize Luke's body is hovered over them and I break down. "I'm sorry... I'm sorry."

Luke lunges forward when I move to cover my face. "Don't touch your face." He grabs my arm, pulling it back while his free hand applies a towel to my bloody thigh. "Hold these. Here, apply pressure," he says, grabbing my clean hand and forcing it down to hold the towels. "Your hand is covered in blood. Did you cut it?" I don't speak. "Damn it, Danica! Did you cut your wrist?" he asks angrily as he carefully wipes the blood away. He relaxes as the blood disappears, revealing no cuts, before I'm able to answer him.

"What happened? Why did you do this?" he asks, cursing as he lifts the towels on my leg to survey the damage I've done. I grit my teeth as he probes the cuts. "Sorry, they're mostly surface wounds. This one's deep though, we need to get you to an urgent care center."

"No, no hospital," I beg grabbing his hand.

"Yes, the hospital. You're bleeding too much, you've already bled out too much... look at this." He motions to the blood soaked towels and floor. "Babe, please."

"No. There's liquid glue in my make-up bag. Just use that." He tenses, looking at me skeptically. "It's fine, here give it to me, I'll do it."

He sits back, reaching for the bag sitting on the counter, and hands it to me without a word before he scoots my feet to the side and sits on the floor. He lifts a hand to his head, stopping mid-way looking at it. Its covered in my blood now and I watch him through lowered lashes as he lifts and looks at his other hand as well. Silently, he pulls the bath mat towel from the edge of the tub and turns on the bathtub water soaking it. I'm expecting him to clean his hands, but instead he turns back to me.

"Let's clean you up first," he says and I nod, allowing him to tend to the wounds his eyes never looking up at me. He swipes at the blood, checking the cuts and applying more pressure before repeating the process until he's satisfied with the results. Turning my head, I rest it against the bathroom wall, staring at the shower curtain in front of me as he applies the liquid skin glue and blows lightly on my thigh. I'm mortified he's seen me this way and my mind races for the right words to explain it all.

"We can't get this wet, but you need to clean up. Let me get you a clean shirt and some shorts," Luke says standing. He returns and pulls the last clean towel from the rack over the toilet along with a wash cloth sitting folded into a flower-like design next to the soap. Turning on the water once again he mops up the floor around me before he begins to wipe the sides of my thighs and calves.

"You don't have to… " I start, and he looks at me, his face reminding me of a parents scold, and I shut my mouth allowing him to do as he pleases. It's the least I can do.

"Come here," he finally says after lifting my legs and wiping the backs of my thighs too. I place my hands in his and he helps me up to my feet. "Can you stand here and not put any weight on that leg?"

"Yeah."

Kneeling down, he picks up the razor from the floor and turns on the sink. "I'm going to stand right outside the door. Take off your clothes, clean up, and change. I'm right here if you need me," he says, looking at me one last time before disappearing, leaving the door cracked. I strip off my underwear, they're wet with blood and I wipe at the streaks they left along my rear and legs. Next, I check my upper thighs and clean the bit of blood on my lower abs. I'm lightheaded as I stand there, the rush of the adrenaline long gone now and the pain from my cuts is now making its presence known. Slipping on his shirt, I lean against the wall and try to figure out how to slip his shorts on as my head spins.

"Luke," I call his name softly, hating myself more every minute that goes by for putting him in this position. "Will you help me?"

He looks exhausted when he pokes his head in and I hold up the shorts for him. Kneeling down, he slips the athletic shorts onto one foot and then the other while letting me lean on his shoulders for support. When he pulls them up, he's careful around my thighs and turns his head, considerate of my nakedness, as he pulls the shorts over my rear and into place at my waist. When he's tugged the drawstring into a knot he slides one arm under my knees and one around my back picking me up and carrying me back to the bed, gently setting me in the middle.

"Don't move," he says. I nod. I have no intension of moving, my head's spinning, and I lean back closing my eyes. The sink goes on in the restroom and a few minutes later Luke returns cleaned up. He slips a shirt on and props some pillows against the headboard before slipping into bed beside me. "Do you feel alright? You looked pretty pale in there."

"A bit lightheaded, I'm fine."

"Kay. Well, come here," he says, moving closer and pulling me into his side. My cheek presses against his chest and I turn my body enough to wrap an arm around his waist while keeping my leg from pressing into him. We lay there, his hands combing through my hair, his lips brushing over the top of my head over and over until I can't stand the silence.

"You're not going to say anything?"

Luke's breathing halts before he exhales slowly. "What is there for me to say? I don't know... no, actually I do have a question." There's a moment of tense silence before he asks exactly what I knew he would. "Why?"

As usual the answer to why eludes me and I try my best to explain. "I had this dream, about us, and it freaked me out, and with you leaving today and, and I don't know... I can't explain why I cut. It's something I fight and tonight it won."

"I'm sorry it was because of me," he says sadly. "You've been out of Crestdale for five months, I thought you were doing better. If I'd known."

"Luke, I have been. This was an accident, I didn't mean to do it. It was a moment. One moment... " His hand pauses in my hair. "I promise."

"You scared the crap out of me," he whispers. There's something different about his voice in that moment and I wish I could take everything back.

"I'm so sorry… I can't say that enough," I tell him, pushing back my tears.

"I'm just happy you're safe. Get some rest and we'll talk later."

The crash always makes me lethargic and I'm fast asleep in Luke's arms within minutes.

Luke's whispered 'goodbye' wakes me, the soft glow of sunlight streaming through a crack left in the curtains telling me it's morning. As I stir from sleep, my stomach drops for one hazy moment as I panic, thinking he's saying goodbye to me. Looking around, I'm relieved to find him sitting in the chair by the windows, cell phone in hand.

"What time is it?" I ask, rubbing my eyes.

"It's after nine. I have to leave for the airport soon," he makes a face, his finger smoothing over his brow before he adds, "and your grandparents are on their way here."

"What? Did Gram call all freaked out now that she's had time to think about me being here with you?" I sit up, quickly scanning the room. He's picked up our clothes from last night. My jeans, bra, and sweater are folded neatly on his dresser, his clothes in his suitcase. I realize he's fully dressed, shoes and all, and I have a sinking feeling as I study his granite face. "You called them, didn't you?"

"I'm not keeping this a secret."

"That's not for you to decide." Irritated, I push myself into a sitting position, grimacing at the soreness in my thigh.

"Like hell it's not. You said last night was an accident, that it was one moment." He raises his index finger, emphasizing 'one'.

"It was. I had a dream we were in this hall and it was on fire and you disappeared and I couldn't find you… seriously, Luke, when I woke up it was as though the whole world was sitting on my chest. I had this feeling I would never see you again. I panicked. I need you, I don't want to lose us."

"Do you care about me?" he asks, and I nod fiercely. He sighs, "Then don't lie to me."

He sits there, waiting for me to offer up something, but all I do is nod. With a shake of his head, he massages the back of his neck as he looks at the floor.

"I saw the marks. Your grandparents don't check you anymore, do they? You have fresher marks on your thighs. You said you haven't cut since rehab, but those marks are new… or newer."

"So what, you're an expert now?"

"No, I'm the guy who's falling in love with a girl who needs help. When you went to Crestdale last summer I did research. I wanted to know what you were dealing with since you wouldn't talk to me about it. Honestly, I thought maybe your grandparents were overreacting, you seemed fine to me. You never said anything to let me know you were struggling. I thought you were over it."

"You're no different from them, the therapists and my grandparents, you think I'm going to simply *get over it*," I make quotation marks to mimic his phrase. "Please tell me how in the hell I'm supposed to get over it and I will. By all means, enlighten me!"

I stand, beyond angry, and Luke copies me. "That's not what I meant and you know it. I want to help you, and keeping this a secret is not going to help you."

Ignoring him, I try to shove past him to grab my clothing, "Please move out of my way."

"Let's talk about this."

"Talk about what? There's nothing to talk about. I told you, Luke." I push at his chest when he won't budge and he catches my wrists. "I told you I was screwed up. I told you and you said you didn't care, that you weren't going anywhere."

"And I'm not," he swears, maintaining his grip as I fight it. "Babe, I'm not going anywhere. Don't turn away. Look at me." Luke tugs my arms, moving his face closer to mine, forcing me to look at him. "I can't stay here and protect you. I have to go home and I couldn't go without making sure someone would take care of you. I had to call them, I know you're angry, but I had to."

I can't stop the glower I give him and his lips curve into the tiniest of smiles at my derision. "Do you know what I did after you fell asleep? I laid there and watched you and I thought. I thought about fate, our fate, and you know what I realized?"

"What?"

"Not a damn freaking thing," he says seriously. "I don't have a clue what's in store for us. This could be it, I could get on that plane and we might never see each other again."

"Don't say that." His hands have loosened their grip and I back away, hugging myself.

"Why? You know it's true. If anyone knows the truth about how fragile this life is, it would be you."

In that regard, Luke is one hundred percent correct. One moment my life was stolen kisses and laughter, and the next it was gone. Was that what fate had in store for me?

"If I'd known you were cutting I never would have let things between us go so far. I never would have put that pressure on you."

That admission hurt worse than knowing he called my grandparents. "You regret this relationship?"

"Regret isn't the word I would use. I could never regret you. What I regret is how something with me could make you want to cut."

"But it's not you, not really. Luke, I need you. Having you in my life keeps me happy, makes me feel sane and alive," I explain as I sit on the edge of the bed.

"And there's the problem, babe. I can't be that for you. I can't be the thing that makes you happy. That's too much stress to put on me. I have to go home and sit there and wonder if you're cutting yourself because you miss me too much, or if we fight will you hurt yourself. You can't rely on me because I don't know what my role in your life is. You're not ready for something significant, *we're* not ready for that. Maybe someday, but I need to grow up some first and you need to heal."

"You're scared," I accuse, finally grasping what he's saying. "Are you scared of how I feel about you or how you feel about me?"

Kneeling between my legs, he takes my hands. "Both."

He's spared any further explanation by the knock at the door. Bringing my hands to his lips, he kisses them before standing and letting my grandparents in.

Today's Reality… Savor the memories
March 2015

"And we haven't spoken in two months," I tell Lee. My grandparents brought me straight from the hotel, and Luke, to check-in for another 'indeterminate' inpatient stay. Since I'm now eighteen I considered fighting them, but between Gram's pleas and Luke's sad eyes I couldn't do it.

"You haven't spoken to him. Why?" Lee asks as he pops a chip in his mouth. It's warm for March and we're taking advantage by eating lunch under the large elm in the courtyard at Crestdale.

I shrug because I honestly don't know the answer. "We left it vague. He left me a voicemail when he landed back in Charlotte letting me know he was there and telling me what an amazing week he'd had with me. And of course he apologized, again." I push my lunch to the side, no longer hungry as I recall his voice. It was heavy, I could feel the weight of his words through the phone. "He told me he would be there for me, but maybe it would be best if we took some time apart."

Lee scoffs, shaking his head, "Unbelievable."

"What?"

"He ran pretty quickly. Either he's in love with you and he's scared or he's an ass who got what he wanted and decided he was done."

"Lee!" I throw my wadded up napkin across the grass, falling short of hitting him. "He didn't *get what he wanted*," I point out, clarifying our night spent together as purely innocent; or mostly innocent. "Honestly, I think I scared him. His face when he saw me cutting. He was upset, but he was scared, too. Dr. Schaffer and I have talked about it often. She's done a good job of reminding me how he's merely twenty-one and I threw a ton of pressure on him when I fell apart that night. It wasn't fair of me."

Checking his watch, Lee wads his trash and stands. "Lunch break's over, I better get back to it."

"Thanks for listening."

"Anytime. I'm glad you finally decided to talk. I was getting sick of pestering you for details," he teases as he leans down and swipes my trash from the ground. "You coming in?"

I give him the best smile I can manage. "I think I'll stay here. You know how I love the shade of the tree."

"And the sound of the basketball," he points out knowingly, and I nod, waving him off as I lay back and close my eyes. The not-so-distant sound of basketballs slapping against the court takes me back to better days and I savor the moment. I savor the memories.

It's how I spend my daylight hours every day for weeks. I wake up each morning and do my required meditation, group meetings, and therapy sessions, and then I spend all of my free time outside. Under the tree and, if I'm lucky, listening to someone playing ball on the court. I don't play ball myself unless it's with Lee and I don't watch the patients who do play. I simply listen. Closing my eyes and remembering all those years spent sitting under a tree similar to the one here at Crestdale and watching Jonah practice. Jonah, his dad, my dad, Kadence, the neighborhood kids... these are the mental pictures and memories I have when I hear rubber meet asphalt, and I smile.

Smiling is a relief. Thinking of those days and not wanting to drown myself in my sorrow is a huge leap for me, and after two more weeks of hashing out my last breakdown and my relationship with Luke, I'm able to go home again, feeling stronger and expecting better results this time.

Today's Reality…What might have been
June 2015

I'm journaling, something my therapists have been after me to do for a while, at the kitchen table when an old quote comes to mind and I jot it down:

Sylvia Plath said, "It is so much safer not to feel, not to let the world touch me."

It's such a powerful quote. *Sylvia knows what she's talking about.* I scribble the words, circling the phrase and thinking about the last time I let the world 'touch' me. The last time I let myself feel. I haven't made a cut since the beginning of May. It's one month, but with the exception of my stays at Crestdale, it's the longest I've gone. And the May cut was understandable — because Luke called. It was out of the blue, it'd been four months since we last spoke, and he'd been drunk. *"Nothing good ever comes from calling an ex when you're drunk."* I write the words, looking over my shoulder to be sure Gram is occupied before I decide to write the whole story. *"Not for you and not for them."*

"Hey, gorgeous, how are you?" Luke slurred when I picked up my phone.

"Uh, hi." That's all I could think to say in my befuddled state. Four freaking months ago he'd told me he was falling in love with me then he turned me over to my grandparents and disappeared. And now he calls. The fire in my belly shoots off sparks.

"That's all I get? Uh, hi?" he mumbles. There's laughter in the background followed by the slamming of a door.

"Luke?"

A crash and several curses later, Luke speaks, "Oops, dropped the phone."

"You sound wasted, are you okay?" I'm torn between hating myself for caring and wanting to tell him how much I miss him.

"Yeah… I'm great, we're having a party," he slurs, his voice so loud I pull the phone from my ear.

Silence. I lay there, waiting for him to speak. When I've counted to twenty and all I've heard is his breathing I try again. "A party, huh?"

"Damn, I miss you."

Well, hell, I don't know if I can handle drunk Luke telling me he misses me at two a.m.

"I wish I were stronger. I wish I had it all together and I could be the guy you need, Danica. I suck... I'm sorry I suck so much."

I bite the inside of my cheek to keep from saying anything. What can I say? I miss you too, I wish you were stronger too? I don't know if that's his fault. Was he not strong enough or was I too damaged? It's irrelevant really.

"It comes in waves. My missing you... I feel fine and then my phone rings and I smile thinking it's going to be you. It's never you... not anymore. I want it to be you, but it can't be. We can't be." He's nearly incoherent, but I let him speak, his voice filling me with sadness.

"Luke!" A female shouts in the distance and Luke grunts, "I'm talking to Danica, Court, go away."

Courtney. I should hang up. This call is a train wreck you can't pass up. I'm the innocent bystander who's going to stand here and watch until I'm forced out of the scene. It happens faster than I expected though. There's a shuffle and more cursing through the line. "Danica?" It's Courtney now.

"He called me," I say quickly, as though I have to explain myself to her.

"He's drunk."

Thank you, captain obvious. "Obviously," I snap.

"Don't encourage him, okay. You know he wouldn't have called if he wasn't drunk." Wow. Luke's angry 'don't' sounds in the background.

"As I said, he called me. Just take care of him, okay? Don't let him drive or anything."

Whatever her angry reply was, I didn't hear it as I hung up the phone.

Biting on my pen cap, I think about the aftermath of that phone call. That night I let the pressure of his painfully sad voice and confessions drive me to make one small cut. It was a surface wound, deep enough to feel a pinch before all of my therapy sessions kicked in and I put the blade down and cried instead. He never called me back, never apologized. And I didn't expect him to. I didn't tell Gram or my therapist about the small slip. Instead I chose to savor it as a victory. I didn't resist, but I stopped. I write that down, underlining it twice and adding, *"Savor the victory!!"*

"Sweetheart," Gram says, breaking my thoughts. "I think I heard the mail, will you go check? Your grandfather is expecting that reimbursement check and if we don't get the mail first, he'll pull himself up from his chair and hobble out there himself." Gram's hands are covered in flour as she kneads dough for homemade bread and she holds them up as the reason she's asking me this favor.

"Sure." Leaving the kitchen, I walk through the family room and, sure enough, I spot Gramps struggling to get out of his recliner. "Stay there, Gramps, I'm checking the mail now," I tell him, waving him down. He slipped two weeks ago, wrenching his knee, and has been under strict orders from both Gram and I to stay seated and rest. The June air has a sweet zing to it and I check the sky, studying the thick rainclouds rolling in. I love the smell and sound of rain. An evening storm is the perfect accompaniment to the piano. I snap open the mailbox, my mind now on music, and pull out the mail. An oversized envelope jams itself in the box and I have to tug to dislodge it and pull it out. The corner is crushed, but otherwise it's intact and I fold it around the other letters in my hand, my eye catching the return address at the last moment.

Hall. Grove Pointe, North Carolina.

Jonah? My bare feet move as though they're being sucked down into quicksand with each heavy step I make back to the house. Dropping down to the brick steps, I set the rest of the mail to the side and stare at this one envelope. The handwriting is too cutesy, with large bubble swoops and swirls, to be from either Jonah or his mother. *Kadence*. Knowing it's from Kadence brings me a moment of reprieve and I drag in a long breath before tearing the seal. Deliberately, I ease the contents of the envelope out. It's a five by seven photograph card and staring back at me, his blond hair darker and shorter than it was a year and a half ago, is Jonah. He's leaning his back against a brick wall, his white shirtsleeves rolled up his forearms, his thumbs hooked in his pockets, his face angled down. It's as though he was staring at the ground before the photographer called his name because those eyes — those piercing, warm, drown-in-them eyes — are looking straight at me. They're flirting with the camera in a way that would turn any girl to putty. The Jonah Hall signature look ladies and gentlemen. He's still got it.

The first fat rain drop hits my foot as I read the words on the card. Along with his name and a 'Congratulations Class of 2015' is the note across the bottom. 'Jonah will be attending the University of North Carolina, Chapel Hill in the fall.'

Torn between joy and pain, I flip the card over, finding a handwritten note on a post-it note adhered to the back. It's in Kadence's handwriting and there are no salutations or pleasantries. Just six powerful words: *You were supposed to be here.*

My tears fall in sync with the rain as it moves in swiftly, slapping at my feet and legs not covered by the front porch. I think of the words I finished writing in my journal moments ago *'Small victories in the battle of depression are huge'* and I laugh at myself. Small victories are huge, but often times the attacks are larger. And today I've been struck by a sneak attack so powerful it takes my breath away.

The front door opens behind me. "Oh, it's raining? What are you doing, I thought you were bringing Gramps the mail?" Gram says. Swiping at my face, I remove the sticky note from the back and hold the card up over my head without turning around.

"What's… this?" She takes the picture from my hand. "Oh, I see. How do you feel about this?"

The wind picks up, sending the rain slanting into my face and I finally stand, grabbing the mail by my hip. "It's kinda wet now," I tell Gram with a shrug, "sorry."

She takes the mail and after a long, thoughtful look at Jonah's announcement, she holds the card back to me repeating her question, "How do you feel about this?"

"I don't know," I tell her honestly, fanning the air with the card. "I… I'm jealous, I'm sad, I'm happy and angry. And that's for starters, give me a few hours and I'm sure there will be more. I'll be in my room." I excuse myself, my wet feet leaving a trail behind me. I go straight to my closet pulling out a box I've tucked away. It's full of school stuff — notes, cards, and memorabilia — I couldn't bear to put out, but I couldn't throw away either. At the bottom, under old movie tickets and photographs, newspaper clippings, and my old spirit tee, is my freshman yearbook. I flip it open, knowing exactly where to look. Eight pages in, left side:

"D-

One down, three to go! We're not fresh meat anymore! You know the only reason I'm writing this is because you threatened to tell Kathy about Kristen. You're EVIL, Bambi! You said you wanted 50 words so here you go- 50 sappy words that make me sound like a wuss. Love you as much as Coach loves Tuesday death drills at practice. Summer baby, it's gonna be on!!!!

Always - J

Ps. 73 words! Hope you're happy now"

The note makes me laugh to this day. Jonah wrote it under duress, during lunch, after I excitedly flipped open my yearbook looking for his message the period before. He'd taken it from me before homeroom that morning and kept it for three periods. Three whole periods, so of course I'd been looking forward to something amazing, yet when I opened it to where he said to — his picture, naturally — there was only a huge circle around his face and his signature with a smiley face.

"A smiley face," I attacked him the moment we were in the hall after class. "It took you three periods to drawn a freaking smiley face and sign your name?"

"What! Did you not see all of my notes," he asks, jumping back as if he's scared of me.

"All of your notes? You said pull up your picture, that's all I saw."

"Yeah, all of my pictures. I left you something in every shot." He yanked the book from my hands and flipped to his team photo. "See."

There in the margins he drew a number eight, his jersey number, with little basketballs, and scribbled his initials.

"And here, two pages away, I drew this little guy making a slam dunk," he points out.

"But you didn't write anything, Jonah."

"What am I supposed to write?" he asks, and I seriously consider hitting him with the book.

"A note, something I can read when we're thirty and I want to look back on all the memories we made, you idiot. That's what yearbooks are for."

"You act like we're not going to be talking to each other anymore when we're thirty. You won't need notes in a book, you'll have the real thing." He spreads his arms wide, wagging his brows, and I swear a half dozen girls cat call him throughout the crowded halls.

"We're not always going to see each other every day, Jonah."

"Why the hell not?" he complains, and I roll my eyes. Hard.

"Jonah Hall, you will take this book back and you will write me, your best friend in the whole world, a note. And not a 'woohoo yay it's summer' note. I want a real honest note with a minimum of fifty words. Got it?"

Several of our friends have joined us as we're walking to our usual seats for lunch, but they maintain their distance when they see my angry face.

"What if I don't, angry-girl-I-do-not-know?" he asks making a face.

Looking around, I devilishly grin and pull on his shirt, bringing his face close to my lips. "Then I will totally tell Kathy about Kristen and your summer is bound to be ruined, lover boy."

"You wouldn't."

"Try me," I smirk, knowing I've won. Jonah sighs, taking the book and walking away.

He sits as far as he can from me at lunch, the book covered on the table in front of him so no one can see what he's writing. The guys sitting with us give him crap for how much time he takes and I fully expect him to quit, but he doesn't. He looks up at me a few times, a little smile playing about his lips, and I know he's up to something, but I don't care. At this point he can draw me another cartoon character and I'll be happy because he did it for me. He hands me the book back at the end of lunch and walks right out of the cafeteria door without another word. I flip open the book, searching the back and front covers for his note and find nothing. It takes me all of fourth period, discretely flipping around the yearbook, before I finally find it on page eight and I laugh, out loud, while Mr. Troyer talks about genocide. The outburst earns me a nasty glare, and I give my thanks there's only two days of school left.

Gram's standing in my doorway when I come back to the present. "I missed it all," I tell her sadly, closing my yearbook and placing my hand on the cover. "You know that last fight I had with Jonah was about how I was supposed to be there for senior year. He seemed so convinced I would be coming back when they were here, he mentioned it."

"Darling, you live here. It's not fair of him to be angry with you for not being there anymore."

"No, no that's not it, it's more." I shake my head, a memory, nagging to be recalled tickles the back of my mind. "Why did you fight with the Halls, Gram?" She looks ready to deny and then I fully recall Jonah's words when he was here and his comments on the phone back in December. "Jonah told me his parents wanted me to come back with them. He was angry about you guys not telling me something. That's it, isn't it? They wanted me to stay with them back after my first hospital stay?"

Gram crosses my room and sits on the bed with a sigh. Twisting around from my spot on the floor, I wait for her response. "Yes, Virginia was concerned we weren't going to be able to handle you. She said you needed more help and she was worried we weren't prepared for it."

"Because you're older?" I guess, and she nods. "So why did you update them after that? Why didn't you tell them to back away because this was family business?"

"It wasn't that simple, honey, your parents loved them and... well it doesn't matter now. I know they were acting out of love for you and your mom and dad, but we weren't going to lose you. Not after losing Brad… and your mother, too."

"Gram."

"Hmm?"

"I want to go back to Crestdale," I tell her firmly and she looks at me with concern. "You have Gramps to take care of, with his knee and he's so cranky and… well, I'm fighting the urge to cut right now. I'm hurting and you can't watch over me." Gram's lower lip quivers as she nods. "I need somewhere safe, at least for a few days, and Crestdale always makes me feel safe."

"Okay, whatever you need. We'll call in the morning and make sure they have a room."

The rain outside is an ominous reminder of the first time I cut and I choose to sleep in between my grandparents to ensure my own safety that night. The next morning we confirm a spot at Crestdale and, once again, I pack my belongings and head to rehab. I wasn't honest with Gram about my reasoning for going back. Yes, I wanted to cut and, yes, I'm sad. But more than that, seeing the picture of Jonah, remembering the plans I once had, hearing from Luke last month, all of these things were adding up in my head and I *didn't care*. Not really. I didn't care if Luke missed me and how sorry he was. I didn't care that I'd missed out on everything in high school. That Jonah, and all of my other friends, graduated without me. I don't care about anything anymore. I'm an empty body walking through the days. I'm moving forward, but I'm not living. I'm pretending. How do you know if you're dead or alive? I wouldn't know, I feel dead even as I live and breathe.

Today's Reality… I have a new project. His name is West.
June 2015

Being back at Crestdale is a balm to my broken soul. The depression lingers, taking refuge deep down within my gut, and my desire for the release of a blade continues to cause my fingers to twitch and my scars to burn, but being here helps. This place provides so many hands, so many 'in case of emergency break here' escape routes that being at home didn't. When I'm down I open my room and find someone: a doctor, a nurse, another patient, and especially Lee. I'm surrounded by people who get it, who know. It doesn't help me find the answers I need, but it helps me get through the days and for now that works.

I'm heading to my first group meeting since returning when I spy someone new hesitate outside the door of our group room. New blood always peps me up, gives me something to look forward to. I know it sounds crazy, hell, I *am* crazy, but I've decided my new goal is helping others. Perhaps I'll make some friends this stay. Perhaps I'll make a difference for someone.

I head into the room behind the new guy, taking a seat and nodding politely to the other repeat offenders around our usual circle of chairs. I know everyone here, which is sad in its own right. Only two of them are inpatient though, the others come back weekly for this meeting. It's part of the process — the part I refused to follow through with before. I chose seeing my own therapists instead of coming back to the meetings at Crestdale because I hated making my grandparents trek one hour each way every week. This is a simple 'surviving your depression' type group. The patients vary in issues and in habits, but we all have one thing in common, we don't know how to deal with life normally when bad things happen. While we wait for Hannah, the group therapist, I watch new guy loiter around the exterior of the room. He's the new kid in school, trying to look as though he belongs while every bit of his body language disputes it. He's young, my age most likely, and tall. *Wow*, he's ridiculously tall judging by the height of his head in relation to the posters on the wall he's standing by. I smile at my first thought - Lee would love to shoot hoops with him.

Hannah walks in moments later and, true to her style, she singles the new guy out immediately calling him over, "You must be West. Come, come join us. We're glad to have you join us today."

West. New guy has a name. He approaches our circle cautiously as Hannah introduces him.

"Everyone, this is West and he's going to be joining our group…" she explains, and West interrupts her.

"For the day," he drawls. "I'm only here for the day."

He's in denial. The thought is immediate as though I'm an expert and then I almost snort aloud as my inner voice laughs — you *are an expert at being in denial.* Shaking my head, I focus back on Hannah as she pokes at West, trying to get him to tell his story. He doesn't particularly look to be buying into it all and I'm surprised she's pressing him until he explains his situation.

"My therapist said I had to attend one of these group meetings before I could be released. I don't get the point."

There's a smattering of laughter and Hannah makes a note in a small notebook sitting in her lap as she prods him again for his story and explains the facility policy: "Everything said in group meetings is confidential and remains within the group." I've heard this policy so many times, I wonder if I should market the saying: 'What happens in group therapy, stays in group therapy.'

After a moment he speaks, kicking at the floor as he starts. "I'm West. I'm here because I have a habit of giving up everything I love."

"Will you explain that, West?" asks Hannah. She has no mercy.

"Do I have to?"

"Well, you could wait and try to explain it at next week's meeting. It's your choice."

He shakes out his shoulders, straightening in his seat. "According to my therapist, I give up things I love to punish myself."

"From what?" *Oh, crap! I said that.* I'm shocked I asked it out loud and I sink back into my seat as he looks my way. His glance is more curious than mad and it prompts me to go on. "What are you punishing yourself for?" I ask, sitting straighter, "What did you do?"

"Danica," Hannah warns, but I ignore her, raising a brow at West.

"Why are *you* here?" he counters, leaning back in his chair.

Around us the others sink into the background. *Now or never, Dani. You want to open up and do things differently this time, now's your chance,* my inner voice tells me. It's not the mocking voice of doubt and fear I've heard so often over the past two years, it's the new voice. The voice of the girl who said she'd do her best this time. Without blinking, I pull the sleeve of my long, black tee up, flashing my arm at West and showing him the scars I've given myself. His eyes go wide, but I don't stop there. Leaning over, I pull up one pant leg and then the other, allowing him to see the scars my accident left behind. Out of the corner of my eye I notice the others lean forward getting their first look at the damage I've never shared. I sit there vulnerable, opening myself up, before I speak again.

"I punish myself because I lived," I confess without emotion. Then I cover my body as though the entire moment wasn't a big deal. But it was, it was huge, and West says nothing; he merely looks away and Hannah moves on to another patient. I slide back, mentally counting in my head to calm my rapid heartbeat.

After the meeting, I'm surprised by West's deep voice standing over me. "Soooo… I feel pretty low now."

"Oh? Why is that?" I ask, standing.

"I shouldn't have asked why you were here. It's not my place," he explains, taking the metal folding chair from my hand. He follows the lead of the other patients who leave their chairs against the wall.

I follow behind him, laughing at his apology. "You really haven't been doing group meetings, huh?"

"No. It wasn't part of my deal," he says.

"Deal?"

"Never mind," he replies. I study him and he breaks, shifting nervously under the scrutiny of my gaze. "I give up. You know, it's not really that big of a deal, but I screwed up and my dad made me come here, thinking I needed help for my *issues*," he mocks, making air quotes at the word issues. Walking back to grab the chair he'd been sitting in, he places it in the pile with the others. "I get out in two weeks."

Two weeks, huh? I'm perplexed and intrigued by his story, what he's saying and what he's not saying. "Are you sure?" I ask.

"Sure that I get out of here? Pretty much."

Denial. Checking my watch, I grab his arm and pull him out the back doors and into the courtyard. I take a deep breath of the fresh air and allow the sun to warm my face as I lead him to the big tree. "Are you sure what you're giving up isn't a big deal?"

"You ask lots of questions," he points out, leaning against my tree. "Look – I did something stupid, and to keep people from getting into trouble, I took a deal that landed me here. End of story."

"Is that what your therapist says, or you?"

"I told you inside. My therapist thinks I'm punishing myself. It's a load of crap."

"Why does he think that?"

"It's a she – Dr. Steel – and she thinks that because I had to walk away from my life when I came here."

"And?" I cross my arms, watching him carefully, trying to mimic all those doctors who've questioned me a million times.

He explains his story, how he takes things to extremes, how his own mother died six years ago and he gave up something he cared about because he was angry and blames himself. I want to tell him I totally get where he's coming from. I know all about blame and running away... and then he mentions his girlfriend. I lower myself to the grass and West follows as I ask about her and what happened, and I know. I know by his explanation, and by the pain in his voice. He's me, he's in denial and needs to fix himself.

"You're not ready to leave," I tell him boldly.

"I need to leave. I need to find her before school starts in a few weeks... to win her back."

"Of course you do! You're willing to give it all up for her, right?" I laugh, partly at him and partly at myself for trying to be the voice of reason. "You have to take care of *you* before you can take care of *her*."

He claims to be fine, the same as I always have, and I resolve myself to backing off — what business do I have butting into this guy's life anyway? And then I push one last time, because I can't help myself.

"This isn't my first trip to the rodeo. You're *not* fine. You're in denial. Do you love your girl? Then get strong for her."

"Damn, you're pushy. You remind me of Jules."

I chuckle. "Jules, huh? Pretty name."

"It's beautiful. *She's* beautiful," he insists, and I want to simultaneously swoon and hurl my lunch.

"Look, I'm no expert, but I could be for all the therapy I've had. I don't know your whole story, but until you admit your issues, you'll never be healed. You want to end up here again? It may feel like a bunch of B.S. they're feeding us here, but it's not," I tell him honestly.

Dr. Thomas calls my name from the doors and I check my watch seeing it's time for our session. West looks to be thinking about what I've said — I guess that's all I can hope for.

"Sorry, I have a session. I hope I'll see you around, West. Think about what I said." He doesn't reply and I give him one last look before jogging toward the building.

As I reach the door he calls out behind me, "Hey! Thanks for the advice. Maybe you're right. Maybe I'm not ready yet, but what do I do?"

That a boy, I allow myself an internal smile. Sending him a nonchalant shrug, I tell him the one thing I know, "You stay. You get better."

"Thanks."

It's a week before I see West again. "Hey," I call across the courtyard, "you stayed?"

He looks about, before spotting me and nodding. He's sitting on a bench, near my favorite tree, and I'm excited by the rare bit of happiness seeing him sparks within me.

"Did something I say change your mind?" I ask as I reach his side.

"You think I'd make a life decision based on our short conversation last week?"

I'm momentarily stunned, and then he smiles. It's endearing, the slightly crooked smirk he throws my way as he pushes his dark hair up.

"I'm playing," he assures me. "I have a week left, but you were right. I've decided to stay longer."

"Good, I'm glad." And that's the truth. I'm glad he's going to take some time to help himself and I'm glad I played a part in it. Taking my usual spot in the grass under the shade, I pull a rubber band from my wrist and throw my hair up in a knot. It's stifling today, almost too hot to be outside, but the fresh air is a must, the antiseptic smell inside gets to me after a while and I enjoy breathing in the sunshine.

"So, why haven't we run into each other before last week?" he asks.

"You got here in November, yeah?" I confirm, trying to remember what little he told me when we met, and he nods. "I actually checked back in last week. I'm here voluntarily."

"Really? *Back* in? You said the other day you've been there, done that. Exactly how many times have you been here and done this?"

I snicker despite myself. "Here? Um, several. Before here it was therapy sessions and different group meetings at other places. I've been exorcising my demons for two-and-a-half years." West attempts to keep a straight face, but he isn't able to hide the flicker of shock. I imagine he's wondering why he ever listened to my advice the other day. Who am I to tell someone what they should do? I'm a hypocrite. The truth hits me as I think of all the times I've sat in group therapy and laughed silently at the others. The ones who played the weak my-life-is-over card. In reality, I'm no better. It's easy to judge and tell others to step up and change their reality. Doing it, facing the demons of your past? It's not as simple as the counselors make it seem.

"So how long do you think you'll stay?" I inquire, steering the conversation away from me.

"A month or so, I guess. I need to report to school after the Fourth of July. How about you? You have plans for school?"

"College? Nah, not right now. I... I don't think I could handle the pressure of classes, honestly." I didn't mean to give that much away. I'm sure he's taking mental notes, diagnosing my own particular brand of crazy. Uncomfortable with the thought, I pop up, making a decision.

"Okay, thirty days. Come with me," I wave and I'm kind of surprised when he follows.

"Where to?"

"I heard you've never talked to Lee, let me introduce you. He's gonna love getting you on the court."

Today's reality… Thirty days goes fast
July 2015

It's time and it sucks.

I knock on West's door, peeking my head in when he calls out. "You done with your exit interview?" I ask, slipping inside and falling onto the bed beside him.

"Yeah. I'm a free man," he says, rolling to his side and I laugh halfheartedly.

Over the last few weeks we've spent countless hours together. Group meetings, lunch in the courtyard, endless rounds of one-on-one and Horse with Lee. I shared my story with him, as he shared his with me, and now he's leaving. The sickening brick in the pit of my stomach is appearing and I swallow my sorrow back, focusing instead on West and his plans. "You're going to go straight to her, aren't you?"

"Am I that obvious?"

"You're that in love. You're that full of regret," I point out, kicking his leg with the toe of my sneaker.

He begins to waffle, his resolve for getting his life back already shaky when the reality of actually doing it starts to sink in. As much as I get it, it also makes me angry and I tell him so.

"B. S."

"Excuse me?"

"Don't give me your lame wishy-washy answers, West Rutledge. I've been there. Done that. Remember?"

He rubs at his forehead before pulling out a thick, heavy manila envelope and handing it to me. Scratched across the top in black marker is the name 'Jules'.

"I wrote to her. Every night. Sometimes twice a day. I wrote her songs, letters, and rambling explanations of what I was doing here. I told her about you, about the trees in the courtyard, the posters in the counseling room. So much crap, I'm almost embarrassed by it. Almost…but not."

"Because you love her."

He nods. "Because I love her."

My eyes water at the gesture and I bite my top lip as I turn the envelope in my hands.

"I have a favor to ask of you?" West resumes packing as he talks. "Will you hold onto those for me?"

Hold onto them? "The letters! Why? You should give them to her. Mail them. This would show her where your heart lies, West. You could prove to her you did it all for her."

"I want to win her back. I don't want to show her all of that pain if I don't have too. I want to get myself together, get started at school, and then go after her. Start fresh."

"Do you doubt her feelings for you?"

"Surprisingly, no." A strange sort of jealousy comes over me at his steadfastness.

Not jealousy over Jules, but over his conviction. Of his readiness to go after his goal. "I envy you," I admit, setting the letters on the bed.

"Ha! You envy me? How many times have you called me out on my crap in the past few weeks? What is it you envy, exactly?"

"All of it. You've never faltered when it comes to how you feel about Jules. Not really. You've tried to throw a bunch of 'I don't know' and 'what if it wasn't real' crap at me, but we both know that's exactly what it was. Crap. You're in love with her, and you've made it clear that you believe she was in love you. Most days I struggle to believe I deserve to live, I envy you for knowing it."

"Dani." He pushes my legs aside, sitting on the edge of the bed, and I know he's not happy with what I said.

"Sorry," I apologize with a shrug. His imminent departure is bringing me down. I wonder if there will ever be a day when moments such as these will merely make me sad, like a normal person. *I so long to be a normal person.*

"You know what? If it weren't for you, I wouldn't be here. You're going to figure it out, too."

I'm not sure if I believe him, so I change the subject again. "Why don't I help you finish packing before we go down to dinner?"

We eat our last meal together, sitting outside and talking about his school and football and everything he has coming up, and I wait for the inevitable break in the damn. It's coming, I know I won't be able to stop it from happening, and when we return to his room before lights out so I can grab his envelope of letters, it happens. I crack and West pulls me into a hug.

"Win her back and live happily ever after for me. Okay?" I murmur, my forehead pressing against his chest. It's the closest physical contact I've made with anyone, other than my grandparents, since Luke. Seven months since I've been hugged. The reminder makes me needy, and I lean my head on him, grasping the sides of his shirt as I seek comfort the way a crying infant would. When his hands rub my upper arms it's a wonderful moment. I feel comforted by someone who cares, someone who expects nothing from me, and I come to an understanding as to why our friendship has worked where my other relationships have been so hard. There's no pressure. I don't have to be the granddaughter, the old me, the strong girlfriend — I get to be me, all broken apart and messed up and West doesn't care.

I'd planned on heading home soon after West left, but I find myself spending the next few weeks fighting depression again. I don't eat, I don't sleep, I rarely leave my room. I miss him, I miss having a friend. Gram and Gramps visit me on the allotted visitation days, and each time they ask if I'm ready to leave. My answer is no, every time. I've become afraid of myself. It's a no-win situation. If I leave I'm afraid I'll cut and if I stay I'm afraid I'll never find normal.

It's a surprise visit from West, with Jules in tow, that finally convinces me to go home. We sit and chat for a few hours, and I'm so happy for him, that he fought and won. I allow myself to wish out loud as we're saying good-bye. "I want that someday."

"You'll get it, you need to take care of you first," he says, repeating my own advice from the day we met,as he gives me one last hug.

Once they're gone I allow myself a good measure of self-pity and then I dream. I dream about finding a love, my own personal fairy tale, like West and Jules have found. *Luke?* His name flits in and out of my mind.

I wonder how he is and if he was my 'Jules' and I let him get away. It's rather silly to think considering he's the one who gave up, but then again how could I blame him. He gave me the same advice I gave West. The advice West turned around and gave back to me. Get better first. I gave West a hard time about getting out there and being brave when it was his time to leave Crestdale. Now it's my turn. I set a hard check-out date of Thanksgiving. I'll spend the holidays at home, I tell myself, my therapists, and my grandparents and we all work together to make that day a reality.

But there's a funny thing about reality. Like the calendar Mom used to keep in our kitchen said, 'Our expectations and our reality do not always match.' Sometimes we have no control over the reality of our lives. I never expected to lose my parents at the age of fifteen, and I never expected what fate planned for me next.

Today's Reality... This is unreal
November 8, 2015

Words are full of power.
'I love you' makes one soar. 'I hate you' can tear out your heart.

The 'hello' of a long awaited beloved's voice may cause your stomach to dance.

The angry shout of a lover's goodbye has the power to squash you as though you're nothing but a bug under their heel.

Words. They hold a special power. A dangerous, deadly power.

The black and white words I read folded in a white envelope addressed to me when I return home from Crestdale after five months? Those words, that news, fill me with despair.

Every. Last. Word. They're a cut, a burn, a break. Each one tearing away at me until there is nothing left. He's dead and it's my fault.

There's nothing left...
Nothing left...
Nothing...

My Reality… The cycle
November 2015 through Present day

My journal has but one entry after November 8, 2015.

Cycle: a set of events or actions that happen again and again in the same order; a repeating series of events or actions

My life is but two cycles. Those I love die and … Cut, heal, cut, heal. It's an endless cycle of crazy I'm on.

Today's Reality… I'm to blame, as usual
January 15, 2018

"Danica?"

The familiar voice jolts me from the past and I twist around to see a small blond striding my way. Her large sunglasses cover half her face as she stops, standing over me. Confused by her sudden presence, I mumble, "What are you doing here?"

"You called me. This morning, remember? Are you all right?" Her voice is full of trepidation as she kneels beside me on the slope.

"I… " My mouth shuts, and I think for a moment. The moisture, clinging to the shaded ground on the side of the road from the storm three days ago, has seeped into the seat of my jeans making my rear wet. "I'm cold," I remark absently as my gaze shifts back to the open space ahead of me.

She sniffs, her gloved hand touching my arm lightly as she speaks. "Of course you are. It's wet, and it's getting chilly now that the sun's going down. Why don't we get some coffee?"

"The sun's going down?" I focus on the sky then, noticing the pink and orange brilliance on the horizon and I'm stunned. I've sat here for hours and my mind clears. "Oh my gosh, I was supposed to meet you. I'm so sorry."

She shrugs, shaking her head, "No harm done."

Scampering to my feet, I wipe at my wet jeans as I study her from lowered lashes. She's roughly my height and frame, judging by the way her oversized cardigan swallows her. Her hair's the kind of blond you get in a box, a bit too platinum for my taste, but not trashy.

This is Courtney Johnson. This is the girl I unknowingly stole Luke from.

After extending my apologies, again, for the way she found me, I follow her to the same coffee shop I'd stopped in yesterday. My mind works the entire way there. This morning I'd awakened with two goals:

One: Stop by the crash site.

Two: Stop by the cemetery to see both my parents and his grave.

I'd called Courtney, hoping she'd be willing to bring me to the cemetery since I didn't know where his plot was. She didn't owe me anything, so it was surprising she'd agreed without any begging on my part.

I ride around the shopping center looking for a parking spot and replaying the last few hours in my mind. Once I'd found the courage to make it to Burkeside Avenue I'd gone numb. Leaving my car along the side of the road, almost exactly where Luke and Courtney spun out that cold December night, I crossed over to where I'd lost control and landed. There was nothing there. Nothing to prove that five years ago two people died in this spot. No skid marks, no charred grass where the flames licked at the ground, where they'd licked at my body. Nothing. Anger bubbled up, making my stomach churn at the serene site along the grassy embankment. I'd seen entire memorials erected at crash sites along the interstates on my drive from Texas to North Carolina, yet there was nothing for my parents. In that moment, I sank to the ground, overcome by the feeling of loss this place awoke within me. My parents, two caring, beautiful, vibrant people, died here.

No, I thought, pulling my knees to my chest as I sat in the wet grass. *Four people lost their lives because of that night. My parents died at the scene, I lost myself, and the fourth? He was collateral damage. Luke.*

He was my hero that night and became everyone else's hero after. In the end, being a hero cost him his life.

Another death I blame myself for.

New Reality… of all the people, I run into you.

We sit at a small table while we wait for our drink orders. Courtney swipes at her phone, her thumbs flying over the screen as she sends a message to someone, and I excuse myself to wash up. The lines of my palms are covered in dirt. I use the facilities and splash lukewarm water on my pale face. I'm a wreck, tear tracks streaking my face, dirt smudged across my right cheek. Flipping my head upside down, I shake out my hair to give it life before I slick some coral gloss across my lips. Taking a page from the movies, I pinch my cheeks to give them color and return to the table where Courtney waits, my coffee now sitting at my spot.

"Feel better?" Her hands are wrapped around her drink and I notice her perfect manicure. Deep red polish, squared off nails. I tuck my free hand in my lap under the table to hide my neglected fingers as I nod and take a cautious sip of my hot beverage. "Hope you don't mind I ordered a bite. I haven't eaten since breakfast," she says as she cuts some sort of pastry pizza looking thing. I nod, I could eat too, but somehow I'm not hungry.

"That was your first time at the site? Since it happened?"

I nod.

She hesitates before asking another question, "Do you not have anyone here who could have gone with you?"

Taking a slow sip of my drink, I glance around the shop before answering. "I haven't talked to anyone here since I left." I cough, clearing my throat. "Um, I was pretty withdrawn for a while."

It's her turn to nod. Her lips curve upwards and I get the feeling she knows all about me by the look on her face. "He told me about you," she confirms, licking her lips and leaning forward in her chair. "Not right away, of course, but eventually. How have you been? I know it's not my business and yet, I feel as though it is, we're connected by everything… that's happened." Her eyes shimmer as they water.

"It's okay, we are connected. I'm okay. I'm not sure if I'll ever be healed, not one hundred percent, but I'm okay."

"I'm sorry I was so hard on you that night. When he called you drunk… it wasn't my place. I'm surprised you called me today, considering."

"Honestly, Courtney, I don't know what to say," I admit as I watch her eat.

"He was never the same after he came back from that trip to see you."
My heart constricts. "He came to see me in March, what — two months
after he saw you, and told me we should date again. Told me how stupid
we were being by always fighting and how it was time we grew up." She
shakes her head, a small sad smile on her face. "I think he wanted me
back more because he didn't want to be alone than because he loved me,
and because he felt helpless after what happened with you. Of course at
the time he didn't tell me about being with you. That came later."

I'm barely able to get the next question out. "So did you two get back
together?"

"Oh, no way. I'm not that dumb or blind. I knew he'd been up to
something although I didn't know what. We became friends again
though, or I mean we started hanging out again and talking. We were
never not friends. The day after he made that call to you he broke down
and told me everything."

The image of Luke running from me into Courtney's arms turned my
stomach although I knew that wasn't her intention for telling me this
new fact. Being the person who might have kept them apart shoots pains
of guilt through me. That familiar call for release tickles the backside of
my brain as I add this new addition to my list of sins. My hand squeezes
the coffee cup I'm holding.

"Courtney, I'm so sorry. I hate myself knowing if I'd stayed away, you
two could have possibly been happy together, you could have stayed
together."

"Oh please, no." Her hand stretches across the table to settle on my
sleeve. "Don't blame yourself. Luke and I were always on and off.
Neither of us were good to each other for long."

"Maybe that was my fault, though. Maybe if I…"

She refuses my apologies. "If anything you gave him direction and I
thank you for that. Saving you that night changed him."

"And killed him."

"No, the job killed him. He died doing what he loved. The rush he
got when he ran into a burning building, or when he pulled someone to
safety… he once told me it was better than sex. He loved it. He saved
three lives in that fire, he was the hero he longed to be. Don't blame
yourself for what happened to him. Please. He cared about you, Danica.
I realized it the night he called you drunk. He wanted you back, but he
was scared for you, knowing you weren't ready for anything serious. He

said it was poor timing and that maybe someday things would fall into place."

I want to believe her, I want to think of Luke and pretend that somehow I'd been good for him in the long run, but all I can see is his beautiful face and his pale eyes staring into mine. I see the laughter on his face as he forced me behind the wheel again for the first time since the wreck and the way passion darkened his features the one night we spent together. He should be here. Standing, I remove my bag from the back of my chair, throwing it over my head. "I need to run."

"Danica… "

"I'm sorry," I tell her over my shoulder as I rush out of the coffee shop.

Heaven help me, my eyes fixated on the knife she'd used to eat with while we were talking. Maybe coming to North Carolina was a terrible idea?

Rushing from the coffee shop, I push the door open and run smack dab into a group of girls. *What is it with this place and run-ins?*

"So sorry," I mutter, dancing back and forth with the small girl in front of me as we try to pass one another.

There's an audible gasp in front of me and the girl stops. "Oh my… Dani?"

I knew if I stayed in Charlotte or Grove Pointe for longer than a few days I was bound to run into someone. I'm not naive enough to think I could get away scot-free, hopeful, but not expecting it. However, the face staring at me when I look up isn't one I'd anticipated seeing.

"Kady?" The beautiful teen in front of me is the perfect female version of her brother.

"What are you…" she breaks off, throwing her arms around my neck and I stumble back at the force behind it. "You're here, I can't believe it."

My arms go around her as my shock wears off and I take a peek around at her friends who are all watching our reunion curiously as I sniff back the tears my conversation with Courtney brought to my eyes.

"Please tell me you're back for good, are you?" she asks, her eyes bright with excitement.

I have no idea what to say to her. How am I so awkward at this? "Uh, I don't honestly know what my plans are at this moment."

Her eyes narrow on me now that we're standing face to face. "Are you crying?" She looks behind me at the coffee shop and back at me.

"Oh, it's nothing. A reunion with an old friend," I lie, taking her hand in mine as I plaster on a fake smile. "My goodness, you're so grown up, how are you?"

"Why don't you guys go on in, I'll be there in a minute?" Kady suggests to her friends with a nod.

As the door opens I see Courtney sitting at the table, she's talking animatedly on the phone and I want to get away before she comes after me. I know running wasn't the smartest thing to do and now that I'm outside in the fresh air, my head is clearing and I'm feeling guilty. There's barely any light in the sky now and I shiver at how cold the air has turned as I give Kady another smile.

"It's been four years since we saw you last, five since you left... I suppose you could say I grew up," she says, her light brows arching over her pretty eyes. "Does my mom know you're here, or Jonah?" she asks before correcting herself. "Of course they don't."

"I'm sorry, it was honestly a last minute decision. I had something I needed to do and... "

"And you'd no intention of calling any of us. Did you?"

My mouth goes dry as she turns bitter. She used to worship me, following Jonah and I around and looking up to us since we're older. Now she looks bored and angry. "I'm not sure," I admit and she moves around me, ready to open the door and leave me standing there. "Kadence, wait."

"What? Why should I wait, look we can pretend we never saw each other, Dani. You can go on and I won't utter a word to my parents, and especially not my brother, you've hurt them enough. You look well, I hope you are."

"I'm not sure if I can stay," I say to her back as her hand pulls on the ornate door handle. "I came here to make amends, but I'm not sure if I can. It's harder than I thought it would be."

"So run away then," she says over her shoulder with disdain, "again."

The heat rushes out of the coffee shop as Kadence walks in, her long hair swirling around her shoulders as she leaves me standing there. *Run,* my head tells me, but I hesitate, Kadence's words swirling around. Run, again. I came here to stop running. I'm going to stop running. *Stop. Running.*

The thought is loud and clear and it's not doubt speaking in my head. It's West and Luke, Lee and Jackie, my doctors and the other patients I've met over the past few years. It's Gram and Gramps who took me in and tried to make me whole again. It's me — Dani. The one who celebrated her twenty-first birthday a few days ago by making a vow to get back her fairy tale life. To get any life back.

Stop. Running.

My fingers touch and then wrap around the door handle firmly. I pull the glass door open and am assaulted by the heat and coffee scent as I step inside. It's as though I'm standing there naked, the way people glance up and look at me, and I want to back right out of that door, but I don't. I stand there. I stop running, and then everything goes back to normal. Kadence and her friends are standing by the counter laughing loudly as they each talk over the other, except for Kadence. She's stands there, her eyes narrowing on me before she looks away.

Ignoring her for the time being I straighten my shoulders, take a breath, and walk back to Courtney, sliding down into the chair I'd hastily vacated a few minutes earlier.

She gapes at me, hanging up her phone with a quick 'I'll call you back' and leans back waiting.

"I'm sorry," I admit. I push at the cup I'd left sitting there when I got up the first time and take the plunge. "Sometimes it gets to be too much. I'm a work in progress, you know. The cutting was an easy stress reliever, so without it now I panic. I shouldn't have walked away, especially since you were kind enough to meet me."

She nods, her face understanding and soft and so pretty. I never noticed that before. Luke showed me a picture of her once after he'd first broken up with her and left school, it was a grainy cell phone shot and I'm glad it was because I probably would have hated her so much more if I'd realized how pretty she is in person.

"I don't know what I can and can't say to you," she confesses, it's almost a whisper, as though she's trying not to scare me away again.

"You can say anything," I tell her, dismayed when she disagrees.

"We both loved, or cared deeply for, the same guy. At the same time," she tells me needlessly. "He cared about you and I don't want to say anything to hurt you or make you feel vulnerable again, but I think we could be friends. If you want, of course. I'd be happy to take you to the cemetery and if you want to talk about anything with me, about Luke or about the night of the accident, I want you to know I'm here."

My eyes water at her generosity. Thinking of the two times I spoke to her on the phone before Luke's death I ask, "You were so angry with me back then, why don't you hate me anymore?"

"I was a twenty-one year old girl who was jealous. I was worried about Luke, he always acted so impulsively and I was afraid he'd ruin his future…" I grimace. *Didn't he though? He chose a career that killed him too soon.*

"But more than that I was jealous you held his attention so easily. You didn't live here and he'd never truly met you, but what he felt for you was so real. He was never one for commitments."

I smile at the wry look on her face. "He told me it was fate that put us together. It seemed so romantic at the time, but when he died… I took his words and let myself think I killed him. I killed him, but he saved me."

For the second time, Courtney reaches across the table and touches my hand. "You didn't kill him. Did you know he wanted to go into the military straight out of school? The Marines. His parents talked him into school first. He talked about joining the police before, too. He wanted to be dangerous, to do dangerous things. I firmly believe he would have done it with or without you."

A girly screech across the coffee shop steals my attention and I look up, confirming Kadence and her friends haven't left. They've moved to the chairs near the front door and are talking to two boys with floppy hair and beanies. One reaches out and tugs on Kadence's hair in a noted intimate way and I'm thrown into turmoil. Simultaneously jealous of the carefree teenage life she's so lucky to have and protective of this girl who was barely past playing with Barbies when I left town.

"Friends of yours?" Courtney asks, evidently following my eyes.

"Yeah kinda, one of them is. Family friends."

"She's been casting glances at us since you walked back in."

"I abandoned them when I left Grove Pointe. I don't know how to make it right," I confess.

"Can I give you advice? As a friend?" Biting my lower lip, I nod. "Start with I'm sorry."

Newer Reality… I'm sorry

"Kadence?"

Getting up and walking to the front of the store was difficult. Interrupting the party of five and having four pairs of eyes looking me over quizzically? That was darn right embarrassing. The last set of eyes, Kadence's, barely register concern as I stand beside her.

"Can I speak to you for a moment?" I beg, "Please?"

She eyes me wearily, her fingers lifting to the boy by her side and touching his side in a way that silently tells him to release his hold on her hair. The moment he does she stands and moves from the table. Her head swivels around, as though she's looking for a private spot before she pushes on the front door, exiting and looking over her shoulder at me. I follow her out into the cold night air.

"I assumed you would want privacy," she says, turning on me and tugging her jacket closed over her chest.

"I'm sorry. I know you're disappointed in…"

"Disappointed?" she asks interrupting me.

I clarify. "Or mad."

She laughs under her breath, shaking her head. "I'm not mad or disappointed. None of us are. Well, Jonah maybe, but my parents were hurt. I was hurt. We missed you. Now you show up in town and, from what you said earlier, you might have left town again without a word if I hadn't spotted you." Folding her arms over her chest, she sighs, "That hurts."

"I didn't mean to hurt any of you."

"That doesn't make it better."

I get the picture. I can see it in her body language, she's unforgiving and I should go. "Okay, I understand. It was good to see you, Kady," I tell her backing away. I'm stuck. All I want to do is run away again, but I didn't say goodbye to Courtney and I hate the idea of walking out on her again after she was so kind. I dig in my bag, deciding to call Courtney from the car to explain as I step into the street without looking at Kadence again. I'm halfway to my car when her voice shouts behind me.

"I'd never hear the end of it if I told them I saw you and didn't invite you to dinner."

Time stops. "Really?" My pulse races at the thought of finally confronting the Halls.

She nods. The boy she was with inside opens the door behind her and she shrugs him off, jogging my way. "I said we were hurt, that doesn't mean you get to walk away again."

Laughter bubbles up filling my chest and I smile, pulling Kadence in for hug. "Can you drive? It's been a rough day and I'm honestly not sure if I can force myself by there again today." I admit as she hugs me as fiercely as I'm hugging her.

Kadence came with a friend, so she runs into the shop to tell them she's leaving and I text Courtney apologizing for the wasted day and thanking her for her help as I wait. Her repeated offer of friendship gives me something to look forward to if I decide to stay and I tell her I'll be in touch. And I will be, regardless of my long term plans, I need the closure of going to Luke's grave. I've yet to say goodbye to my hero.

"Should you call your parents first, let them know I'm here?" I ask as Kadence drives my vehicle on the back roads to her house. Somehow, without my saying, she understood my earlier comment about going by 'there' again. So we drive into her neighborhood the way my old school bus used to. Jonah and I never took the bus, our mothers carpooled, but sometimes we would end up behind the bus and kids we knew would press their faces into the glass as we followed them home. I recall those days so clearly now, especially being back in Grove Pointe. While I was in Texas some of my happy memories faded away, replaced by the unhappy ones instead. The wreck, the fire, the pain — those were the things that stood out. Now, as I sit next to Kadence, I'm finding the good things aren't so terrifying to remember anymore.

"So, you're a senior?" I go for the obvious, dip my toes into the water and see what I can stand.

"Yeah. Can you believe it?"

"Honestly? No," I tell her as a vision of a little girl with pigtails and ponies runs through my mind. "Do you have college plans, any acceptance letters?"

"The family tradition, UNC, most likely."

We turn onto their street and I realize we never placed a warning call to her parents. I contemplate how quickly I can snatch my keys from her hand and jump in the driver's seat as she parks and turns the engine off.

"C'mon," she coaxes, popping the door open. I'm frozen. My eyes fixated on the warm light pouring out through the front windows onto the front lawn. The house is the same, of course, but different. It's no longer my home away from home, the place I could walk into without knocking, the place where warm cookies would always be awaiting my arrival. There's a tap on the window next to my face and I turn to see Kadence standing outside my door, hands on her hips. Taking a long deep breath, I open the door and join her, walking a step behind all the way to the front door.

"Momma?" she yells as she pulls her keys from the front lock, motioning for me to enter behind her.

The scent of childhood hits me the instant I walk in. Heat, food, and cinnamon spice mix together welcoming me home. Nothing's changed about their foyer — it's the same two story entrance, with the large, black iron chandelier hanging overhead, and grand staircase turning up to the second level. Candlestick lamps and fresh flowers adorn the table opposite the door as they always have. I recall the ribbing mom would give my dad all the time about how Mr. Ron bought Ms. Virginia fresh flowers each week for her foyer vase. "Where are my weekly fresh flowers?" she'd tease and I wondered if Mr. Ron got an earful from all of the other men whose wives used his romantic gesture against their husbands.

"She's on the phone upstairs... " Mr. Ron appears at the top of the stair case tugging at the sweatshirt he's pulling on. His right foot steps down one step before he stops dead in his tracks, looking at me as though he's seen a ghost.

You can do this, I remind myself squaring my shoulders and raising my gaze to his and forcing a smile onto my nervous lips. Words fail him, his mouth opens and closes several times before he descends the staircase. I catch Kadence's blonde hair move out of the corner of my eye, her hand lifting out as a warning, but it's subtle. So subtle I imagine she didn't expect me to see it and when Mr. Ron finally speaks I realize he knew exactly what it meant. *Take it easy on her, Dad, she's as skittish as a cat in a room full of rocking chairs.*

"Kady brings home friends quite often, so we're used to it, but this is a surprise," he says.

"A welcome one, I hope?" I manage, impressed by my own composure.

His head moves from side to side, slowly, and for one moment I expect him to say 'no, not at all' instead he opens his arms and steps closer. "Ah, honey... an extremely welcome one."

Like the prodigal son, I find myself swept into a warm, loving embrace. No matter how far I went or how much hurt I caused, I find myself being held by the man whom I once regarded as a second father to me.

"Welcome back, kiddo," he teases into my hair, kissing the top of my head.

We pull apart, his arm slung over my shoulder as he steers me into the kitchen while Kadence runs up the stairs. Pulling out a stool at the counter he tells me to sit while he pours us some iced tea. The kitchen is brimming with the scent of Italian food and Mr. Ron opens the oven door, checking whatever dish is baking.

"You staying for dinner? It's Italian night," he offers, wagging his brows my way, and I nod. I'm waiting for the questions. For the bottom to drop out and someone to be angry the way Kadence was — I'm waiting for Ms. Virginia to appear and flip out on me.

"Since I know my daughter is horrible at keeping secrets I imagine you didn't plan this trip with her, so how in the world did you end up at our door tonight?" His voice is curious, but maintains its light tone.

"It was somewhat of a fluke. I ran into her, literally," I laugh, explaining the run-in at the coffee shop. I'm in the middle of telling him about my semi-cross country drive to North Carolina when Ms. Virginia appears.

"I thought for sure my daughter was lying when she told me you were in this kitchen and yet here you are," she says breathlessly. Her bottom lip is trembling, I can see it from across the room. Her hands are clasped at her waist, demurely, and her head tilts to one side as she gapes at me, sending my emotions into overdrive. I'm sad, happy, scared, and confused all at once. My scars itch, my bravery wavers, my eyes water as my mouth twitches into a smile. I'm a full-blown mess and yet I'm perfectly happy with it all. For the first time in years I sense as though I'm where I was intended to be.

"Surprise?" I offer with a shrug, breaking the tension as I stand.

"The best surprise ever," Ms. Virginia nods, hurrying across the kitchen and pulling me into an embrace.

"I hate breaking up the party, but I'm starving," Kadence complains after a while and Ms. Virginia releases me reluctantly, sending her daughter a disgusted glance.

The conversation remains light over dinner. I point out the changes I've noticed around Grove Pointe and Mr. Ron bemoans the loss of 'his country living' to the masses. Kady fills me in on the high school rivalries and my old teachers. She confirms the hot spots are all the same. Movies, shopping, coffee shops all rank high in the life of teenage girls. *Good to know life hasn't changed that much in five years.*

"So, how long are you here for?"

I set my fork down, giving Ms. Virginia my undivided attention. I knew the question wouldn't stay hidden forever. Thinking of my call this morning with Gram explaining my plans I repeat them to the Halls. "Truthfully, I'm not sure. I kinda ran away from home. So to speak," I confess. I give them the basics — how I left Texas a few days ago without a word to my grandparents. How I'm here to find some closure with 'things'. How my birthday opened my eyes to a few truths.

"You'll stay here," Ms. Virginia suggests when I mention the hotel.

"What? No, that's kind of you, but I can't."

"I insist. You're not staying at a hotel, that's expensive and can't be comfortable. I saw the way you ate your dinner. You're obviously tired of fast food." Real food does sweeten the deal, but I hesitate accepting.

"You know she's going to nag until she gets her way," Kady laughs, standing and clearing our plates. Mr. Ron nods and I'm outnumbered.

"I'm not sure how long I'll stay. I don't have a long term plan," I repeat, making sure they know how uncertain everything is where I'm concerned.

"Danica, this is your home. It's always been your home, you'll always be welcome," Ms. Virginia says.

"And Jonah?" My voice wobbles at the mere passing of his name over my lips. His name causes varying reactions from his family, too. It's Kadence who stirs first, going back to the dishes.

"Hun, he's at school and we're not expecting him home until Spring Break. We could not tell him you're here if that'll help you get adjusted. It'd give you time to figure out your plans, too," says Mr. Ron.

"No. I'll call him, tell him you're here. He'll be… fine," Kadence says confidently, but I don't miss the pointed look she gives her parents. "I mean if you're going to stay for a little while."

Their faces are so eager I find my resistance breaking down, but I hesitate. There are unresolved issues standing in my way and I struggle with a way to bring them up. *Just say it,* my mother's voice whispers in my ear.

"I feel as though I should call Gram and see what she thinks," I admit, trying to gauge their reaction. There was something between them and my grandparents three years ago, I need to know why the animosity arose.

Instead of anything helpful, Ms. Virginia smiles politely, "Of course. You should let them know. Give them a call and then Kady and I can drive over to the hotel with you and get your things."

Agreeing, I step into the front room and dial Gram. My eyes wander over the framed pictures randomly placed in the wall of bookcases framing the room. I'm admiring Jonah's graduation shot when she answers.

"Hi, Gram, how are you?"

"Danica? I didn't expect you to call me again after this morning."

I sigh heavily, "I know. I'm sorry I was a bit short with you. I realize you were worried."

"You left a cryptic note and didn't call me for four days, of course we were worried. You're an adult now, but we will always worry, hun."

"I know," I repeat. I regret our argument from our morning conversation. She'd been frantic when she answered the phone, talking about calling police and reporting me missing and accusing me of going off the deep end, as though I were crazy. Her worry, while understandable, was hurtful and I didn't hold back. "As I said this morning, and in my note, I'm fine. I needed to come back to GP. To see Luke and Mom and Dad and... the Halls." I add the Halls name in as though it's a loaded word and wait for the fallout.

"The Halls," she mumbles and I wait.

And wait.

A shaky breath fills the space between us, a shaking, deep breath and the drumming of my heart, that's it.

"Yes, of course you'd want to see them. Have you?" she asks eventually.

"Actually yes, I ate dinner with them tonight." There's no reply so I continue, "And they want me to stay with them."

"For how long?"

Her acceptance is unexpected. "I'm not sure, Gram. I guess until I decide what I want to do. It would be better than a hotel and it would give me a chance to make amends with... with everyone."

"I think that's a lovely idea. The Halls have so many memories of your parents Gramps and I don't have, if you're ready for that. Promise me you'll call Dr. Green if you need to."

"Gram."

"Promise me, Danica. I know I can't hover over you forever, but I will try."

"Ha, okay, I promise to call if I need to."

She thanks me, telling me to call her in a few days once I'm settled to update her.

"Gram," I nearly shout into the line before she can hang up.

"Yes?"

"You know I might not come back to Texas. I may decide to stay here. I need you to know that, to accept that might be the choice I make."

"Yes, hun, we know and we expected it," Gram admits and I bite my lip as tears spring to my eyes. "Everything we did, we did because we loved you, sweetheart. Your grandpa and I love you very, very much."

"I love you both, too. I'll call you in a day or two." Hanging up, I swipe under my eyes, taking deep breaths to compose myself.

"Everything settled?" Ms. Virginia asks, entering the room, and I nod silently. "Good, let's get your things and move you in."

Tonight's Reality... Peppermint gum is all it takes

I t takes roughly an hour to pack my belonging at the hotel, check out, and relocate to the guest room at the Halls. The plush room might as well be a hotel for all its glory. The queen bed is covered in huge down comforters and stacked with pillows you want to sink into. There's a bathroom attached, the towels fluffier and fresher than anything my hotel could offer.

"All I need is a mini fridge and I'll never have to leave," I tease as Ms. Virginia opens the closet, verifying there are hangers for my clothing.

"If that's all it will take, I'll send Ron out to grab one now."

"Thank you," I offer, smiling at her joke. "For inviting me to stay, and for not asking too many questions."

Her hand stops on the closet doorknob. "I have many questions, but having you here is more important than the answers. Maybe one day soon we can both ask our questions." She makes the offer in a way that clearly tells me she knows I'm curious too, but her answer is spot on and I nod.

"You're right, the answers aren't as important anymore. I'm here."

"Okay, Mom get out now. Time for girl chat," Kadence orders, leaning against the door frame and interrupting our moment. She's changed into long, baggy pajama pants and a tee shirt. They're covered in red lips and little pink and red 'xoxo' symbols and they make her look more the age I remember her as.

"Okay, I'll let you unpack and you two hang out. You," she says, pointing to Kadence as they swap spots at the doorway. "Don't stay up too late, you have school." Kady rolls her eyes and I smother a laugh. "Dani, if you need laundry done make a pile and I'll find a hamper for you tomorrow."

"Yeah, yeah... the floor is fine. Goodnight, Momma." Kady pushes at Ms. Virginia, shutting the door behind her with a firm 'click' and turns on me with a mischievous grin.

"Do you want to unpack or chill," she asks, throwing herself on the bed.

"Chilling sounds perfect, I can unpack tomorrow," I admit, unzipping a bag and rifling for my pajamas. "Let me clean up and change."

A few minutes later we're both on my bed, make-up free, pajama clad, hair knotted on our heads. This is the way I always expected us to be; sisters sharing life. Kady swipes through the pictures on her phone, showing me her friends, some of them people I remember from before, and giving commentary about each one. She's telling me about their ski trip over Christmas break when a shot of her and Jonah pops up.

"About Jonah," I start as she flips over the shot without explaining it. "How does he truly feel? About me?"

"I dunno." Her shrug is too quick, her answer too flippant to be anything but a front. And she knows I know it.

"Earlier you said you were sad, that your parents were sad. You indicated Jonah was mad, though. Is he? Does he hate me?"

"He could never hate you, Dani. Even when he wanted too, he couldn't do it." There's such a sadness there, in her eyes and voice, and I know I left a mess with Jonah. If Kadence feels this way about it, I imagine he's worse.

"Your parents seemed fine with the idea of keeping him in the dark about my being here. How do you feel about it?" I wonder.

"I think my parents want to protect him in case you don't stay."

"Does he need protecting?"

"Perhaps," she says. She's being infuriatingly unforthcoming with details on his feelings and I can't figure out if I should yell or laugh. "He needs to know you're here, though." Her eyes light up and she rolls to the side, jumping to her feet. "As a matter a fact, I'll call him now."

"Now?" I expected a few days first. "Wait, your parents…"

"Nope, I'm calling him," she giggles and I fall back on the bed.

"I'm going to die, heart attack, panic attack… something," I mumble as my eyes follow her.

"Shhh, you'll be fine. It's you and Jonah. You two have been apart for way too long."

Lord knows she's right. Sitting up, I set my feet on the floor. My brain tells my body to jump up and steal the phone from her hands, but I remain motionless, awaiting my fate.

"Well, hey to you too, bro," Kady laughs into the phone and everything stops. "You'll never guess who stepped foot in our house for the first time in years tonight." Her face is pink with excitement and I wish my ear was pressed to the phone so I could hear Jonah's voice on the other end. She giggles, "Nope, not even close. Think prettier."

Now my cheeks are pink, flushing at her praise. *Pretty.* I haven't felt pretty in years. My soul is too ugly to be pretty.

"No, it's not one of Mom's friends. Why would I call you about that?" Kadence rolls her eyes my way, laughing, and the urge to yank the phone from her hand to end my misery, and his, is overwhelming. "She's staying with us…. okay, okay… it's Dani."

In my mind I picture the Jonah of my childhood. I envision him sitting there expecting a simple phone call from his sister and getting this news instead. I envision the way his hand pushes back his shaggy blond hair, the way his brows scrunch over his eyes. The way he tugs at his lip with his thumb and index finger, how he used to when he was deep in thought.

"No, I'm not kidding. She's standing right here." There's a pause, knocking some of the excitement from Kadence's face before she stretches her hand towards me. "He wants to talk to you."

My breath lodges in my chest. I can't believe this moment is here. My hand shakes as I accept the phone from Kadence. Turning my back, I step closer to the windows overlooking the Hall's picturesque backyard and raise the phone to my ear. My shallow breaths reaching Jonah before I'm able to speak.

"Dani?" he asks and he sounds scared, or nervous. I close my eyes, a wall to hold the tears at bay, as his soft, questioning tone reaches through the line and hugs my heart.

"Hi," I whisper, clutching the phone in both of my hands to keep from dropping it.

"Shi… you're really there? I thought she was screwing with me. Are you… why? Dang it, I…" he rambles, nothing making sense other than the curses he's spewing between words. "Dani? Seriously, you're home?"

I have to chuckle or else I'll break into tears, I can't help it. "Yeah, I'm home."

"Kadence said you're staying there, at my house."

"Your mom kind of insisted, is that okay?"

"Okay? You're joking right? I'm coming home. I'm… "

"Jonah, no," I interrupt. "I'm sure you have classes tomorrow. Don't come home."

"Are you freaking kidding me? It's been four years. I'm coming home. Don't you dare leave, either," he orders. As though my ears have been deaf to everything except Jonah's voice, noise filters in behind him. He's at a party or a bar. A place with people and music and the sound of a girl's voice saying his name. "D, promise me you'll be there."

Surrounded by girls and always busy, that's the Jonah I knew. "I won't leave, I promise."

"Kay, I need to take care of a few things and then I'll be on my way. Let me talk to my sister."

"Sure." I'm lowering the phone to hand it back to Kadence when I hear him call my name through the line.

"Dani?"

"I'm not leaving, Jonah. I will see you tomorrow." I promise, all but throwing the phone at his sister before I break down. Kadence mumbles into the phone as I pace the length of the room, shaking my arms out and resisting the pressure. *You can do this, you CAN do this,* my mother's voice soothes.

"Wow," Kadence murmurs and I swing around on her. She looks shocked as she waves her phone in her hand.

"Wow, what? What did he say?" I ask. In my agitated state I claw at my arm. Kady's eyes flick to my fingers creeping under my long sleeve. She doesn't comment, but I feel the need to explain. "It helps me cope. It's safer than making a real cut, it's okay," I tell her, nodding. I know it's complicated for someone who doesn't understand what cutting is like to grasp the coping skills as good and not bad. Gram used to think my scratching at myself was a precursor to doing the real thing. It isn't. It's similar to a smoker who uses nicotine gum to help quit smoking. It's a safer alternative to control the urges when the urges scream louder than my strength.

"When was the last time?" Kadence asks.

"Jonah first, and then I'll answer some of your questions. Please?" I assure her, dying to know why she's so unnerved after ending her call.

She checks her phone before sitting on the edge of the bed. "He was angry… no that's not the word. Crazy, or better yet out of his mind. I didn't expect him to want to come home right away. Mom and Dad are going to be irritated with him for that."

"Maybe we should call back, force him to stay?" I suggest, not wanting to start trouble before I've spent one night in the house.

"Ha. You're as crazy as he is if you think he's not on his way already. He pretty much made me swear on my first born that I'd make sure you didn't leave. He seemed worried you might run, again.

"I suppose I don't instill much confidence after my last disappearing act, huh?" I mean it as a joke, but I know it's not one. I hurt this family by withdrawing from them. It'll take more than one day to make that up to them.

"I don't blame you, you know. I did at first because I missed you, but after a while, especially as I've grown up, I've slowly come to understand it all. You ran away from the pain, sometimes I wish I could run away from things, too." Kadence gives me a sheepish expression. 'Even the seemingly perfect people have their moments,' it was something Lee told me once.

"I haven't lost control in over a year now. I've slipped, but when I do I catch myself and seek help." Kadence's eyes go wide and I touch her arm for reassurance as I sit beside her. "It's been a few months since I slipped, though. I'm getting better, I'm a work in progress."

She wraps her arms around me, in an awkward side hug as we sit on the edge of the bed. "I'm so glad you're here."

"Me too," I tell her. And I mean it. This won't be easy, but I'm glad to finally be here doing this.

Her phone rings and she glances at the screen, releasing me from her death grip. "Oh, do you mind if I get this?" I shake my head. "I'll see you after school tomorrow, okay? I'll come straight home." I wave as she leaves my room, closing the door behind her.

The moment the door clicks shut my body cries out in protest, it's wiped out. Today has been exhausting between facing the wreck site, Courtney, Kadence, Mr. and Mrs. Hall, and then hearing Jonah's voice. I'd planned on baby steps, but today was a crash course in 'Danica Evans, this is your life'. I unearth my phone charger, finding an outlet and setting my phone on the bedside table before crawling into bed. Sinking down into the mattress, I shift and fluff the pillows until I'm settled. Tomorrow I will see Jonah for the first time in four years. We'll speak for the first time since our final conversation three years ago when I'd all but given up hope of ever seeing him again. I fall asleep attempting to picture Jonah today, but instead I dream of the sixteen year old who pulled me into a dark corner in this very house five years ago and kissed the living daylights out of me.

There are few sounds that send shivers down my spine. A moving love song, the shrill of a first responders sirens, the crushing grind of metal, and now Jonah Hall's voice at two in the morning. The shiver tickles my spine before I'm able to open my eyes. My body reacting to his presence before my brain fully realizes he's there, kneeling by my bedside and saying my name.

197

"D?" he whispers, the sound caressing each nerve in my body, sending them into full awakening.

Shifting in the dark, I search for his shadow as I rub the sleep from my eyes. "Jonah?" The light on his phone pops on, illuminating the immediate area and casting an eerie glow over his face allowing me to see him. "I thought you were being dramatic saying you were on your way tonight," I admit, shifting to sit.

"Nope," his head shakes, a ghost of a grin on his face. "Don't get up... actually can I lay down next to you?" He mutters in the dark. "Damn, is that creepy?"

I laugh, or I aim for a laugh, but it turns into a snort cry as the jolt of him being here hits me. "If it's creepy, then let's be creepy."

His phone dims, then cuts off as he stands, and I follow his shadow as it rounds the room to the other side of the bed. The bed sinks under his weight as he settles beside me, on top of the covers, and I turn to my side facing him. He remains on his back as I lay there silently, counting my breaths and waiting for him to speak.

"I'm pretty sure I called Kady twenty times to make sure you hadn't left," he confesses. "She finally quit answering her phone, so I drove faster."

"I told you I would be here," I remind him, feeling bad for his poor sister.

"Yeah, I wasn't sure that was real." He chuckles low and my stomach dances at the sound.

"I can't believe you came straight here. What time is it?"

He shifts, his foot brushing my leg, as he yawns. "Around two a.m., sorry for waking you, but I couldn't stand it."

His voice sounds huskier than normal, the way he's whispering low and I match it. "Couldn't stand what?"

"I couldn't stand having you under the same roof and not seeing you, if only for a minute."

Carefully, slowly, I lean forward until my forehead touches his shoulder. Nothing else touches, but my forehead to his shoulder and I close my eyes, sinking into the bliss. The soft knit of his shirt is warm on my skin. His scent filling the air around us. Peppermint gum, a heavy woodsy cologne, and the sharpness of alcohol — that's the smell of Jonah Hall at two a.m. That's the scent I want to smell again and again and I know my plans are now set in stone. I'm not going back to Texas. I'm staying in Grove Pointe and I'm winning this boy back.

Today's Reality… Life's a walk in the park
January 16, 2018

Perhaps my last thought early this morning, as I fell asleep next to Jonah, was premature. His early morning wake-up call certainly changes things.

"Poppy, calm down. I told you I'd be gone for a few days." He's rolled to the edge of the bed and is whispering into his phone as if I could sleep through it. "Nooo, I'm not angry at you for last night. I know you drank too much… it's fine. Go to class and I'll call you later. No? Rest then, feel better and… yeah, I'll explain it all later." His heavy sighs and cut off sentences are all the proof I need to know there's a clingy girlfriend on the other end of the line. Sliding to the far edge of the bed, I self-consciously rub my hands over my face and fluff my hair as I sit up. Jonah looks over his shoulder, his face scrunching up as he offers me a silent apology while he ends his call. "I've got to go, talk to you later. Yeah, bye."

"Morning," he says, falling to his back and slinging one arm over his face. "Sorry about that, did I wake you?" He peeks out from under his sleeve and smiles. "Don't answer that, I can see from the look on your face the answers yes," he groans.

I clear my throat. "What time is it?"

He yawns and pushes up to a sitting position next to me. "A little after eight."

"Eight? I thought college students didn't get up until noon," I tease and Jonah laughs under his breath.

"I have an early morning class on Mondays and my alarm was set," he says.

"And your roommate called to complain," I ask, knowing darn well that wasn't his roommate.

"Something like that," he murmurs and I get the idea he'd rather not discuss the call. I change the subject. We have enough heavy stuff to talk about without adding a mysterious girl who happened to have been at his place when his alarm went off. "So, you slept in here, with me, last night. We haven't been allowed to have sleepovers since we were, what? Eight, nine?"

"Yeah… Mom's gonna be pissed," he jokes, his hand reaching out and nudging me gently.

I push him back, laughing as I repeat a long forgotten rule of our childhood. "As long as she knows it's your fault."

"Still trying to play favorites?" he teases and my smile fades.

"I wish." His laughter evaporates as quickly as mine does and we sit there. I tug at the cuffs of my shirt, pulling the sleeves over my palms, effectively hiding my scars. The physical ones. The mental ones are there, though, and when I sneak a glance at Jonah and meet his questioning eyes I crumble inside.

"Dani," he pleads. I shake my head, letting my hair fall around my face. Jonah's hand snakes out and tugs on my shirt, finding my arm and pulling me back with him as he falls to the bed, hauling me into a hug. I'm nestled in the crook of his arm and I hide my face in his chest, content in being held.

"I swear I'm in a constant state of PMS," I attempt to bring levity to the moment. "I go from happy to sad faster than…"

His fingers tangle in the hair at my neck. "Don't make jokes, D. This isn't a joke to me, you're not a joke."

"No jokes, got it," I quip and he huffs, his chest rising and falling against my cheek. "Sorry," I apologize. Pushing away from his chest, I slide off the bed and stand.

"You look good, D," he offers, sitting up and leaning against the headboard. He crosses his legs at the ankles and stares at me intently. *Not unnerving at all, Jonah.*

"You look good too, Ocho," I compliment him, slapping my forehead as I realize what came out of my mouth. "Oh my gosh, that came out of nowhere. I haven't called you that since eighth grade." Spanish I, my favorite class of all time. Jonah and I sat next to each other all year googling Spanish curse words and passing notes while Seniorita Torres' looked the other way, because she loved us and we aced every test despite our goofing off.

"Dang, I miss those days. Middle school was a cake walk." A response isn't necessary. I'd go back to middle school in a heartbeat. We both know this and I'm restless standing there. It was one thing to play nice with his parents and Kady last night, walking on eggshells. I can't handle that with Jonah, though. If I'm going to do this, stay here, we need to get everything out. Now. I brace myself for what's to come. "Are we going to do the memory lane thing or are we going to get real now?"

"Well, okay then… pleasantries over," he says sardonically and I'm spared anything more by the knock at the door.

"You two hungry?" You two? So his presence in my room has been noted by his mother. Fabulous. I yank the door open quickly, to ease her mind more than my own, and she straightens, startled.

"Good morning, sweetie," she says to me as she eyes my appearance. "Jonah."

"Mother," he mocks her tone, a smug smile on his handsome face.

"Imagine my surprise this morning when your father woke me on his way out saying your car was in the drive way and you weren't in your bed. There was a moment of concern, as my first thought was perhaps you'd been kidnapped on your way from the car to the front door. But then I thought, what in the world could convince my responsible, studious son to skip his classes and drive three hours in the middle of the night to come home?"

I swallow back a smile as Jonah clasps his hands in his lap and gives his mother his best innocent face. "I can't imagine what would corrupt me so." His playful tone turning my cheeks pink and he winks when I round on him, admiring this flirtatious Jonah. Gosh, he was incorrigible as a teen. As a man, I get the feeling he's downright impossible.

Ms. Virginia shakes her head. "Come down and have breakfast. While it's warm, okay?" She looks between the both of us. I agree immediately and pin Jonah with my gaze, too, studying him for the first time this morning. Something amazing happens to Jonah Hall when he's thoughtful. His face twists to the side, reminding me of a curious puppy, and his right eye narrows as he sucks in his cheek, his lips puckering up. It's impossible to tell if he's being playful or serious with his own brand of smolder. His blond hair sticks up in the most alluring, sexy bed head I've seen, and I wonder how I've spent the last few minutes staring at him without noticing these things.

"We'll be down in a minute," he promises. Ms. Virginia huffs a resigned 'fine' and pats my shoulder as she leaves.

Jonah slides from the bed, meeting me at the door, his shoes dangling from his left hand, phone in the right. "We'll do breakfast with her and pretend everything is great, and then you and I are spending the day together. Got it?"

"Excuse me?" I blink at his mild demand.

He softens. "Sorry, should I say please? We're going to talk. Today. Alone. Mom will steal you all day if I let her and I'm not letting her. Agreed?"

"I get it, agreed."

He leaves, closing the door behind him and, as much as I want to sink back into the bed and hide from an intense conversation with Jonah, I pull out some clothes and jump in the shower instead.

After breakfast, Jonah drags me to a local park. We park in the back of a mostly empty lot and sit there quietly watching the groups of tennis moms on the courts in front of us.

"It's nice out, wanna walk?" he suggests after a few minutes and I agree

He leads me into the woods, following a well-worn bike and walking trail, kicking at the dead leaves as we go. Each kick startles me and after twenty steps I'm ready to turn and run simply to get away from his anger. "Jonah," I finally warn when his next kick sends a hidden rock flying across the path in front of us.

"Where do we start, D?" He toes the ground, stopping and looking at me.

Back to before the accident? My head cries as I shrug. "Where do you want to start?"

"Are you staying? Here, in Grove Pointe?"

"I don't know." I'm completely honest, it's all I can be now. "I'm not sure if there's anything here for me to stick around for."

"I'm here," he offers as he resumes walking, his hands stuffed in the front pocket of the pullover he's wearing.

"You're in Chapel Hill," I remind him. "But, you're right. You, and your family, are here and I don't want to lose you guys again."

Another pile of leaves fly around the ground and I smile inwardly, thankful for the small bit of emotion he's releasing. Each kick of his shows me he's struggling with something and that means he's not indifferent, that means he cares about me. About us.

"Jonah, I'm sorry. I told your sister and now I'm telling you. I'm sorry for blocking y'all out the way I did… especially you."

"Believe it or not, I understood." I challenge his admission and he backtracks. "I mean I understood after a while. I understood you weren't you. You were dealing with so much pain, you couldn't deal with anything else."

My throat burns as I think back. "That last phone call though, the things you said to me. That broke me, Jonah."

"It broke me, too. I've never regretted something more than I did telling you goodbye that day." I nod, picking up a stick and breaking off the little twigs sticking out from the thicker stem as we walk. "Crap, please don't tell me I made you cut." His face pales as the thought hits him and I'm baffled. Does he really not know? My cutting was because of him, it was because of his family, my youth, my loss, my pain. It was because of so many things, and yes he was a part of it. My answer is written all over my face. I know because he turns to face me when I don't answer, and the moment his eyes touch my face, his head shakes in denial. "No, no, no," he argues, storming ahead of me and stopping in front of a tree.

His booted foot kicks at the tree and I tease him, "What did that tree do to you?" His answer is his fist making contact with the bark and a curse-filled shout. *Apparently he doesn't find jokes in serious moments all that humorous.*

"Jonah, geez what the hell?" I shout rushing to his side as he curses and shakes his fist out. "Seriously, are you crazy? Give me that," I yell at him, trying to grab his arm as he fights me. "Quit jumping around and let me look at it," I order, punching his side.

"Damn it, hit a guy when he's down," he mumbles, letting me grasp his fist in my hand. Turning it over, I survey his red knuckles. They're scratched up, a few specks of blood smear his middle finger, but otherwise he's fine.

"You're lucky you didn't break anything, you idiot," I admonished, giving him the fiercest angry face I have.

His face is wreathed in pain and I'm rethinking my diagnosis when my face crashes into his chest and his arms crush me. They're solid bands of steal, welding themselves around my body and locking me in place until I can barely breathe. "I broke you," he whispers harshly.

"No, Jonah… no you didn't. It wasn't your fault. It was all me. I'm solely to blame for what I did." I attempt to pull back so I can force him to hear me out, but he refuses to release his grip.

"I can't blame you, you're the one who was hurt."

"Yeah, you're right. And I did it to myself. I hurt me. I wasn't strong enough to fight the depression. Nobody can take blame for my behavior but me."

"No, I don't agree with that. We could have done more, we should have known…"

"Stop. Jonah, look at me," I order, tilting my head up. "Look at me."

His grip loosens, allowing me to put a few inches between us, and he looks down at me. The pain on his face makes me want to cry. I hated seeing the pain on my grandparents' faces, I hated seeing it on West's face when he came to see me after Luke's death, and Lee's broken eyes killed me, too. But Jonah, Jonah's pain is different. His pain is mine and mine is his and I'm starting to understand exactly how much hurt he went through when I left. I swallow hard, words escaping me with my new awareness. His head falls forward, his forehead meeting mine, our faces inches apart. His eyes search mine, our shallow breaths mixing as we stand there. One arm releases from my back as his hand slides up the side of my neck and wraps around my nape. My name escapes his lips, a feather light whisper on the wind. "Dani."

I lose myself in the depths of his eyes. I lose myself in the moment, and losing myself feels exactly like being found. For one minute. Then a vibration surrounds us, causing Jonah to jump and me to trip backwards as his arms release me. I stumble on the uneven ground and his hand shoots out to steady me as he produces his phone from his pocket.

"Hey." He answers the phone, his eyes glued to mine before he releases me and turns away, tugging his hand through his hair as he goes.

Kicking at the leaves, much the way he was earlier, I walk ahead to clear my head. *What happened there?* Time erases when I'm standing in front of Jonah. The past five years melt away and it's as though I'm standing in that dark laundry room again, ready to leap into a relationship with him. I'm ready… but I'm not. I can't be. We need to find our way back to friendship, back to the us we were before. *Don't we?*

"I'm not sure… I might stay a couple of days. Yeah, if the guys don't mind, stay. It's fine, I'll shoot him a text and let him know. Poppy, it's fine." Jonah's voice reaches me and I speed up to get away from his conversation. His tone is strangely patronizing and I find myself overly curious about this Poppy.

"D! Hold up, we're going to the left." I stop, looking at the path and realizing I'm at a fork in the trail. Per Jonah's shout I turn left, he jogs to catch up.

"Poppy, I need to go. I know, I'm sorry I'll talk to you later, okay?" His eyes roll and he pulls his phone away from his face looking at the screen.

"Guess she didn't care for your apology," I snap against my better judgment. *Stay out of it, Dani,* my head yells at me. He shrugs and it's infuriatingly uninformative and I tell myself I'm stupid for prying, for getting into this conversation. Inhaling and exhaling, I push the hair out of my face. "So, she's your girlfriend?"

No reply.

"Bed buddy? Friends with benefits, latest conquest in a long string of many?" He doesn't crack and I turn walking backwards. Again, turning to humor to get my answers, I raise my arms beseechingly and dramatically, "Come on, help a girl out. Give me the deats."

The tiniest of smiles breaks on his stone face, and he shakes his head, closing his eyes.

"Ha, I saw that. I win. Who's the girl, Hall?"

He stops cold, his face void of emotion again. "Wow, you're a piece of work."

"I... what?" I'm perplexed.

He chuckles under his breath, it's not a humorous laugh, but a disgusted irritated one. "We were this close to something happening back there," he reminds me, holding his thumb and index finger up, as though I need the visual aid.

"Uh, yeah. And then Poppy called," I drawl, making her name sound dirty and ridiculous. "What kind of name is Poppy anyway? Couldn't find a good Rose or Daisy?" *Oh. My. Gosh, I'm lame. That was a horrible jab.* Jonah's not amused and I resume walking, pulling the collar of my jacket up as a cool wind whistles through the trees around us. "I don't need you feeling guilty on my behalf, Jonah."

"I don't feel..."

I shoot lasers at him, now it's my turn to laugh. "B.S. You do feel guilty. If I'm going to stick around for any length of time, you need to stop. Let it go, no more punching trees or asking if what I did was because of you. Okay?" I don't allow him time to answer, but instead pick up my pace, racing through the trail now. He remains behind me the rest of our walk and it's not until we've circled back to the parking lot that he speaks again.

"What did you do? What have you been doing for the past three years?" he asks.

Every time I look at him I see a different guy. One moment he's this sexy college guy I barely know and the next, he's the Jonah from my past. The Jonah who knew all my secrets once upon a time. I'm not sure how to reconcile the two. The innocent boy and the alluring man.

"No guilt, D. I just want to know."

Maybe this is how we move on. Instead of hiding my past I share it with the people closest to me. My therapists always believed in sharing, in opening up. That's what group meetings were for. It's the mantra behind AA and other group step programs. You have to be honest with yourself and oftentimes to be honest with yourself you have to be honest with those around you. "Okay," I glance around, spotting the picnic tables by an empty playground. "You should know. You should understand what life's been like for me."

Today's reality… You didn't really want to know everything, did you?
January 16, 2018

Sitting on top of the table, I cross my legs, picking at the frayed edge of my jeans. "What do you want to know?"

"Everything."

"It's not a pretty picture. It's still not a pretty picture. You need to know that now, because if you can't handle it, then… "

"I can handle it," he tells me, his eyes meeting mine as he takes my hand, his thumb rubbing my palm.

Perhaps I mean to shock him. Test him now before I bother opening all of the deep, dark corridors of my broken soul to him. I'm not sure what I'm thinking, but I take my free hand and push up the sleeve covering the arm he's holding. And I wait. He saw my scars once, four years ago, when there were seven. Now? There's more than seven. Infinitely more than seven, and if he checked my other arm he would find the same thing. Some are light and barely noticeable, while others are pink and ugly with scar tissue because I'd gone too deep, hurt too much.

"Those don't include the ones on my thighs, or my waist." Jonah resembles a beaten man each time I speak. As though each revelation is a punch to his gut. "Or my collar. It was, or is, an addiction."

"Is?" he asks weakly, his eyes remaining on my arm.

"Addiction never goes away, not completely. It's the same as an alcoholic or drug addict. A bad memory can trigger the need, a sad day… too many things can make me want to cut."

"You're saying this to scare me away, aren't you?" His eyes shift to my face and I see it there. He's challenging me, daring me to tell him that's my reason for confiding in him.

"Partially," I admit, "but more than that, I've needed to fix things with you for a long time and this is the only way I know how."

His careful touch over my scars distract me and he has to speak first to pull me from the spell he's weaving. "So why did you cut? Did you figure it out? I mean… "

"I know what you mean. I think it was about feeling alive, or proving to myself that I was alive. I dunno, that's not exactly right because in the beginning… it was different. It changed as I got deeper and deeper into my depression and deeper into the need for that release. The reason evolved and soon 'the why' didn't matter anymore. What mattered was how it made me feel at the time. The pressure cutting released. The high when I was done." Closing my eyes, I focus on the tips of his fingers grazing my forearm and I continue. "I was angry I lived. I was full of so much guilt. I kept thinking if Dad were driving, or Mom, they would have missed Luke's car. They would have been able to control the vehicle better than I did. I hit the gas. Did you know that? That's the truth of what happened. Somehow in all of the confusion and panic my foot hit the gas instead of the brake. It was my fault. Nobody knows I know. I overheard the officers talking with my grandparents at the hospital about it. Everyone thought I was out most of the time I was there those first few days, I heard things, things I wish I hadn't. Anyway, I didn't think I deserved to live. For a few months the pain from healing, the skin graphs and debridement of the burns, they served as my punishment. Pulling away from everyone did, too. But it wasn't enough. Not for long."

"So you cut," he acknowledges softly and I nod. "You mentioned Luke. That's the name of the guy in the other car?" His brows raise in question. *A sharp pain shoots through my temple at my stupidity for mentioning Luke right now.* "Aannddd, I'm going to assume that's a yes by the look on your face," he says suspiciously. "What am I missing?"

The idea of keeping Luke a complete secret has gone through my mind several times. There's no need for anybody to know about our relationship, it's private. Personal. But when I open my eyes and I see Jonah waiting for the truth, I know I can't keep myself hidden forever. Luke is part of my scars. "After you left Texas, I searched him out."

Jonah's hand slips away from mine. "The guy in the other car, Luke?"

"Yes. He'd left a teddy bear and a letter at the hospital after the wreck. He'd stopped by hoping to apologize and to check on me. We never met, but I called him a few weeks after you left. We started texting, you know connecting." Jonah looks away, his entire demeanor changing the more I reveal. "You told me to talk to someone, so I did. He was broken too, having a hard time with his part in the accident... eventually we started a relationship."

"Whoa, wait. You had a relationship with the guy who made you wreck that night, but you cut me out for years?"

"There's a huge difference between you and Luke, Jonah." *Big mistake.*

Jonah flies off the table so quickly he'd make Superman proud. Frustration is written all over his face as he snaps at me. "You bet there is. If it wasn't for him nothing would have happened. Your parents would be alive, you never would have left, things never would've changed."

Maintaining my composure, what little is left of it, I stand too. Hugging myself, I try to reason with him. "That's not fair, you can't blame him, he lost control same as I did."

"Oh, so you can blame yourself, but let's not blame him? Why was he sitting in the middle of the road? Why didn't he move?" He digs the car keys from his pocket. "You know what, I can't do this with you."

"Jonah?" I plead.

He spins on me, his face red, his eyes narrow as he grits his teeth. "What Dani? What do you want from me?" His body shakes with rage, and disbelief. "You've now made it perfectly clear where I stood. You went running to the guy... damn it, the guy... "

"The guy who didn't remind me of everything I'd lost every time I so much as thought of his name," I interrupt, shoving his shoulder to get him to listen to me. "Don't you get it? I didn't cut you out because I didn't care. I cut you out because I cared too much. It hurt too much. I look at you, at Kady or your parents, and all I see is Mom and Dad. I see all the fun times and I couldn't stand it back then. I needed something, someone, else. Luke was there that night, he saw what I saw."

Slowly, he takes two steps back, "Do you know how it feels to hear you say you needed someone else more?" He doesn't allow me time to answer before he backs away, returning to his car. He climbs in, cranking the engine without another word. We drive home in silence, every time I attempt to speak he shakes his head saying 'don't' and eventually he cranks up his radio. An hour later he's driving away, heading back to campus with the excuse of an important class in the morning he'd forgotten he needed to attend and I'm left numb. I expected to get a day or two and instead I got a few hours.

"Have you continued to play?"

I twist around on the piano bench, finding Ms. Virginia walking into the room, a mug in each hand. Nodding, she points me toward the couch along the wall across from the shining piano. "Hot chocolate?" she offers, setting the mugs on the coffee table and taking a seat. It's early afternoon and Kadence isn't home from school yet.

Gliding my fingers across the ivory keys, I stand and pull the cover over them as I answer her initial question about playing. "I do. I stopped for a while, but I started back. I've been writing, too."

Her smile encompasses her entire face as I sit next to her, picking up my mug. The hot chocolate's topped with whipped cream and I'm in heaven when the rich goodness touches my tongue. "What happened with Jonah today?"

"That obvious, huh?" I ask, lowering the mug to my lap and letting the heat warm my stiff fingers wrapped around the porcelain. "There are things, about the past few years, I would prefer to keep to myself." She nods her understanding. "However, I did tell Jonah about a relationship with someone and he was hurt by it."

"Ah, jealousy," she ventures and I almost agree and let it go before I think better of it.

"No, not jealousy. Hurt," I correct her, explaining my relationship with Luke in as few details as possible. "Jonah feels as though I betrayed him and I'm not so sure if I disagree with him," I admit to both myself and her.

"Danica, there's nothing in this world my son wouldn't do for you. He will see reason, give him time."

"Luke caught me cutting. The week he came to Texas I had a meltdown of sorts and he walked in on me cutting. I didn't tell Jonah about this. But he called my grandparents and told them and they picked me up from… from where we were, and I was readmitted that day back into Crestdale. Luke left that day with promises to stick by me and it didn't take but a few hours for him to change his mind." Her shock at Luke's behavior is written on her face, but I shrug it off and press forward. "Did you talk to my grandparents after our last conversation? After I told you to back off."

"I did not. You were adamant and I didn't want to hurt you by forcing anything on you at that point, so we honored your wishes, as difficult as they were."

"No, you don't have to explain. I made my stance clear that day when I told you to back off. I'm so sorry for that. I'm sorry I said you weren't my family. The truth is you've always been my family. My parents would've been so upset with me had they heard what I said to you." I shake my head, disgusted in myself. "I ask because I always wondered if you knew what came next."

The dread of my statement hung in the air. When I think about those months after receiving the letter that brought my world crashing down I can't help but cringe. Ms. Virginia must feel it too, she rubs hers arms and sits back as though she's bracing herself for something she's not ready for.

"On November 8, 2015 I received a letter. The news sent me into a tailspin and I had no desire to pull myself out. I'd just returned from a self-imposed stint at Crestdale. As a matter a fact it was Jonah's graduation announcement that sent me there." Ms. Virginia's face pales and I realize she'd no idea I received one. "Kady." I tell her and she nods, no more explanation needed. "Anyway I received this letter and the only thing that saved my life after I read the words was the fact that I'd recently left rehab. I'd just celebrated getting stronger."

Her fingers touch her lips before she presses her palm to her chest. "What could possibly…"

"Do you recall that large fire here a few years back, that old factory north of town?"

"The old mill? Yes, it was horrible." She shakes her head slowly as realization begins to sink in and I nod as tears begin to fall from my eyes.

"Luke became a firefighter a few months after we connected. He'd always wanted to be a hero and I guess talking to me gave him the courage to follow that dream. He was one of the men, one of the ones who… " I break off, unable to speak of his loss easily. It's been over two years and I can't say it. Some things never get easier.

Ms. Virginia's face is splotchy with her own tears now and we both wipe at our cheeks. "I'm sorry, I don't want to bring up all the horrible things, but I wanted you to know why I disappeared for so long. It wasn't until late last year before I felt healed, or mostly healed. I've spent most of the last three years since I pushed you out of my life fighting my own demons and losing."

"I can't believe your grandparents didn't call me if things were that bad. I can't believe we didn't know. Danica, I am so sorry. I feel as if we failed you, we failed your parents."

"Stop, no. It wasn't your job to protect me."

She rocks forward, her slim hands wiping on the thighs of her jeans as her gaze pins on me and she takes a shallow breath. "It was our job. We should have been there to help you."

"What are you talking about?"

"Honey, years ago your parents asked us to be your guardians if anything ever happened to them, and we said the same for Jonah and Kadence. Their will clearly states we were to get custody."

My stomach drops out and I shift on the couch, putting additional space between us. "What... what happened then, if I was supposed... " *My grandparents.* All the times Gram grumbled in private about having to 'update the Halls', the argument with Jonah where he hinted that I wasn't aware of something and he wasn't surprised I didn't know. How he said 'they' wouldn't ever tell me. "You let my grandparents take me. Why?"

"We were prepared to have you stay with us. Jonah and Kadence, Ron and I. We all discussed it, we were ready to grieve our losses together, with you. Then your grandparents showed up and I couldn't do it. They'd lost their only son, and your mother too, and I couldn't say no. We struck an agreement, we let them move you to Texas and we would keep in daily contact."

"When you came, after I cut myself that first time, did you argue with them about bringing me back here?"

"We did. While you were out with Jonah, there was a relatively large argument. I was so worried your grandparents wouldn't be able to handle your grief and you'd try to take your life. Boy, was Jonah furious with us when we left without you that weekend."

"You talked to my doctors. Jonah mentioned Dr. Panos called you," I recalled, trying to process everything.

"Not that it matters anymore, since you're of age, but legally we were granted custody of you. We could have taken you away from your grandparents at any time, but for your sake we didn't. And theirs, too."

"But you stopped checking in after I told you to stop," I point out, wondering how they could have dropped me so easily. Did they not want the pressure anymore? Rationally I knew that was ridiculous, I'd made myself clear that day — I told her to back off.

"Don't think it, honey. I would have picked you up in a heartbeat if I thought it would be best for you. The one thing we knew at that point was they were getting you the same help we would've. You were adamant we leave you alone and we decided telling you the truth then would cause you more harm than good. So we stepped aside, we asked your grandparents to contact us if they needed anything. I do regret that decision, we should have kept in contact with your doctors until you were of age, but honestly I don't think anything would have changed. Would it?"

I thought on that. Maybe if I never left North Carolina things would have been different. Maybe. But I don't know for certain. What I do know is once the news of Luke's death hit me there was nothing anyone could have done to help me. Here or there, I would've fallen apart. I tore myself to pieces and eventually I picked myself back up, after receiving the care I needed. "No," I told her with conviction, "it wouldn't have mattered."

"I'm so proud of you, your parents would be too — so very proud at how you pulled yourself out of the darkness." I don't want to hear her praise, I'm certainly not perfect. "What changed? What was the turning point for you?"

"A friend," I hint, thinking of those darkest hours. After Luke's death I became the actress again. My 'fake it till you make it' persona turned back on and in full blast. I grieved with my grandparents, and with my doctors. Jules and West called me too, but they didn't know how good I was at pretending. I became creative at first, hiding my cuts in places they wouldn't look and then eventually I didn't care. I cut deep and I cut often. "Gram became so concerned she called Lee, a friend and worker at Crestdale, and asked him to talk to me. I refused to go back to Crestdale, I'd decided, I had no right to live, so what was the point in trying to get better? It was Lee who unearthed the truth. He drove an hour to my house, walked into my room and yelled at me…"

"Take off your shirt," Lee shouted after barging into my room and finding me staring out the window. "Danica, take off your shirt, or lift it, or your pants legs, or whatever it is that's covering your cuts. Show them to me."

"You're a lunatic," I tell him, but I don't shout and I don't bother looking his way. I have no fight left in me.

"And you're cutting," he accuses.

"Yeah… and?"

"And you're going to die," he says angrily. "You will kill yourself, is that honestly what you want?"

Standing, I pull off my sweatshirt and drop it to the floor so Lee can get his fill. There aren't many spots left untouched anymore and I showed them all. His eyes glazed over in such acute pain he would have hurt me if I'd any feelings left. "Yes," I said in a deadly flat tone. "Yes, it is what I want. It's what I deserve."

"You're not suicidal, Danica. You're hurt and you need help to cope. You don't want to die," he says, and for the life of me I will never forget how very positive he was in that statement. And how right he was, but I fought him.

"I don't want to die? Are you so sure about that?"

"Yes, I'm sure…" he starts and it angers me, his confidence in what he thinks he knows about me.

"How do you know, look at me," I move my long hair letting him see the marks along my chest, my collar, and my inner biceps. "I have a purpose for this…"

He walks closer, his eyes shimmering with tears, and I hate seeing them, hate the hurt I'm causing another person I care about. "Yes, I know you do. It helps you feel better, I get that, I do."

"How, how do you know what I feel?"

"Because it's what my sister felt. It's what I watched her go through. The cuts, the pain, the self-destruction, the way she hated herself… Danica, I watched it all and then I walked into the bathroom one day to find her gone in a bathtub full of bloody water." My breathing stops as Lee picks up the shirt I'd thrown to the floor and holds it out for me. Covering my chest, I listen to him tell me her story.

"It was nothing like yours and yet the exact same. It was hurt, loneliness, and pain that festered until she began cutting. And then she couldn't stop. She kept a journal, we found it after she died. Do you know what she wrote over and over and over?" I shake my head, unable to speak. "She wrote 'I don't want to die, I want to feel better.' Danica, she was you."

Backing away, I refuse to hear him as tears stream down my face. "I want to die, I want to…" I stop as I step on the locket Jonah gave me years ago. It's on the floor next to my parents' picture and, of all things, a razor, fresh with blood from thirty minutes ago. "Oh… Lee…. I don't want to die. I don't want to… help me, I just want to stop hurting."

"Hey, hun, I know," he soothes, rushing and pulling me into his chest as my body shakes with sobs. "I'm not letting you die. We're going to get you help, 'kay? You're going to get better."

"He diiieed… because of me. I killed Luke, I killed him."

"No. No you did not. Life happens, bad things happen, and you had nothing to do with it. One day at a time, okay? Will you come with me?"

"He put me in his car and took me straight to the hospital. Lee saved me from myself because he knew, he'd been there. He barely left my side for a year. I got out of the hospital program and went back to Crestdale and then when I was ready to leave there I did more therapy. I've worked and worked at this, to get better. It's been hard as hell," I tell Ms. Virginia and she nods allowing me to share everything.

"You're parents pulled some massive favors to get you some amazing Guardians here on earth, sweetie." She squeezes the hand I hadn't realized she'd taken hold of and I smile.

"They did," I agree. "And you know what? I'm not squandering that anymore. I realized for me to honor their memories, and Luke's, I need to live. I came here to get closure, I want to see their graves and offer up some sort of proper good-bye. I think that's the last thing I need so I can move forward," I admit.

"We can do that. Anything you need, I'm here. Anything, hun," she says, checking her watch and standing as she wipes at her smudged face. "Kadence will be here any minute, we should clean up unless you want her twenty questions," she teases lightly and I stand.

"Thank you for everything, Ms. Virginia. Thank you for being here and understanding now." I hug her tightly, relieved to have finally opened up all of the doors of my past to her.

"Not that you have to thank me, but you're welcome," she says, Pulling back she gives me one more look. "Jonah will be here too, Dani."

I nod, hoping she's right, but a part of me doubts it. Part of me thinks there's no way my parents can pull any more miracles for me. I know he'll forgive me eventually, but will he ever love me again? That has to be too much to hope for.

Today's reality... The unsuspecting chaperone
January 18, 2015

"So, Mom... remember the prospective student night you were against me going to because you don't trust Jonah?" Kady mentions as she passes the potatoes my way at dinner two nights later. I cough to cover my giggle.

"Yes, and I seem to recall happily offering to bring you to the event. You were the one who didn't care for the idea."

"Uh, yeah. It's for prospective students, let me have my mommy and daddy bring me. Please, there's no reason I can't stay at Jonah's and he can't watch me."

"Watch the tone, young lady," Mr. Ron warns, exchanging glances with his wife. "Plus, there is every reason for us to not let you stay at Jonah's."

Kady rolls her eyes, plastering on a pretty pout. She pushes her meat around her plate for a few minutes before trying again. "Well, I was thinking. What if Dani came with me?"

Hold the presses. I give myself whiplash turning to look at Kady's innocent smile. "Wait... what?"

"We'd have fun. It's a weekend event. I get an excused absence at school if I go and there's a mixer event Friday night, a basketball game Saturday, and some campus tours. There's lectures, too," she points out, as though any of us believe that's her intent for wanting to attend so badly. "It would be so much fun and you know, it'd be good for you to check it out, Dani. Maybe you could transfer to UNC next year with Jonah and me." *Oh, the bombs keep dropping.* I'm about to adamantly refuse when Kady's foot nudges mine under the table. She sends me a pleading look, her eyes and head nodding toward her parents — and I give in.

"I'd be happy to go with her. It does sound fun," I offer, albeit unenthusiastically.

"And she could see Jonah's apartment and... "

"Kadence, please," Ms. Virginia says, shaking her head at her exuberant daughter. "Dani, you don't have to go."

"No, I know. The idea of seeing UNC and experiencing a little of what I've missed might be good for me. I've barely spoken to Jonah since I've been back, it'd be nice to see his place and meet his... " *Poppy.* "... friends."

"Ron?"

"Daddy?" Kadence echoes.

He gives me one last chance to withdraw my offer to escort Kady, and when I refuse he agrees, with conditions. Kadence listens attentively as he goes into all of the pitfalls — boys, alcohol, drugs, boys — anything she might think of doing is covered over our steak and potato dinner. Then he turns on me. "Those all apply to you too, young lady," he says with a wink, and while it's meant lightheartedly, my eyes glaze over at the sentiment. My dad never got the chance to warn me of these things and Mr. Ron's sad smile confirms he knows this. "Of course you are legal so I can't stop you from drinking, but you will not drive, don't drink anything you didn't open yourself. Stay away from mixed drinks. Beer is your best bet and don't mix your liqueurs."

I laugh, "Yes, sir."

"I don't think I have to warn you about the boys, I'm sure Jonah will have that under control. Granted, I think I'll have a chat with him on that," he muses and Ms. Virginia gapes as Kady breaks into a fit of giggles and I catch fire with embarrassment.

Standing and carrying her dish from the table, Kady eyes me meaningfully as she walks by. "Yes, Daddy, I think you should definitely have a talk with Jonah on that exact subject."

After dinner, Kady knocks on my door before letting herself in. "Whatcha doing?"

"Plotting ways to dispose of your body," I tell her, tossing the notebook I was writing lyrics in down beside me. "What's up?"

"Is 'thank you' enough, or do I owe you something more?" she asks.

I wave her over, tapping the bed in front of me, and she happily takes a seat on the end, tucking one leg beneath her. "So, tell me your ulterior motive," I prod after a moment.

"Ulterior motive?" she squeaks, but her wide-eyed and so very feigned look of innocence doesn't work on me. Thankfully she knows it and we don't have to play games. "Fine, there's this party and I was hoping to go, but I can't go to parties with my parents around."

"And... who's going to be at this party?" I dig, knowing she's left off the obvious.

"Did you see the guy I was talking to that day at the coffee shop?"

"You mean Mr. Beanie Hat, Floppy Hair who couldn't keep his hands away from you?" I tease.

"Yep, that's the one. His name is Eli, and he thinks I'm this goodie goodie and won't go out with me, he says 'I can't handle it'."

I bite back the laughter at that statement. "You can't handle it? What exactly can't you handle?"

"I don't know. That's the problem. He's not a player, I mean he dates, but he doesn't do girlfriends and he's smart, and athletic, and I know he's into me, I mean you saw him right? He's always petting at me... I can't figure him out, and I thought a weekend at UNC with him might change that. Maybe he could see a different side of me. You know, my sexier side." Kady bites at the side of her lip and I look her over.

Sexy, she's not. She's beautiful in the all-American girl way. Blond hair, blue eyes, innocent face with full pouty lips, but there's something about her that screams virgin. It's not a bad thing at all. It's simply her and I can see how maybe a more worldly guy would see that and run.

"You know, if this Eli doesn't like you for you, maybe he's not worth your time," I offer, feeling out of practice at the art of offering dating advice.

"It's not that. I know he likes me. He does. He just... I don't know, he just doesn't know it yet."

"Okay then, mission get Eli to notice you commences... um, when is this trip happening?" I ask, realizing I never confirmed a date, not that I have much going on.

"Two weeks. Last weekend in March."

Two weeks. "Okay then. I guess I should call Jonah and let him know we're coming. Make sure he's okay with it."

Kady stands, stretching her arms up over her head as she asks, "Has he not called you since he left Monday?"

"Me? No, why would he?" As far as Kady knows Jonah needed to get back for a class. I didn't tell her about our argument, or disagreement, or whatever it was.

She shrugs indifferently, making an excuse about needing a shower. "Jonah's moody, don't let it get to you; he fell in love with a girl once and she left without a word. He's never been the same." Kady gives me a pointed look and I know she's talking about me. "Call him. Tell him I said hey," she adds, leaving me to myself again.

The two weeks between Jonah leaving and Kady and I going to see him again drag on. I spend my days researching the prospect of transferring my credits from my online program in Texas to the local college in Charlotte and spending time with Ms. Virginia. She's always patient with me, offering up memories and stories whenever I ask, but always knowing when I need time, too. From her, and Mr. Ron, I learn how my parents almost never became a couple due to my mother's extreme infatuation with a guy from the fraternity that was always paired during Greek events with their sorority. Thankfully that guy was a complete jerk, standing her up when his buddies scored tickets to some grunge band on tour, leaving room for my father to swoop in and sweep her off her feet.

The stories of my parents make my heart heavy, but happy, at the same time. I'm grateful I have people like the Halls who can share so many moments of their lives with me. It's why they chose them as my guardians if anything were to happen to them — through the Halls I will never forget my parents. I will get to hear the things they would have told me.

It's a dreary afternoon, a few days before Kady and I leave for UNC when I finally get the nerve up to drive by my old house. I'd been running errands, grabbing toiletries, and buying some new jeans for my trip, when I was hit with this overwhelming desire to see it. I drive carefully as I pull into my old stomping grounds. It's mid-afternoon and school has evidently let out recently judging by the groups of parents awaiting their kids at random spots along the street. As I pull down my old street, my pulse picks up speed. Sitting there is the home I grew up in. The house my parents bought a few weeks before having me. It's not as opulent as the Halls. My parents loved this little house and although they could afford to buy up they decided not to, electing to save instead. Their decision is what afforded me so many otayo at Crestdale, and what makes my current situation easier. Life Insurance and Dad's thrift sense has made my need for a job non-existent for a while as long as I'm frugal. It's one more thing they did which proves how much they loved me.

"Danica Evans?" A tap on my window brings me back to the present. Mrs. Baldwin, our old neighbor, is standing outside my car door and at her side is the little girl I babysat when she was an infant. Mrs. Baldwin slides back as I open my door with a smile. "Oh my goodness, it is you. I thought I recognized you as we were walking from the bus stop," she gushes, moving in for a hug.

"Hi… it's so great to see you. My word, this must be Ava," I smile, bending down to Ava's height with a smile. "I used to babysit you when you were a tiny little thing and now you're what? Sixteen, seventeen?" I tease and she giggles.

"Noo, I'm six," she informs me, holding up her fingers proudly.

"Ohhh, six. Well, you are big for a six year old and so, so pretty." I straighten and smile at Mrs. Baldwin again as she watches our interaction.

"How are you doing? We sure do miss you and your parents here," she says politely and I answer in kind. It's my first interaction with someone who knew me and my parents before the accident. I can't believe it's taken me five years to talk to someone, other than the Halls, who knew me when. It's surreal. She brings up the way Mom loved decorating the entire yard at Christmas, saying the new owners — while nice — are nowhere as festive as we were. When Ava tugs at her arm complaining about needing to use the potty, she finally excuses herself, and leaves me by myself with my old house again. I peek around the cul-de-sac quickly before I jog up to the driveway and stand under what would be the shade of my large tree if there were leaves on it and close my eyes for one small moment. Long enough to imagine Jonah and Dad shooting hoops, and the sound of laughter as Mom and I plant flowers, or the feeling of a bucket of soapy water being dumped on my head while I wash our cars. I flip through them, all memories made in this yard, this house, and I smile. I don't cry or throw up or look for a blade — I simply smile. There is victory in the smallest of battles, I remind myself as I open my eyes and back away from the tree I loved so much.

I return to my car, opening the door and standing there for a moment as I breathe in this new victory. "Thank you," I whisper. "Thank you for the memories, I hope your new family is blessed with as many as I was," I sigh before slipping into my car and driving away. That afternoon I find my parents' graves, for the first time. It's easier than I thought it would be, sitting there on the grass in the cold mist and talking to them. I don't pour my heart out because I know they already know what's within me. Instead, I talk randomly about Gram and Gramps, Crestdale, Luke and Lee and the Halls. I mention Jonah last.

"You were right, Daddy," I sniff with a nod as I recall the smile on his face moments before we crashed. "Jonah and I were planning on dating before the accident. I don't know how it happened back then, I wish I did so I could copy the past and make it happen again. I think he's the answer. This…" I muse, looking up and looking around the cemetery. "Grove Pointe, the Halls, being home… I think this was the answer all along."

My last order of business before I see Jonah is to say goodbye to Luke. Courtney and I make lunch plans on Thursday, the day before Kady and I are heading for UNC.

219

"So, have you made any long term plans?" Courtney inquires over chicken salad sandwiches at the small deli we're at.

"Well, kinda. This weekend will help me finalize things, I think," I tell her, thinking about Jonah and how he's the last of my unresolved issues now.

Luke's plot at the small cemetery is one of the most perfect spots I've seen. In the shade of a large tree and resting next to his grandparents, the grey granite headstone is shiny and new compared to many others nearby. Courtney walks up before me, setting a rose she'd brought down and closing her eyes for a moment before she steps away and leaves me alone.

"Hi," I whisper, kneeling and running my fingers over the engraved letters that make up his name. "You saved me, Luke Claborn, more than once, and you loved me when I needed someone to love me. Thank you. I promise I'll never forget you or what you did for me and I'll always love you in a way I think nobody but the two of us will ever understand." I pull a penny from my pocket. It's one of several pressed coins we'd made during his week in Texas, and I press it down into the ground at the edge of his stone. Pressing a kiss to my fingers, I touch the four letters at the bottom of his marker, below his name and the dates of his birth and death is one inscription — 'Hero.'

Today's reality… A college life for me
January 30, 2018

Prospective student weekend is totally a ruse for a bunch of kids to party on a college campus. Of this I'm certain, because once the sun goes down and the lectures and tours are done, the crazies come out. Of course there are the school approved and sponsored events, but Kady has her eye on mixers of a whole other kind. The kind involving Fraternity Row, keggers, and a certain guy's older brother.

"How's this?" Kady asks, stepping out of Jonah's bathroom wearing skin tight skinny jeans and a crop top.

My jaw drops at the show of skin and she laughs. "I think you're going to freeze to death."

"I have a cardigan to wear over it," she points out, pulling a chunky knit sweater from her bag and sliding her arms in. "Better?"

"Ah, yes. Much." I admire her relaxed look. Her long, blond hair is curled into large waves, her eyes smudged to a smoky perfection. We've primped and fussed for an hour, taking over Jonah's room and giggling like little girls.

"You're the rock star here tonight. Where were you hiding that outfit back home?" Kady pouts as she sits on the edge of the bed. "I did not see that in your closet."

Tugging at my layered look for the tenth time, I brace myself for her certain disappointment. "Unfortunately, my closet consisted of mostly sweatshirts and baggy pants. So your mom and I went shopping earlier in the week."

One. Two. Three.

"You what!" Her glass shattering squeal makes my ears ring. "You two went shopping and you didn't tell me?" She huffs, standing again and stomping her boot clad foot.

"Is somebody being murdered in there, should I be worried?" Jonah's voice calls through the door.

"You two are on my list," Kady warns as she pulls the door open with an angry jerk. Jonah steps back, startled, as his sister stops in front of him. "They went shopping. Without me," she whines and his face contorts as he manages to hold a smile at bay. Barely. His eyes sparkle with suppressed laughter and I busy myself by grabbing my purse and phone to cover my amusement. Shaking out my hair as I leave the room, I bump into Jonah who's standing in the doorway. "Sorry," I mutter, backing up a step so he can move. We haven't spoken since our fight two weeks ago. I tried to call him, but the calls went unanswered. He did send a text after the third missed call saying he was sorry we keep missing each other, but he's swamped. He also said his parents told him we were coming and he'd see me then. That was it. When we made it on campus earlier today he was in class. We finally exchanged our awkward hellos two hours ago, over pizza at the dining room table, when he made his appearance. He rents a house right off campus with a few friends who we met earlier. At dinner, his roommates and one of their girlfriends ate with us and spent the time monopolizing conversation while Jonah and I sat across the room pretending to ignore each other before Kady pulled me into Jonah's room to get ready. Now here we are standing face to face for the first time since our fight.

"You went shopping huh?" he asks as he stands in my way. His eyes peruse my outfit and a smile curls the left edge of his mouth. "And without Kady... Did you not know the mall is her mother ship? She may never speak to you again."

I sink my teeth into the inside of my cheek to keep from bursting into laughter as I raise a brow, standing there patiently waiting for him to move. Jonah clears his throat, sliding to the side and making room for me to exit his room. I step through the door to make my escape and he leans in, causing me to turn sideways so we could both fit through the frame. It was that or bump into him, so I turn, and his lips throw a wicked smile my way as our chests skim. The contact causes me to trip over my own feet.

I turn my head from his so we're not face to face and am almost clear when his warm breath skims across my cheek as he leans in and speaks. "I like the polka dots, by the way. So sweet and innocent." Snapping my attention to his face, he chuckles, his eyes drinking me in again as he clears the door and moves to push it closed. "Sexy as hell, too," he adds a moment before the door clicks shut.

Looking down at my jeans I smile to myself. *Best outfit ever.*

Thirty minutes later we're smashed between hundreds of sweaty bodies, pushing through a throng of partiers filling a one story house off campus.

"This is Eli's brother's house," Kady shouts over her shoulder as we weave our way into the back of the house past all of the dancing. "Oh, there he is." She tugs on my arm excitedly, nearly pulling me to the floor.

I scan the crowd ahead, looking for anyone resembling the teen I saw at the coffee shop before spotting him in the middle of a small group.

They're circled around a table filled with plastic cups, beer cans, and a large tower of blocks.

"Eli," Kady calls out, moving faster as the crowd thins, her hand leaving my arm. I stand back for a moment, watching as she reaches him. He lights up when he looks at her and I smile inwardly. *Yeah, he's into her.* Eli leans in, whispering something for her ears only, and I move forward again. I reach their sides as Kady slaps at his arm, blushing prettily at his comment before introducing us.

The group he's with is a mix of guys and girls playing some version of college Jenga I realize as I get a closer look at the blocks in the center of the table. Each person removes a brick, does some sort of task — handwritten on the brick they chose — and then places the brick back at the top of the pile.

"Wait," I question the random stranger in front of me as I watch a guy across the table read his block and take two sips of the beer he's holding. "So, this is Jenga with dares?"

"Yep," he mutters before looking my way and smiling. "Want in? Grab a drink. We just started a new round."

"Oh… I'm good, thanks though." I imagine my alcohol tolerance is about that of a goldfish and tonight I'm on Kady duty. A pretty brunette laughs over everyone shouting out 'Rhyme Time' before she randomly yells out 'art'. Cheering goes out as the people around the table start calling out words, mart, tart, fart, cart, and I laugh as understanding dawns. They go around three times before one of the guys repeats the word fart and is booed. He takes a long sip of his drink and the game moves on.

"I'm Everett by the way," the guy next to me offers. He's shifted little by little since I've been standing there, bringing me into the circle without my knowing, until we're now side by side. I take him in and immediately see the resemblance to Eli.

"You're Eli's older brother?" I blurt, and his eyes confirm it to be true. He looks over his shoulder to where Kady and Eli are standing against a wall. Eli's arm is around her shoulder and their heads are close as they chat with each other. I wonder if I should pay more attention to what's going on there, but Everett's next comment derails me.

"How the hell did my little brother score the prettiest girls at the party?"

"Ha, well hate to break it to you, but your baby brother isn't 'scoring' with anyone tonight, or at least not that girl," I point out protectively and he laughs, checking them out once more and raising his brows suggestively my way. "If you disagree with that I can grab 'my girl' there and we can leave," I tell him.

"Hey, Ev, your turn," a voice shouts and Everett holds up his hand. "Hold that thought," he tells me, plucking his piece from the game and turning it from me as he reads it. "Well, well, well. Strip one." The girls hoot as Everett holds his drink out to me and I take it automatically. *Strip one?* He shimmies as he tugs his shirt over his head, revealing hard abs as his tee shirt sticks with the shirt he's wearing. *Ahha, strip one. Got it and thank you, drinking Jenga.*

"Thank you, madame," he bows, removing his drink from my hand.

"Nice shirt," I tease, complimenting his form fitting Iron Man tee shirt, and he puffs his chest as he turns, throwing his shirt over his shoulder at Eli and Kady.

They look our way and Kady waves. "You met Dani," she calls to us and Everett looks between us and nods as she sends a thumbs up and Eli tosses the discarded shirt onto the nearby counter.

"So you're Dani, I presume?"

"You presume correctly. Danica, actually." I correct. Dani is for Jonah, and his family.

"Okay, well, Danica, it's your turn," he tells me and I try to shake my head, but he insists, nudging me to the table. "Sorry, you're in the circle. Come on, it's fun."

With a sigh I check out the tower, leaning forward and tapping on an end piece halfway up. The piece slides out effortlessly and I read the tile with Everett over my shoulder. "Give two." I wait for an explanation of what this means and Everett fills me in.

"You get to make anyone in the circle take two sips of their drink."

"Oh? Okay then I choose you. Take two, Everett," I order, placing my tile back on the pile. Everett sends me a look, clearly calling me a traitor with his eyes as he finishes off the drink in his hand. I shrug with a smile. "Sorry, you did force me into the game."

"As long as you remember turnabout is fair-play," he warns, leaving me standing there as he retrieves more drinks.

Drinking Jenga ends up being a great way to pass an evening with a bunch of strangers. I've drank several sips, rhymed lock, bell, and Scooby, and stood on one foot. The challenges of those around me have been vastly entertaining. The random 'kiss the person on your left' couple. The girl who twerked for thirty-seconds, Everett needed to explain that one to me. I sadly, or perhaps thankfully, missed the great twerking craze of 2013 while recovering from the accident. While

Everett is taken aback by my lack of knowledge he doesn't mention it and I'm grateful. The more we play, the more pop culture references people make, and I realize I'm woefully ill-suited to college life. I feel so green. The more out of place I feel the more I drink and soon I'm picking up a second beer at the exact moment the 'waterfall' challenge is called.

Seeing my questioning look as everyone around us starts drinking, Everett leans in. "You drink until the person with the tile quits," he explains his beer at his mouth. "Cheers." I've chugged half the bottle by the time the girl calls it and my stomach flips.

"Geez Poppy, take it easy on us, girl," the bottled blond next to me complains and my head snaps at the name. *Poppy.* She's the pretty brunette who did the rhyme 'art' when I first joined the group. If Poppy is here, where's Jonah? I'd assumed he'd headed off to find her after separating from us almost two hours ago, but she's been here the entire time and he's not been around.

Arms circle my waist and Kady's chin rests on my shoulder, startling me as she sighs into my ear. "Having fun?" she giggles. "I wanna dance, come with me."

"I'm playing this game I can't just leave," I tell her as Everett looks on.

"Boo, come on. Can she quit Everett?" Kady pouts and Everett looks between the two of us. "Don't you guys want to watch us dance?" she teases and I'm in awe. Maybe all-American Kady has more play than I gave her credit for.

Everett throws up his free hand to the group shouting, "We're out."

"Yay," Kady sings, turning me about and dragging me into the dark and significantly more crowded room where the DJ is set up. The boys follow behind us and I smile at the brotherly punch Everett gives Eli as they laugh about something. Kady grabs my beer, stealing a sip before I think to stop her, and makes a gagging face. "That's gross and warm," she complains and I laugh, tipping the bottle up and finishing it off, setting it on the floor next to a pile of other empty bottles before we maneuver our way to an area big enough to dance.

When you spend five years in varying states of depression and hospitalization or solitary confinement you miss out on the latest songs and dance steps, but dancing — like riding a bike — isn't something you forget how to do. It takes two or three songs before my body remembers the feel of the beat. Kady and I playfully bump and grind with each other until the guys step in and I find myself the sole subject of a guy's attention for the first time in almost three years. Everett's hands grasp at my waist as he moves to the music, his thighs rubbing against mine as we dip and sway. The two beers I drank have kicked in, erasing inhibitions, and when the song slows, my hands wrap around his shoulders without thinking.

"Why haven't I seen you on campus before?" It's the first thing we've said since hitting the floor since the dance beats were too loud to talk over.

"I'm not a student here. I'm actually visiting from Texas. I'm staying with Kady's family for a while."

"So I may not see you again?" I'm surprised to see genuine sorrow on his face. It makes me sad because I don't want him to think I'm interested in him or that he has a chance at anything with me. Panic invades me and I push at his chest shaking my head.

"I'm not free," I blurt out at the same time a pair of strong arms yank me back by the shoulders, twisting me around.

"Jonah!" I shout as Everett reaches for me.

"Man, what's your deal?" Everett asks, but Jonah's face is all the answer he needs. He is pissed and most likely mentally stabbing Everett as he takes my arm and tugs me to the side.

"What the hell are you doing? Everett Brand, seriously? Dude's a colossal player and you should stay away from him. And where's my sister?" he growls.

"First, where do you get off pulling me away from a guy? I was dancing and so is Kady, she's right over… there," I argue, motioning to where Kady should be. *Oh crap. Kady's missing and Eli too. Crap, crap, crap.*

"Too busy working on another conquest to keep an eye on her, huh?" he practically shouts, spinning on his heel and walking away.

Another conquest? He means Luke. I'm two seconds from breaking down when Everett speaks next to me. "When you said not free, you could have said you were with Jonah. I would have stepped off."

"It's not like that, or… I don't know, it's complicated. Hey, did you see Eli leave?" Everett looks around, but has no clue and offers to help me search and we split up. I don't make it ten steps before I look up to find an angry Kady flying my way with an angrier Jonah at her heels.

"We're leaving," he orders as he keeps walking past me, and Kady stops.

Trying to not sound all motherly, I ask as nicely as I possible, "Where were you?"

226

"I was using the bathroom," she snaps, her bottom lip pouting. "And freaking avenging Jonah came flying out from nowhere the moment I stepped out and tore into Eli."

"Was he in the bathroom with you?" I hate asking her. I don't want to embarrass her and I certainly don't want to judge.

"Heck, no," she frowns. "I was going to the bathroom. That's it." Suddenly, I feel as though I'm in a comedy. Poor Eli, and Everett. "He's never that with me. He's always cool about things, but he's in rare form tonight," she says.

Behind her Eli makes his appearance and Kady looks crestfallen at the prospect of leaving, and now I'm the furious one. "Stay here and I'll tell your brother we're not ready to leave. Eli, can you drop us off at Jonah's place if we need a ride later?" With his agreement, I storm my way to the back of the house where Jonah went. I expect to find him outside or waiting by his car, instead he's at the large table in the kitchen where drunken Jenga continues. And Poppy is on his arm. The moment his eyes meet mine his face stiffens and he leans into Poppy, whispering something that makes her laugh. *Ugh, I don't know the girl and I hate her laugh*, I cringe as I walk his way.

"Hey! Ev's new girl, where'd he go?" Poppy slurs, obviously recognizing me from earlier and Jonah's eyes bore into me. Maybe I like her a little just because her calling me Ev's girl clearly ticks Jonah off, big time.

Plastering on a huge smile, I shrug and send Jonah a meaningful look, "I don't know, but I'm back. Can I get back in the game?"

"I thought you were leaving," Jonah says pointedly and Poppy perks up at the tone.

"Waaait, do you two know each other?"

"I'm Dani, Jonah's friend from childhood. I'm visiting his family. I'm sure he told you that's why he came home a few weeks ago."

"Dani?" She turns to Jonah tapping his chest. "Naughty, naughty boy, I thought Dani was a guy. You didn't tell me she's a... she," she purrs.

"Of course he didn't," I mutter as the bar maid (that's the person who has to serve drinks for the remainder of the game, because they pulled the bar maid tile) hands me a drink. Looking at the punch-like liquid, I take a whiff and a hesitant sip. *Whoa, that'll put hair on your chest*, I cough.

"What's that supposed to mean?" Jonah whispers angrily, turning my way and I shrug. "Nothing, it's your turn I think," I point out innocently.

Jonah and I exchange angry glances for a few turns as the game moves into ridiculous territory. At this point most of the people around the table are wasted. Poppy has been groping every body part of Jonah's within her reach for the last ten minutes when she pulls the 'kiss the person to your left tile' and attacks him in front of me. When his hands wrap around her I can't watch anymore. Feigning the need to refill my drink I leave the table, finding the back door and stepping out into the cold air. There are few people outside by the fire pit at this hour and every breath I take is a puff of white smoke in the frigid night air. I throw back the remainder of my punch and fall into a chair. Tossing my plastic cup into the flames, I watch as it catches fire turning from black smoke to blue flames.

"Dani?" Kady calls my name and I look up to find her walking my way. "Eli can take us back to the house now," she offers, wrapping her sweater around her bare midriff.

I don't realize I'm crying silent tears until we're halfway to the car. Silent tears I'm not sure I can explain, except I can. I hate the way this night turned out. I hate how I ended up dancing in the arms of some guy I could care less about, I hate how Jonah was kissing a chick named after a freaking seed, and I hate how I'm going home right now while he's staying behind, with her.

By the time we make it back to Jonah's place I have three arms and feel like a million bucks. Or maybe it's the alcohol talking? Kady walks arm-in-arm with me to the door, propping me up against her side as she digs for the spare key Jonah gave her earlier in the day. The house is dark, so we must be the first ones home. "Eli, your brother was nice…. are you nice too?" I mumble.

Pushing the door open, Kady steers me in. "Yes, Eli is nice and you should get some water and go to sleep." She speaks to me as though I'm a child and I stop in the doorway as Eli moves to follow us in. I'm the adult here, not Kady. *Right?*

"We should go out dancing some more," I gasp as the mood to burn some energy hits me. "Why did we come home? It's early, we should be out. Be young… be free…"

"BEyond drunk," Kady deadpans and a deep laughter behind me causes me to twirl around in a perfect little pirouette. *See I am a dancer. I think.*

"Eli! Hey, come in. Oh gosh… your brother. He was fun, please tell him I'm sorry for leaving." Stumbling, I try to kick off my boots when something comes to mind. "Wait, no that was Jonah's fault." I straighten turning back to Kady. "Gah, Jonah. What's his problem?" I whine and then I'm crying again.

Pushing me toward Jonah's bedroom, Kady mumbles something to Eli and follows behind me, her hands firmly upon my biceps. I shuffle straight to his bed and plummet face first into it. Resting my head on my folded arms, I sniffle as Kady yanks at my boots. "He hates me. Why does he hate me? Doesn't he know how much he means to me?"

"He doesn't hate you. Stop, it'll be better in the morning." Her voice is motherly and I want to cry some more.

"Did you see the way she draped herself over him? That... that Poppy. Ugh, Poppyseed, who names their kid that? They're going to get married and have a billion kids named Mustard and Rainbow and Weasel, and and..."

"Oh my... Weasel?" Kady laughs. "Move up some," she orders, tapping my now bootless legs.

Crawling up to the pillows, I fall back to my stomach, inhaling Jonah's scent in the sheets. "Don't make fun, they're probably getting it on as we speak. Oh no!" I flip over and the room spins crazily. "What if he brings her back here? I can't sleep here while they get all nasty together." My mind envisions Jonah and Poppy kissing and I want to puke. Sweat pops up on my forehead as my stomach clenches.

"Dani, awe crap... don't get sick in his room," Kady begs as I stumble to the bathroom, giving the contents of my stomach up to the porcelain bowl. I'm hovering over the toilet, one hand clinging to the edge of the tub, the other on the back of the bowl as everything I've consumed tonight comes up. My hair lifts up and out of my face, but my focus is below me as another round of stomach pumping ensues.

"So this is college, huh?" I mumble once I'm sure I'm done.

"For some, yes," Jonah's voice sounds behind me and I fall back from my knees to my rear, knocking into his legs. He's the one holding my hair. He's not out getting busy. He's here.

Crap, here comes the tears. "This is pleasant, so bummed I've been missing out," I sniff as Kady appears, handing me a wet washcloth. I wipe at my mouth and face as Jonah kneels down beside me.

"Can you get up, Lindsey Lohan, or should I carry you?"

"I can crawl if I have to, I'm fine... go back to *Poppy*."

"Be my guest," he offers, standing back, and I scamper to my knees. Reaching up, I hoist myself into a standing position and glare at Jonah. He's in my way, standing there like earlier, in the doorway — a big wall blocking my exit. I want to punch him. Him and his smug face and his stupid girlfriend, but I control myself, barely. My mouth and throat have seen better days and I lean over the sink, rinsing the taste of acid and alcohol away, my entire body swaying side to side. When I straighten again, Kady is there instead of Jonah. *Was he really here?*

"Bed," she orders softly and I nod. She helps me pull off my damp sweater and shirt, leaving me in a tank top, and throws a blanket over me, tucking it around my sides the way a parent tucks their toddler in for the night.

"Did I imagine him, Kady?" I groan, my eyes closing. "I used to dream of him, all the time. Even when Luke was in my life it was Jonah who filled my head. Jonah who always occupied my heart… "

Sometime later there are voices, hushed and whispering, around me. "Go sleep on the couch. Eli's gone."

"Does she really think I hate her?" There's a heavy sigh, a muffled curse.

"She drank too much. She wasn't thinking clearly… at all."

"How do I do this again? I keep waiting for her to walk away, what if she walks away? I can't lose her again. I want my best friend, if nothing else."

The softer voice, a girl, makes a shushing sound and their voices lower until I hear nothing but parts of broken sentences. "Thought… break up…. decide."

The deeper voice responds, "There's nothing there. She's just hanging on. I should have told her."

"Yeah, you should have. Go get some sleep."

A door clicks to the left, the muffling sound of water and the unmistakable noise of things being shifted around the bedroom hit me. My befuddled senses recognize the voices I've been listening to, but as I lay there fear sinks in. Fear that I'll forget their words, forget what I've heard. I hate fear. Fear always leads to panic and pressure, and pressure makes me want to cut. I don't want to cut and soon I'm shaking, counting in my head and trying to control myself.

"I miss my best friend, too," I manage to whisper between shallow breaths as I roll to my side and pass out.

Today's reality… I need my best friend
January 31, 2018

I sleep away most of Saturday's events, trusting Kady to be the girl her parents expect her to be. I figure she deserves some freedom after putting up with my antics the night before. When I wake I'm alone and for a moment darkness creeps in as I try to recall the night before. The memories are vague, but I remember Jonah showing up and I remember seeing him staring down at me before I fell asleep — or maybe that was a dream? I'm not sure, until I find the note he left behind.

D~
I needed to take care of a gardening issue.
I'll be back with coffee and presents. Game
time is 6 so grab a shower and be ready for
dinner by the time I get back.

~ Jonah

Take care of gardening issues? Gardening… Oh! It comes back to me — the things I said about Poppy in my drunken state. The voices swirling around the room before I passed out. My heart soars and I smile into the empty room, hugging Jonah's pillow to my chest. I shower and take care to apply my new make-up the way the perfectly groomed cosmetology girl at the counter showed me. It took me three tries, and many blackened cotton swabs, before I mastered the small hooked line at the edge of my eyes. I pull my long hair into a ponytail atop my head, tying the cute UNC bandana Ms. Virginia bought me around it before taking a large curler to the ends to create a messy look. Dressing up and styling myself are so foreign. I'm a twenty-one year old girl who's seriously been living in a fog for five years. Last night's game and conversations proved how much I've missed out on. It's close to four when Jonah arrives knocking on the bedroom door.

"You decent in here?" he calls through the crack. I can't suppress the smile on my lips when his hand pops in holding a coffee cup.

"As decent as I get," I reply, accepting the proffered coffee. "This will go a long way to help, though."

"You feeling a little under the weather?" he teases.

"It's not too bad. The water bottle and aspirin helped. Thank you."

"Hey, I've got practice with that sort of thing," he admits as he pulls his arm from behind his back and holds up a plastic shopping bag. "I come bearing presents."

"Oh, that's right, you did say you were bringing back presents. Give me, give me." Setting my coffee on his dresser I clap excitedly, finding an immense amount of pleasure in the smile playing on Jonah's face.

The bag contains a Carolina blue tee shirt with UNC emblazoned across the chest. "You can't go to your first game without the proper gear," he tells me as I pull the shirt out.

"I love it." I gush, looking at him and realizing he's wearing the guys version of the same shirt. "Plus now we'll match," I tease with a wink. "Twinsies."

Jonah laughs as I head into the bathroom to change shirts. "Yeah, us and a few thousand other students."

He wasn't kidding about the thousands of other students. Dean Smith Center is packed, the intensity ramping up the closer to game time we get. When tip-off arrives I'm beside myself, joining everyone else, with excitement for the game. With Kady and Eli to my left and Jonah and a few of his buddies to my right I watch my first 'real' basketball game since I was fifteen. The cheers I grew up with come back easily — the fight song, the school chants — these are things any kid growing up in North Carolina learns. You're either Duke or UNC; pick one, hate the other, that's life. There's a moment, halfway through the game when we're all clapping and cheering, and I look to my right finding Jonah staring at me. My hands pause, mid-clap, as our eyes meet. All around us people are screaming, the band is playing, an announcer is talking through the sound-system, my feet are numb from the vibrations of all the stomping on the bleachers we're standing on. Yet, the world effectively stops as Jonah's hand sweeps up, taking hold of my neck, and pulls me to him. His mouth crashes down on mine. It's not a deep kiss, or extremely long, but it's enough to steal my breath and rock my world. Then as unexpectedly as it began it ends as his hand releases me and his focus returns to the game where it remains until the final buzzer.

"Can we stop by the restrooms?" Kady asks as we join the mass exodus out of the arena. The guys agree and sigh when Kady and I join a long line for the ladies room. "How are men so much faster?" she complains, pointing over to the men's restroom where Eli and Jonah disappeared.

Once we finally exit the ladies room, I spot Jonah and Eli off to the side waiting on us. They're deep in conversation, although it's mostly

Jonah talking and Eli nodding, and I wonder what they're discussing. I get my answer almost the moment we reach them.

"Hey," they both say innocently, and I smile as Eli takes Kady's hand and she beams at him.

"Kady, you mind if Dani and I skip the after parties? I think she consumed her fair share of liquid fun last night," Jonah says looking my way for confirmation. "Do you mind?"

My supposed guardianship goes to war with my desire to see what Jonah is up to and I buckle. "Um, no I guess we can skip." *It wasn't really a war, more of a tiny, little skirmish. It was a no-brainer.*

"But I'm going with Eli, right?" she asks and Jonah assures her she has his blessings to go out.

"Remember, everything you do will get back to me," he promises and Kady rolls her eyes, pushing him.

"Okay, Dad." She gives me a hug. "Be good, you two," she calls as they walk away.

"I promised your parents I'd keep her on the straight and narrow this weekend. You did too, did you not?"

"I did," he says, taking my hand in his and pulling me in the opposite direction. "Don't worry, Eli knows exactly what will happen to him if he brings her back in any condition other than the one she left in."

"So that's the conversation I witnessed? Brotherly intimidation?"

"You know it," he laughs shamelessly. "As for you, I think you proved you're not up to being a chaperone last night."

"Hey, that's not fair. I didn't realize I was such a light weight. I don't drink ever," I pout and he pulls my hand into the crook of his arm, bringing me closer to his side.

"I know. And you're so dang tiny, you never stood a chance against the power punch they served you in the end."

"Power punch?" The red liquid in the last cup I drank. "What the heck is power punch?"

"The strong cheap stuff. It knocks everyone on their asses."

"Nice. So what are we doing if we're not going to partake in frat parties and debauchery?"

"Who said there'd be no debauchery?" He smiles and acknowledges a group of students in a huddle as we walk by. Letting go of me, he opens the passenger side door when we reach his car. He leans over the open door as I buckle in and makes a thoughtful face. "So are you ready for whatever the night holds?"

"Ready as I'll ever be," I agree, my heart racing at the playfulness he's exuding.

"I was hoping you'd say that."

"Uh, did I miss something or are we heading back to your place?" I wonder out loud when I recognize the street we've turned on.

"Observant, aren't we?"

"Cocky, aren't you?" I throw back as he pulls into his driveway. Jonah puts it in park and turns in his seat, his headlights bouncing off the garage door and back into the car. He looks a bit unsure of himself.

"With anybody else I am cocky and I'm sure of what I'm doing and what will work," he admits, and I'm not sure I want to hear about his success rate. "With you though, I'm nervous as hell. Will you trust me tonight? Humor me?"

"You're kinda scaring me here, do you have a giant well you're going to throw me down? Make me lotion myself up?"

His shout of laughter echoes through the car. "Oh my gosh, I can't believe you brought that up. 'It rubs the lotion on its skin…' "

" '…Or else it gets the hose again,' " I finish, shivering for effect. "Of course I remember. That movie freaked the hell out of me. I can't believe I let you persuade me to watch it and I can't believe my parents saw that on their first date."

"I can. Horror movies are the best for dates, instant closeness."

"So that's your trick, Ocho, you scare the daylights out of your date to get them in your arms?" I jest.

"I don't need to scare them into my arms, Bambi."

Bambi. Emotion washes over me and I take a calming breath. "I can totally see that about you," I admit, a bit defeated. Jonah was a ladies' man before he was a man, and the years have been nothing but absolutely freaking wonderful to him. Of course he's good with the girls. So why me? Why did he say I make him nervous?

"Hey, I don't want to compare notes…"

"That's good because I don't have any notes to compare," I admit.

"Dani," he warns and I bite my tongue to keep from making any more remarks. "I do have a surprise for you."

We exit the car and he walks me through the small house, into the garage where he flips on the light. "A half-empty garage?" I look around at the extra fridge, bikes, a few boxes, and weight sets.

"There," he says, pointing to the pile of things stacked up by the door leading to the back yard. I step closer and realize it's a pile of camping gear. Lanterns, a tent, sleeping bags, all the basics for camping, and I'm confused. "Remember when we were kids, how we always begged our parents to go camping?"

"And your mom was too much of a priss to agree to sleep in tents, yeah. Gosh, we hounded them until Dad set us up our own campsite in the backyard. How many nights did we spend that summer sleeping outside?" I smile at the memory and look at the pile again.

"That was the best summer," Jonah admits. He looks down at the gear and nudges a pile of logs. "Wanna go camping for the night?"

I don't think twice. "Heck, yeah!"

Jonah starts a fire while I change into warmer clothes, grabbing him an extra sweatshirt and making a pile of blankets and pillows to carry out once the tent is set up. Joining him in the back yard, I laugh as he fumbles in the dark with the tent. "Why don't you turn on the back lights of the house?" I suggest.

He scoffs. "Psh, there's no house here," he says, waving around the area. "We're camping."

"Ohhh, right. Okay, so what can I do then?"

"Grab a lantern and shine it this way." He motions to two lights on the ground and I turn them both on, setting them in either side of the 'camp site' and then pull out my cell phone, shining the flashlight app on him. "Better?"

With proper lighting he makes quick work setting up the two man tent and soon we're covering the floor with our pile of blankets and pillows until it's one huge bed. Jonah surprises me again when he runs inside and comes back carrying a box full of provisions. Peeking in the box I find the ingredients to make s'mores, water bottles, two mugs, and hot chocolate. There are also two bags of white cheddar popcorn, my favorite.

"So this is what you did all day? I mean besides *gardening?*" I ask as he sets up two tailgating chairs side by side and pours water into a camping kettle. He grins at my mention of gardening. "It was rude of me to call her names. I'm not thirteen, I'm sorry."

"Sorry? Really?"

"Okay, fine maybe not totally sorry. I mean Poppy is so, so... I don't know." I shrug, sitting in a chair. I feel retched for poking fun of the girl I assume he broke up with earlier.

"D, I'm more offended by the names you presumed I'd name my children. Mustard, Rainbow, and Weasel? What is that, do you have no faith in my sense? Weasel, where did that come from?"

Mortified I cover my face as laughter bubbles up. "You actually did hear everything I said last night didn't you?" He nods. "Weasel... you know 'pop goes the weasel.' " I explain through my embarrassment, covering my face.

"Pop goes the weasel," Jonah repeats and I peer through a crack in my fingers at his face. He's trying hard not to laugh. His teeth grip his bottom lip, but his shoulders are shaking and I drop my hands.

"You're laughing, don't pretend you don't think it's clever," I accuse when he gives me an innocent look. We stare at each other, the small fire casting eerie shadows across his face as he leans over and sets up a grate for the kettle to sit on over the fire, and I resolve to win this contest of wills if it kills me. I expect him to crack, to laugh any minute. Instead he straightens, stuffing his hands into his pockets.

"Dani, you do know talk of marriage and kids with Poppy was completely asinine. We were casual," I can't cover the frown the truth puts on my face before he spots it. "I don't mean casual sex. I mean... hell, this is awkward." He rubs the back of his neck. *The typical male S.O.S signal.* I'm not sure how to make discussions of sex partners and exes any easier though, so I sit there wearing my best clueless face.

Pulling his chair to my side, he faces me, leaning in and resting his elbows on his knees. "Okay, I think it's best we get this out of the way now. We're both adults and I'm going to assume we can talk sex without freaking out, right? Poppy and I started hanging out, it was chill. Then she began to get a little clingy, but she was cool so I shrugged it off. We were never serious, though. I haven't dated anyone seriously. I didn't want to, my heart wasn't mine to give." His eyes close, his head shaking as he chuckles softly. "Man, did I seriously say that? How do you do this to me?"

"How do I? What did I do?" I don't understand why he's blaming me.

"You make me crazy. You make me say things I never thought I'd say. You've always been able to do that to me, you know. All the other boys hated girls, but you owned me. I was wrapped."

I kick at his chair playfully pushing mine back in the grass. "Oh whatever. That's not my fault, blame our parents... they're the ones who forced us together for years until we didn't know any better. I did nothing."

He sits there, looking at me thoughtfully before standing and moving his chair next to mine. "Maybe it was just me," he says, poking at the fire.

No, it wasn't just you, my head screams. *Can I do this? If we go down this road, will it mess everything up?*

"Tell me about school. You've been taking classes right?" he changes the subject, breaking the moment for my confession and I jump at answering him. *Coward.*

"Yea, online… all the general courses, marketing and business stuff. I don't know what I'm doing it for."

"What do you want to do?" he asks as though it's an easy question to answer.

"I want to go a full year without cutting. I want to be happy and not feel guilty. I want…"

"Wait," he drops the stick he's holding and pulls me from my chair. "Why do you feel guilty when you're happy?" I drop my head and he bobs around trying to force me to look him in the eyes. "Dani?"

"It's hard to explain. I can't."

Jonah's hand dropped to my hip after he pulled me up, his fingers pressing into my side. I try to turn away and he tugs my hip back square with his, lifting his other hand to the back of my head and tugging it back gently by the hair. If any other guy were to tug my hair this way I'd slap them, but his tug is gentle and purposeful. He rubs the spot he tugs once I look up and I'm tempted to close my eyes and rest my forehead on his chest as he massages my scalp. It feels glorious. "At the party last night… you disappeared. I barely had the chance to process your disappearance before Kady ripped into me."

"Did she, why?"

"I guess she took issue with the way I was treating you, and her too. She called me some pretty nasty words too, that sister of mine has a mouth when she's angry," he frowns, causing me to grin. "Anyway, she yelled at me for letting Poppy kiss me in front of you the way she did." *Ugh. Kady, the mother, strikes again.* "I said something I sincerely regretted afterward though."

Thinking he insulted her I asked, "What did you say?"

"She slapped my arm, like a girl I might add, and yelled I shouldn't be kissing another girl in front of you and I, being the ass I am, laughed in her face and said you could go back to Luke for all I cared."

I sucked in a breath so deep I'm surprised I didn't take the whole world in with that gasp of air. I can't move, I'm stung by his flippant comment, and by the truth. *I could never go back to Luke, if I wanted to or not.*

"Now two things happened next that you need to know before you slap me the way she did, because I can see you want to."

"You're right about that," I manage, smiling and wishing I'd seen her slap him.

"First, that was the biggest lie I've told in years. I was jealous after seeing you with Everett and I was being petty. At the same time, as my brain was trying to think of a way to take the comment back, Kady found a way to bring me to my knees. She told me about Luke. She told me he's gone."

"She knows? How did she…" I must wobble on my feet because Jonah's hands wrap around my back, holding me up as he explains what Kady told him. She'd overheard my conversation with her mother two weeks ago. She'd overheard the whole thing and never said a thing to me.

"I wish you'd told me yourself. I got so upset with you that day at the park. You walked away from me. You threw us away and I'm not talking about a romance, D. I'm talking about our friendship. I tried to understand. My parents kept telling me to be patient and give you time and I knew that. I knew you were hurting, but damn… I didn't expect the dead air for three years." The glow from the flames allow me to see the pain written across his features. "Knowing you found someone else to take my place, to fix you. I know it's crazy and not fair, and messed up, but I hate it. I hate it so much, why didn't you tell me?" he asks.

"I don't know," I tell him honestly. "Luke's hard to understand. The reasoning, I mean, for why we clicked. What we were, why I lost him, how he died… all of it is so damn confusing, Jonah. I can't explain it all." A sinking feeling pounds in my chest, that familiar pressure moving in wanting to set up a home and I shake my head. Blowing out a deep breath I lift my hands placing them on his chest. "I'm sorry, I was completely screwed up, Jonah. That's all I can offer you, I'm sorry I can't give you the answers you probably want."

"No. You listen to me. I'm sorry. I had no right to be the jealous guy. Trust me, I'm no saint. You have nothing to be sorry about, you have been through hell and back over the last five years and you owe me nothing. I'm sorry I acted as though you owed me something, I promise I won't ask anything from you." He crosses his heart with his index finger.

We snuggle into the chairs, sipping hot chocolate and making s'mores as we sit peacefully looking up at the clear night sky. Jonah brings me a throw blanket as the temperature continues to drop and I pull it to my chin, leaning my head back in the seat and watching the fire. The deep red and orange embers of a log near me keep changing shapes, and I'm hypnotized for some time simply watching them shift and morph before I'm compelled to speak again.

"After the accident I was terrified of fire," I recall, my eyes watering from staring for so long. "I flipped out when Gram lit a candle, it was so bad."

"You were? What changed?" he asks.

"Luke." My eyes slide to the side to gauge Jonah's reaction. He pokes at a log with his stick, but doesn't move otherwise. "It was one of the things he insisted we do when he came to Texas. He wanted me over my fear. I hated his job, for obvious reasons, so he wanted me to find a way to be more comfortable. Fire is beautiful... the way the flames twirl and lick at the logs until they consume them whole. He reminded me of that beauty. 'It's okay to fear power, but admire the beauty,' that's what he told me."

Jonah shifts down further in his seat, propping his shoes up on the stone ledge of the fire pit. "I think he was talking about more than fire."

"You think?" My mind goes back to that day. Jonah's right, Luke had been talking about something else, he'd been talking about falling in love.

"He was right, it is beautiful and powerful and scary as hell." He rests his hand on the armrest palm up. "Both fire and love," he says and I smile, because Jonah always knows what I'm thinking. My hand sneaks out from under the blanket in my lap and I set it on his, allowing our fingers to line up as though we're comparing hand size. "I think I would have liked him."

"I think you would have too," I agree as I weave our fingers together and squeeze his hand with mine.

"He saved you, more than once. And he was smart enough to fall for you, I know I would have liked him. I wish I could have thanked him."

"I think you are," I whisper, looking his way. "Being here, doing all of this for me... you're thanking him for making sure I was able to live."

"How is what I've done anything? He saved your life. He pulled you from that car, he found a way in when I couldn't, and then he gave you up to save you again. This is nothing..."

"No, Jonah, this is everything."

"I thought I could make you better! Damn it, I wanted to save you..." Jonah blurts unexpectedly, his voice breaking. The pain cuts into my own the way a blade would slice through my skin. My heart is bleeding.

I shake my head, gasping back the raging river of tears trying to break free. "Jonah, you couldn't save me. You still can't."

"I'm worthless then."

"Don't be crazy, you will never be worthless to me," I argue, pulling my hand from his and standing. I hold my hand out and he stands too, wrapping my arms around his stomach I hug him closely, measuring my words carefully. This moment is important and I want to get it right. "I need you now. I know I ran, but I'm not running anymore. I want to remember the past and I want to smile at the memories. That's why I stayed, you're why I stayed."

"But... "

"But nothing. You can't save me, I don't want you to save me. What you can do is hold me." His arms tighten around me and I let the tears loose. "I don't need you to save me. I need you to hold me and stand by my side, supporting me, while I save myself."

He lets go, moving his hands to grab at my face, his fingers sinking into the hair at my temples. "Dani, there is nothing I've wanted more than to hear you say that. I'm here, whatever you need from me, I'm here."

I'm smiling and crying simultaneously as we hug. "I need this, Jonah, I need my best friend to keep me in line."

"You said it and I'm holding you to it. It's a done deal, I'm never leaving your side again," he laughs lightly.

"Good, because apparently I can't be trusted around alcohol and college parties."

"Huh, you don't say?" his voice's dripping with mockery,

"Yeah shocker, huh?" I reply on another laugh.

Today's reality… I'm home
February 1, 2018

"I don't want you to leave," Jonah whispers against my temple, waking me. We're huddled together in the cold pre-dawn hours wrapped in a mountain of blankets and a tangle of limbs. I'm not sure how we became so close in the middle of the night. When I feel asleep I'd been on my side and he on his, but now his arm is under my head, my face is on his chest, and my legs are between his. My hand is actually under his shirt, touching his warm skin, and I pull back slowly, but purposefully, rolling to my side and coughing to cover my retreat.

"I wish I could stay too," I confess as I sit up, pulling a blanket around my shoulders.

"Then stay."

"What?" I ask, wrapping a throw blanket over my shoulders as I sit up. The smell of smoke from last night's fire lingers on everything around me and I smile because the heavy smell no longer makes me think of the accident, but instead I think about Jonah, and everything we said last night. Every barrier we finally tore down.

"Stay, D. Stay a few days with me and let's figure things out now. If you go back to GP, what will happen? Will we talk on the phone, see each other on weekends when I have time to come see you? Let's not do that, please," he begs, his eyes searching mine in the grey morning light.

"What do you want to do?" I ask hesitantly.

Sitting up, Jonah takes my hand between his, rubbing my cold fingers vigorously. "I want to be with you. Friday night you told Kady I'd always been the one to occupy your heart. If that's true, if your feelings haven't changed — then I'm here, because the truth is, for me… there's never been anyone but you."

I'm not entirely sure what to say as thousands of words fight with each other to explain how I feel, where I've been, where I want to go. I lead with my heart.

"Do you know the last thing Luke said to me?" Jonah shakes his head. "He was drunk and he called me missing me and he said he wished he could be the man for me, wished he was strong enough and then he said we'd never be." Lifting my hand from his lap, he brings it to his lips, kissing my knuckles softly.

"You're that man. It never was Luke, it was you. From day one you wanted to be there, the letter in the hospital, the Valentine's letter and necklace, when you came to see me in Texas, the three emails you sent the past three years on the anniversary of the wreck…"

"You saw those? I didn't know if you ever read them."

"I didn't, until my birthday. They're the reason I came back. You're the reason I came back. You never gave up. I sat at my desk and I read those emails full of so much hope and love for me and I knew. I knew to move on, to find my happily ever after, I needed to come back home. I needed you."

Blinking, he takes a shaky breath and lets go of my hand. "Come here," he says, moving to the tent zipper and handing me my shoes. "I have another surprise for you."

"Another?" He slips on his shoes and climbs out of the tent. "Out there? It's freezing," I complain as I follow him. The sky above us is dusted with stars, but in the distance the first peek of sunlight is creeping its way into the day. Jonah removes his phone from his pocket, playing with the screen and setting it in his chair from last night. A moment later music sounds around us. "Whoa, where… "

Jonah laughs, pointing toward his back patio. "Wireless speakers."

A guitar strums acoustically, a beautiful Spanish sound and I know it. I know it before the soulful words begin, I know it deep in my heart. '*I Won't Give Up*', *by Jason Mraz*. It was such a huge hit and favorite of mine before the wreck. Jonah pulls our intertwined hands to his chest and presses my face to his shoulder. "This is the song we danced to at homecoming sophomore year. Remember? The one dance you allowed me."

"You mean the one song I dared because I was afraid of Carrie Hoyt," I confess on a laugh. "I knew she'd be pissed about us dancing together. She hated me."

His free hand spreads lower on my back, pulling me closer. "She had reason to be. She knew before I did. When I broke up with her — not thirty minutes after dancing to this song with you, by the way — she accused me of being in love with you. I denied it, but she was right."

I swallow hard, pushing the emotion down. *I will not cry. I will not cry.* "Eighth grade."

"Eighth grade, what?" he asks, his voice thick with the emotion, too.

"I asked you about Nicole Remy, what you thought of her." I lean back in his arms, looking up at him. His face scrunches as though he's trying to recall the conversation. "We were shooting hoops at my house. It was the day you started calling me Bambi… "

"I know. I was waiting to see if you remembered," he smiles, a self-satisfied smile and I grin, too. *So very Jonah Hall, incorrigible.* "So what about it?"

"Last night you said 'maybe it was just you' you were trying to say maybe you were the only one who had feelings — it wasn't just you. I asked you about Nicole all those years ago because all the boys were going crazy over her and I was so worried you would, too. I was constantly waiting for the day when you'd stop wanting to hang out with me."

"I never wanted to stop hanging out with you. That's crazy."

"I know, but I was falling for my best friend and I had no idea what to do," I admit, pressing my cheek back to his chest. "I wanted you to know I felt it, too. Way earlier than that night you finally got up the nerve to ask me out."

"So what do we do now," he asks solemnly.

I step back and he gives me a strange look, but allows me to leave his arms, standing there and waiting for me to speak. "Ever since the accident I've felt as though I were a puzzle everyone wanted to analyze and put back together. I was this whole wonderful picture and then someone stole pieces of that picture, and try as they might — the therapists, my grandparents, and even me — we couldn't complete the picture without those pieces..."

"So I broke down. I was like a kid who'd stumbled upon this messed up puzzle and when I couldn't force the pieces together, to complete the picture, I would fall. Cutting away the frustration and pain until I was ready to try again. Over and over I tried to find those lost pieces. I tried to be the doting granddaughter, I tried school, I found Luke and thought maybe he was the key, my fate, but fate had other plans. I tried saving others by staying at Crestdale and giving advice. Advice I didn't follow myself. None of these things worked. Then it hit me, this past week."

The moment I started speaking Jonah froze, his eyes never wavering from my face. "What hit you?"

"The things I lost, the puzzle pieces? It wasn't my parents, I mean they're missing pieces and they'll forever be a huge part of me, but it's so much more than that. That one last missing piece, the one the little girl in me kept trying to replace and fix was my very being, my soul. It was everything I lost the day my parents died and I left North Carolina. My life, my past, my present, my future... I gave it all up because I chose to focus on Mom and Dad and blame myself. I made them the whole picture and forgot all of the little pieces that made me. Me."

Tears roll down my cheeks as I finish. Jonah's hands are fisted at his sides, his head tilting as he watches me and I can see the battle he's waging internally to stand there, to not comfort me. I hold my finger up, shaking my head, a silent plea for him to let me finish.

"Dani?" he sighs, his voice filled with tension.

"You're my missing piece, Jonah. You're the one who completes my wonderful picture." I'm barely able to get the last word out before he steps in and kisses me. His mouth slanting over mine and removing every trace of fear, doubt, and hate that may have been between us and replacing it all with perfection. "We don't give up. Okay? We have five years to make up for, we're not the same people we were back then, but we'll make this work. We can start slow, be friends if we have to," he says passionately when his mouth leaves mine

"I think we're already past friends, Jonah Hall. Why torture ourselves?" I point out, sliding my hands up his chest and wrapping my fingers around his neck, bringing him down for another kiss before pulling him back into the tent. The sky is turning a brilliant pink and orange with red streaks as we crawl back into the tent and lay together bundled up in blankets. We watch the stunning picture in between yawns as our lack of sleep hits us both. Jonah's phone is now playing a collection of love songs both new and old, and I assume he's fallen asleep until he hums softly with a song playing. My eyes water as I listen to the lyrics. It's a song about coming home and everything she sings, hits me,

I'm home.

I'm a million miles away from being perfect, but I'm a thousand steps closer today than I was yesterday. And tomorrow I'll be closer still.

"Jonah, I'm happy right now and I don't feel guilty," I whisper, thinking about how he asked me what I wanted last night.

"Yeah?" He rolls to his side so we're face to face and kisses my nose. I tighten my grip around his waist, wanting our bodies as close as possible.

"Yeah. When you can say you are where you should be, need to be, and want to be. That's when you know."

"Know what?"

"Everything."

Today's reality… This is my kingdom

I'm stepping out of the shower after returning home from a Christmas concert I performed in, when I hear his voice. Expecting to find him in bed, sound asleep, I pull on a robe to see who he's talking to so late. But when I open the bathroom door, the bed is empty. His low voice carries into the bedroom and I smile, knowing where to find him. I listen as I walk towards his beloved voice…

"Once upon a time, there was a beautiful princess and she was funny and talented and loved, so much, by everyone who knew her. She was especially loved by the King and Queen, but they were forced to leave her, and the poor princess was lost, and it made everyone sad.

"But you know what happened? A handsome and extremely brave, and I should add brilliant, prince — that's me, in case you weren't sure — went after her. He fought every obstacle thrown in his way and eventually he was lucky enough to find his princess again and bring her home…"

"The princess is the lucky one," I interrupt softly when I reach the door.

Jonah turns, he's wearing his dress slacks from earlier, but he's shirtless. His bare torso makes me as breathless tonight as it did on our wedding night three years ago. Surprisingly more so now, because cradled against him is our two-month old son.

"There she is," he whispers smiling, his cheek resting atop Lucas' pale blond fuzz-head. "Our beautiful princess."

"Everything okay?" I ask, walking into the room and smoothing Lucas' patch of hair as I press a kiss to his temple.

"We're perfect. He missed us, that's all. I was telling him a fairy tale."

"He does love your fairy tales," I smile. "Did you tell him how much his mommy and daddy missed him tonight?"

"Of course I did. I also told him how beautiful his mommy looked all dressed up in red singing on that stage with the lights and the chorus. You blow me away every time, Bambi," he teases sweetly.

"I'm so in love with you, Jonah Hall, you know that?" I ask.

"Not nearly as much as I love you, Mrs. Hall," he winks and I'm not sure I'll ever get used to that name. *Mrs. Hall.* "Would you care to finish the fairy tale tonight?"

Sliding under his free arm, I wrap myself around his side and rub Lucas' back. "Of course. You see, my sweet one," I continue softly, smiling as a pair of baby blues, so much like his father's, blink sleepily and focus on me. "The prince thought he was the lucky one, but he wasn't, not really. It was the princess who was lucky, for she despaired of ever finding her own fairy tale, and your daddy changed that. He gave her the fairy tale life she'd always dreamed of, complete with her very own Prince Charming," I finish, kissing his chubby cheek. Tilting my head to Jonah, I smile. "Two Prince Charming's," I amend, stretching up and kissing him.

"The End?" he asks, a smile playing on his lips.

"No," I shake my head, my heart overflowing with love. "And they lived happily ever after."

The End

Dear Reader -

You were introduced to West and Jules in 'Into The Fire' but you can read their entire story in the 'From The Wreckage' series available now. Here's a sneak peek at book one, From The Wreckage...

"Is this on?"

Jules' eyes flick to the small television across the room and she takes her place in the faded velvet wingback chair. Her own face stares back at her from the screen, indicating the camera is indeed working. Out of habit, her hands run over her strawberry blonde hair. She twirls a curl around her finger and brushes her long bangs to the side. Satisfied with her appearance, she takes a deep breath.

"Okay, Hi," she says softly; her hand lifting in a small wave. "I'm Jules Blacklin from Tyler, Texas. Oh, crap. No, I shouldn't wave," she tells herself.

Shimmying backward, she tries to find a comfortable sitting position; her sundress catching against the velvet nap of the seat cushion.

With a low sigh, she moves to run her hand between her skirt and the chair. Freeing the fabric, Jules adjusts the dress again and crosses her legs daintily, while stealing another glance at the television screen to check her appearance. She'd set up the small twenty-inch screen on a side table so she would be able to see herself as a video camera recorded her story. Although now the camera only makes her more uneasy. Sitting here, watching herself speak to nobody makes her question her sanity. It feels like something a crazy person would do.

With a thoughtful eye, she watches herself lean forward and rest her elbow on the armrest, and decides to go with the pose; thinking it makes her look studious.

"Okay, yeah...that's good," she speaks aloud.

With a demure nod of her head, she begins again.

"Hi. My name is Jules Blacklin, Hillsdale High class of twenty-fourteen. I'm making this video essay as my contribution to the class of twenty-fourteen time capsule. I..."

She pauses; her mind blanking out for a moment as she smiles into the lens recording her. She takes a moment to steady her thoughts before continuing. "I want to tell you about myself. About what I've been through, and what the town of Tyler has been through. Winston Churchill once said, 'Sure I am of this, that you have only to endure to conquer.' Rest assured —I have endured. I have endured, and now I am ready to conquer."

Jules gives herself a mental high-five for remembering the quote and releases a deep breath. With her hands clasped, she leans forward in her seat. Her blue eyes stare directly into the red blinking light used to indicate the camera is recording.

"I'm inviting you on a journey. A journey through my senior year. Actually, if you're watching this, then I'm going to ask you to be a bystander. See, I'm not making this for you. I'm recording this for the ones who didn't live, the ones I will forever be mindful of. For the ones I knew, the ones I didn't...and especially for the ones I loved. This is for you."

Uncrossing her legs, she leans back in the chair again; her eyes continuing to connect with the nameless faces that will someday watch this DVD. She settles back for her long story, her finger tracing the scrolling pattern across her skirt. She gathers herself, her thoughts and memories. It's only a few moments — a flash of time — but for her, in her mind she sees everything. Once more, her pale gaze meets the lens and she decides where to start.

"Let's begin with your ending. The last night my life was normal. The last night we were *all* normal."

Acknowledgements

Whenever I finish a book I come to this spot and I debate on what I'm going to say. I'm nothing without the people behind me. My readers, bloggers, Facebook and Twitter friends, my family, and my local fast food providers (I kid, kinda!) all of you are the reason I survive day to day as stories consume my life and mind.

I want to give a special shout out to Mandy with I Read Indie for falling so deeply in love with Jules and West last year and for sharing them all over the net for the past six months. You, my dear, are a gem!

The professionals who back me up:
My editor, Samantha - you're available for my random questions at just about any time I need you. Thank you for your support, laughter and fabulous editing skills.

My cover designer, Regina - you are freaking amazing. Your talent is beyond my comprehension and your heart and dedication to making beautiful things is legendary. I will love this cover forever and ever!

My cover model, Savannah - you had no idea you were *the face* of Dani when you went on a photo shoot with Regina one day. Thank goodness you did!

My PR agent, Rick Miles and the crew at Red Coat PR - You're the best pimps ever. Thank you for your advice and for making me look good.

My agent, Italia Gandolfo, and Gandolfo Helin Literary Management - We're just getting started. I'm looking forward to all of the trouble we can cook up.

My biggest supporters:
J, Gray, Gabe and Belle - my family, my life, my first and best fairy tale. I love you like crazy.

My Fierce sisters Starla, Mindy and Christy (aka Iron Man, Captain and Black Widow) sharing this writer life on a day to day basis is a pleasure with you ladies by my side. I heart you.

My alphas - Jessica and Megan. I couldn't do this without you. I don't know how I managed to snag you two, but I'm forever grateful.

My Chele's Belles and Mischief Makers - Ali, Amanda, Chelcie, Cheri, Courtney, Danielle, Destiny, Kayla, Laura, Mandy, Marla, Megan, Nancy, Tanya, Tess, and Veranda. Thank you for supporting me in whatever way you're able and always lending an ear when I need one.

Occasionally, I ask fans on my Facebook page to help me with random names or thoughts. These ladies stepped up and their ideas landed in Into The Fire. Thank you FB fans for answering my random calls for help. Charlotte Grange gave us Poppy, Kelly Coles named Kadence, and Megan Henry offered up the name Grace.

Playlist

If you follow me on social media you know music is a huge inspiration for me. Here are just a few songs I listed to while writing Into the Fire. You can find the entire playlist on Spotify as 'Wrecked #1 Into The Fire'

Photograph by Ed Sheeran
Breath Me by Sia
Bring Me To Life by Evanscence
Chandelier - Piano Version by Sia
Words by Skylar Grey
Cactus in the Valley by LIGHTS
I'm in Here - Piano/Vocal by Sia
Lost by Kris Allen
Stay by Thirty Seconds to Mars
Distance by Seconhand Serenade
Like A Knife by Secondhand Serenade
I Won't Give Up by Jason Mraz
Coming Home - Part II by Skylar Grey

About the author

Michele writes novels with fairy tale love for everyday life. Romance is always central to her plots where the genres range from Coming of Age Fantasy and Drama to New Adult Romantic Suspense.

Head over to my website and sign up for my monthly newsletter (or type this in your browser http://bit.ly/MGMNews) to keep up with all the latest, exclusive first peeks and other perks.

Email: authormichelegmiller@gmail.com
Facebook: https://www.facebook.com/AuthorMicheleGMiller
Twitter: https://twitter.com/chelemybelles
Pinterest: http://pinterest.com/chelemybelles/
Website: https://michelegmillerbooks.squarespace.com/

Printed in Great Britain
by Amazon